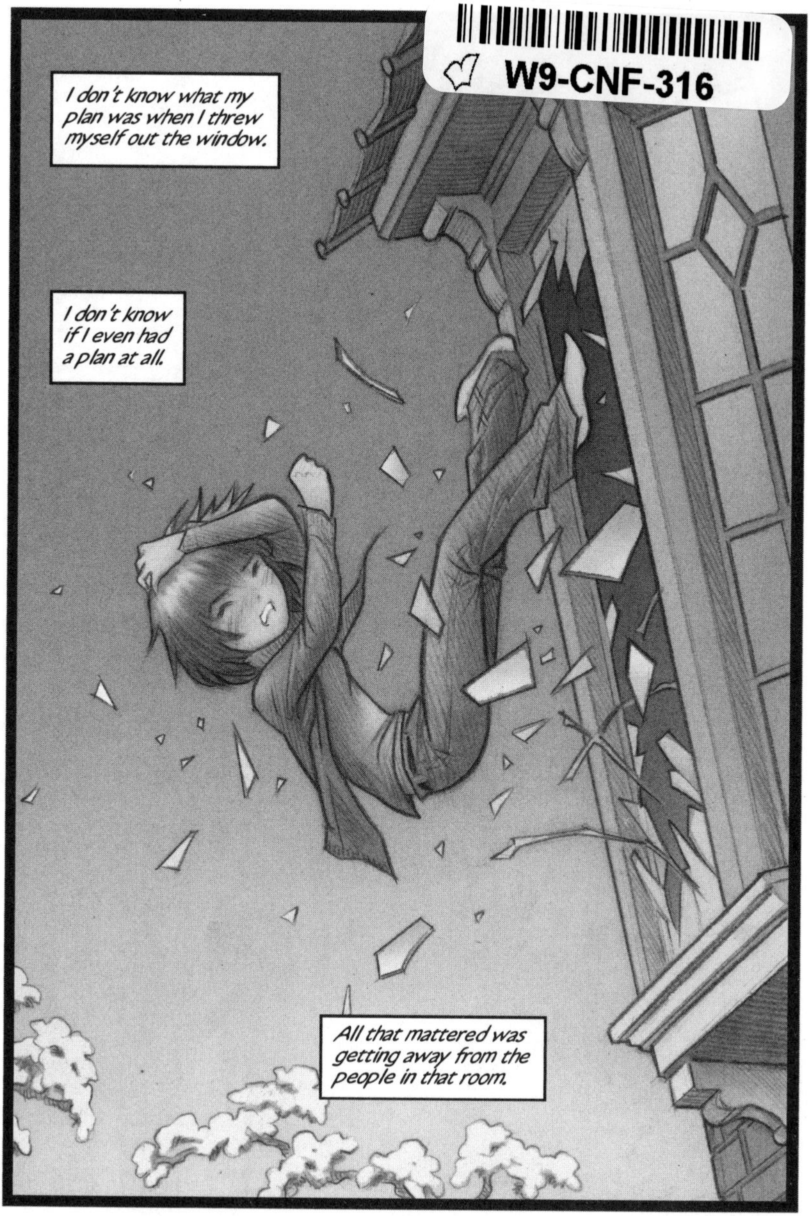
I don't know what my plan was when I threw myself out the window.
I don't know if I even had a plan at all.
All that mattered was getting away from the people in that room.

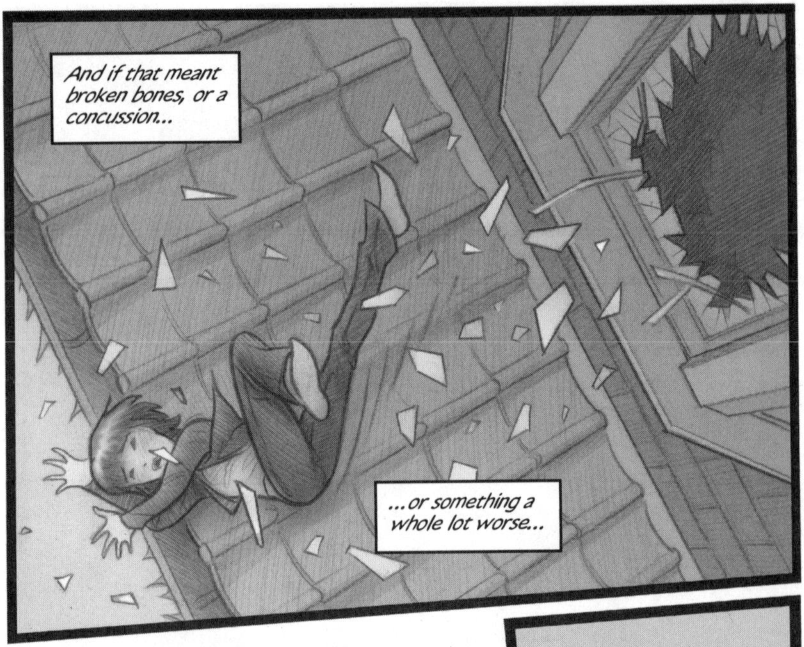
And if that meant broken bones, or a concussion...
...or something a whole lot worse...

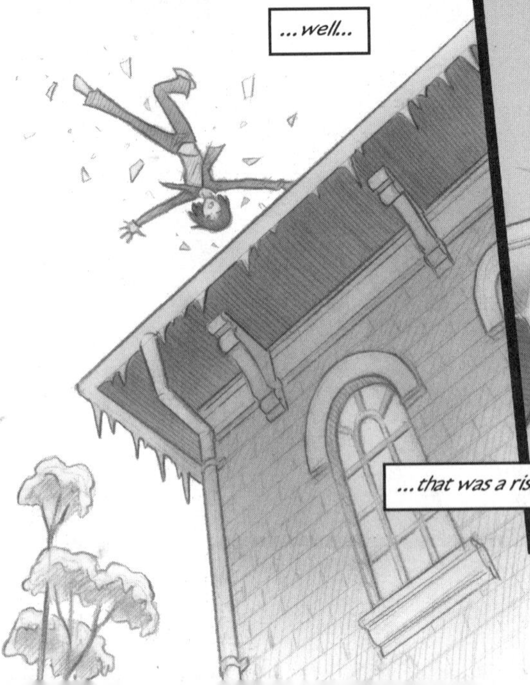
...well...

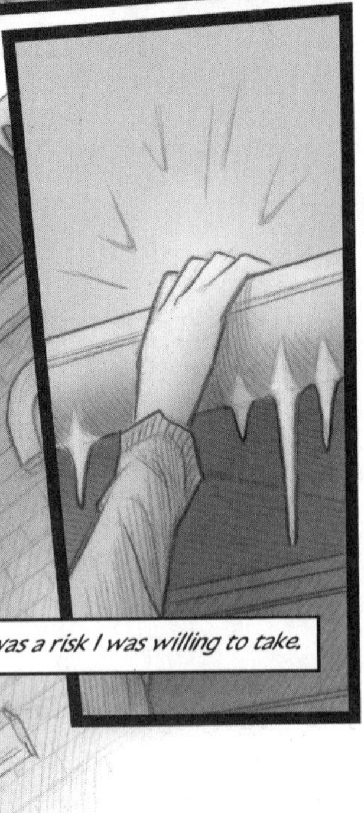
...that was a risk I was willing to take.

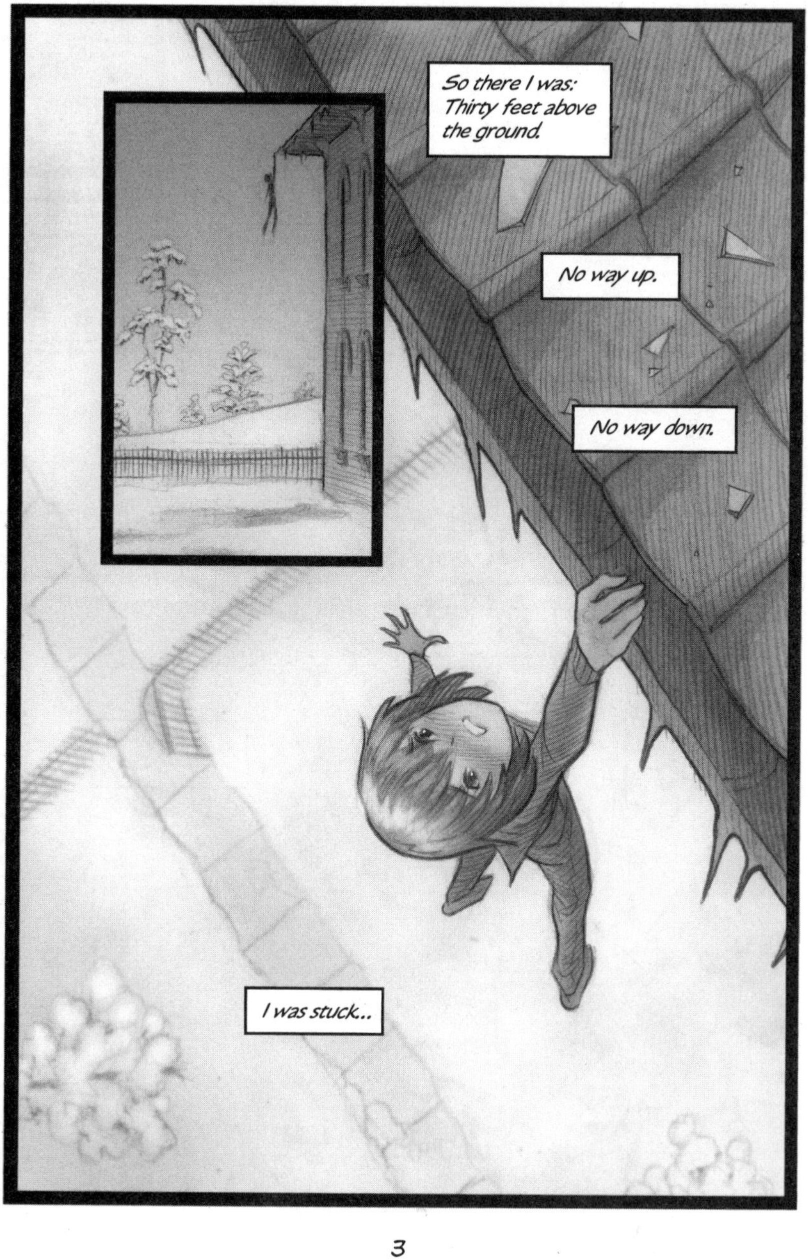
So there I was: Thirty feet above the ground.
No way up.
No way down.
I was stuck...

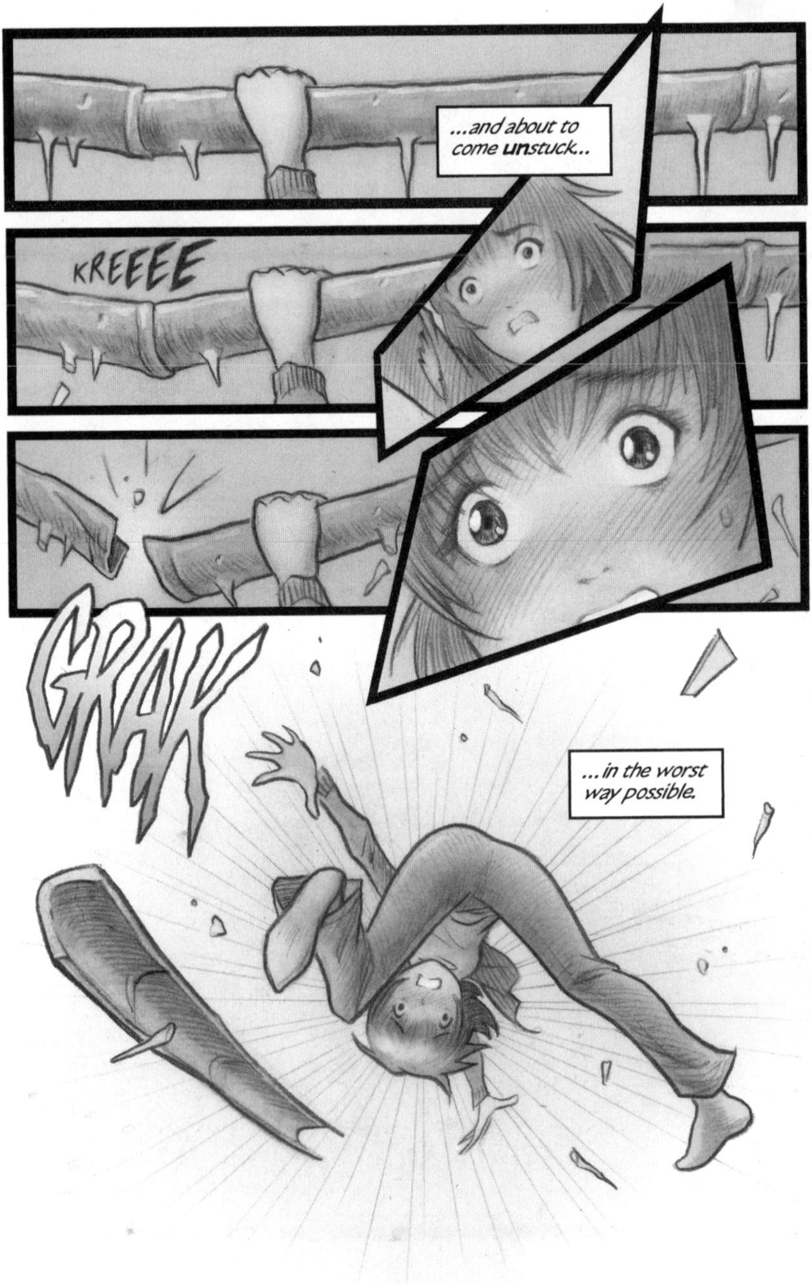
...and about to come **un**stuck...
KREEEE
GRAK
...in the worst way possible.

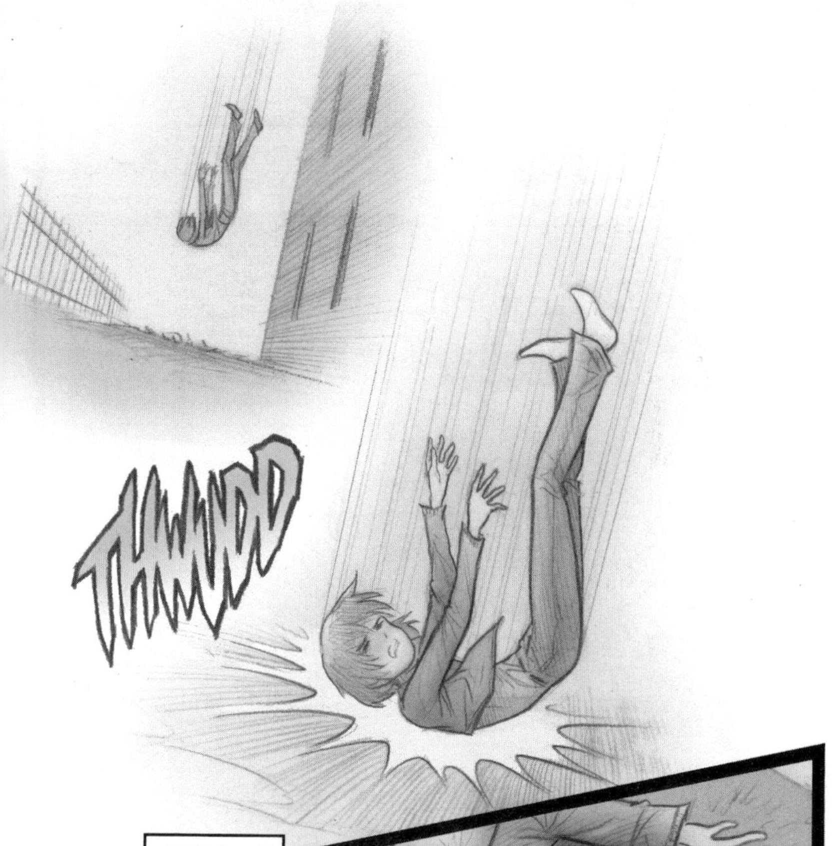
THWUD

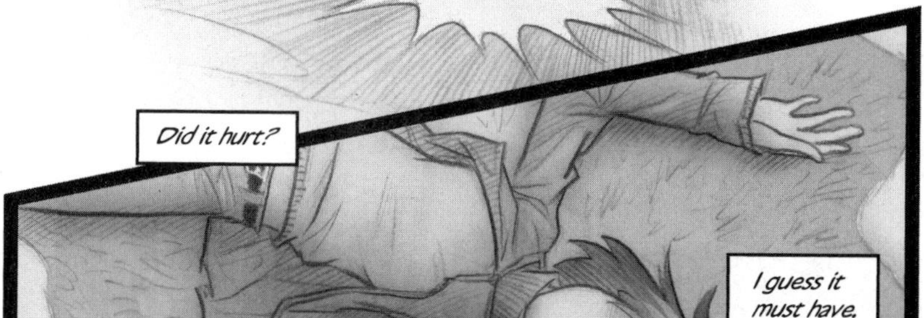
Did it hurt?
I guess it must have.
I don't recall.

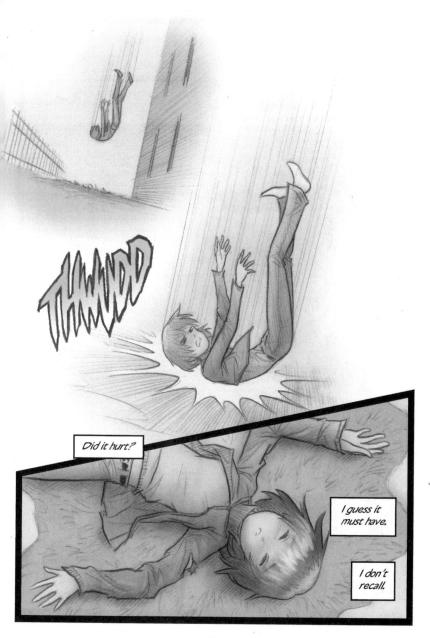

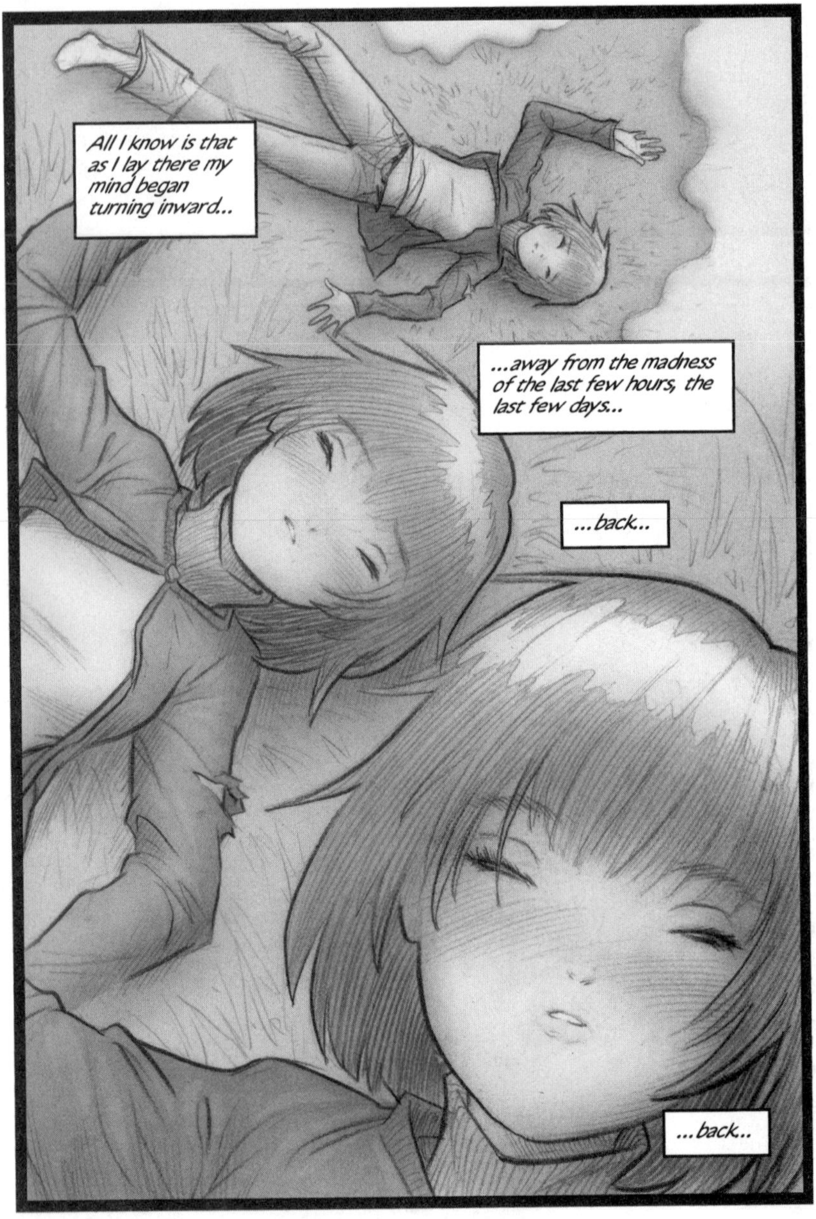
All I know is that as I lay there my mind began turning inward...
...away from the madness of the last few hours, the last few days...
...back...
...back...

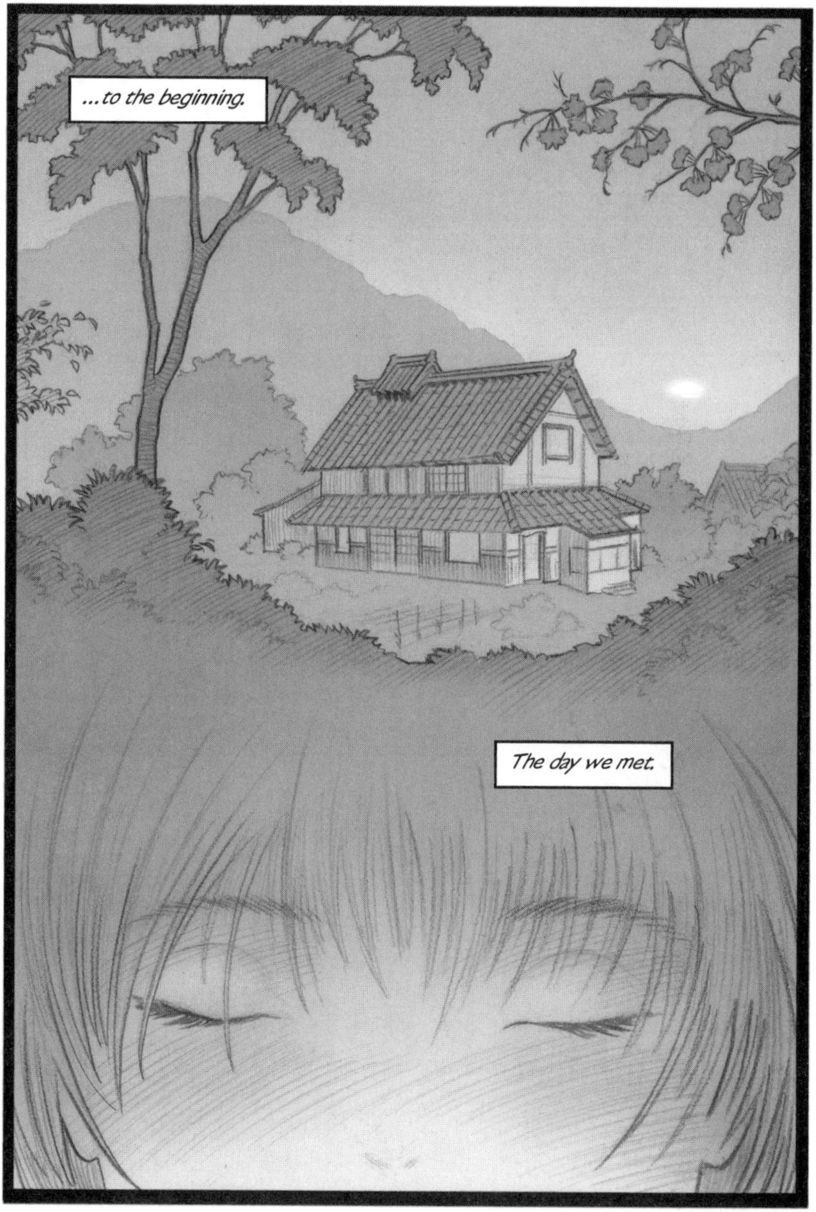
...to the beginning.
The day we met.

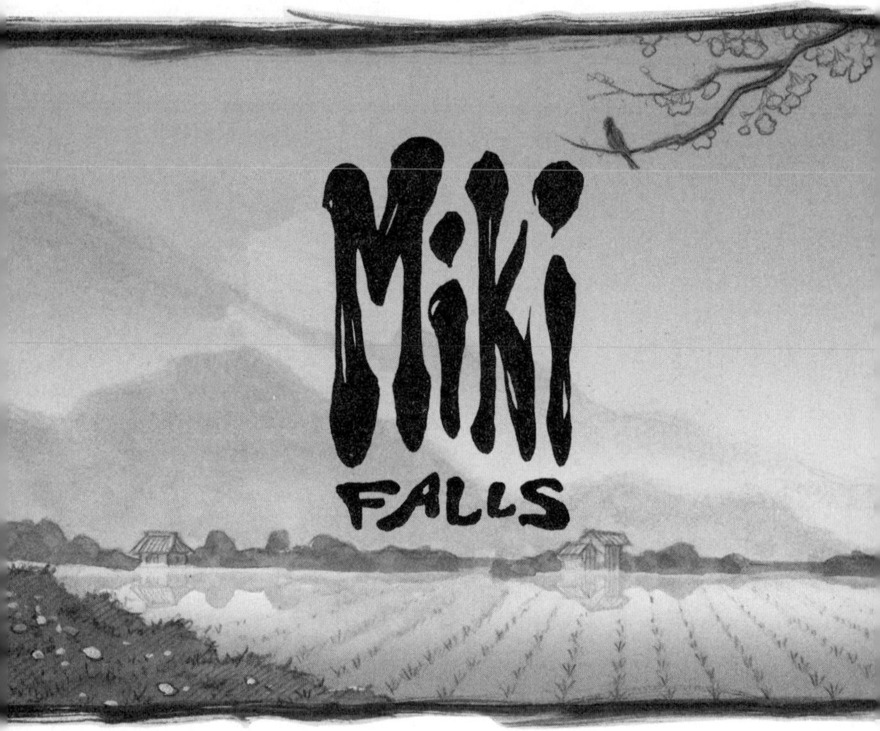
Miki
Falls

MARK CRILLEY

HARPER TEEN
An Imprint of HarperCollins*Publishers*

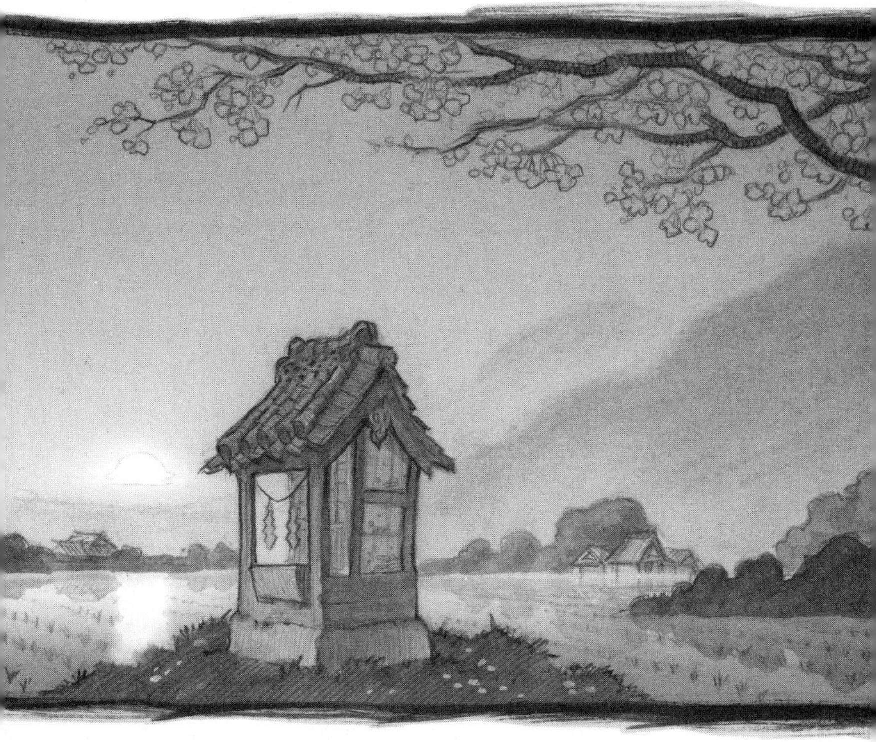

•BOOK ONE•

春 SPRING

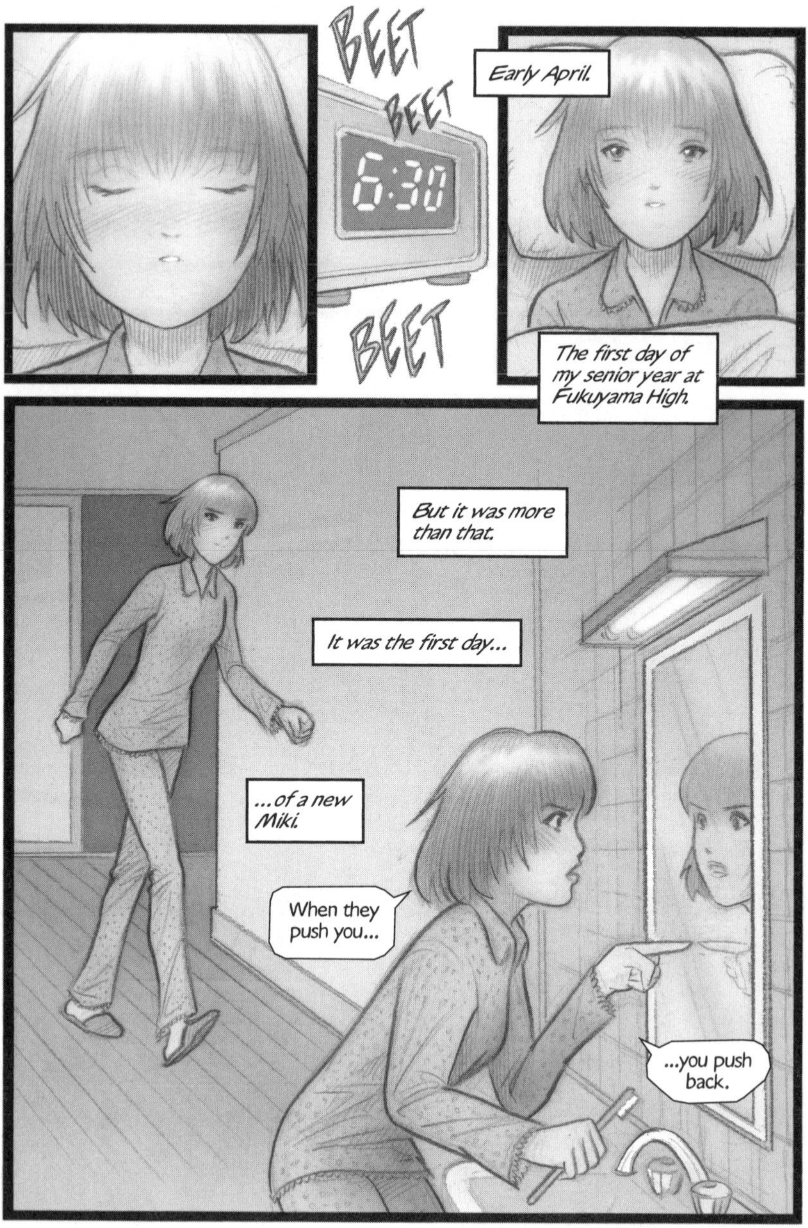
BEET
BEET
6:30
BEET
Early April.
The first day of my senior year at Fukuyama High.
But it was more than that.
It was the first day...
...of a new Miki.
When they push you...
...you push back.

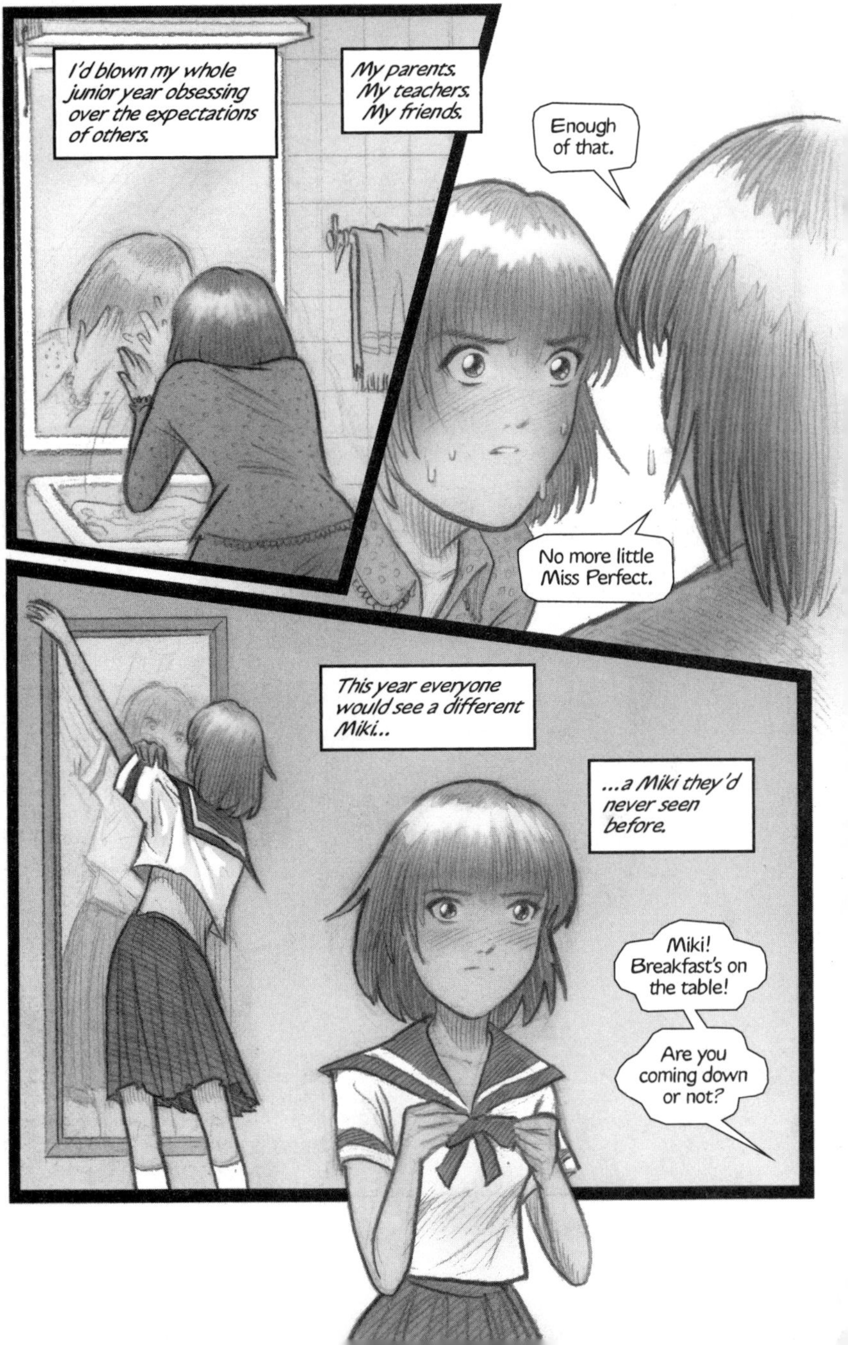
I'd blown my whole junior year obsessing over the expectations of others.
My parents. My teachers. My friends.
Enough of that.
No more little Miss Perfect.
This year everyone would see a different Miki...
...a Miki they'd never seen before.
Miki! Breakfast's on the table!
Are you coming down or not?

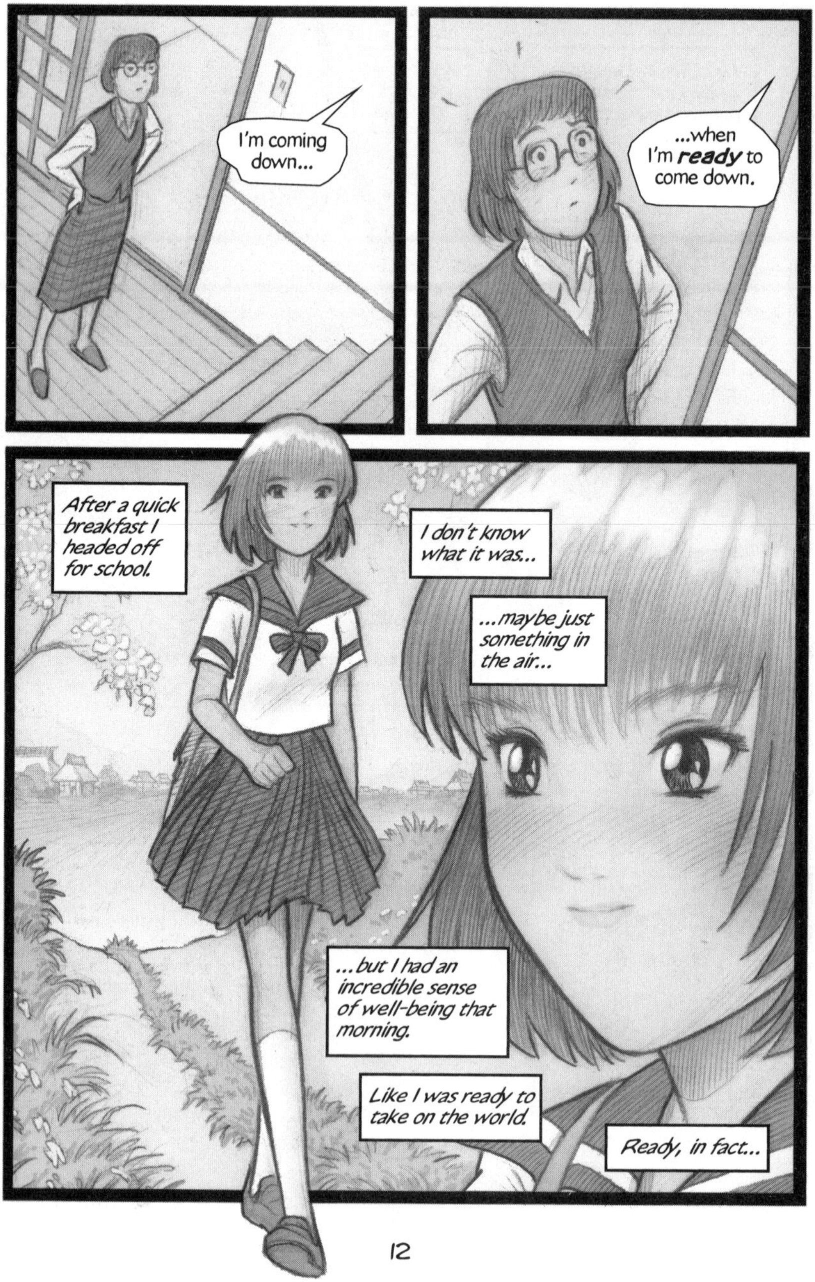

I'm coming down...
...when I'm ***ready*** to come down.
After a quick breakfast I headed off for school.
I don't know what it was...
...maybe just something in the air...
...but I had an incredible sense of well-being that morning.
Like I was ready to take on the world.
Ready, in fact...

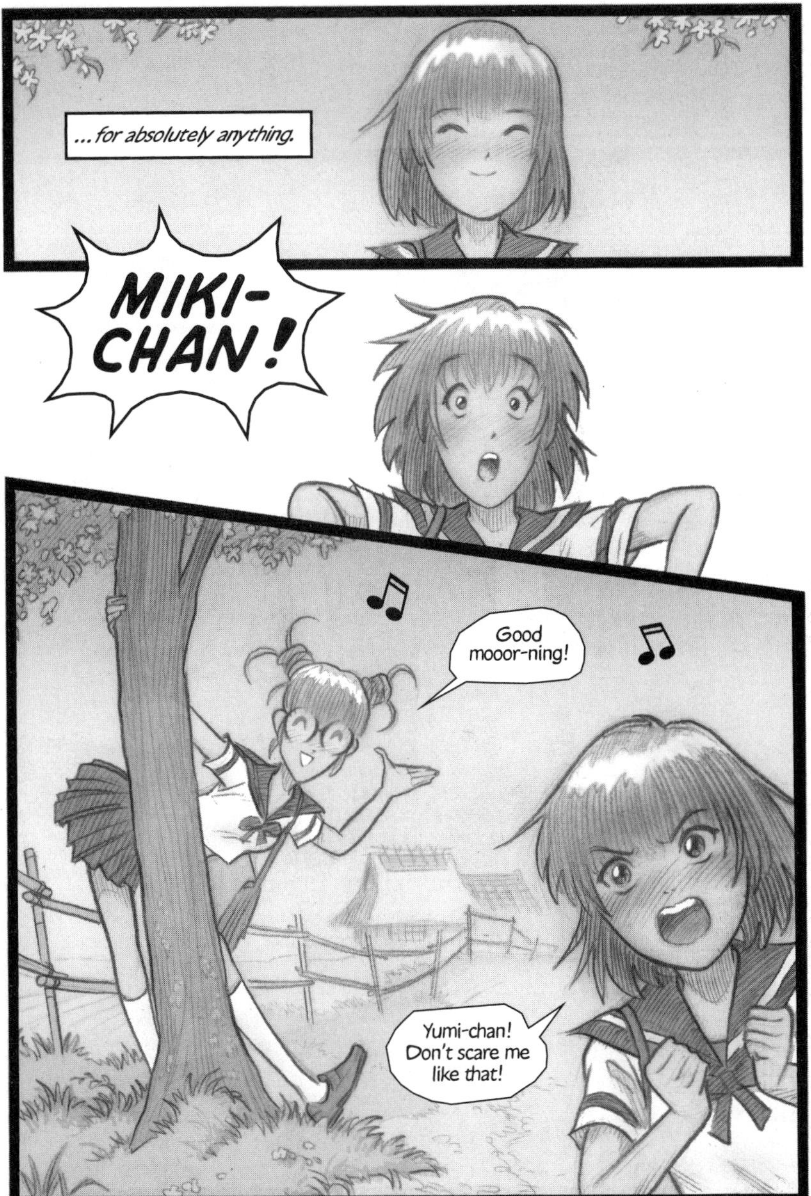

...for absolutely anything.
MIKI-CHAN!
Good mooor-ning!
Yumi-chan! Don't scare me like that!

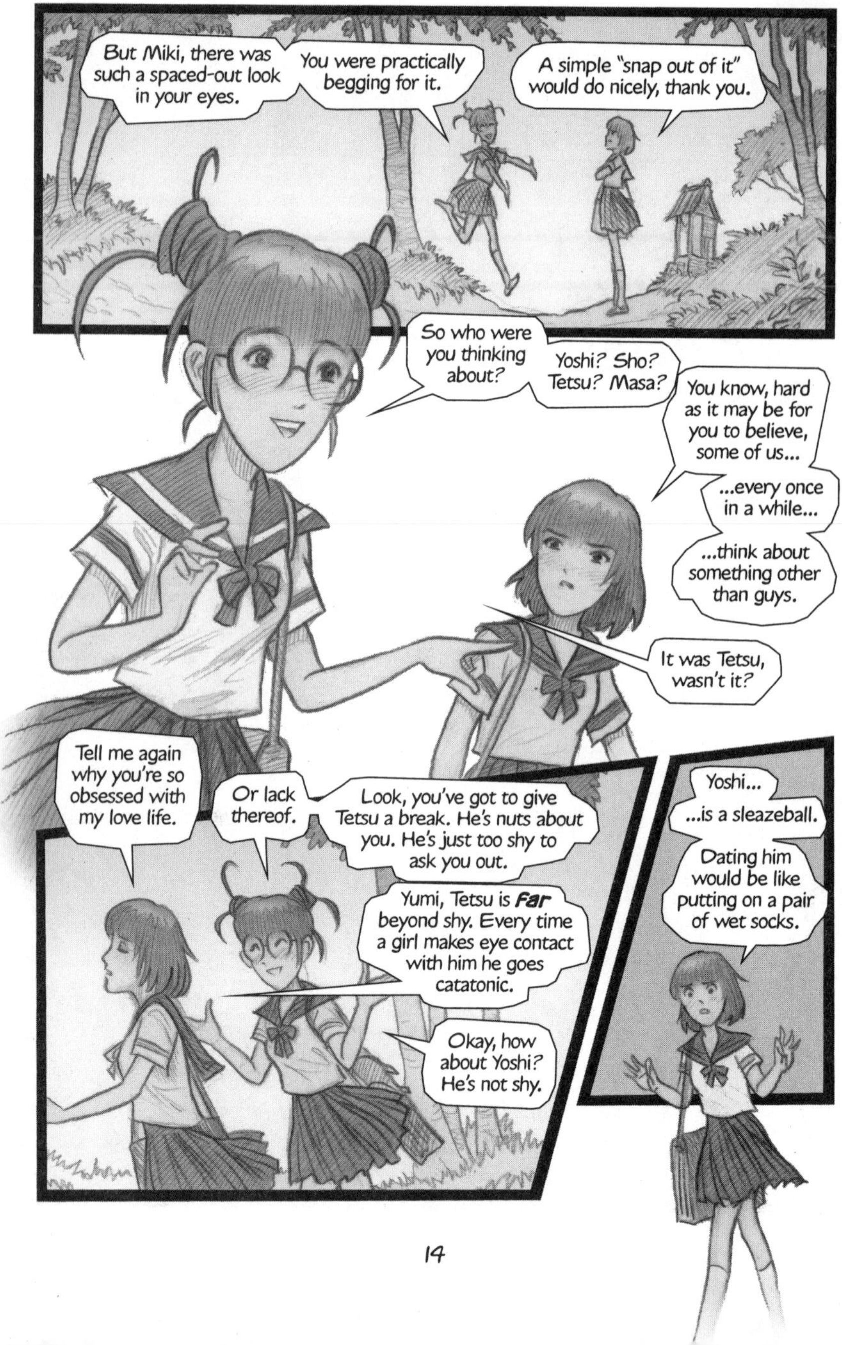
But Miki, there was such a spaced-out look in your eyes.
You were practically begging for it.
A simple "snap out of it" would do nicely, thank you.
So who were you thinking about?
Yoshi? Sho? Tetsu? Masa?
You know, hard as it may be for you to believe, some of us...
...every once in a while...
...think about something other than guys.
It was Tetsu, wasn't it?
Tell me again why you're so obsessed with my love life.
Or lack thereof.
Look, you've got to give Tetsu a break. He's nuts about you. He's just too shy to ask you out.
Yumi, Tetsu is ***Far*** beyond shy. Every time a girl makes eye contact with him he goes catatonic.
Okay, how about Yoshi? He's not shy.
Yoshi...
...is a sleazeball.
Dating him would be like putting on a pair of wet socks.

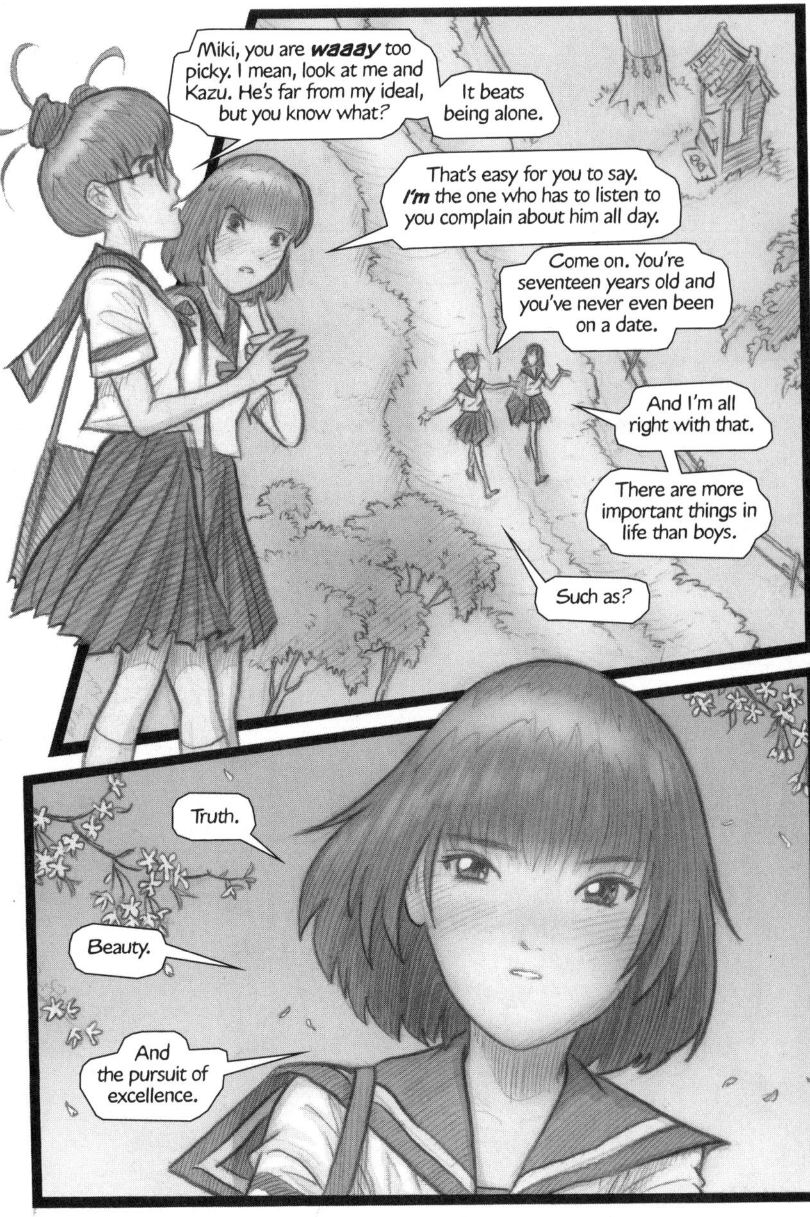
Miki, you are **waaay** too picky. I mean, look at me and Kazu. He's far from my ideal, but you know what?
It beats being alone.
That's easy for you to say. ***I'm*** the one who has to listen to you complain about him all day.
Come on. You're seventeen years old and you've never even been on a date.
And I'm all right with that.
There are more important things in life than boys.
Such as?
Truth.
Beauty.
And the pursuit of excellence.

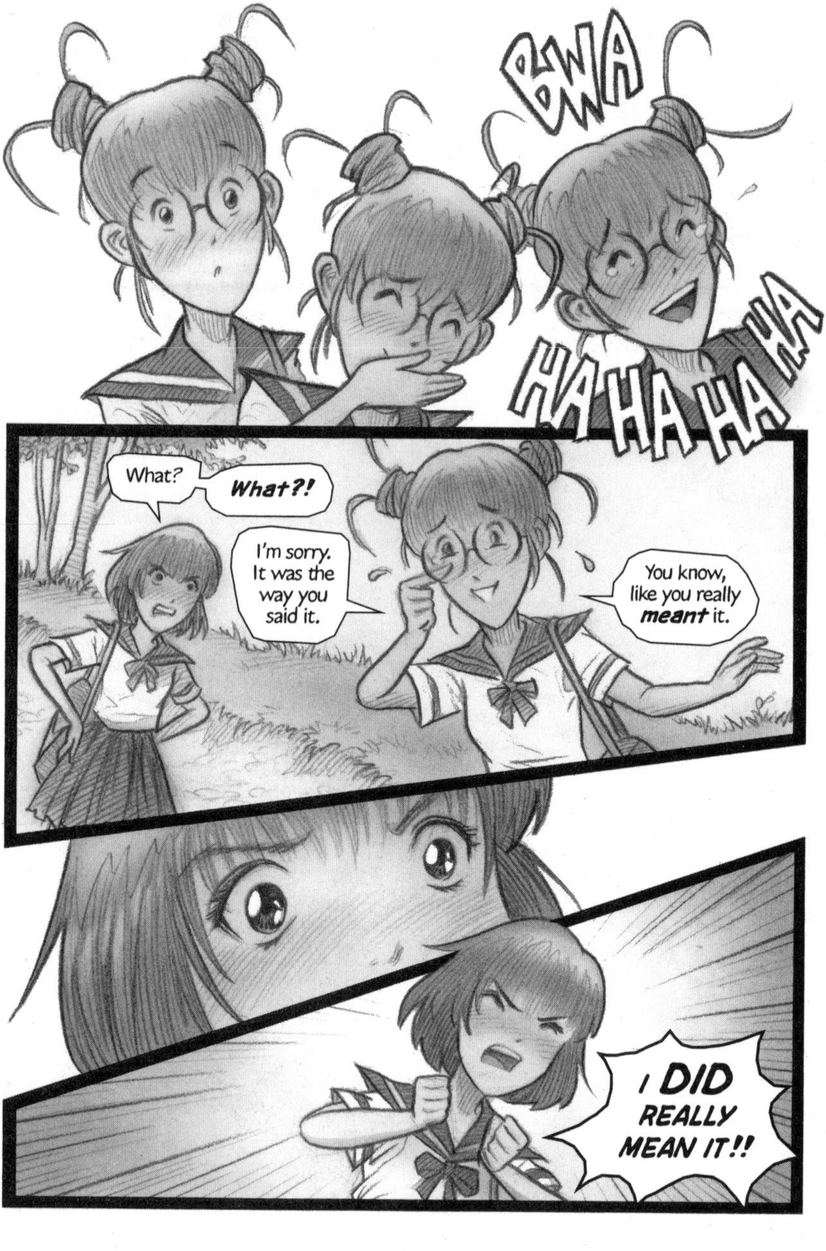
BWA
HA HA HA HA
What?
What?!
I'm sorry. It was the way you said it.
You know, like you really meant it.
I DID REALLY MEAN IT!!

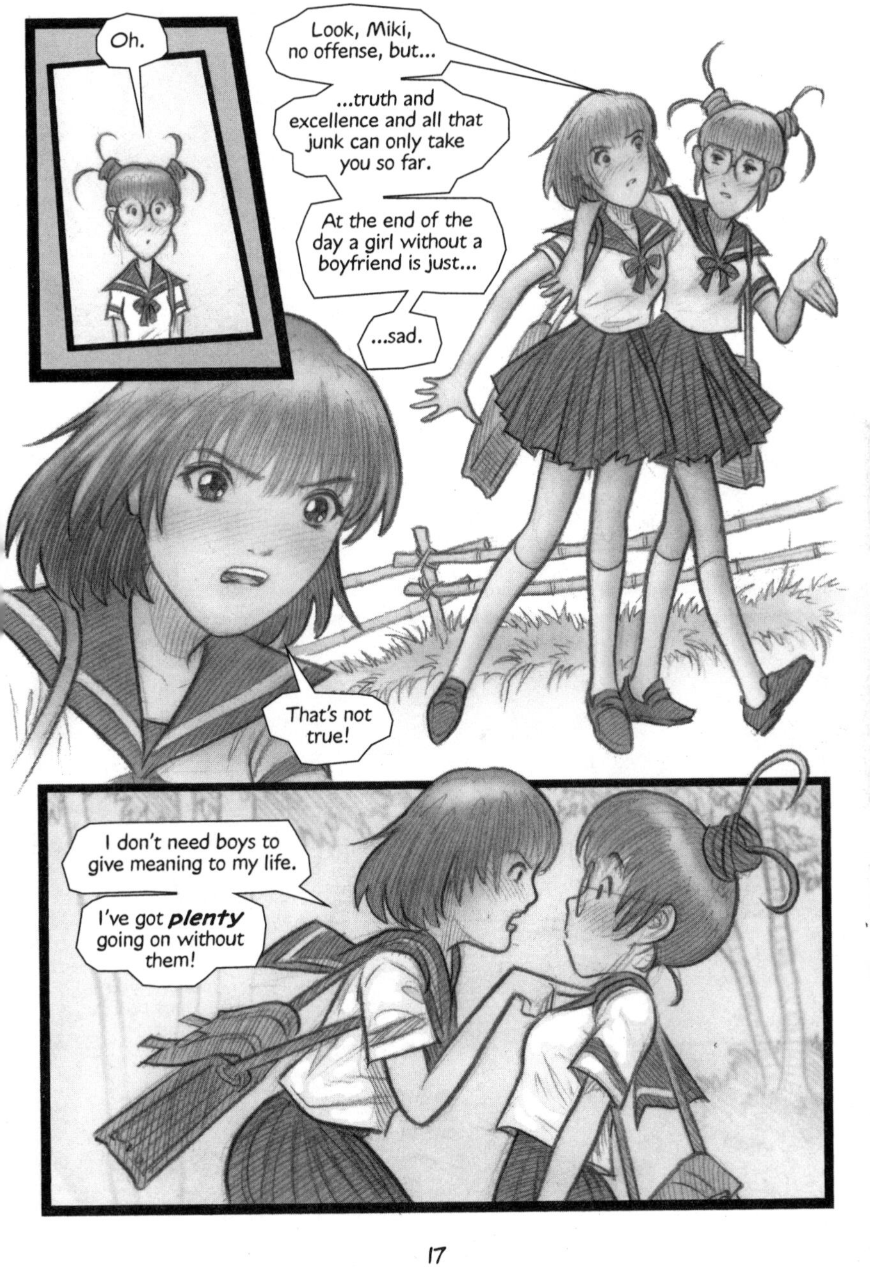
Oh.
Look, Miki, no offense, but...
...truth and excellence and all that junk can only take you so far.
At the end of the day a girl without a boyfriend is just...
...sad.
That's not true!
I don't need boys to give meaning to my life.
I've got **plenty** going on without them!

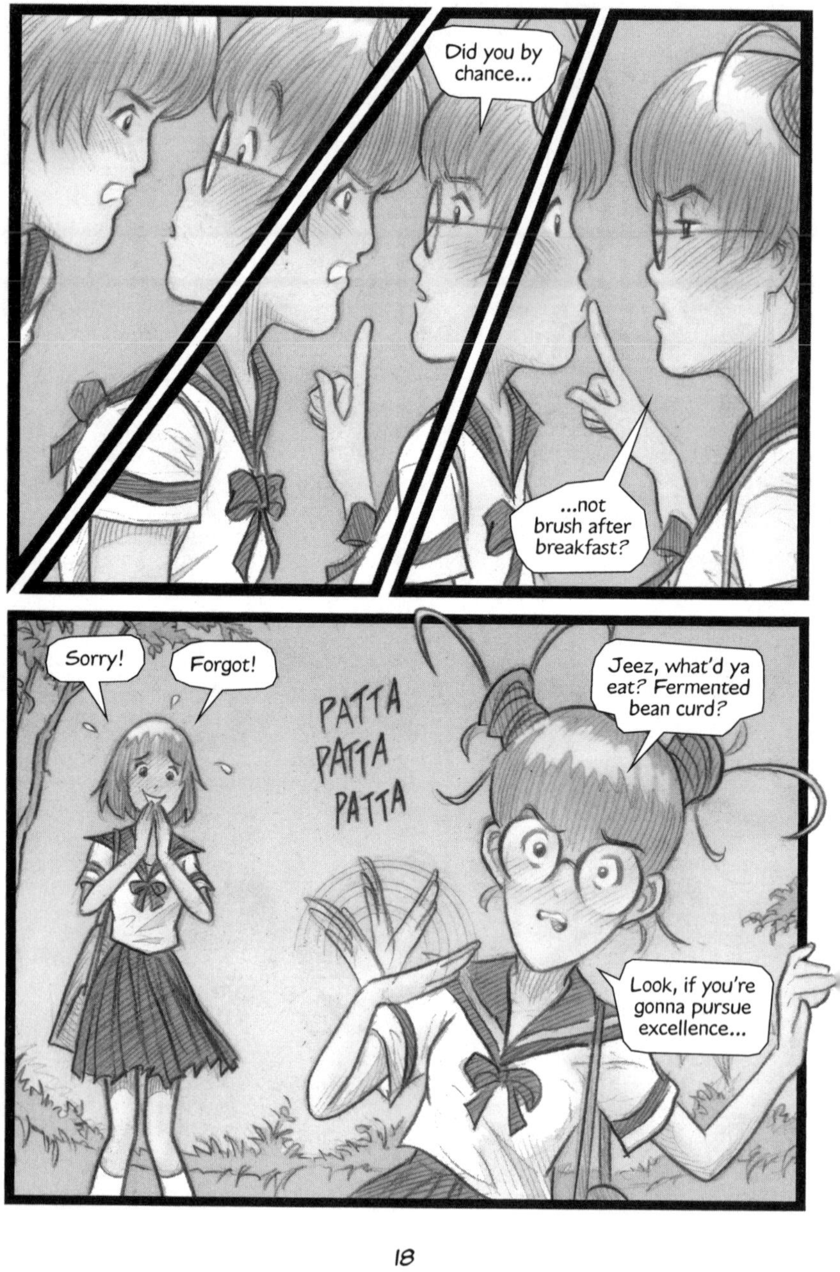
Did you by chance...
...not brush after breakfast?
Sorry!
Forgot!
PATTA PATTA PATTA
Jeez, what'd ya eat? Fermented bean curd?
Look, if you're gonna pursue excellence...

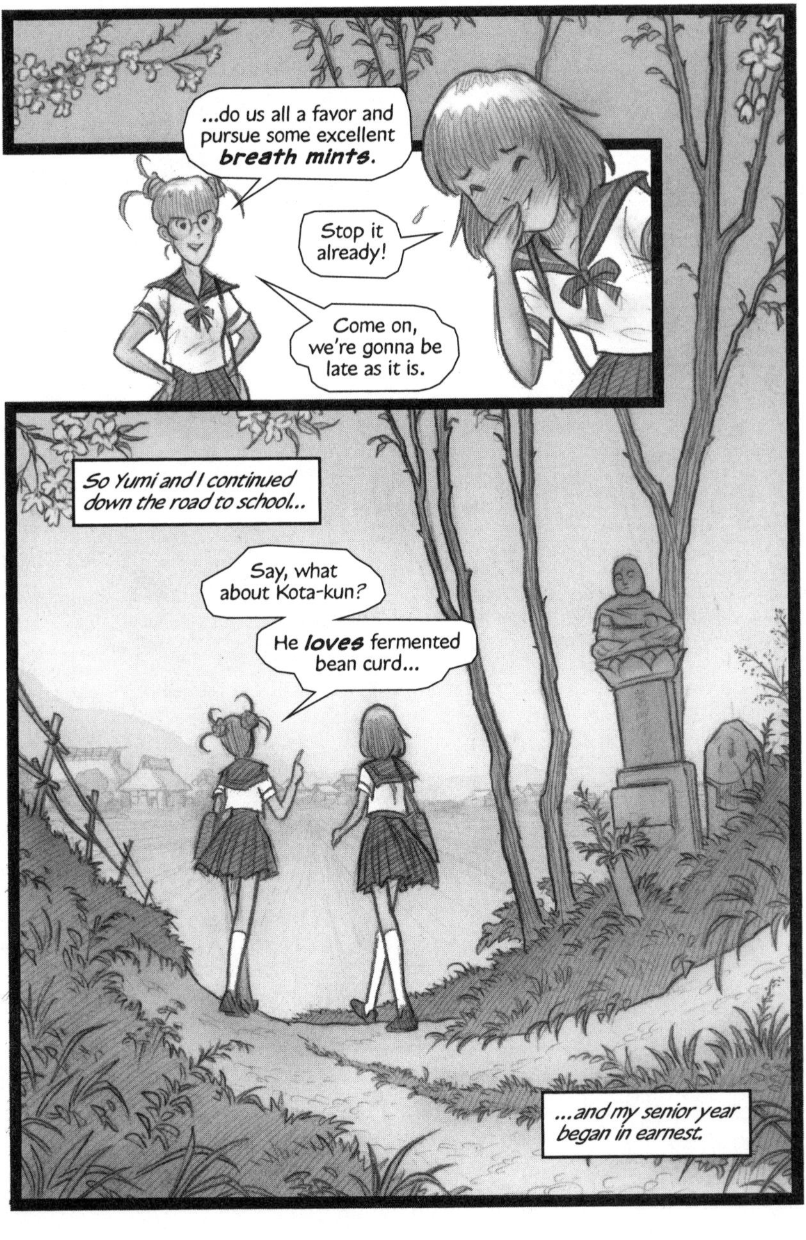
...do us all a favor and pursue some excellent **breath mints**.
Stop it already!
Come on, we're gonna be late as it is.
So Yumi and I continued down the road to school...
Say, what about Kota-kun?
He **loves** fermented bean curd...
...and my senior year began in earnest.

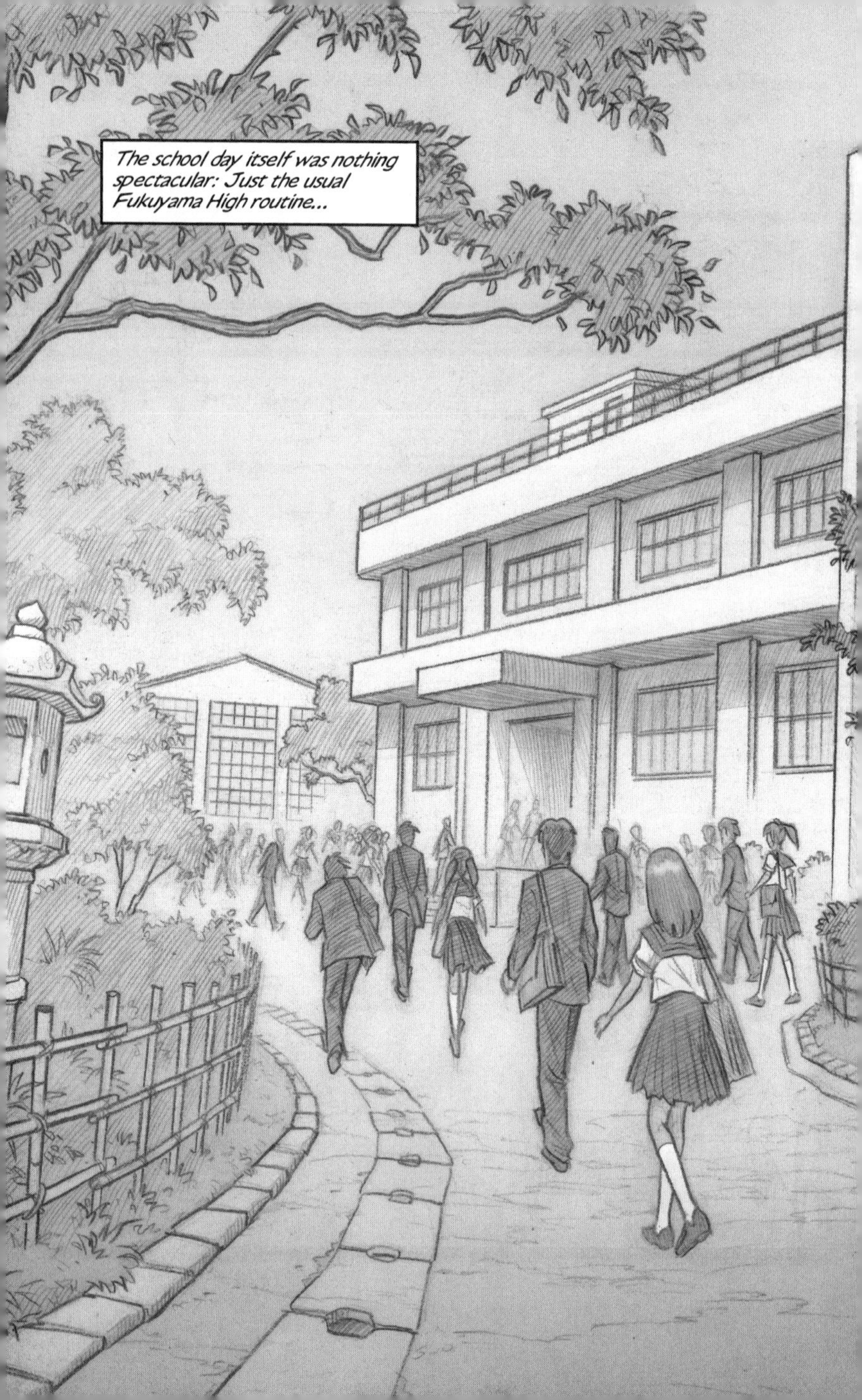
The school day itself was nothing spectacular: Just the usual Fukuyama High routine...

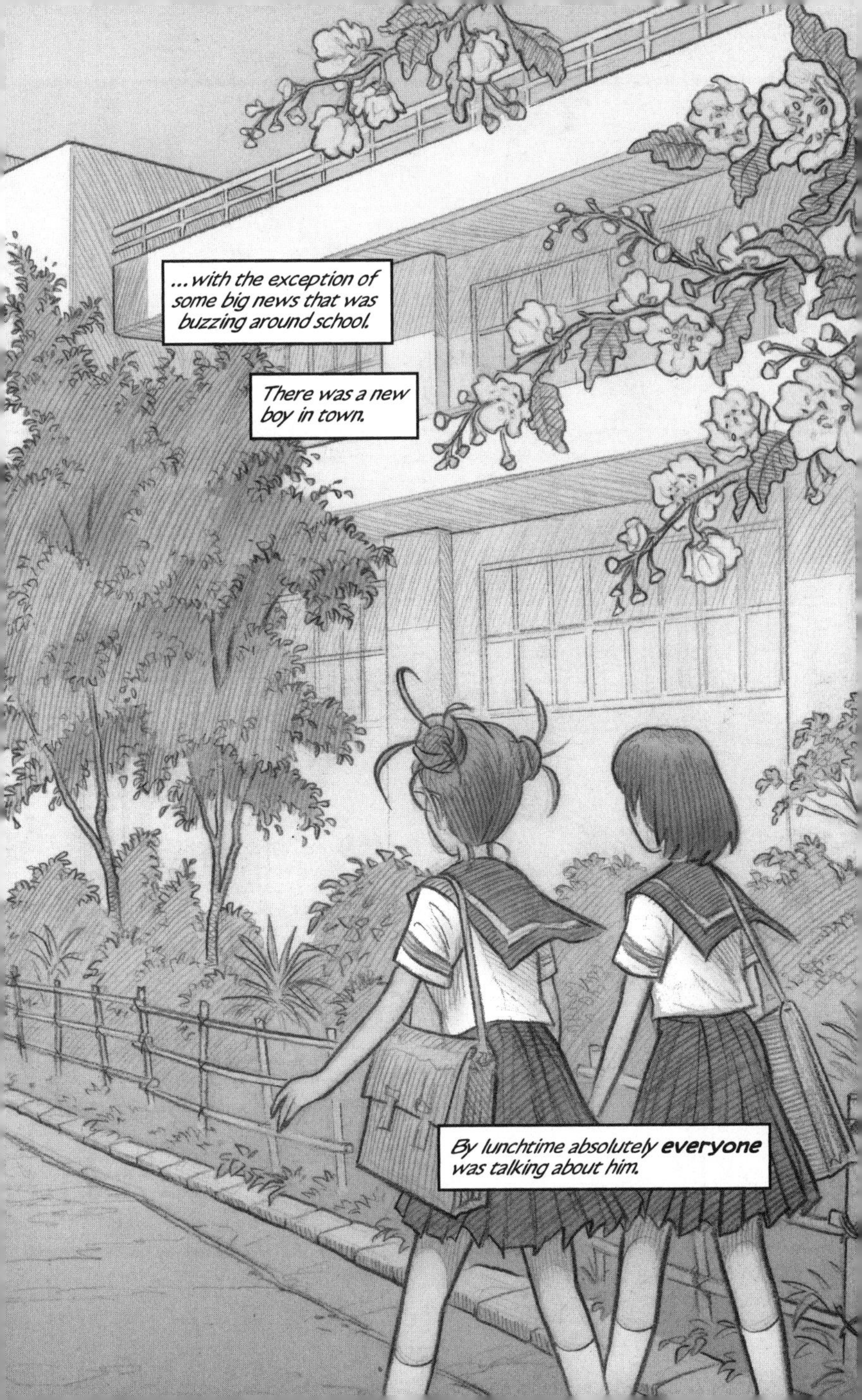
...with the exception of some big news that was buzzing around school.
There was a new boy in town.
By lunchtime absolutely **everyone** was talking about him.

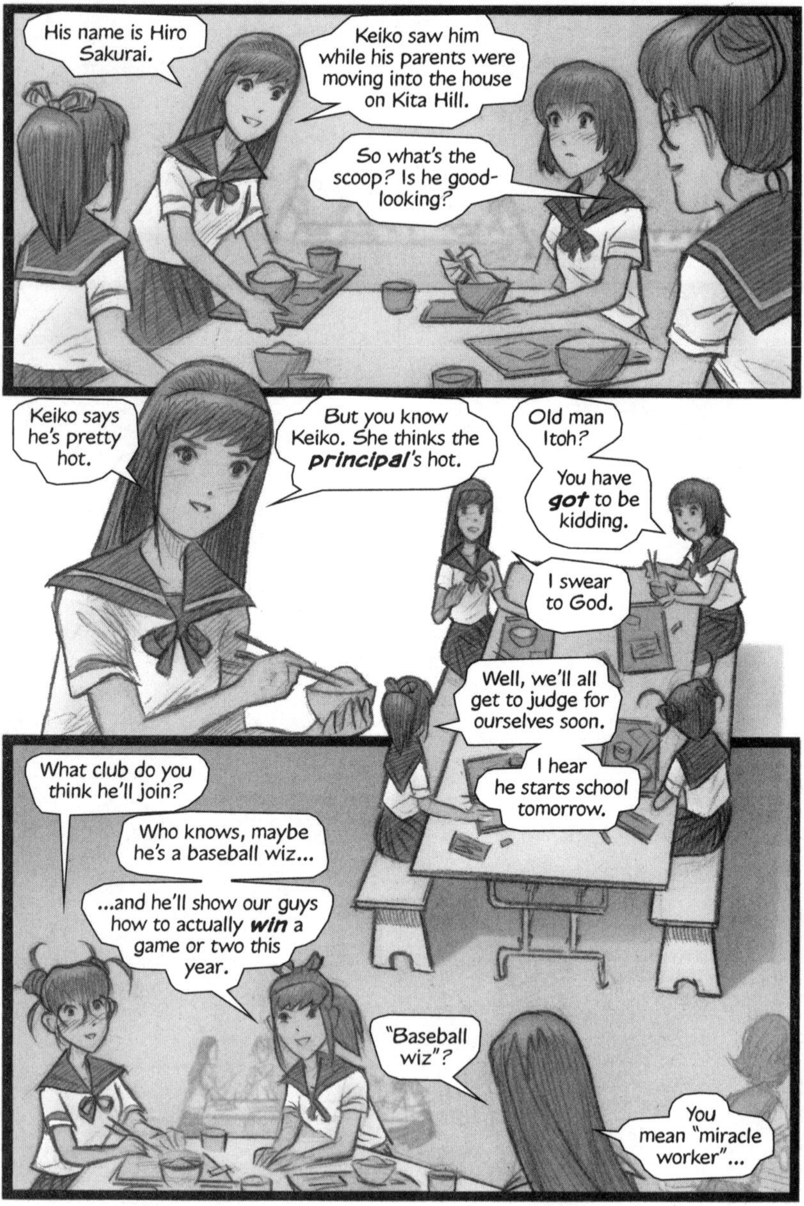
His name is Hiro Sakurai.
Keiko saw him while his parents were moving into the house on Kita Hill.
So what's the scoop? Is he good-looking?
Keiko says he's pretty hot.
But you know Keiko. She thinks the **principal**'s hot.
Old man Itoh?
You have **got** to be kidding.
I swear to God.
Well, we'll all get to judge for ourselves soon.
I hear he starts school tomorrow.
What club do you think he'll join?
Who knows, maybe he's a baseball wiz...
...and he'll show our guys how to actually **win** a game or two this year.
"Baseball wiz"?
You mean "miracle worker"...

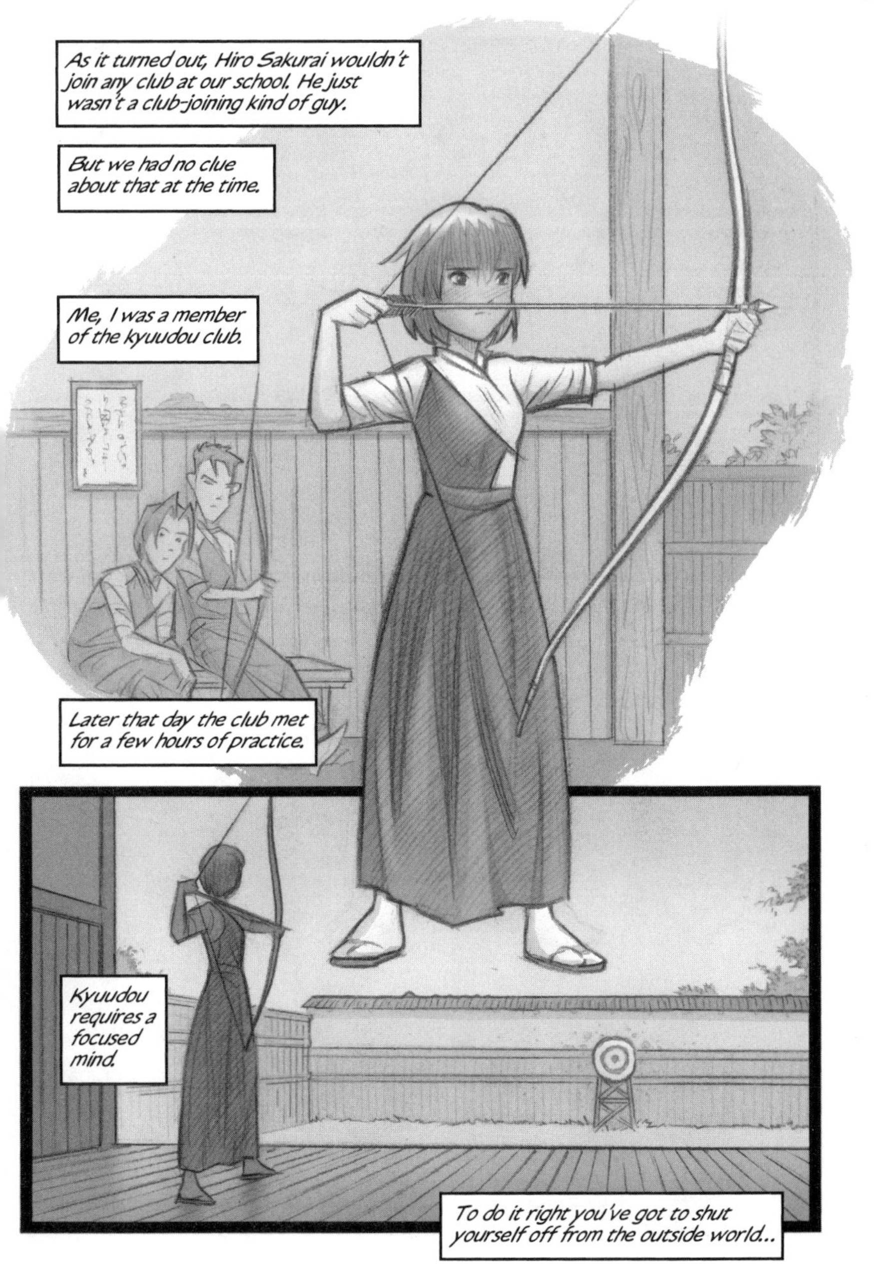
As it turned out, Hiro Sakurai wouldn't join any club at our school. He just wasn't a club-joining kind of guy.
But we had no clue about that at the time.
Me, I was a member of the kyuudou club.
Later that day the club met for a few hours of practice.
Kyuudou requires a focused mind.
To do it right you've got to shut yourself off from the outside world...

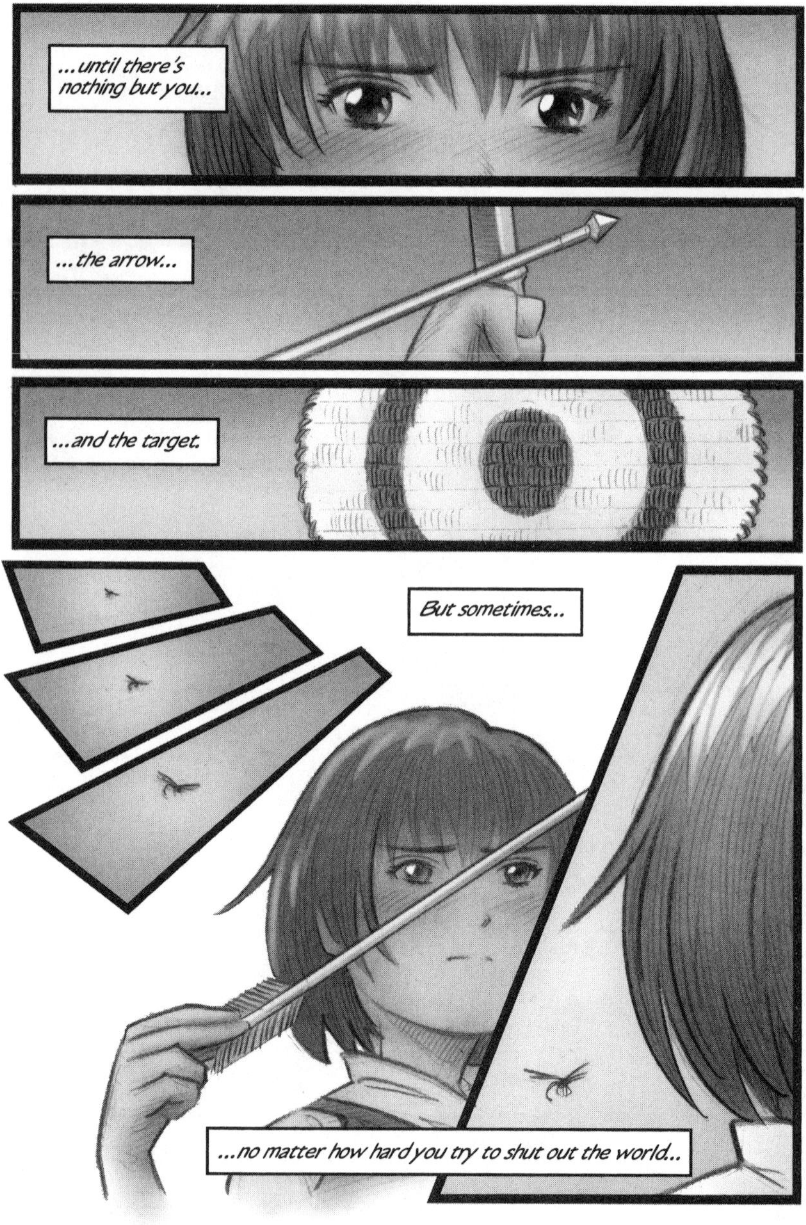
...until there's nothing but you...
...the arrow...
...and the target.
But sometimes...
...no matter how hard you try to shut out the world...

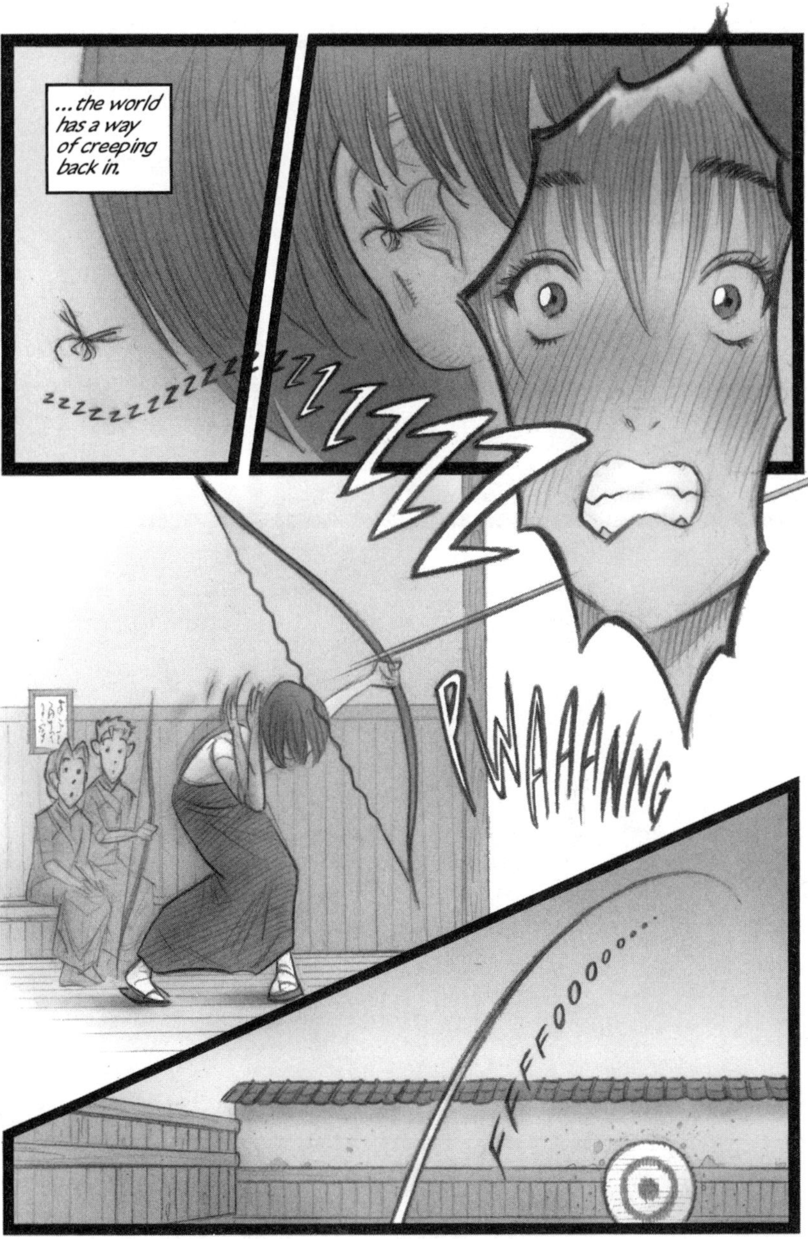
...the world has a way of creeping back in.
zzzzzzzzZZZZZZZZZZZZ
PWAAANNG
FFFOOOooo...

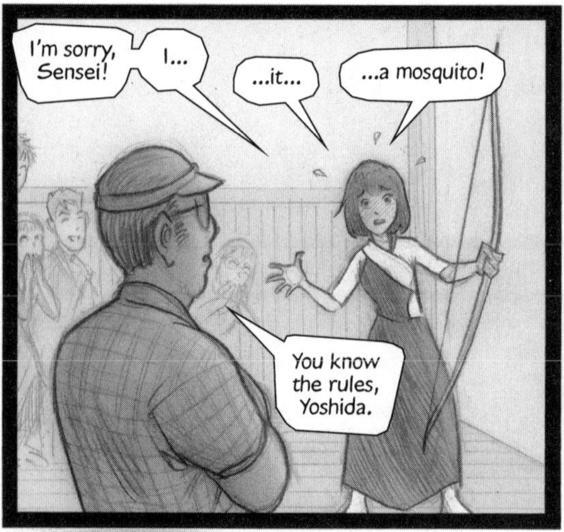
I'm sorry, Sensei!
I...
...it...
...a mosquito!
You know the rules, Yoshida.
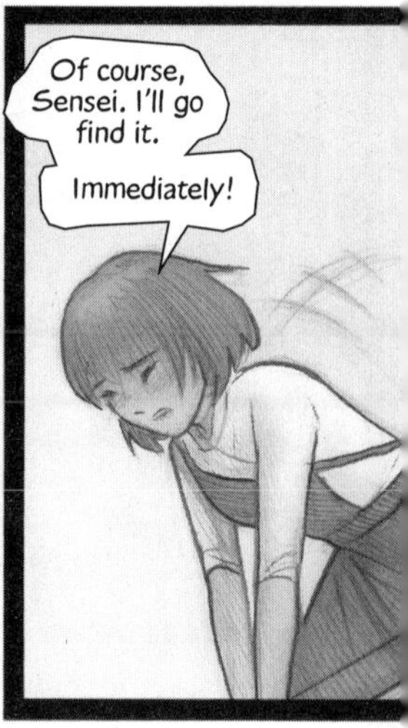
Of course, Sensei. I'll go find it.
Immediately!
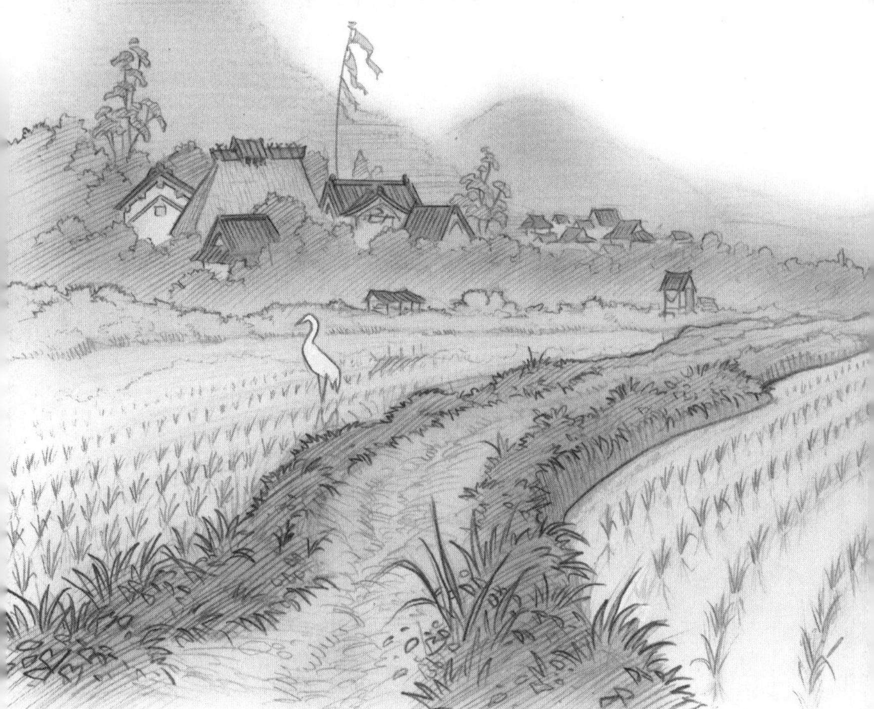

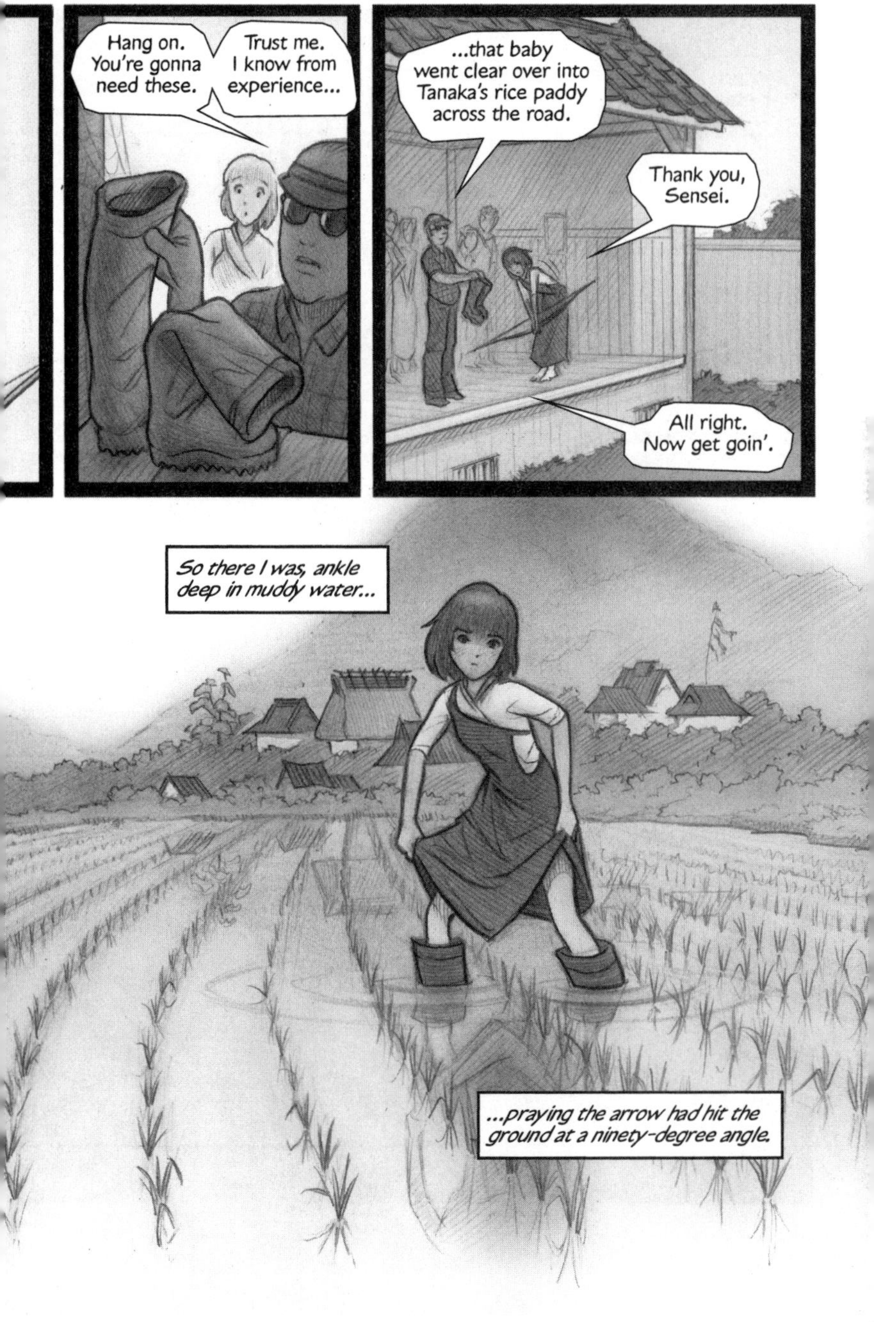

Hang on. You're gonna need these.
Trust me. I know from experience...
...that baby went clear over into Tanaka's rice paddy across the road.
Thank you, Sensei.
All right. Now get goin'.
So there I was, ankle deep in muddy water...
...praying the arrow had hit the ground at a ninety-degree angle.

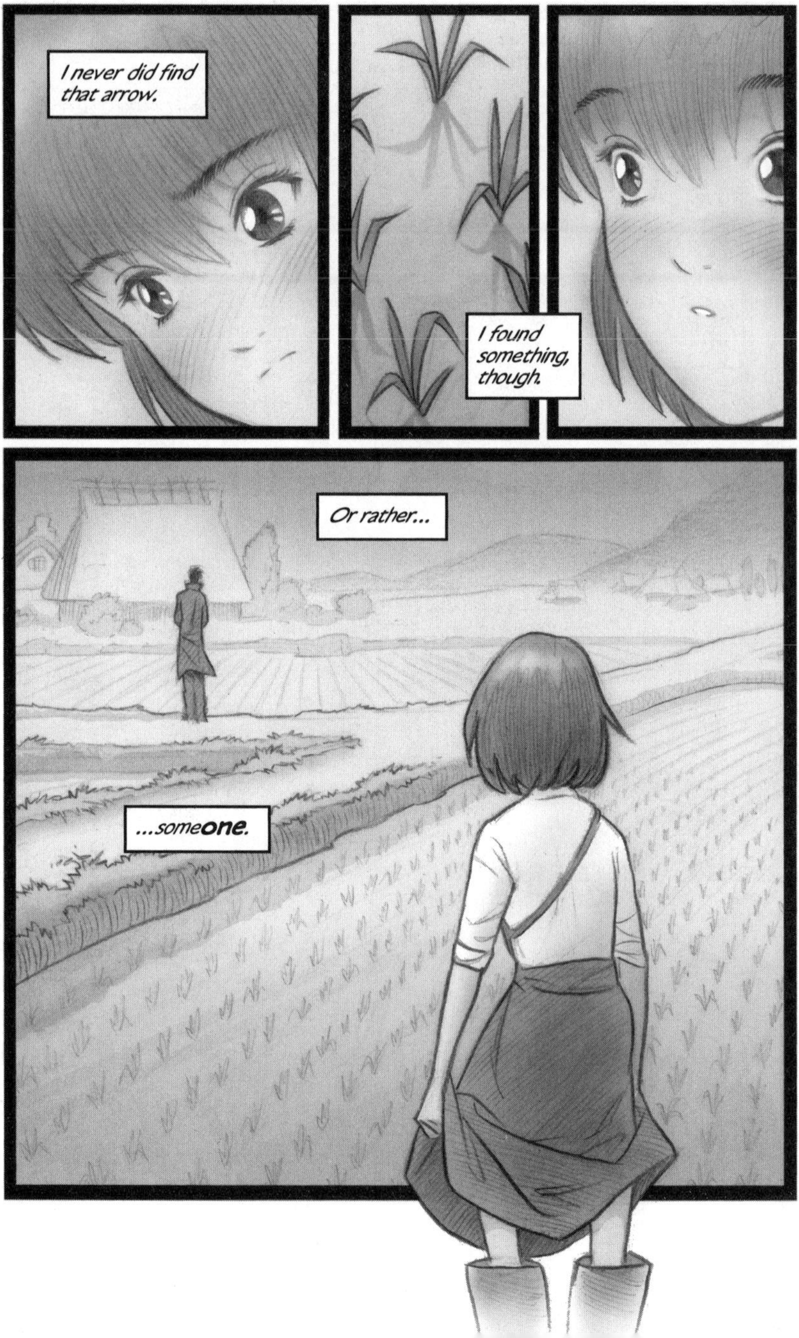
I never did find that arrow.
I found something, though.
Or rather...
...some**one**.

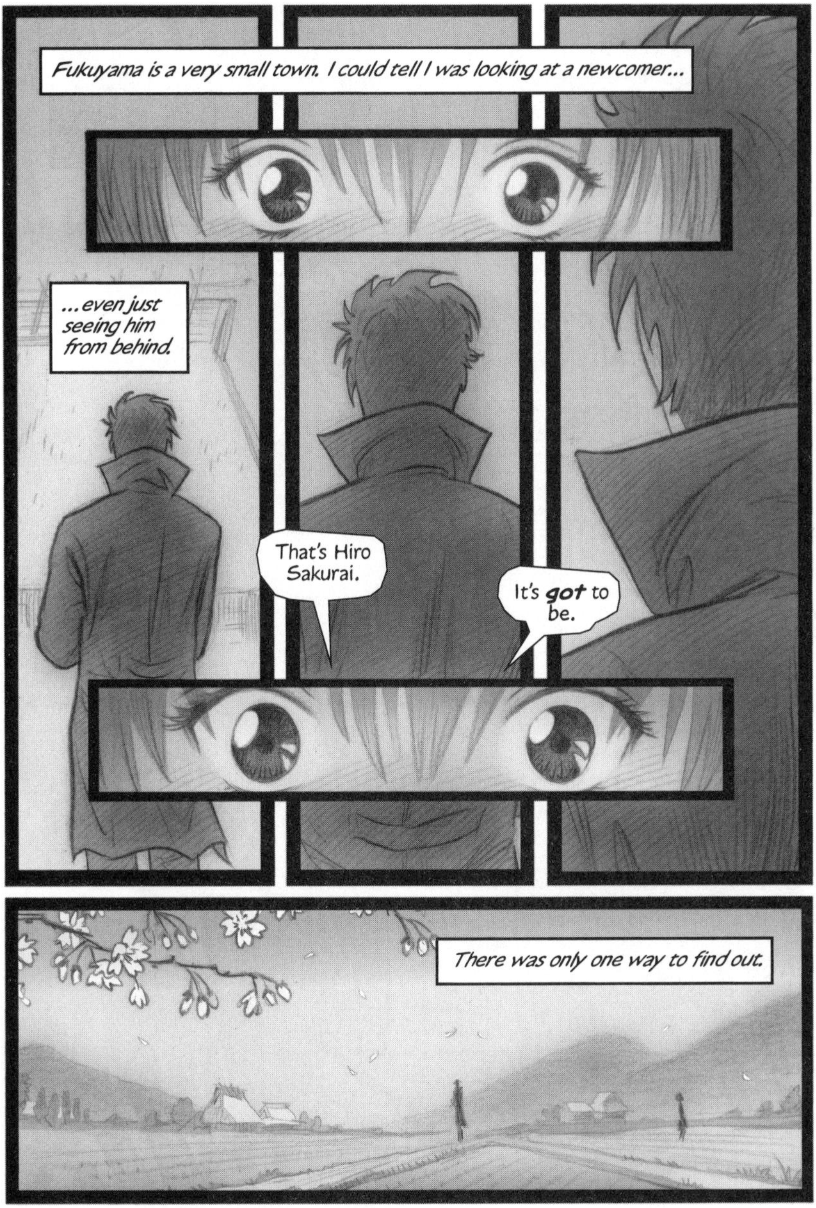

Fukuyama is a very small town. I could tell I was looking at a newcomer...
...even just seeing him from behind.
That's Hiro Sakurai.
It's **got** to be.
There was only one way to find out.

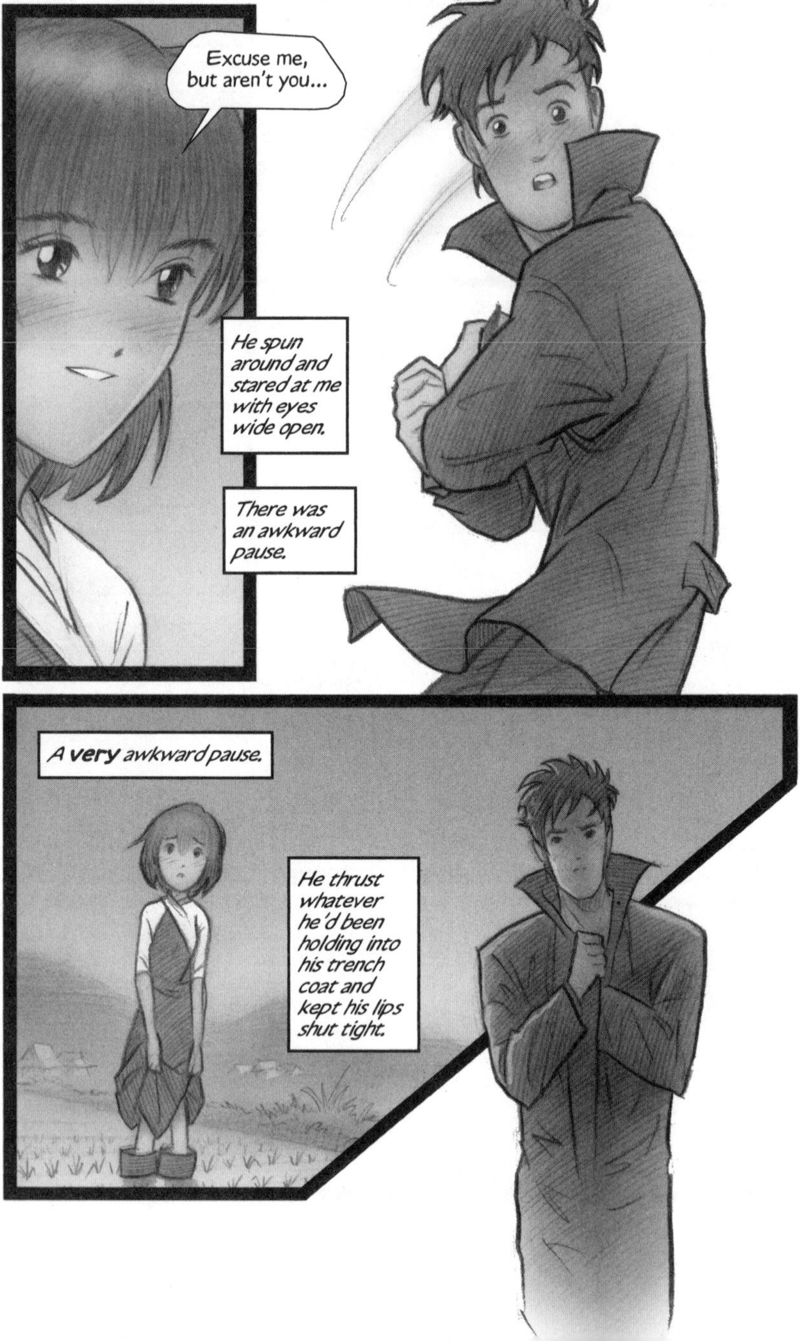
Excuse me, but aren't you...
He spun around and stared at me with eyes wide open.
There was an awkward pause.
A **very** awkward pause.
He thrust whatever he'd been holding into his trench coat and kept his lips shut tight.

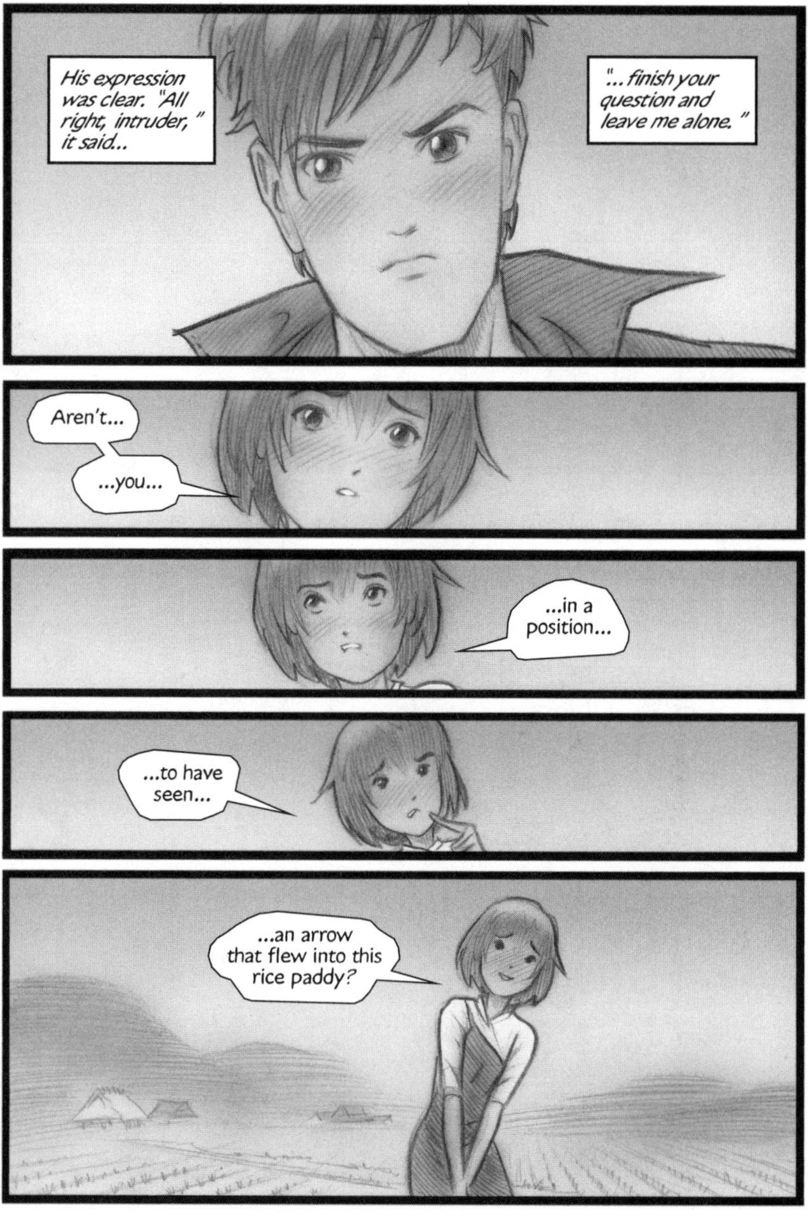
His expression was clear. "All right, intruder," it said...
"...finish your question and leave me alone."
Aren't...
...you...
...in a position...
...to have seen...
...an arrow that flew into this rice paddy?

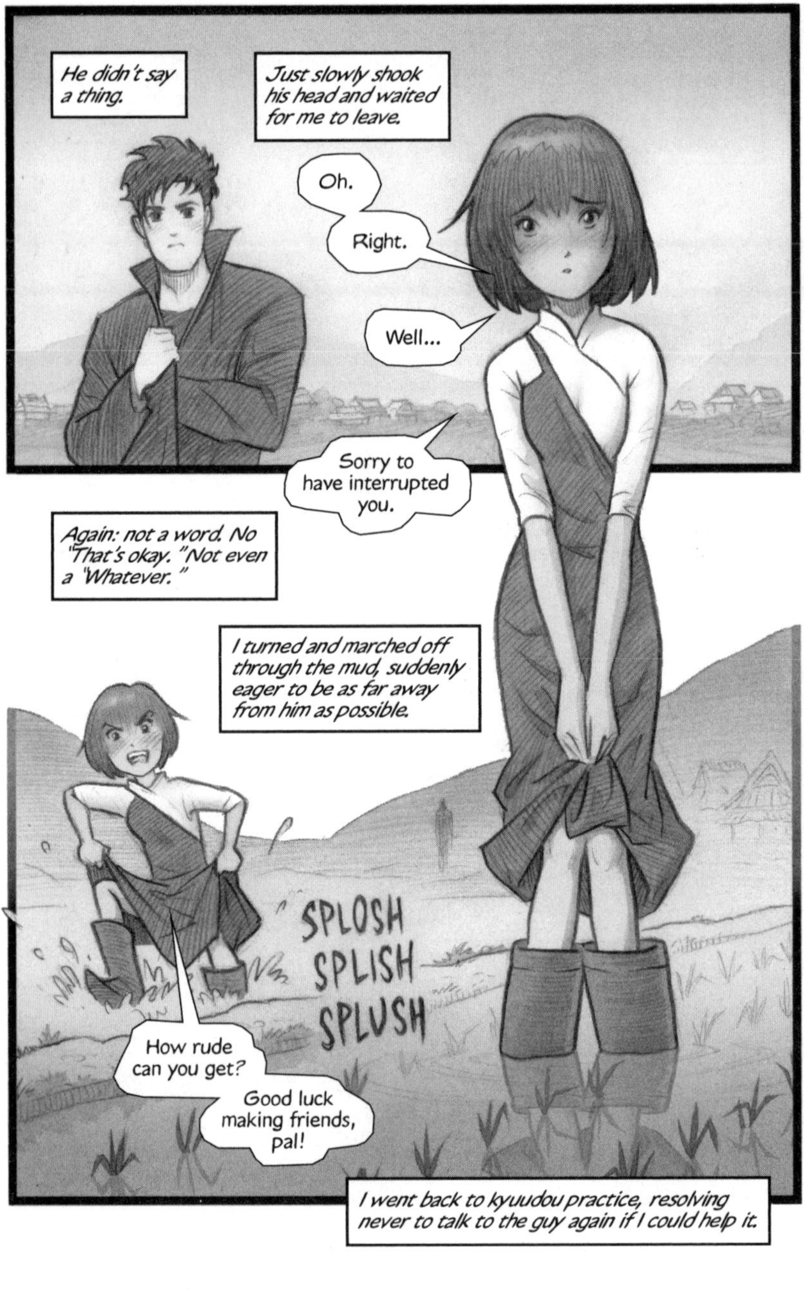
He didn't say a thing.
Just slowly shook his head and waited for me to leave.
Oh.
Right.
Well...
Sorry to have interrupted you.
Again: not a word. No "That's okay." Not even a "Whatever."
I turned and marched off through the mud, suddenly eager to be as far away from him as possible.
SPLOSH
SPLISH
SPLUSH
How rude can you get?
Good luck making friends, pal!
I went back to kyuudou practice, resolving never to talk to the guy again if I could help it.

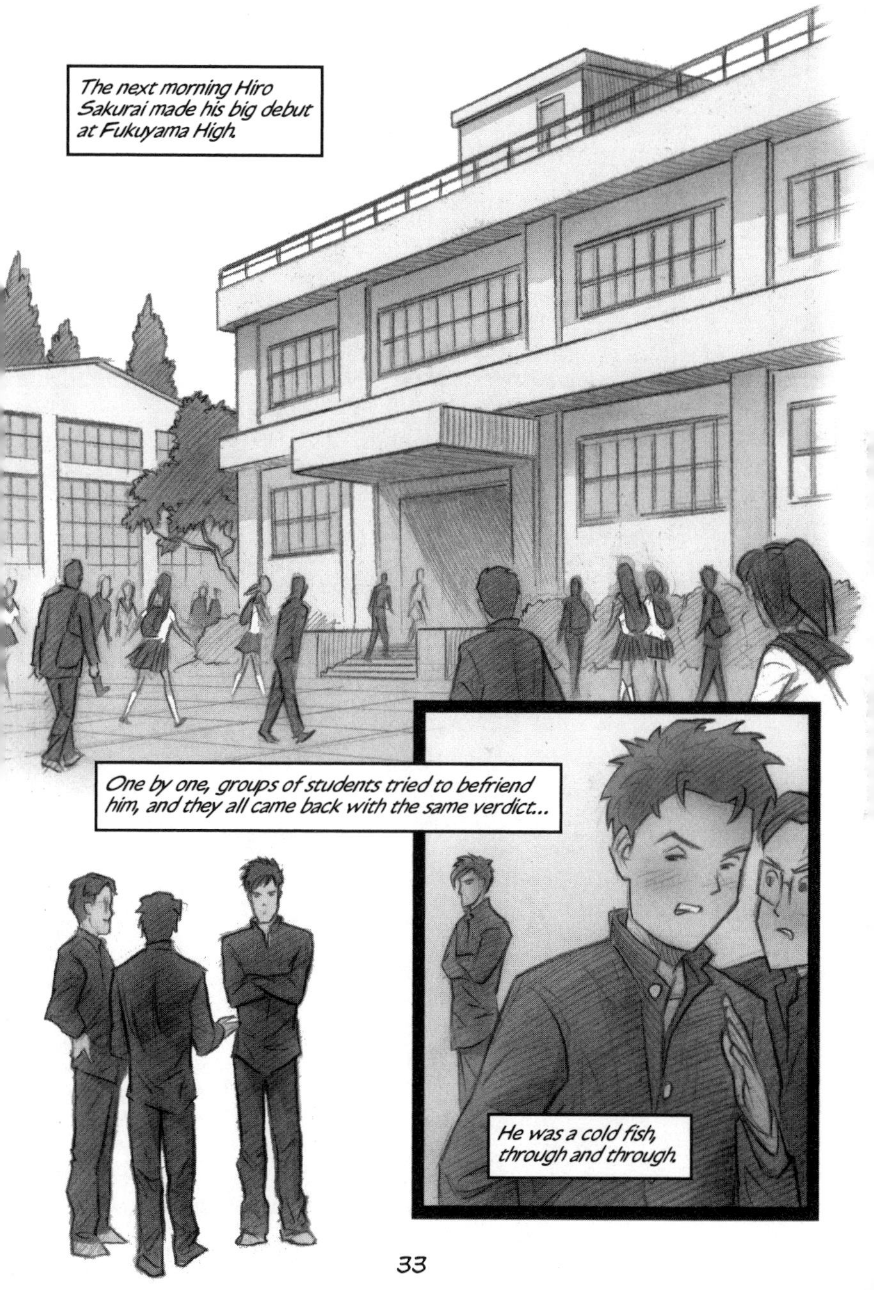
The next morning Hiro Sakurai made his big debut at Fukuyama High.
One by one, groups of students tried to befriend him, and they all came back with the same verdict...
He was a cold fish, through and through.

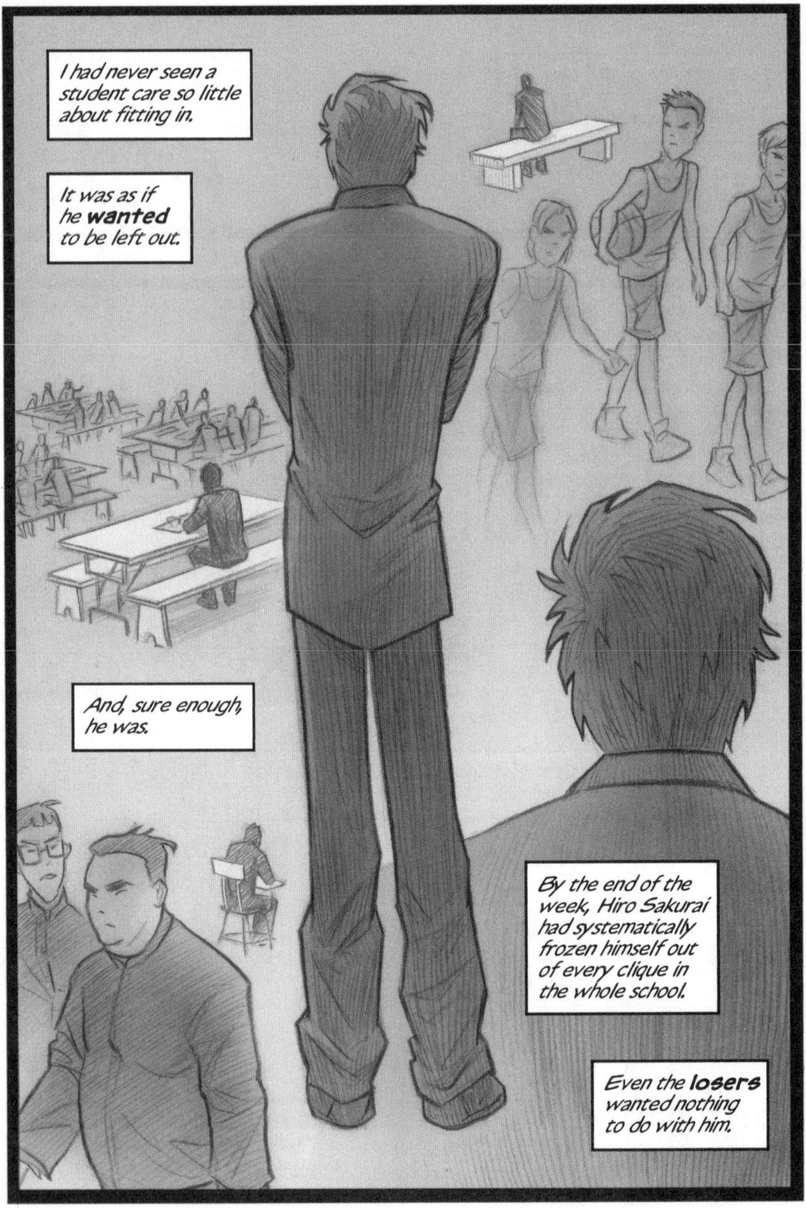
I had never seen a student care so little about fitting in.
It was as if he **wanted** to be left out.
And, sure enough, he was.
By the end of the week, Hiro Sakurai had systematically frozen himself out of every clique in the whole school.
Even the **losers** wanted nothing to do with him.

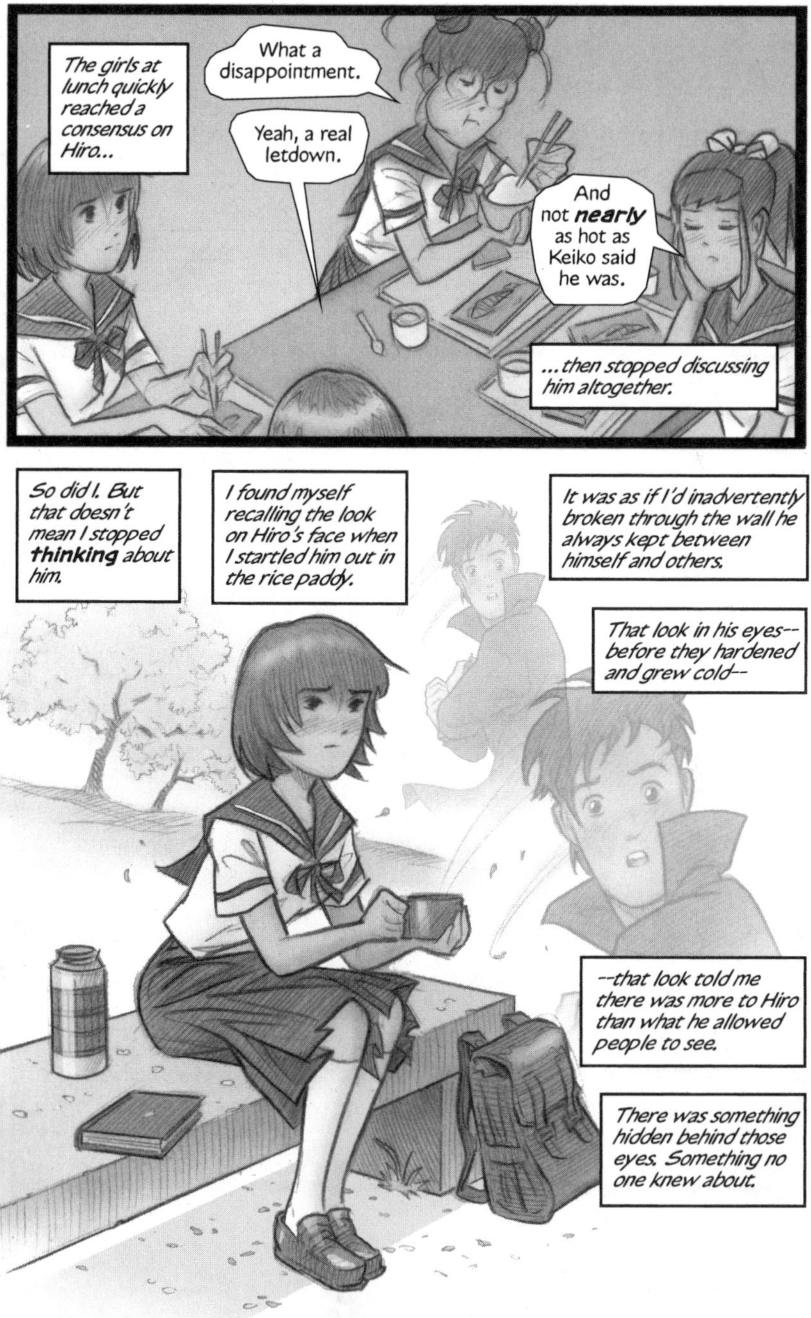
The girls at lunch quickly reached a consensus on Hiro...
What a disappointment.
Yeah, a real letdown.
And not **nearly** as hot as Keiko said he was.
...then stopped discussing him altogether.
So did I. But that doesn't mean I stopped **thinking** about him.
I found myself recalling the look on Hiro's face when I startled him out in the rice paddy.
It was as if I'd inadvertently broken through the wall he always kept between himself and others.
That look in his eyes-- before they hardened and grew cold--
--that look told me there was more to Hiro than what he allowed people to see.
There was something hidden behind those eyes. Something no one knew about.

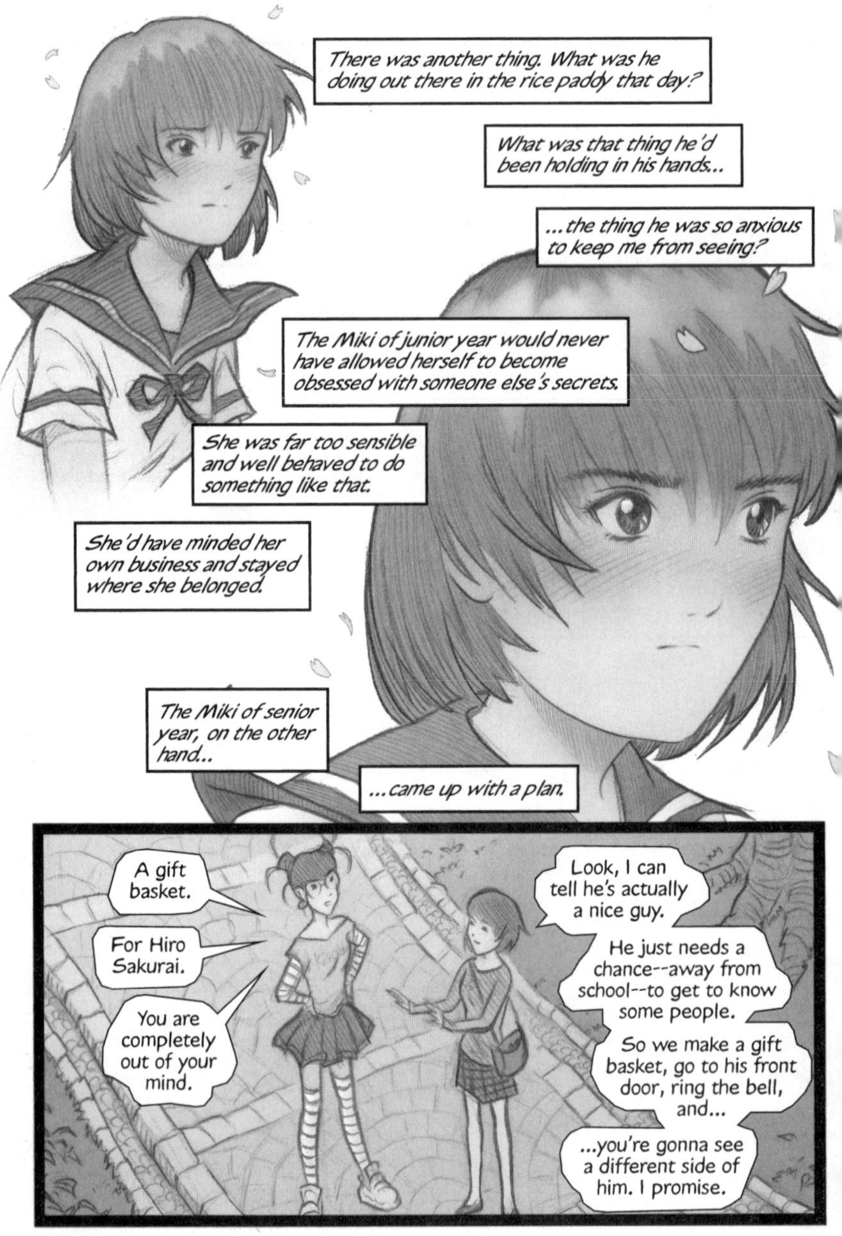
There was another thing. What was he doing out there in the rice paddy that day?
What was that thing he'd been holding in his hands...
...the thing he was so anxious to keep me from seeing?
The Miki of junior year would never have allowed herself to become obsessed with someone else's secrets.
She was far too sensible and well behaved to do something like that.
She'd have minded her own business and stayed where she belonged.
The Miki of senior year, on the other hand...
...came up with a plan.
A gift basket.
For Hiro Sakurai.
You are completely out of your mind.
Look, I can tell he's actually a nice guy.
He just needs a chance--away from school--to get to know some people.
So we make a gift basket, go to his front door, ring the bell, and...
...you're gonna see a different side of him. I promise.

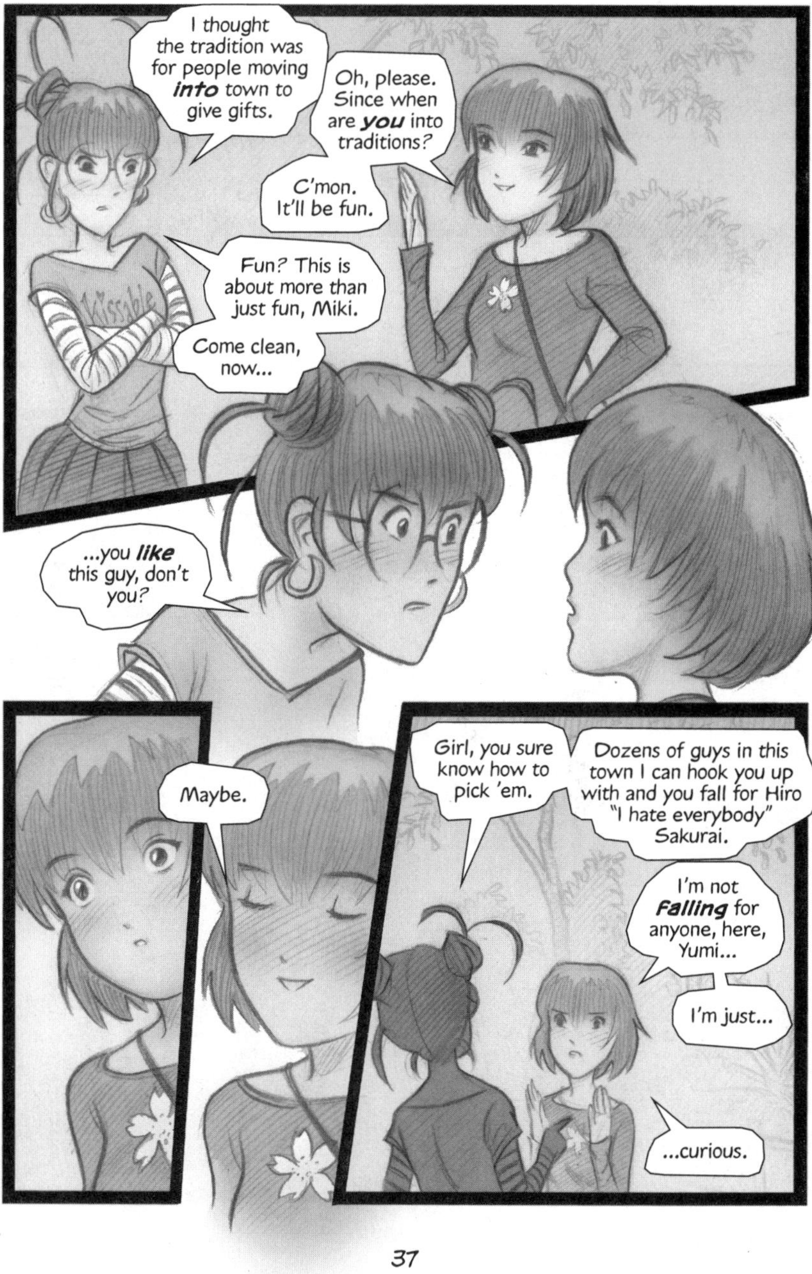
I thought the tradition was for people moving **into** town to give gifts.
Oh, please. Since when are **you** into traditions?
C'mon. It'll be fun.
Fun? This is about more than just fun, Miki.
Come clean, now...
...you **like** this guy, don't you?
Maybe.
Girl, you sure know how to pick 'em.
Dozens of guys in this town I can hook you up with and you fall for Hiro "I hate everybody" Sakurai.
I'm not **Falling** for anyone, here, Yumi...
I'm just...
...curious.

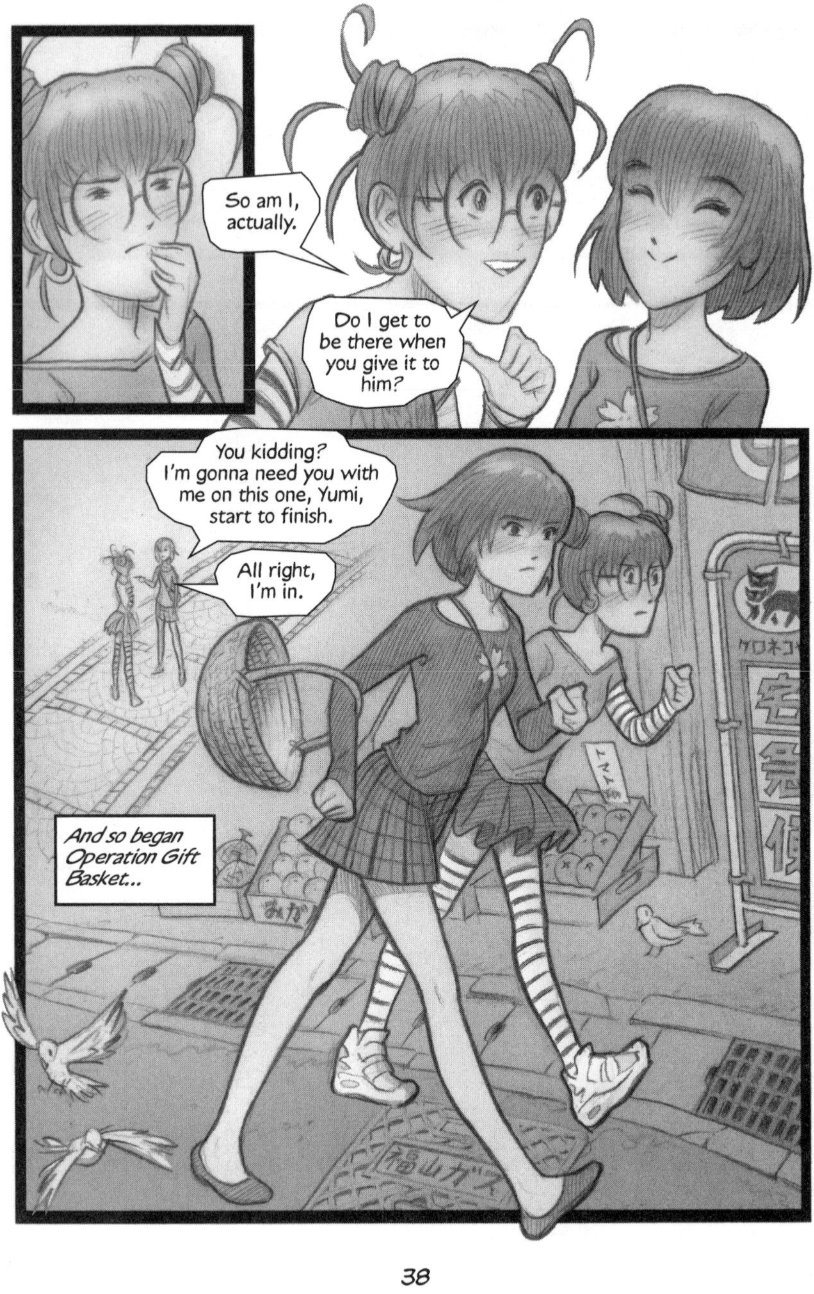

So am I, actually.
Do I get to be there when you give it to him?
You kidding? I'm gonna need you with me on this one, Yumi, start to finish.
All right, I'm in.
福山ガス
And so began Operation Gift Basket...

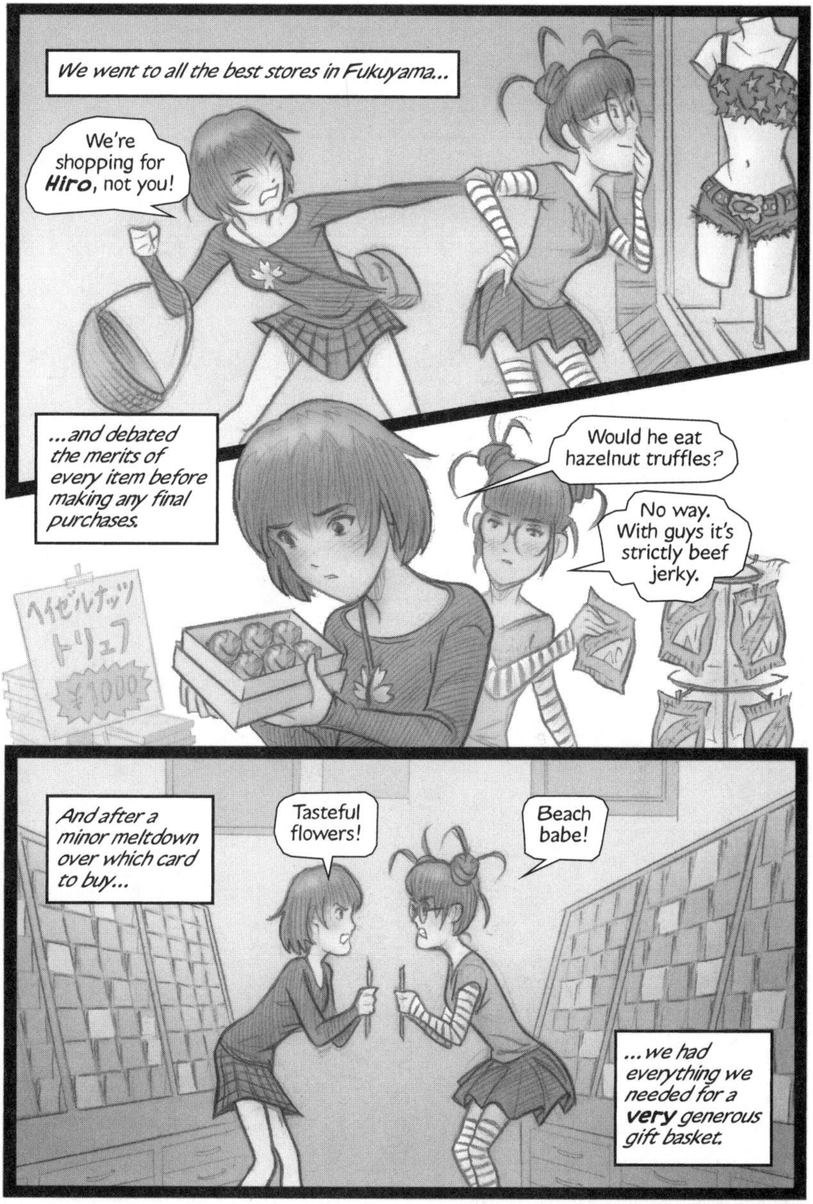
We went to all the best stores in Fukuyama...
We're shopping for Hiro, not you!
...and debated the merits of every item before making any final purchases.
Would he eat hazelnut truffles?
No way. With guys it's strictly beef jerky.
ヘイゼルナッツ
トリュフ
¥1000
And after a minor meltdown over which card to buy...
Tasteful flowers!
Beach babe!
...we had everything we needed for a very generous gift basket.

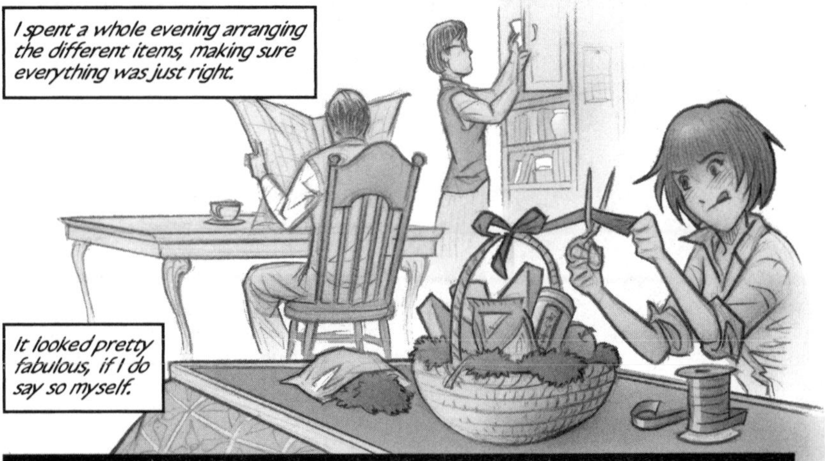
I spent a whole evening arranging the different items, making sure everything was just right.
It looked pretty fabulous, if I do say so myself.
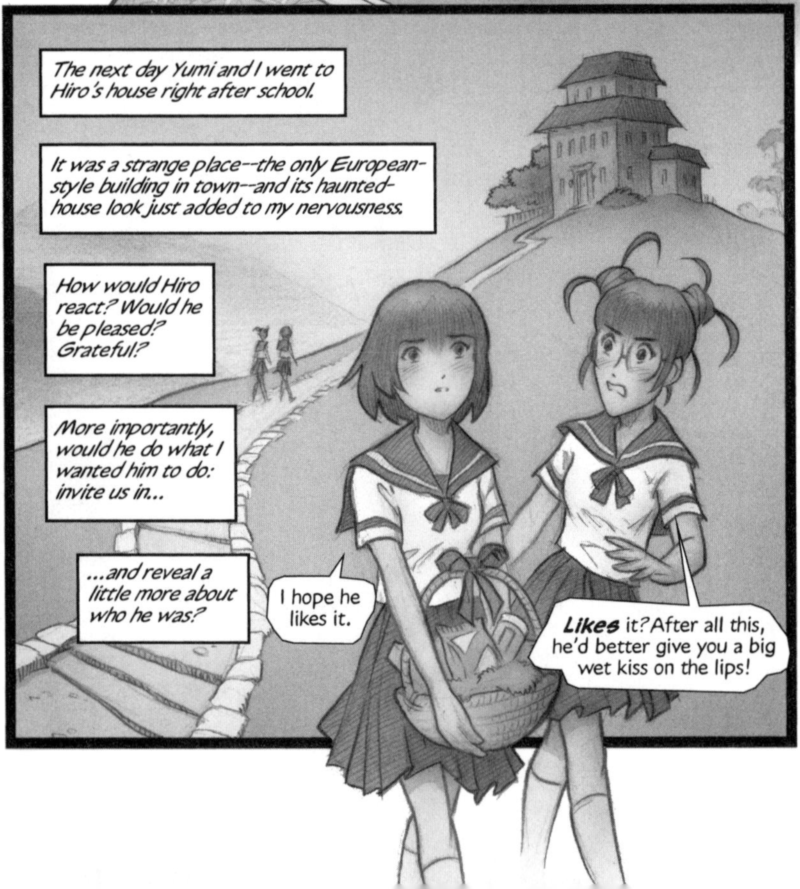
The next day Yumi and I went to Hiro's house right after school.
It was a strange place--the only European-style building in town--and its haunted-house look just added to my nervousness.
How would Hiro react? Would he be pleased? Grateful?
More importantly, would he do what I wanted him to do: invite us in...
...and reveal a little more about who he was?
I hope he likes it.
Likes it? After all this, he'd better give you a big wet kiss on the lips!

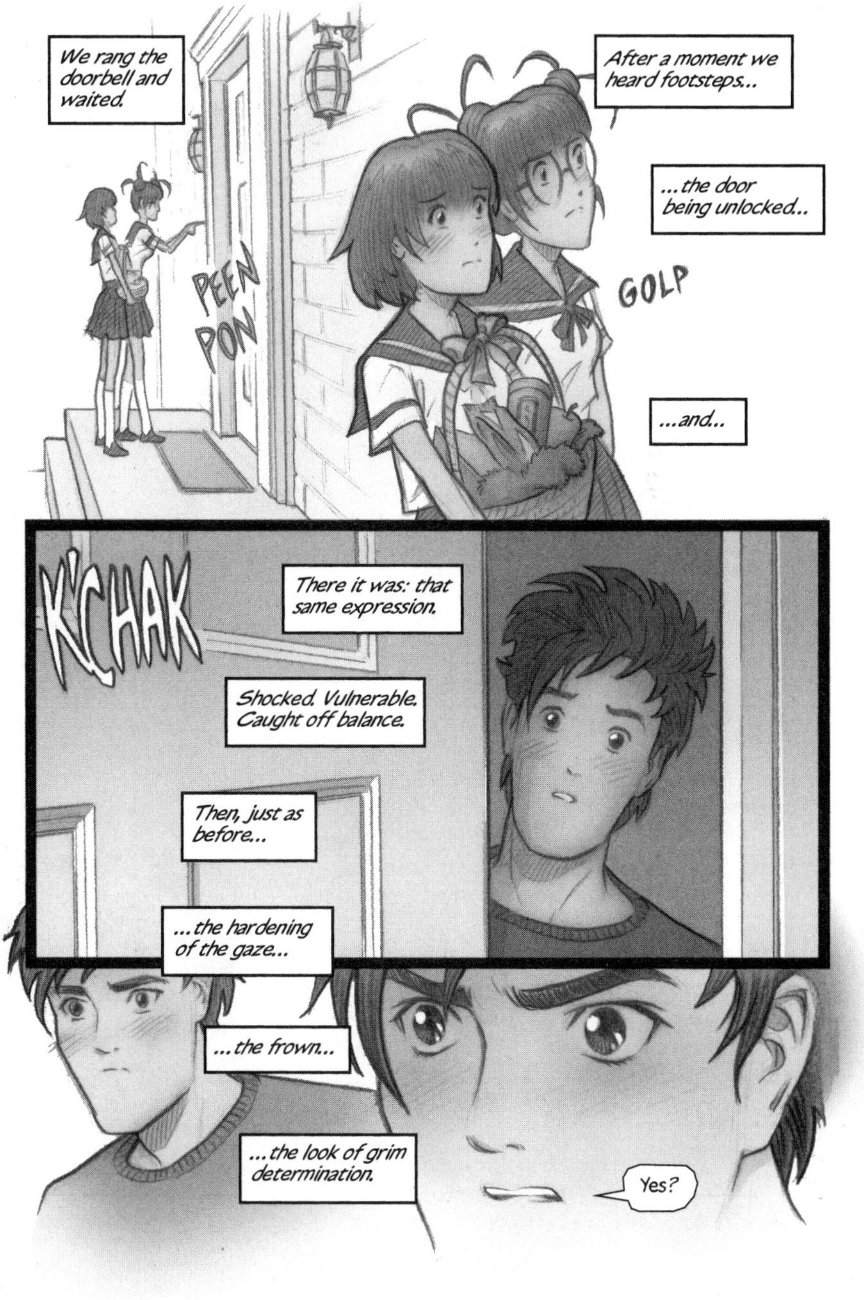

We rang the doorbell and waited.
PEEN PON
After a moment we heard footsteps...
...the door being unlocked...
GOLP
...and..
K'CHAK
There it was: that same expression.
Shocked. Vulnerable. Caught off balance.
Then, just as before...
...the hardening of the gaze...
...the frown...
...the look of grim determination.
Yes?

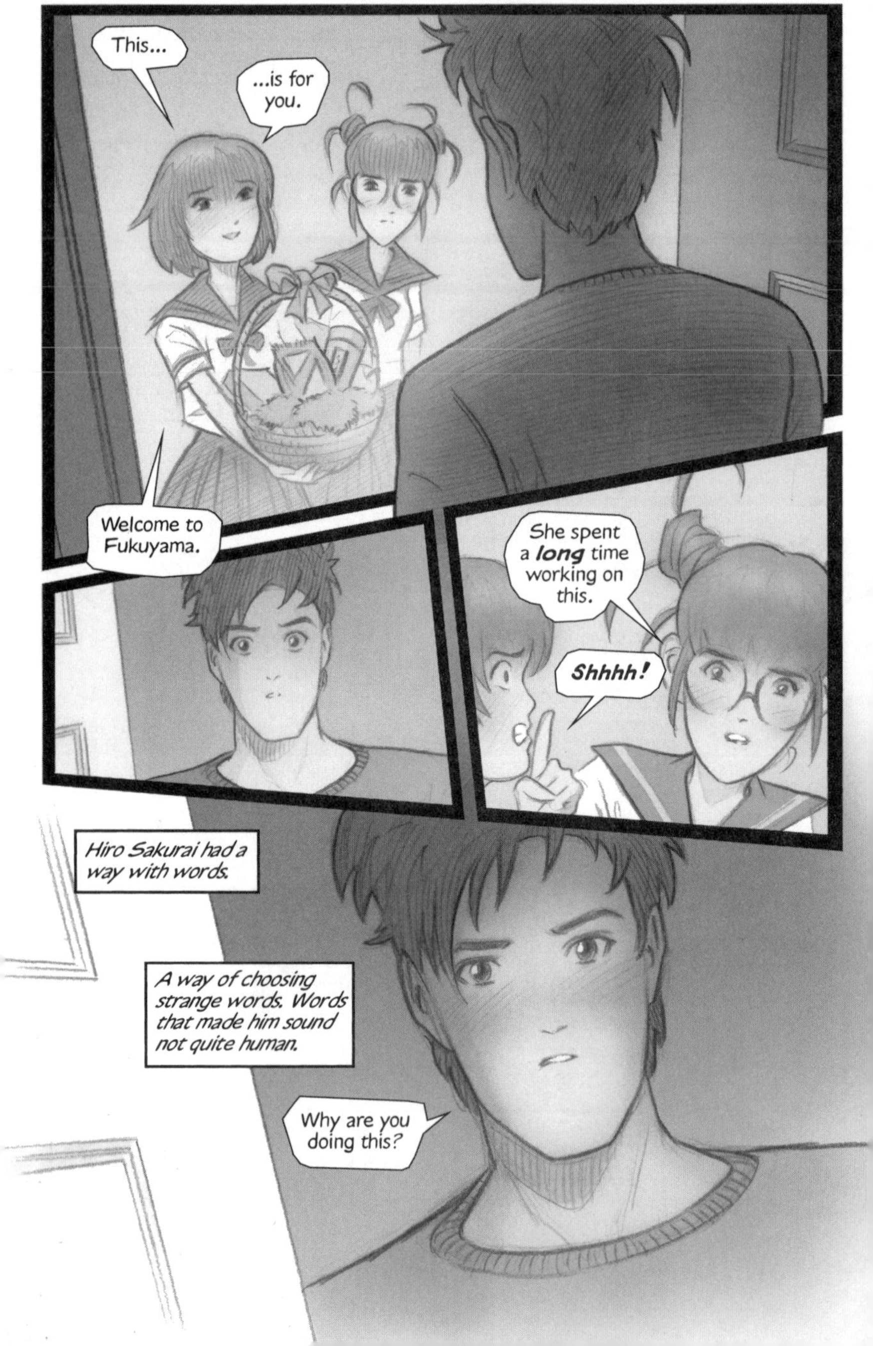
This...
...is for you.
Welcome to Fukuyama.
She spent a **long** time working on this.
Shhhh!
Hiro Sakurai had a way with words.
A way of choosing strange words. Words that made him sound not quite human.
Why are you doing this?

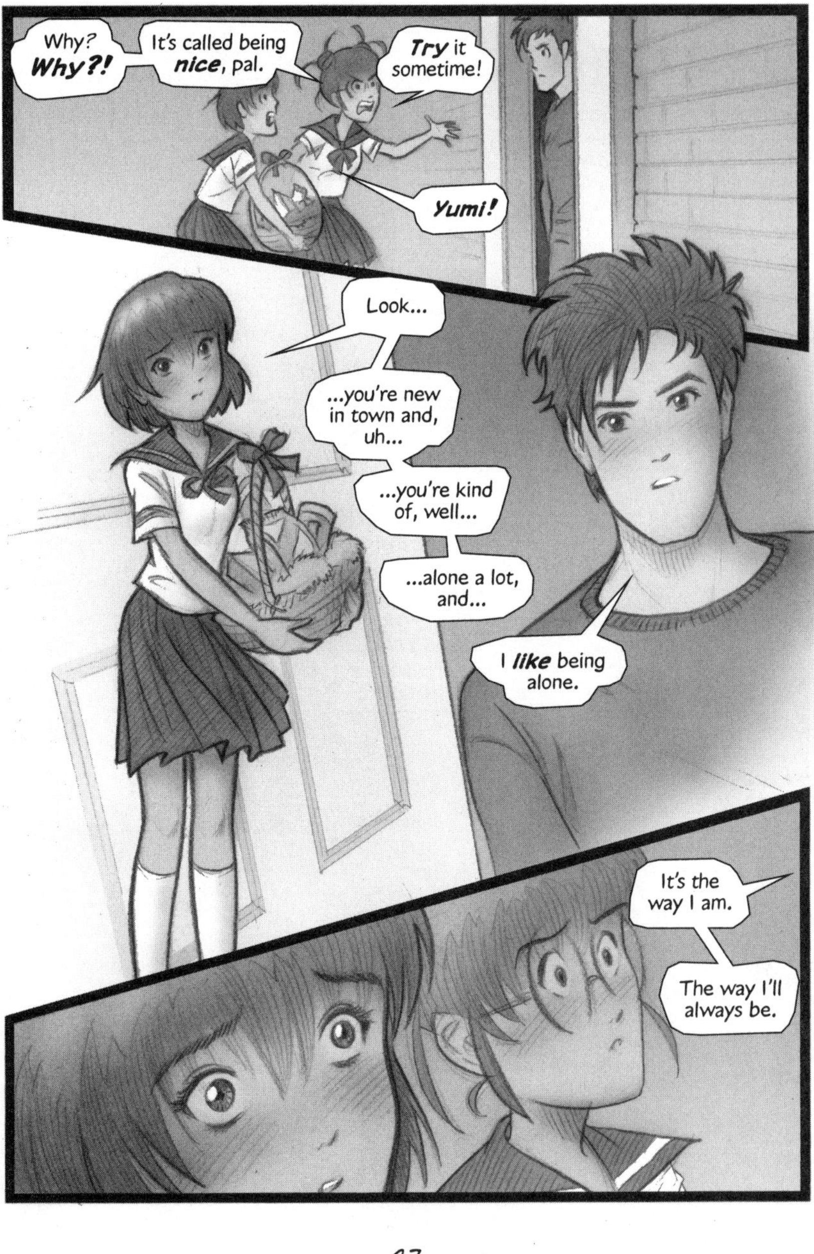
Why? **Why?!**
It's called being **nice**, pal.
Try it sometime!
Yumi!
Look...
...you're new in town and, uh...
...you're kind of, well...
...alone a lot, and...
I **like** being alone.
It's the way I am.
The way I'll always be.

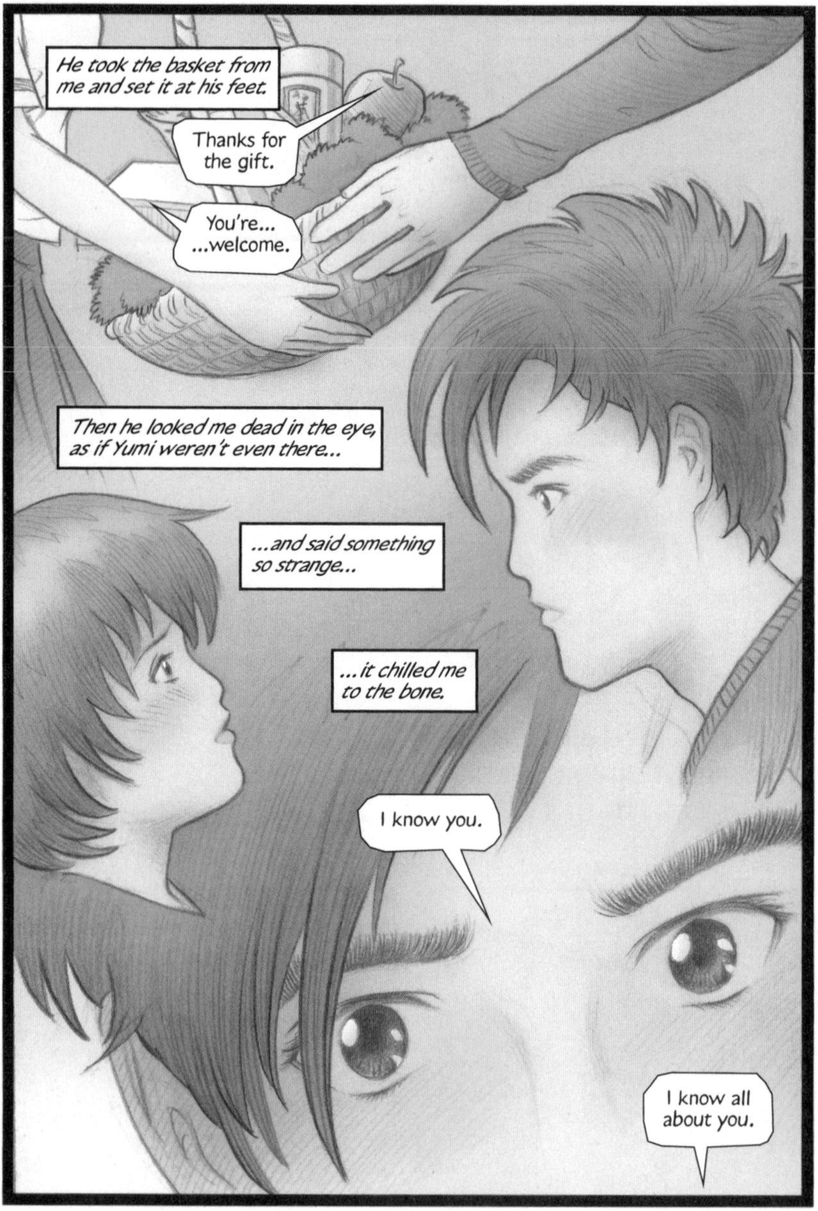
He took the basket from me and set it at his feet.
Thanks for the gift.
You're... ...welcome.
Then he looked me dead in the eye, as if Yumi weren't even there...
...and said something so strange...
...it chilled me to the bone.
I know you.
I know all about you.

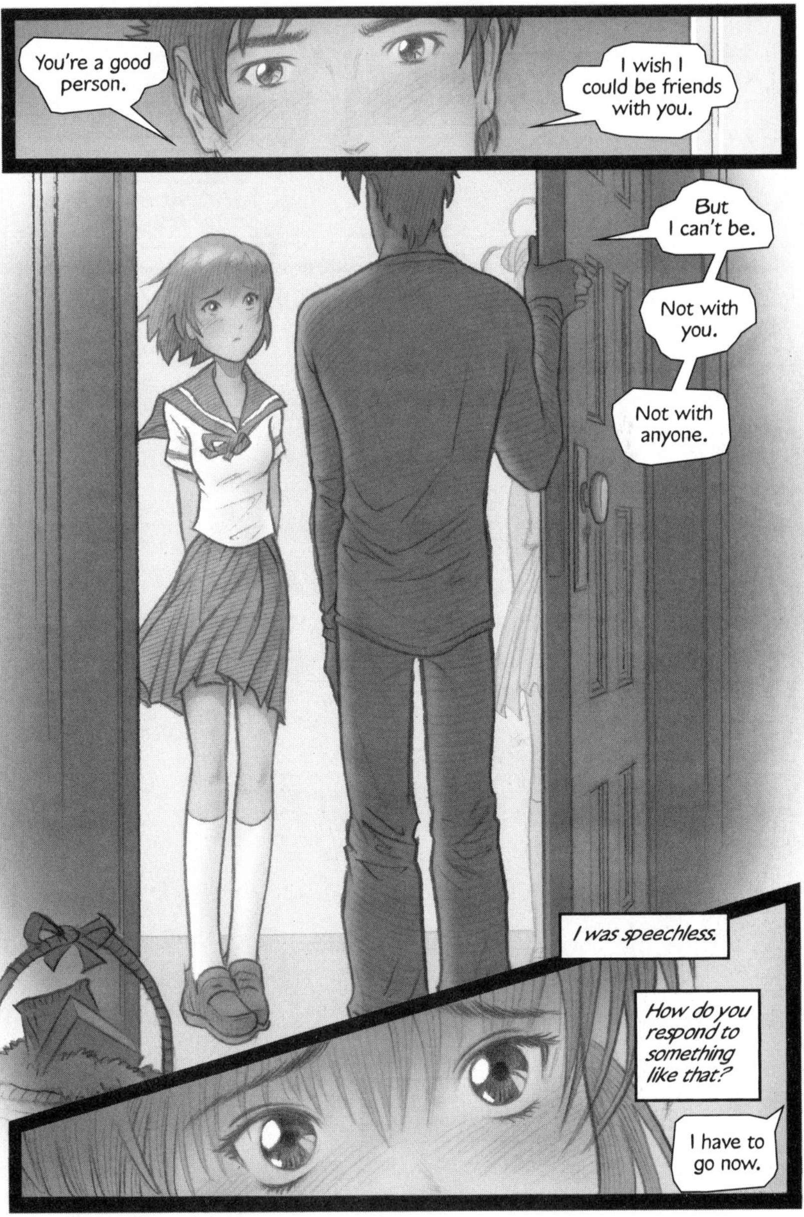
You're a good person.
I wish I could be friends with you.
But I can't be.
Not with you.
Not with anyone.
I was speechless.
How do you respond to something like that?
I have to go now.

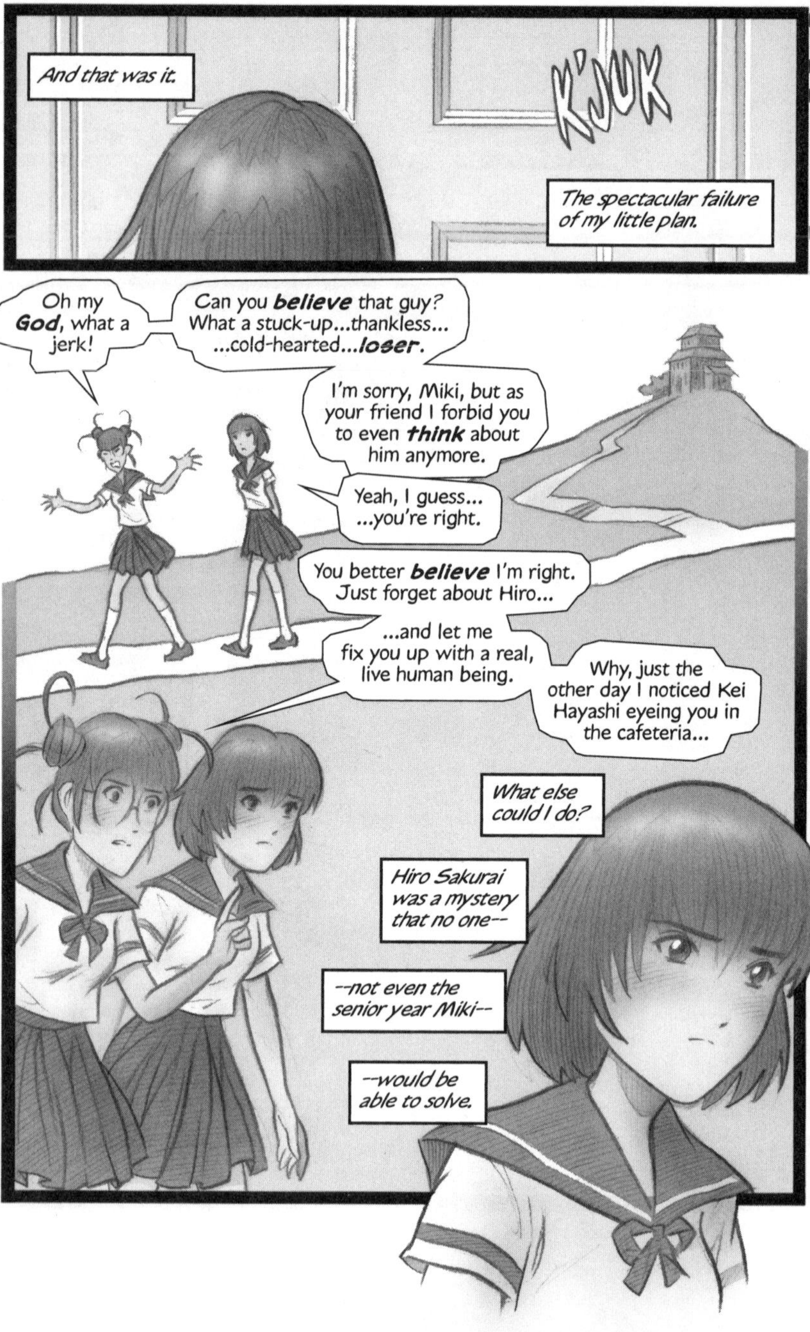
And that was it.
K'JUK
The spectacular failure of my little plan.
Oh my **God**, what a jerk!
Can you **believe** that guy? What a stuck-up...thankless... ...cold-hearted...**loser**.
I'm sorry, Miki, but as your friend I forbid you to even **think** about him anymore.
Yeah, I guess... ...you're right.
You better **believe** I'm right. Just forget about Hiro...
...and let me fix you up with a real, live human being.
Why, just the other day I noticed Kei Hayashi eyeing you in the cafeteria...
What else could I do?
Hiro Sakurai was a mystery that no one--
--not even the senior year Miki--
--would be able to solve.

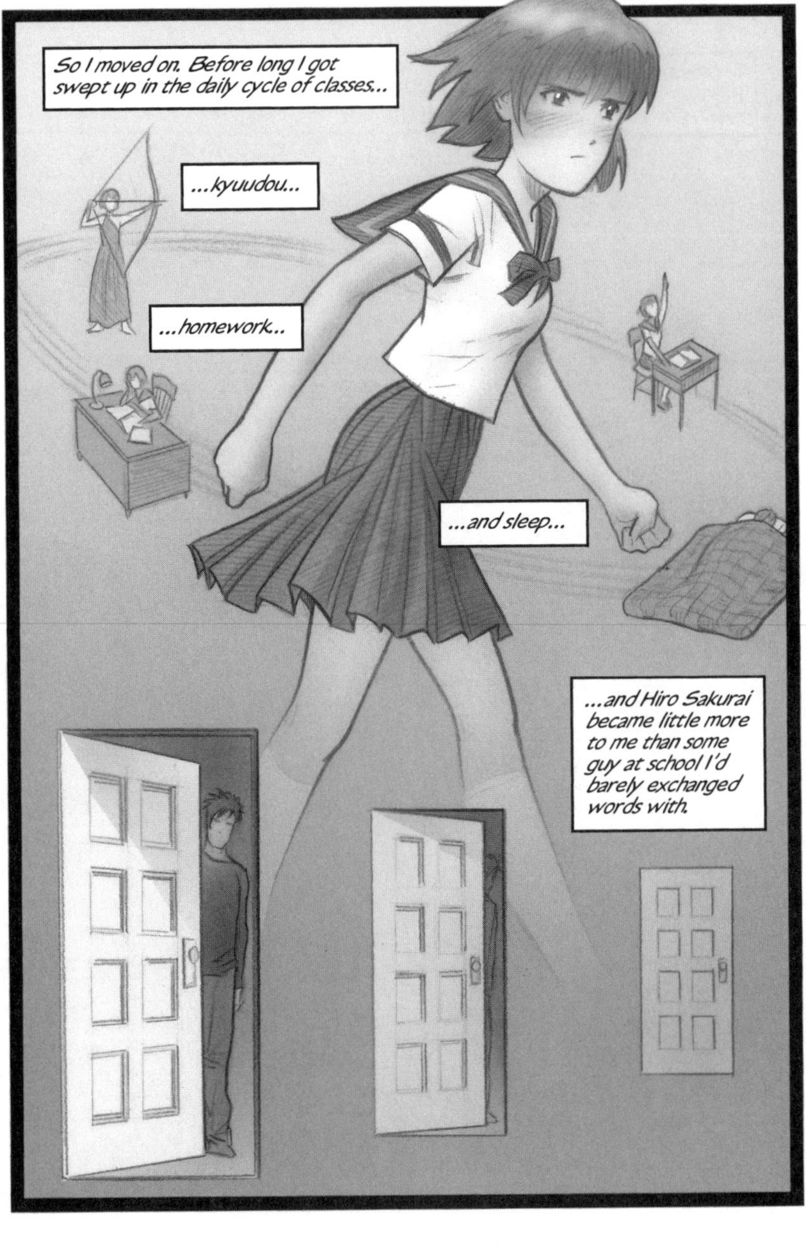
So I moved on. Before long I got swept up in the daily cycle of classes...
...kyuudou...
...homework...
...and sleep...
...and Hiro Sakurai became little more to me than some guy at school I'd barely exchanged words with.

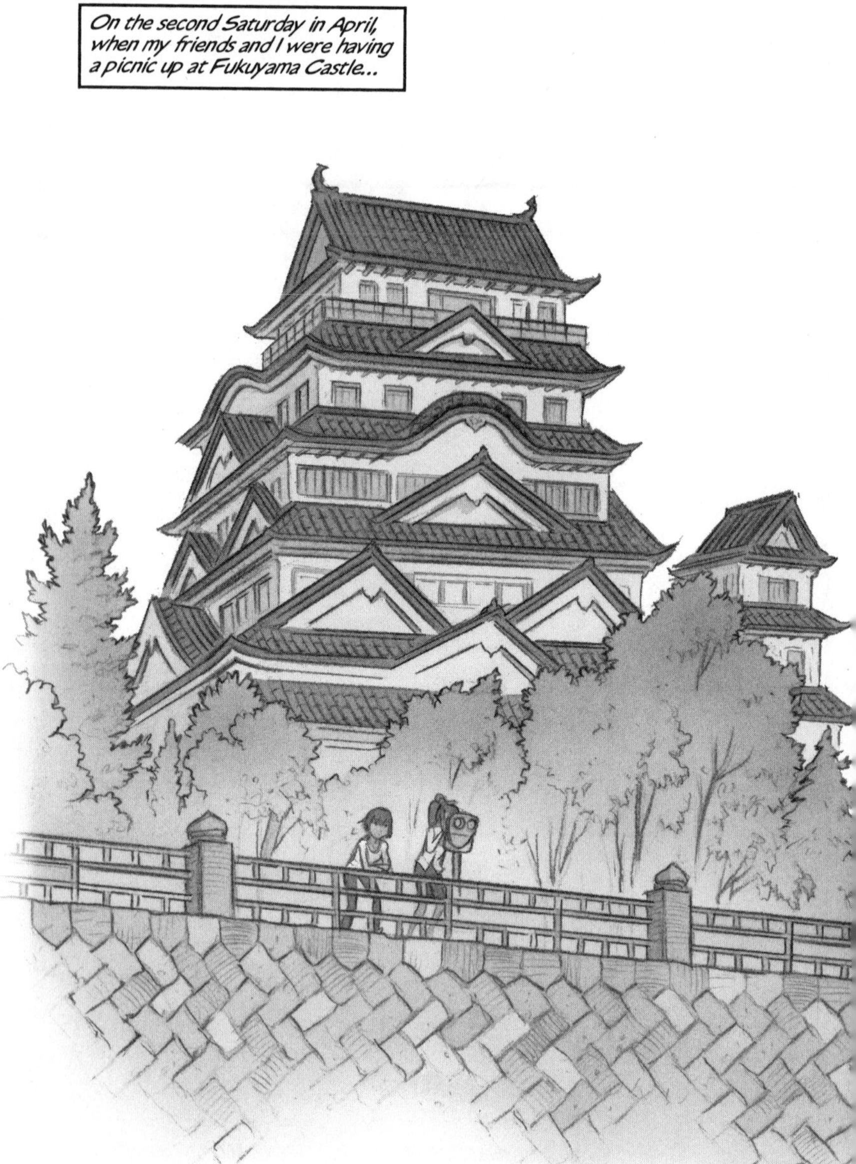
On the second Saturday in April, when my friends and I were having a picnic up at Fukuyama Castle...

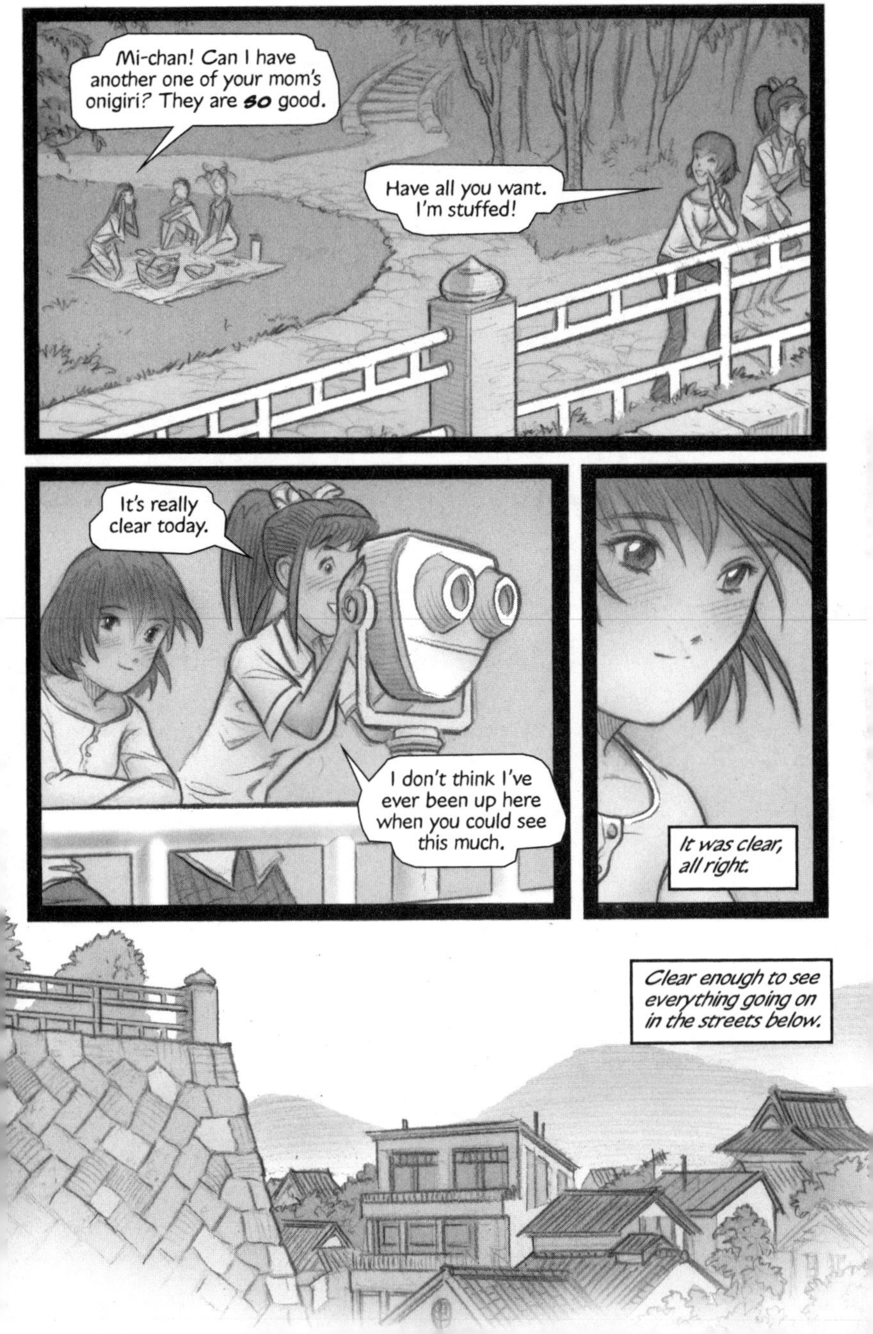

Mi-chan! Can I have another one of your mom's onigiri? They are *so* good.
Have all you want. I'm stuffed!
It's really clear today.
I don't think I've ever been up here when you could see this much.
It was clear, all right.
Clear enough to see everything going on in the streets below.

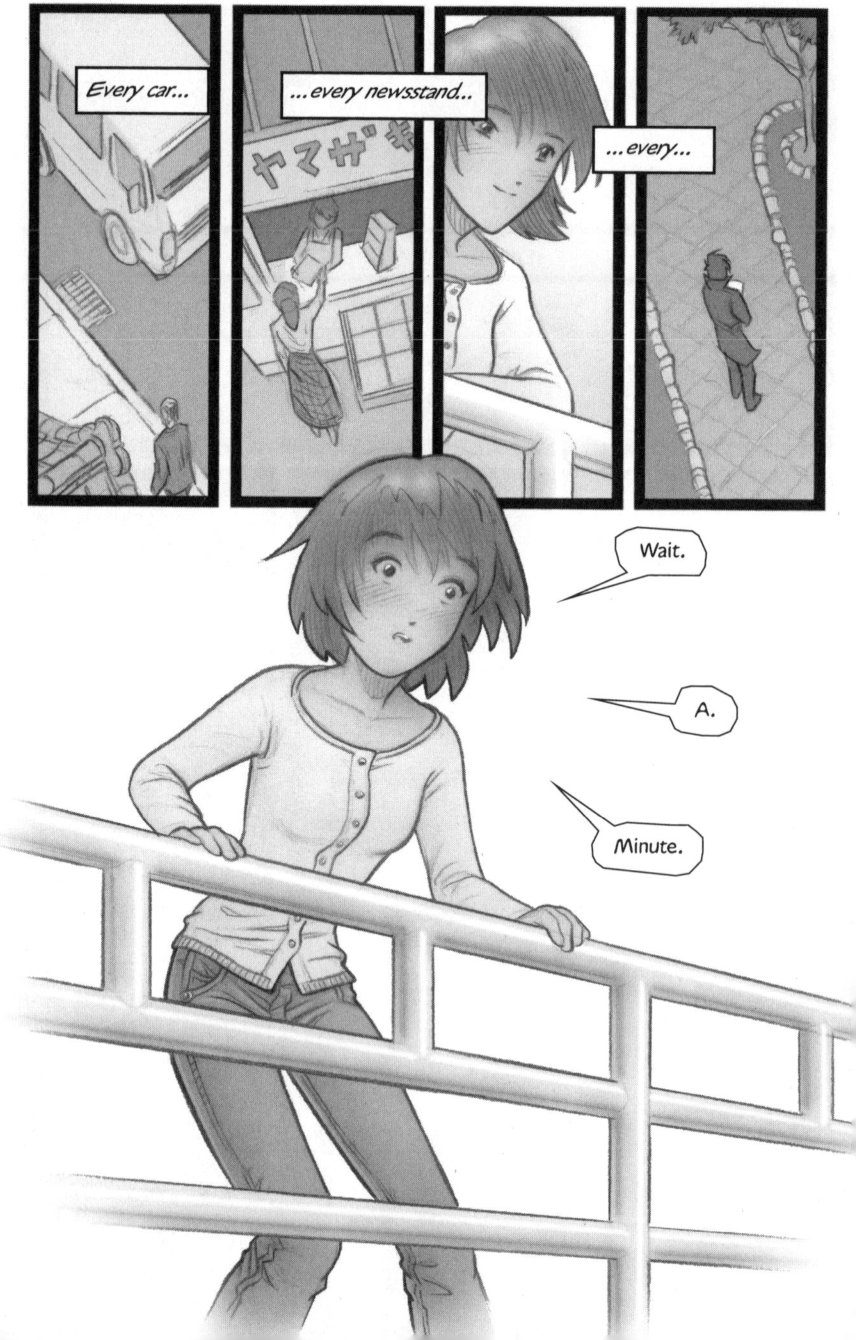

Every car...
...every newsstand...
...every...
ヤマザキ
Wait.
A.
Minute.

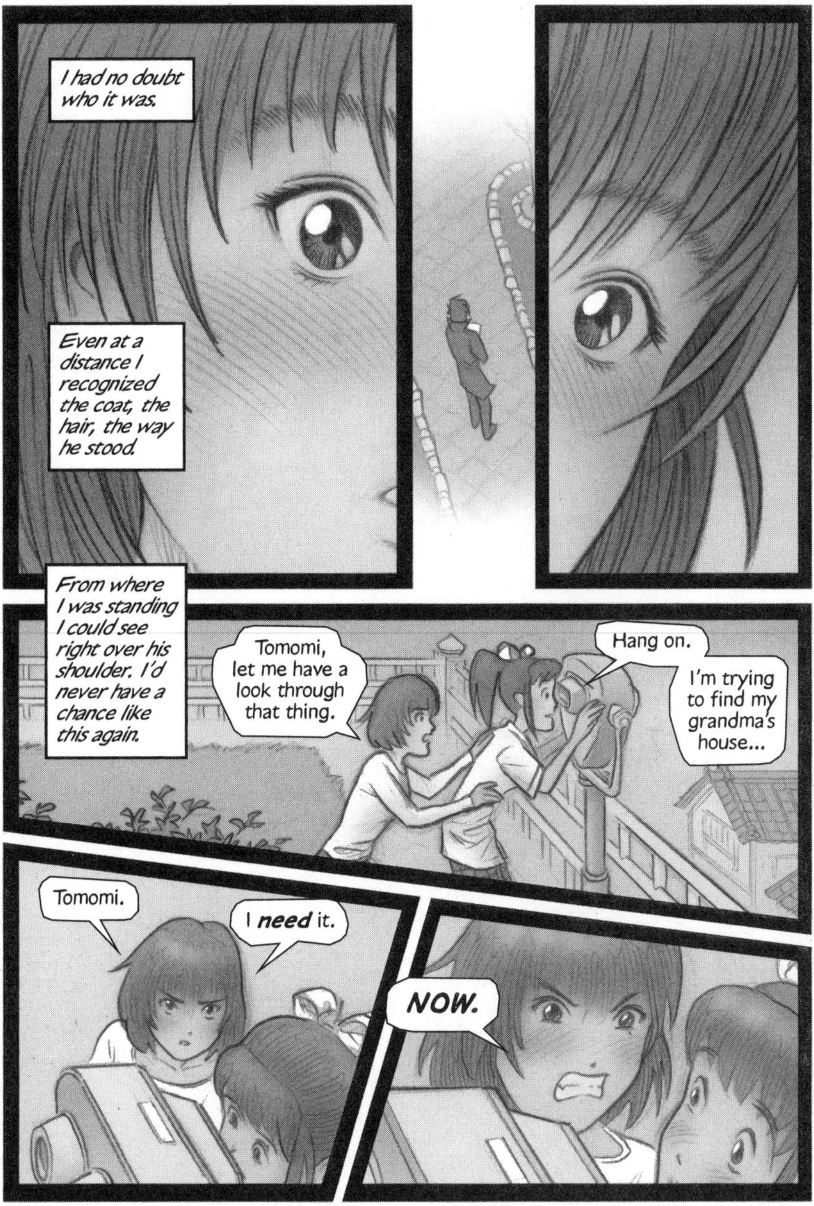

I had no doubt who it was.
Even at a distance I recognized the coat, the hair, the way he stood.
From where I was standing I could see right over his shoulder. I'd never have a chance like this again.
Tomomi, let me have a look through that thing.
Hang on.
I'm trying to find my grandma's house...
Tomomi.
I **need** it.
NOW.

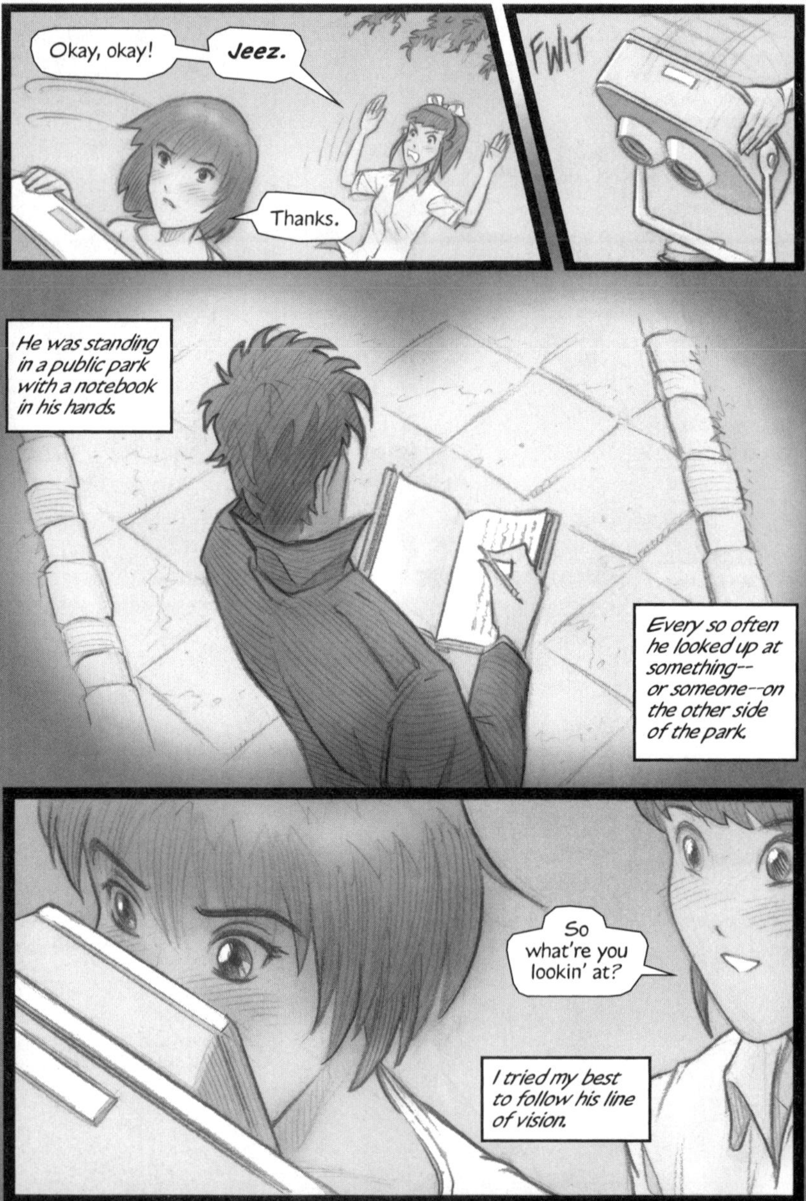
Okay, okay!
Jeez.
Thanks.
FWIT
He was standing in a public park with a notebook in his hands.
Every so often he looked up at something--or someone--on the other side of the park.
So what're you lookin' at?
I tried my best to follow his line of vision.

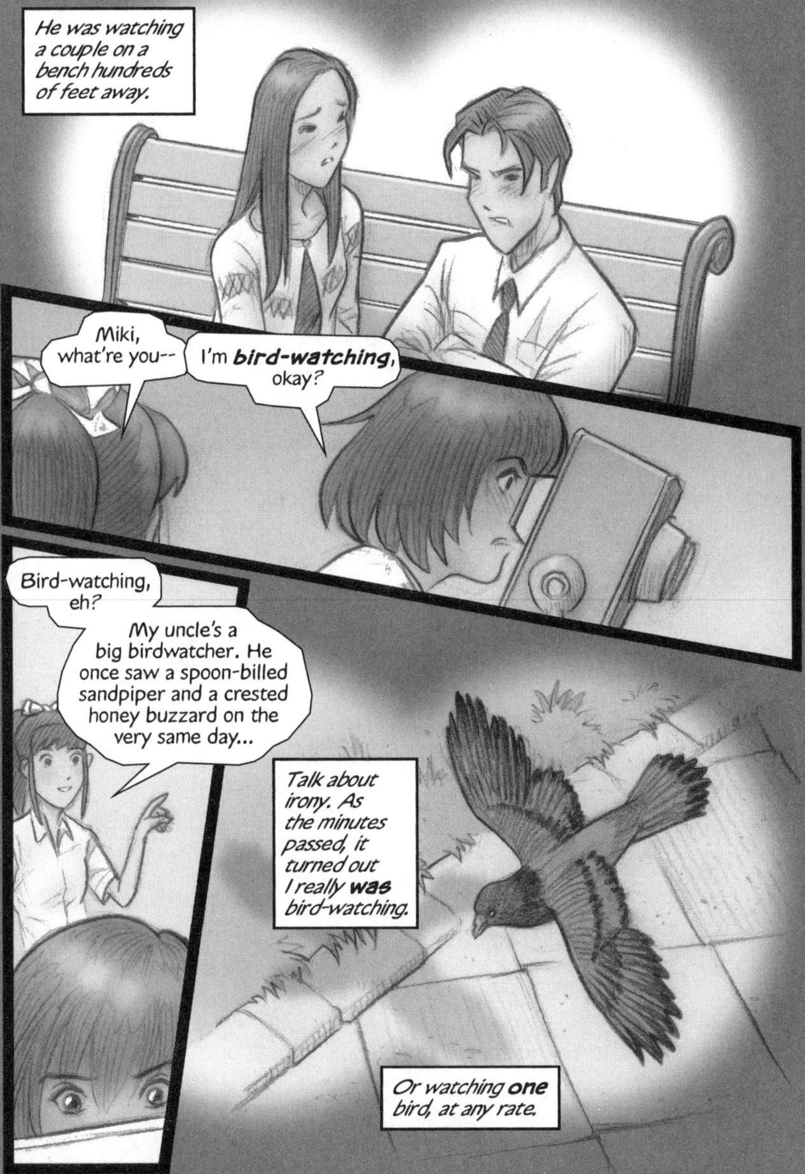

He was watching a couple on a bench hundreds of feet away.
Miki, what're you--
I'm **bird-watching**, okay?
Bird-watching, eh?
My uncle's a big birdwatcher. He once saw a spoon-billed sandpiper and a crested honey buzzard on the very same day...
Talk about irony. As the minutes passed, it turned out I really **was** bird-watching.
Or watching **one** bird, at any rate.

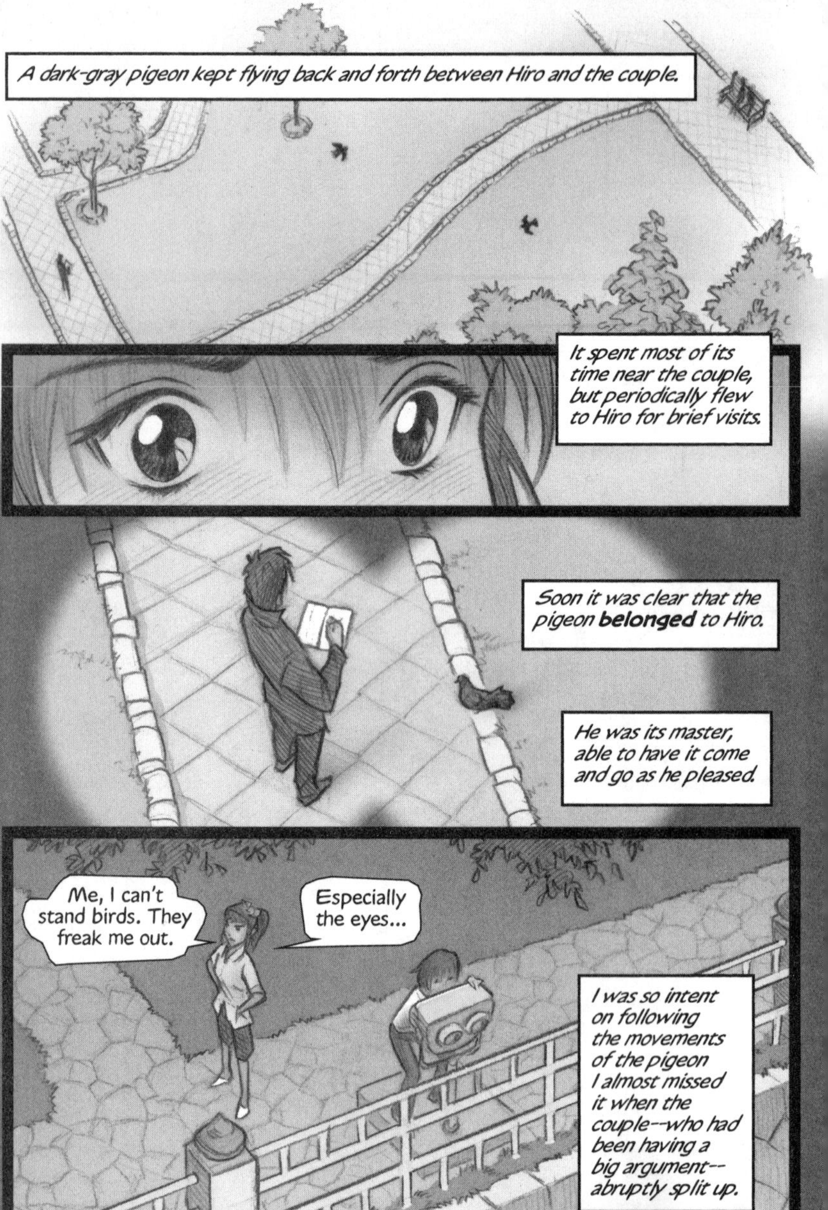
A dark-gray pigeon kept flying back and forth between Hiro and the couple.
It spent most of its time near the couple, but periodically flew to Hiro for brief visits.
Soon it was clear that the pigeon **belonged** to Hiro.
He was its master, able to have it come and go as he pleased.
Me, I can't stand birds. They freak me out.
Especially the eyes...
I was so intent on following the movements of the pigeon I almost missed it when the couple--who had been having a big argument--abruptly split up.

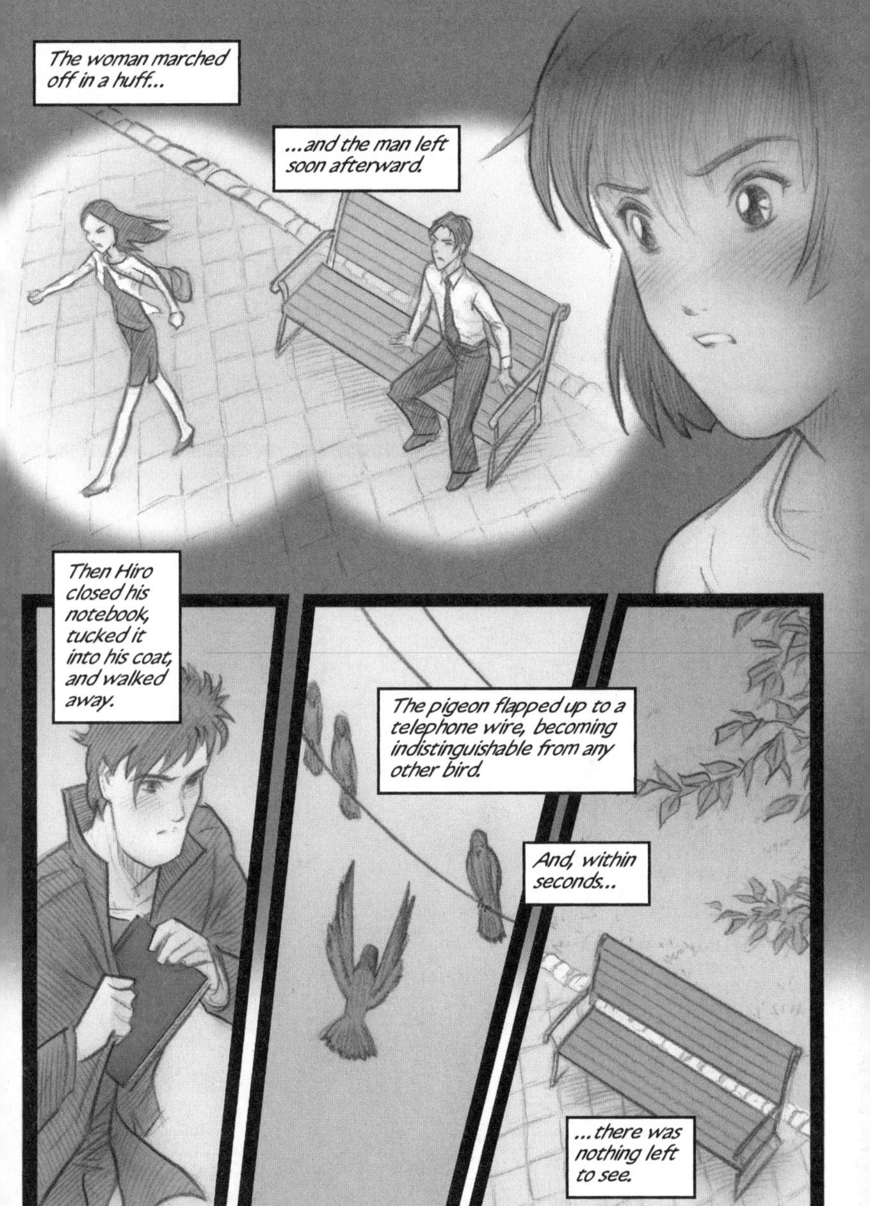
The woman marched off in a huff...
...and the man left soon afterward.
Then Hiro closed his notebook, tucked it into his coat, and walked away.
The pigeon flapped up to a telephone wire, becoming indistinguishable from any other bird.
And, within seconds...
...there was nothing left to see.

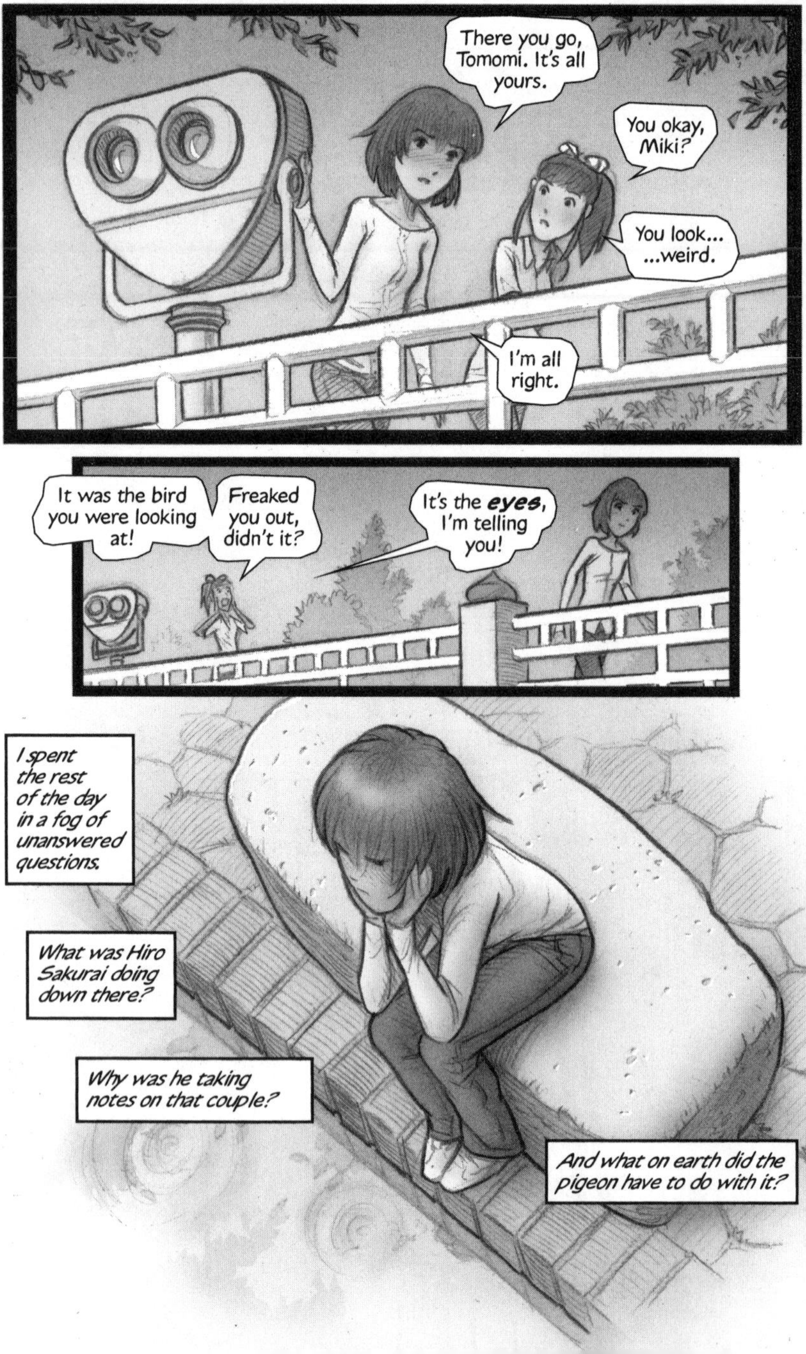
There you go, Tomomi. It's all yours.
You okay, Miki?
You look... ...weird.
I'm all right.
It was the bird you were looking at!
Freaked you out, didn't it?
It's the ***eyes***, I'm telling you!
I spent the rest of the day in a fog of unanswered questions.
What was Hiro Sakurai doing down there?
Why was he taking notes on that couple?
And what on earth did the pigeon have to do with it?

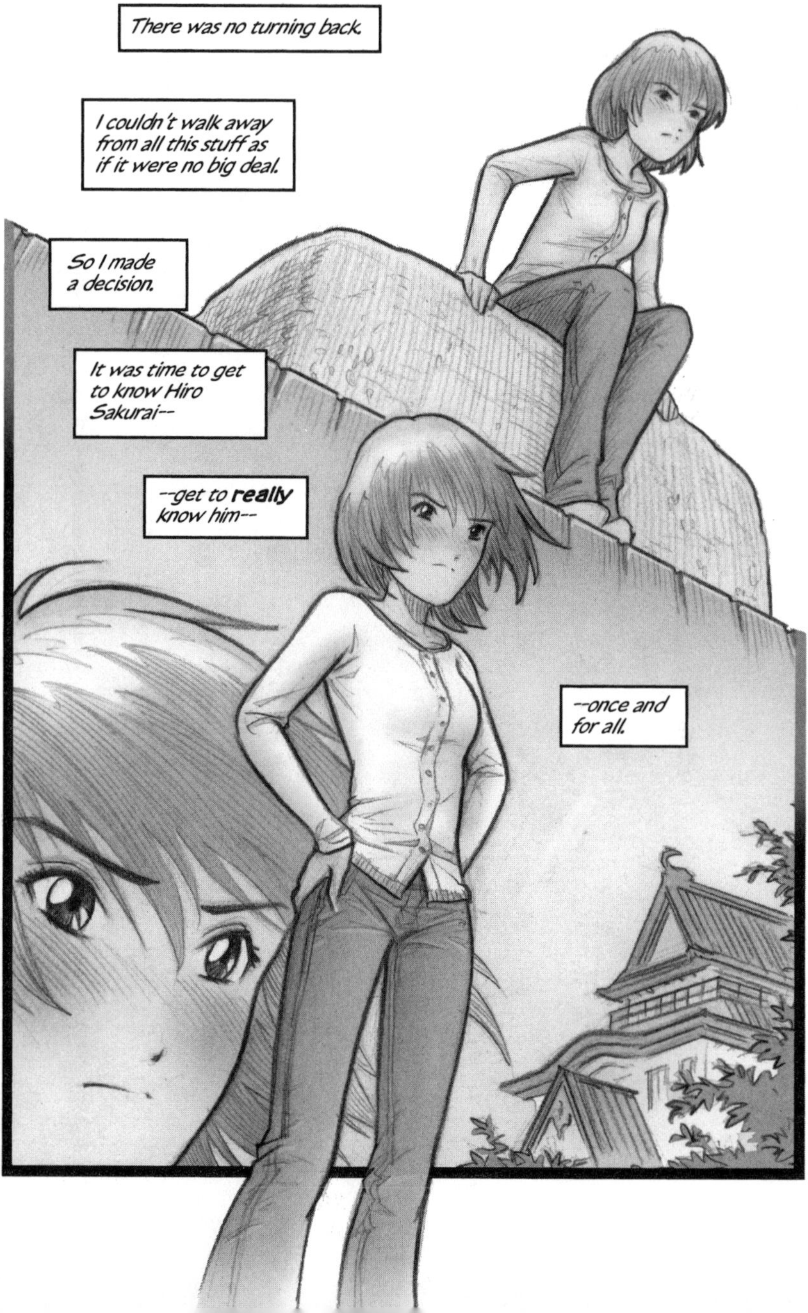
There was no turning back.
I couldn't walk away from all this stuff as if it were no big deal.
So I made a decision.
It was time to get to know Hiro Sakurai--
--get to **really** know him--
--once and for all.

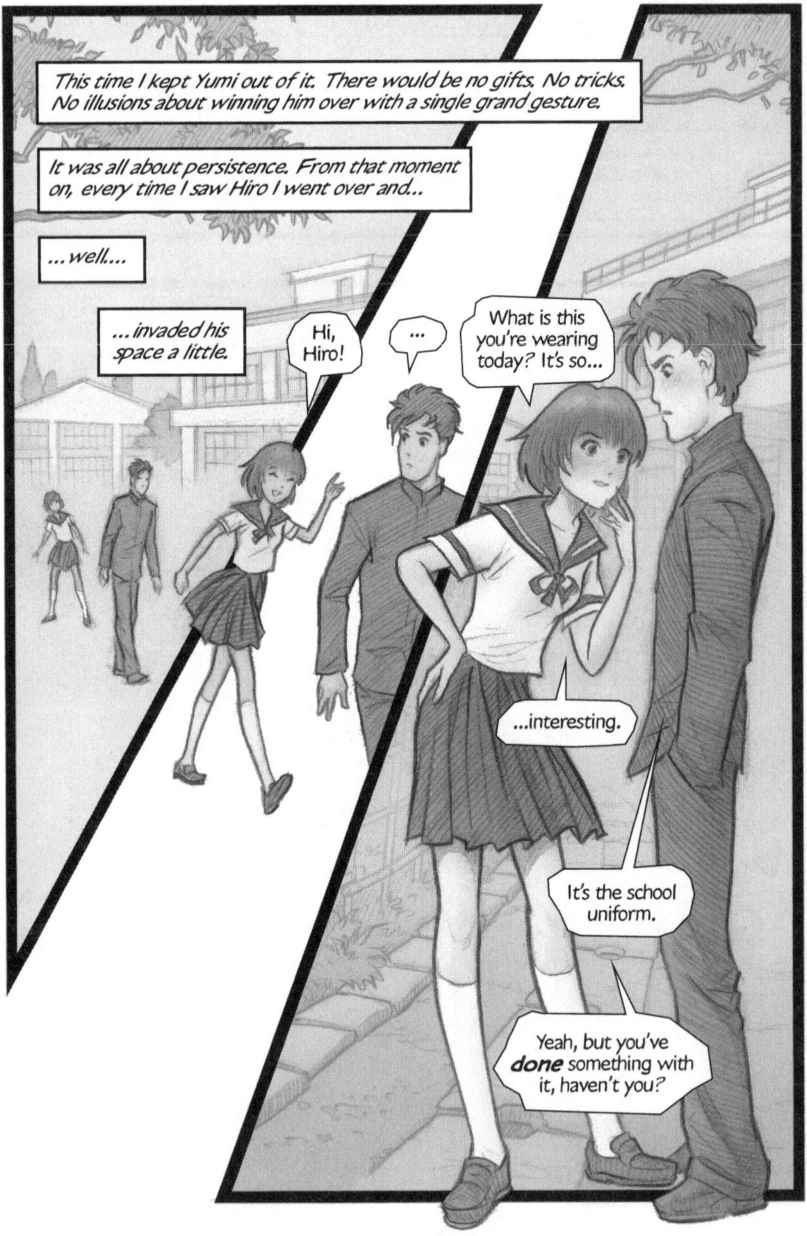
This time I kept Yumi out of it. There would be no gifts. No tricks. No illusions about winning him over with a single grand gesture.
It was all about persistence. From that moment on, every time I saw Hiro I went over and..
...well....
...invaded his space a little.
Hi, Hiro!
...
What is this you're wearing today? It's so...
...interesting.
It's the school uniform.
Yeah, but you've **done** something with it, haven't you?

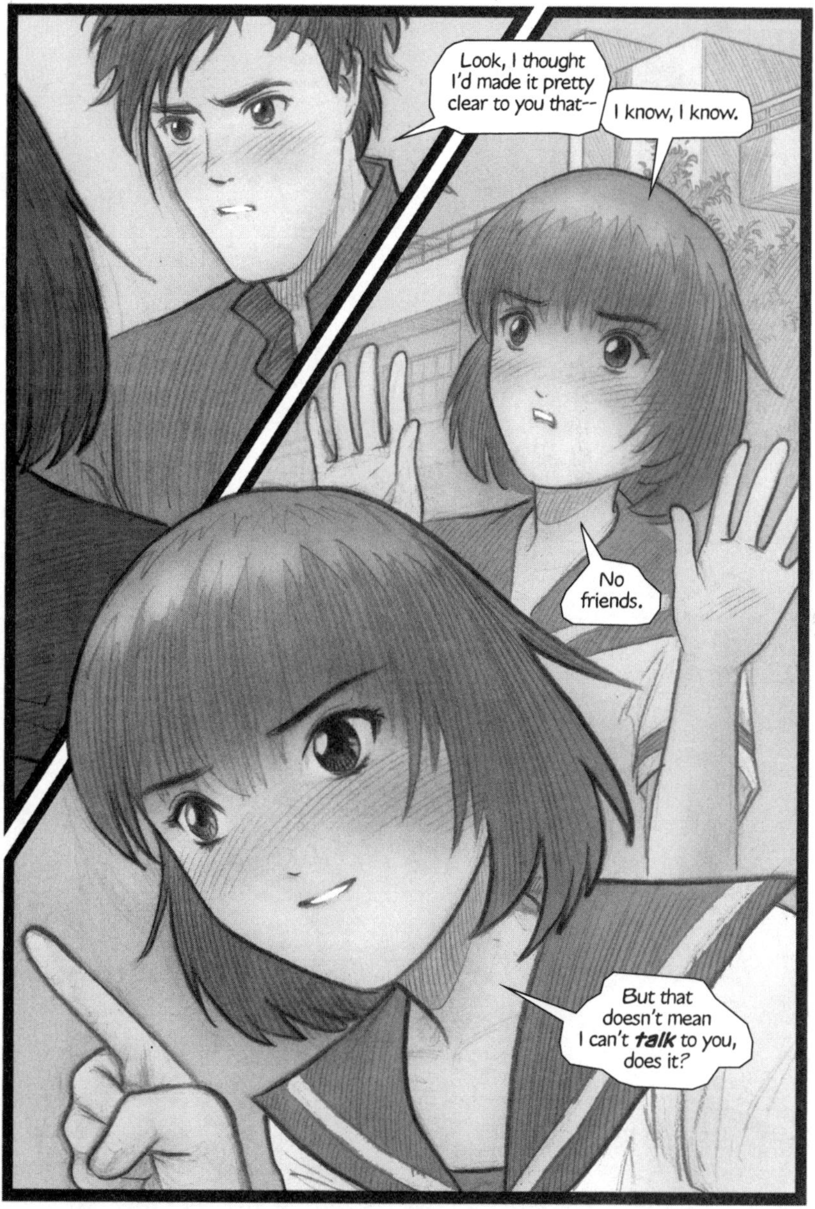

Look, I thought I'd made it pretty clear to you that--
I know, I know.
No friends.
But that doesn't mean I can't **talk** to you, does it?

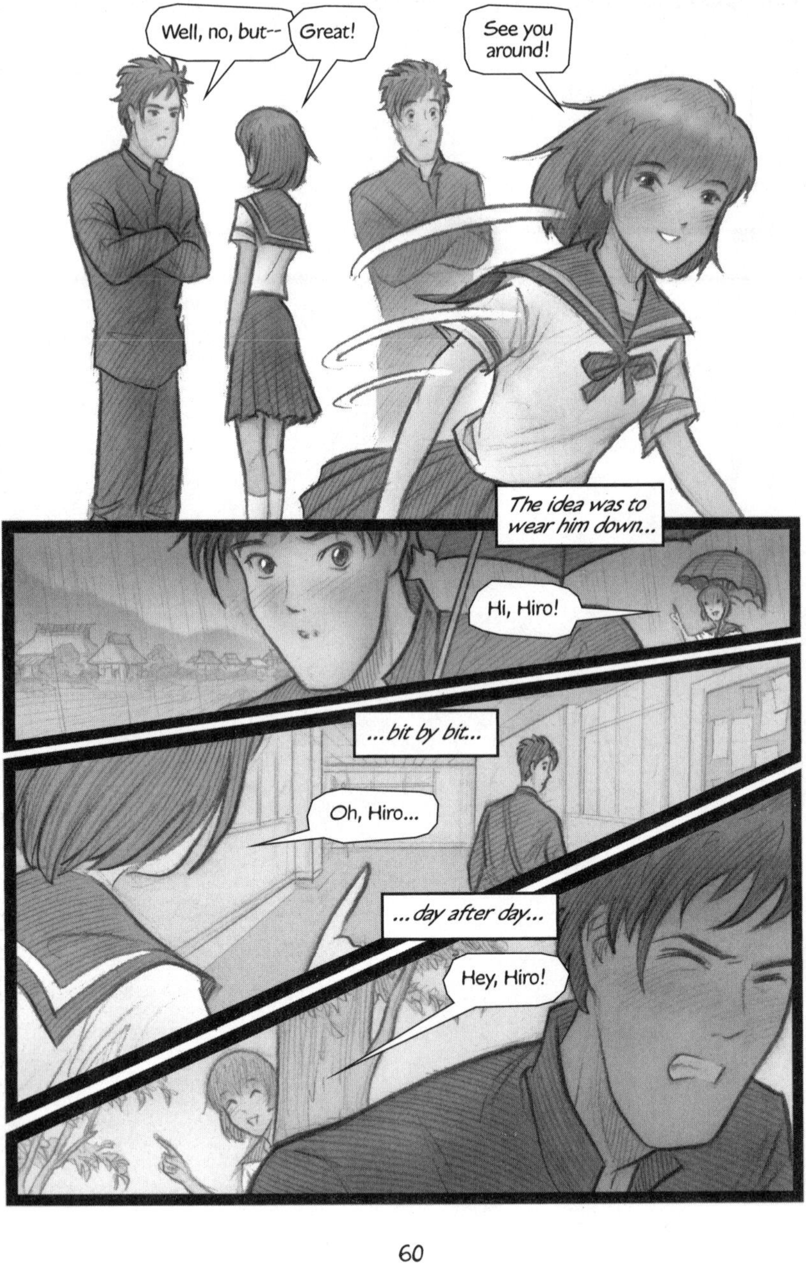
Well, no, but--
Great!
See you around!
The idea was to wear him down...
Hi, Hiro!
...bit by bit...
Oh, Hiro...
...day after day...
Hey, Hiro!

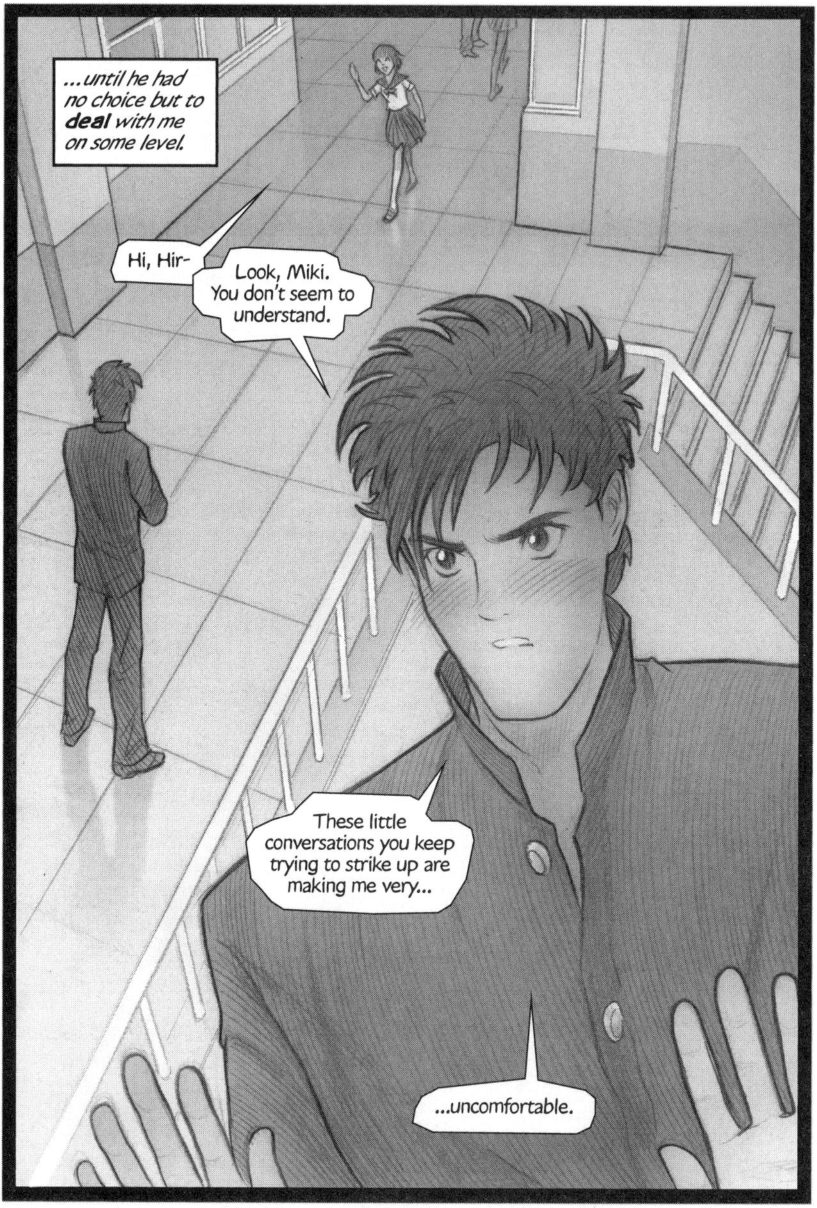
...until he had no choice but to **deal** with me on some level.
Hi, Hir-
Look, Miki. You don't seem to understand.
These little conversations you keep trying to strike up are making me very...
...uncomfortable.

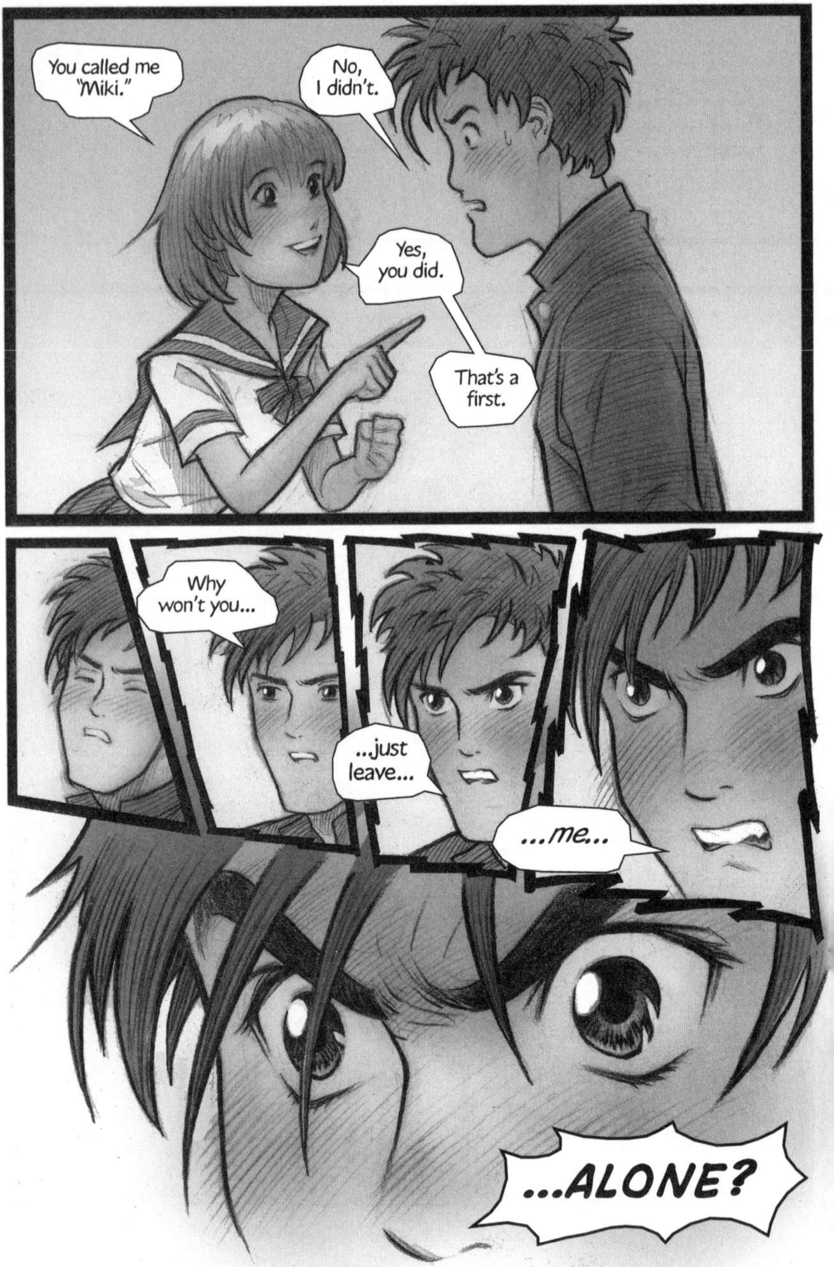
You called me "Miki."
No, I didn't.
Yes, you did.
That's a first.
Why won't you...
...just leave...
...me...
...ALONE?

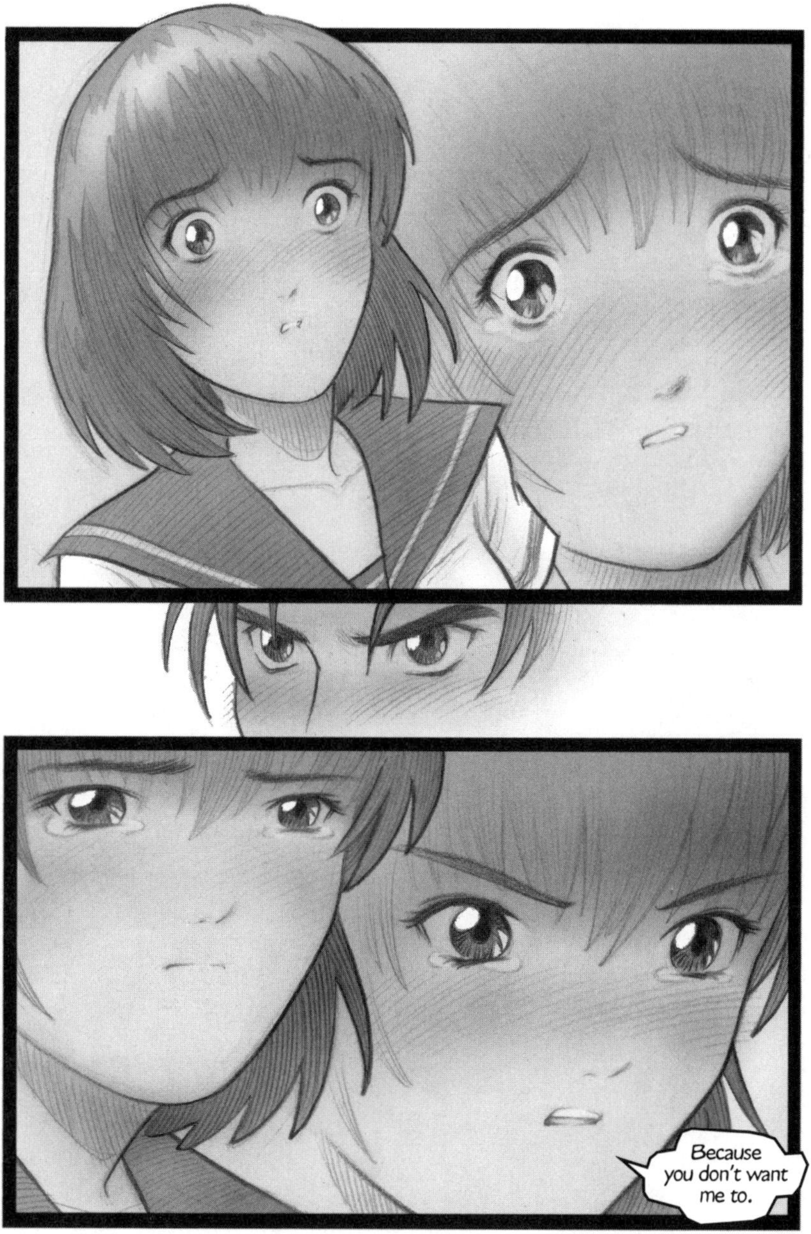
Because you don't want me to.

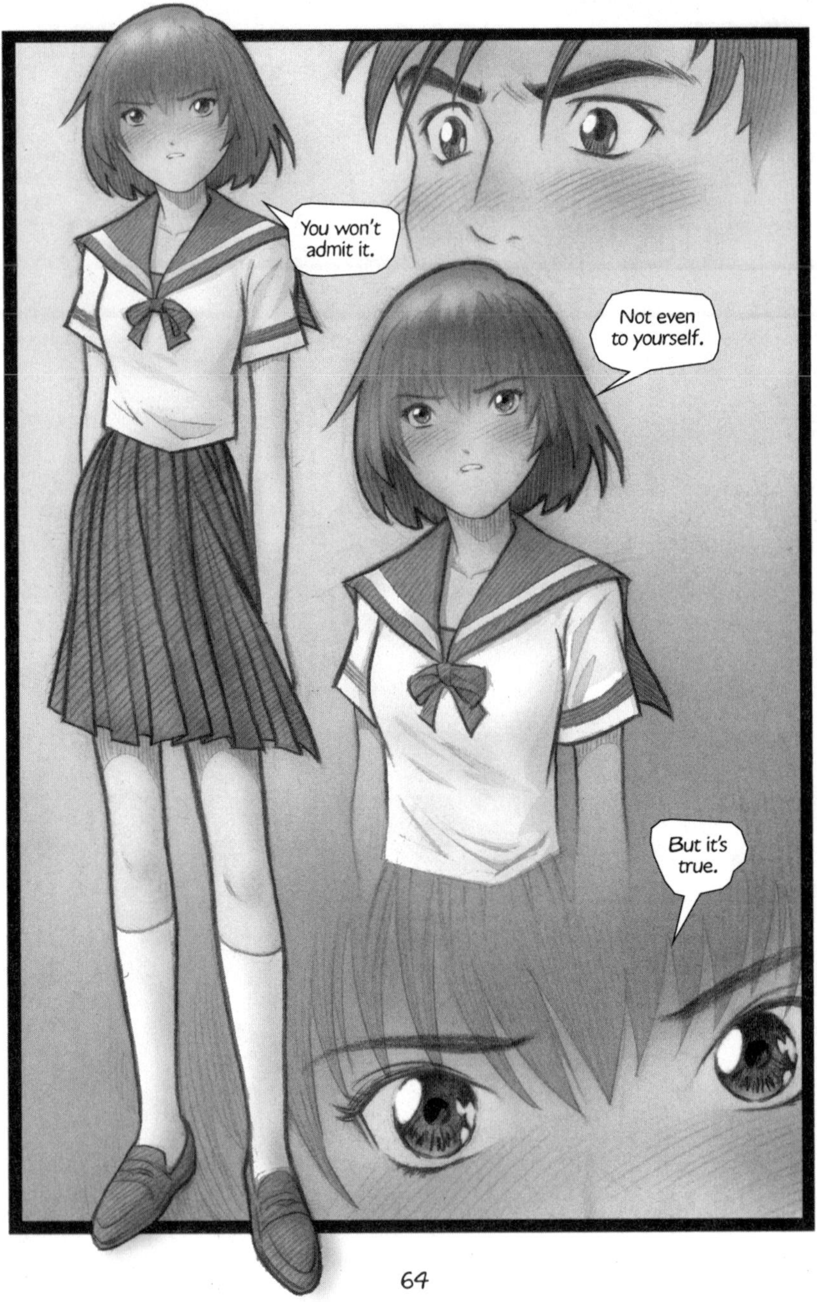
You won't admit it.
Not even to yourself.
But it's true.

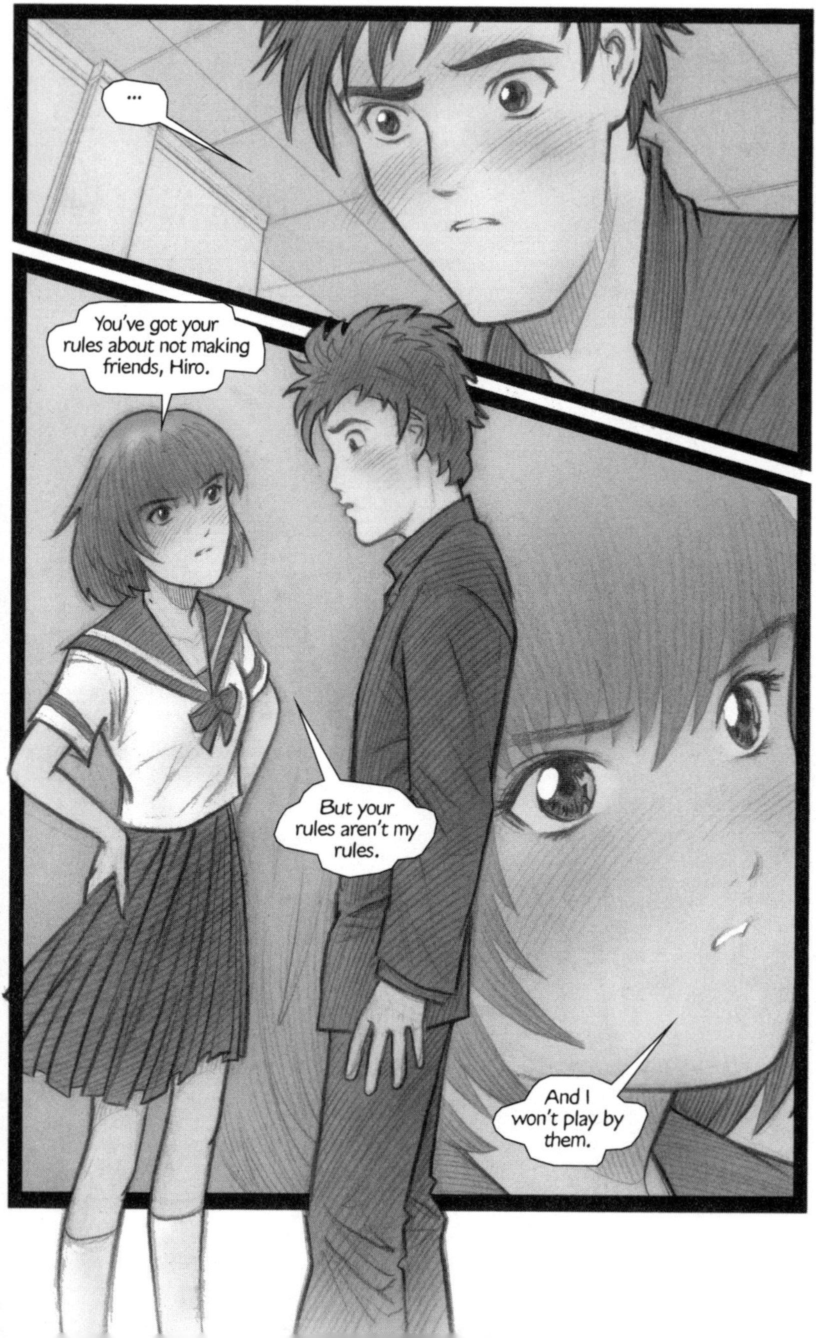
...
You've got your rules about not making friends, Hiro.
But your rules aren't my rules.
And I won't play by them.

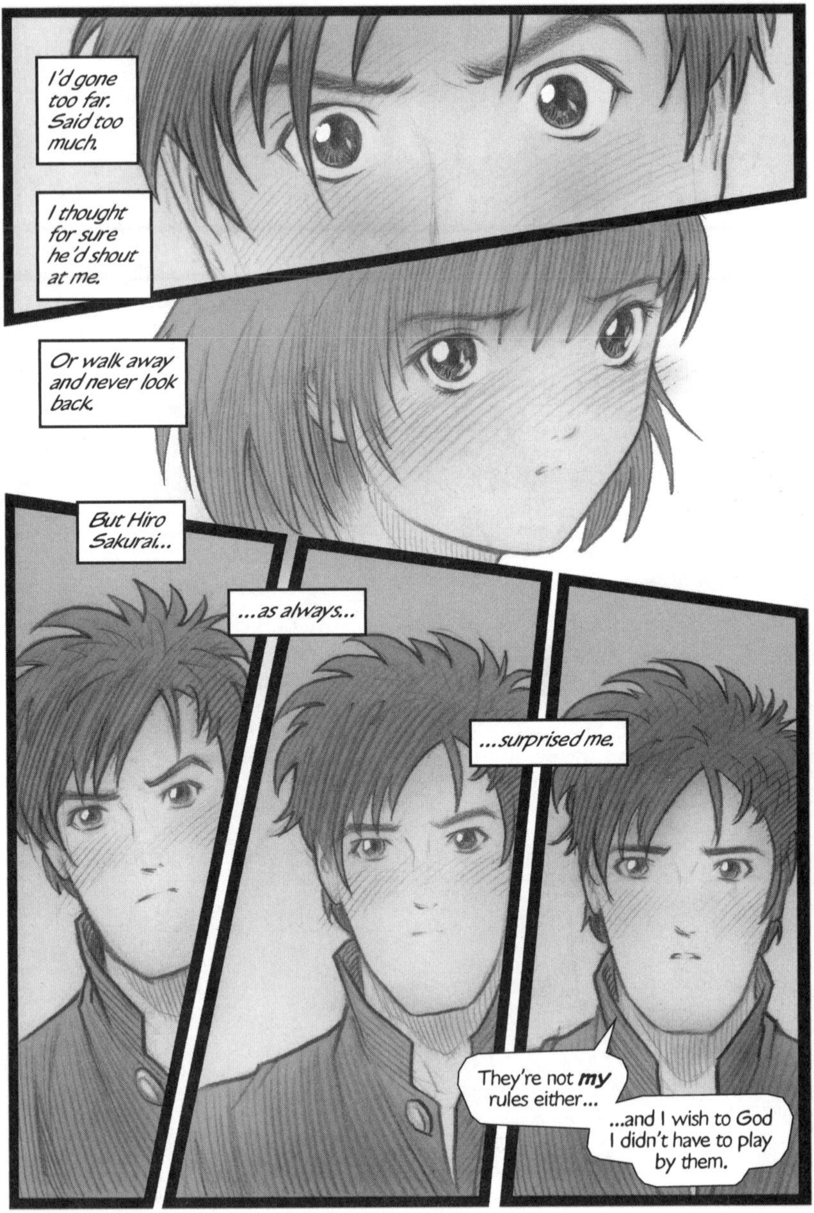
I'd gone too far. Said too much.
I thought for sure he'd shout at me.
Or walk away and never look back.
But Hiro Sakurai...
...as always...
...surprised me.
They're not **my** rules either...
...and I wish to God I didn't have to play by them.

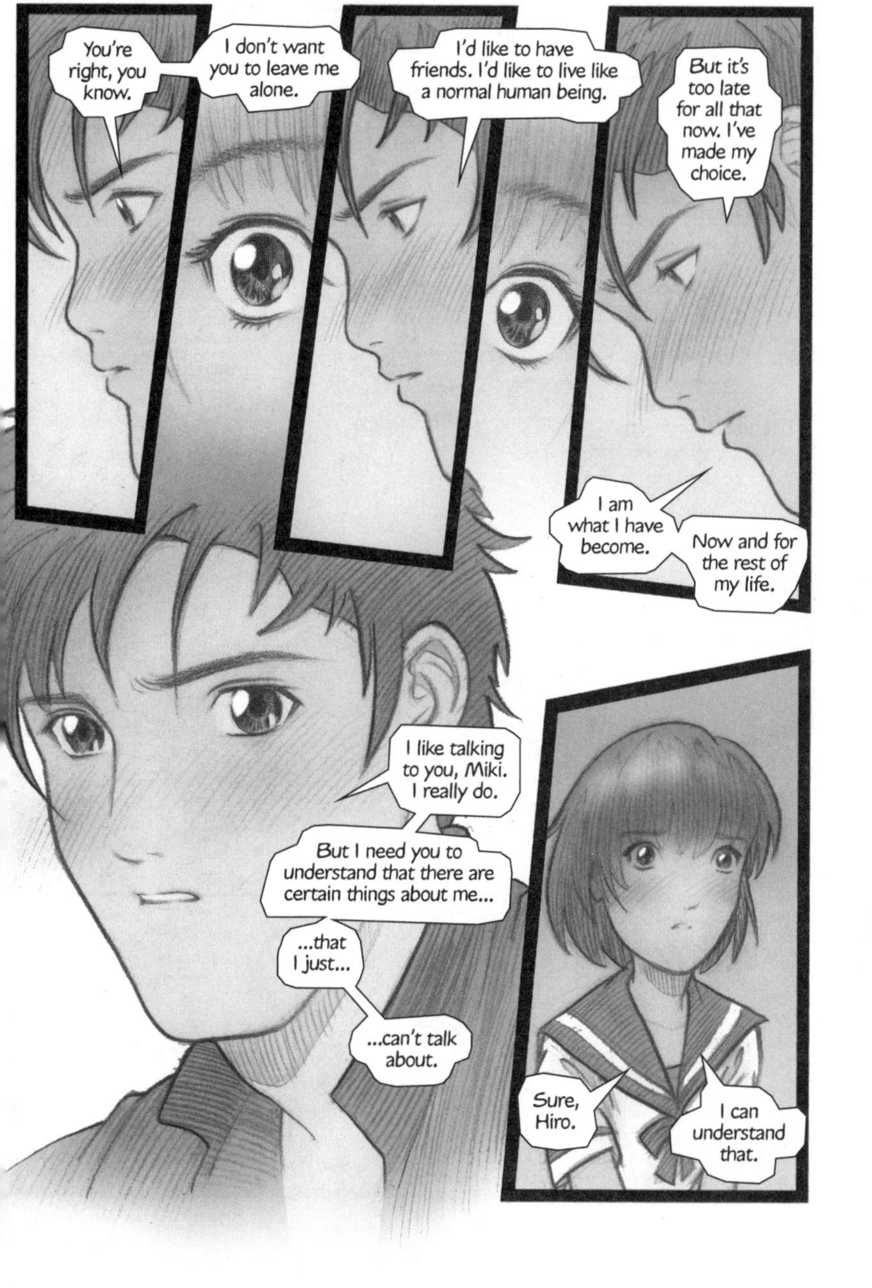
You're right, you know.
I don't want you to leave me alone.
I'd like to have friends. I'd like to live like a normal human being.
But it's too late for all that now. I've made my choice.
I am what I have become.
Now and for the rest of my life.
I like talking to you, Miki. I really do.
But I need you to understand that there are certain things about me...
...that I just...
...can't talk about.
Sure, Hiro.
I can understand that.

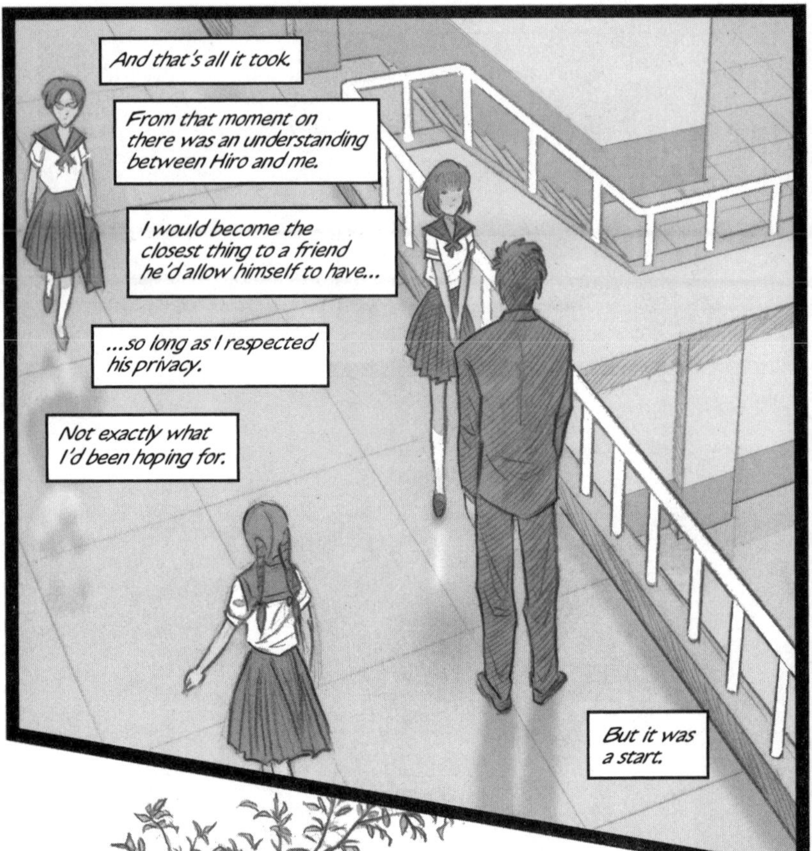
And that's all it took.
From that moment on there was an understanding between Hiro and me.
I would become the closest thing to a friend he'd allow himself to have...
...so long as I respected his privacy.
Not exactly what I'd been hoping for.
But it was a start.

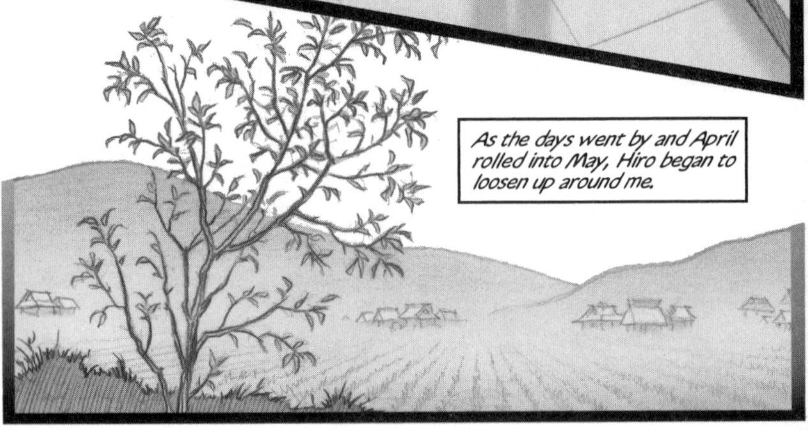
As the days went by and April rolled into May, Hiro began to loosen up around me.

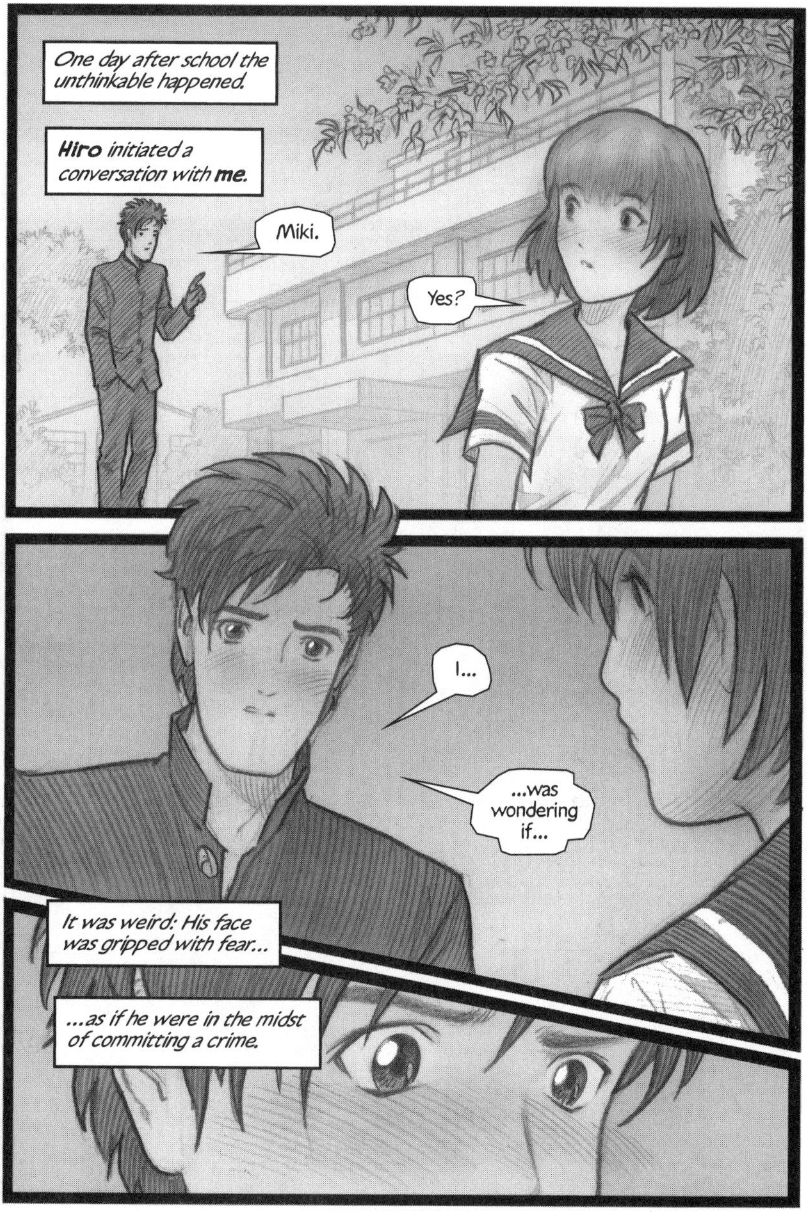
One day after school the unthinkable happened.
Hiro initiated a conversation with **me.**
Miki.
Yes?
I...
...was wondering if...
It was weird: His face was gripped with fear...
...as if he were in the midst of committing a crime.

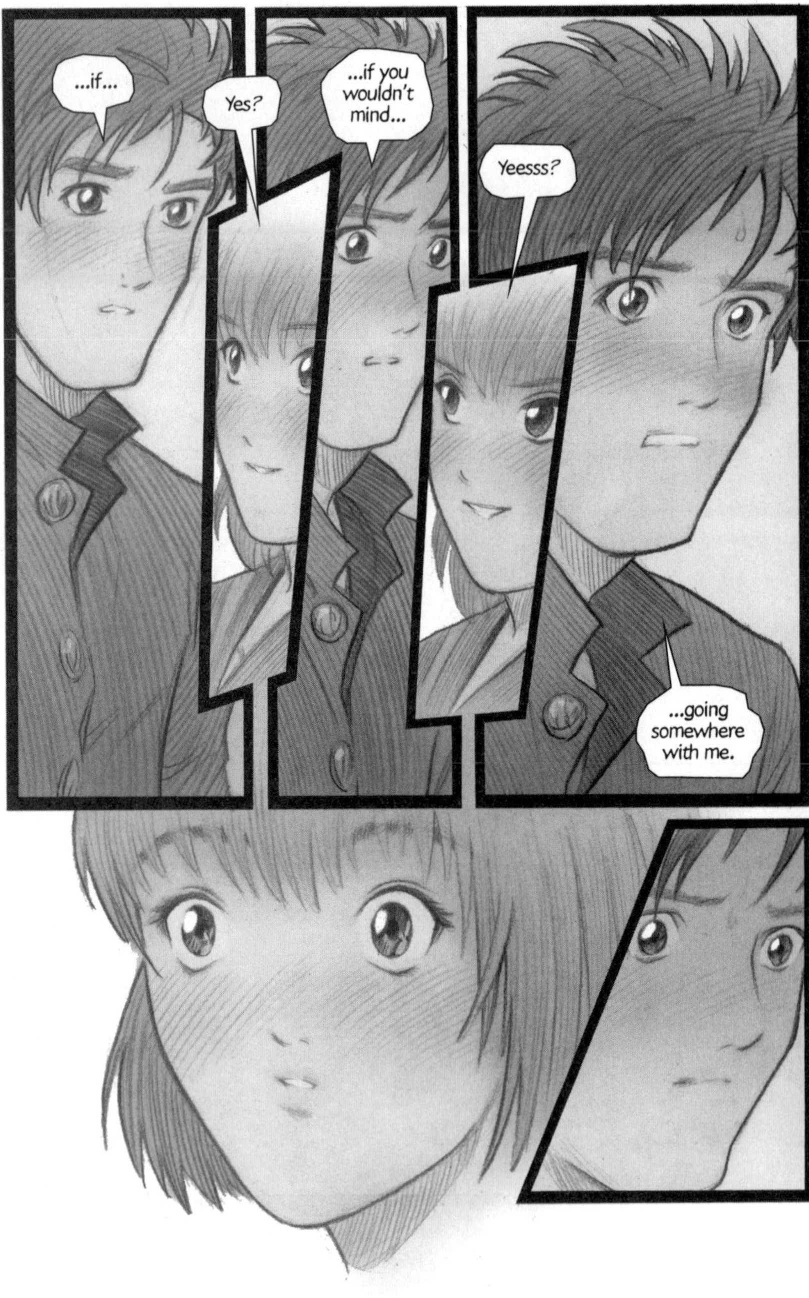

...if...
Yes?
...if you wouldn't mind...
Yeesss?
...going somewhere with me.

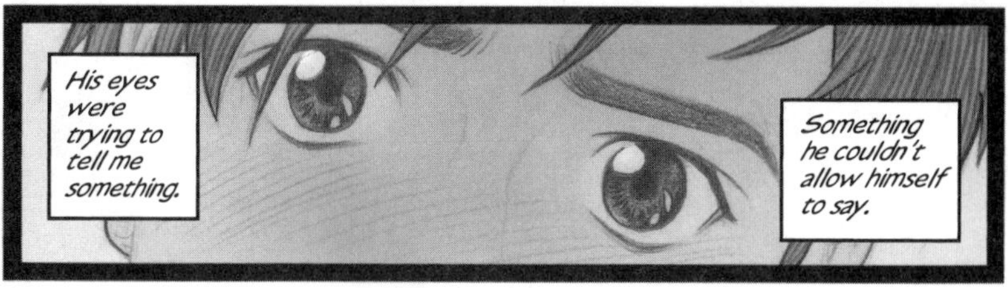
His eyes were trying to tell me something.
Something he couldn't allow himself to say.

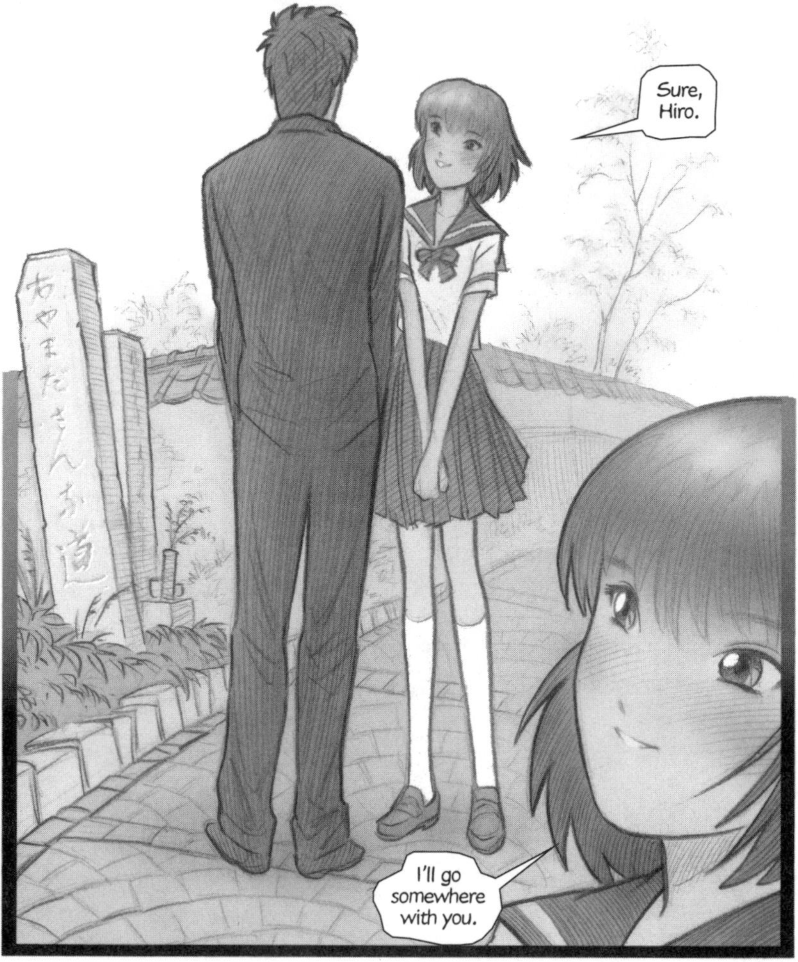
Sure, Hiro.
I'll go somewhere with you.

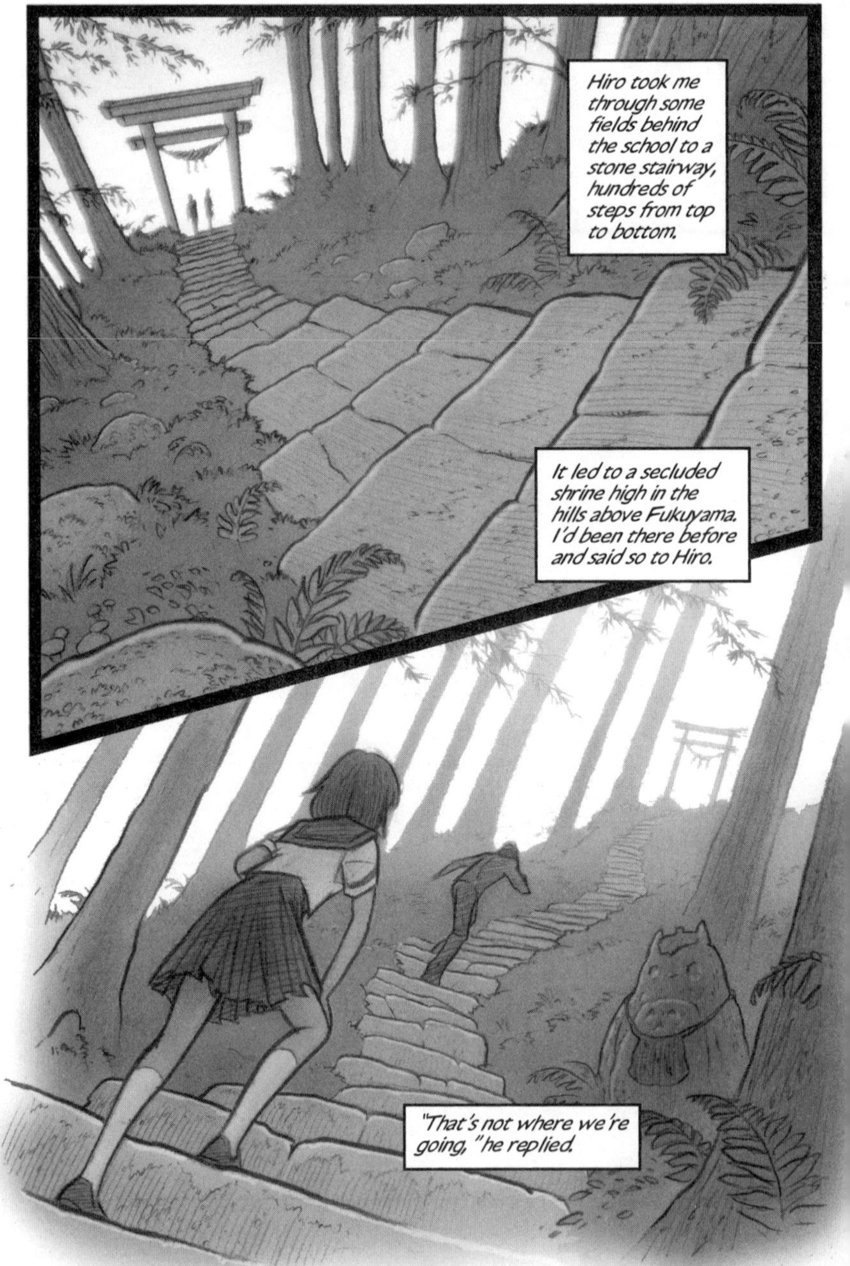
Hiro took me through some fields behind the school to a stone stairway, hundreds of steps from top to bottom.
It led to a secluded shrine high in the hills above Fukuyama. I'd been there before and said so to Hiro.
"That's not where we're going," he replied.

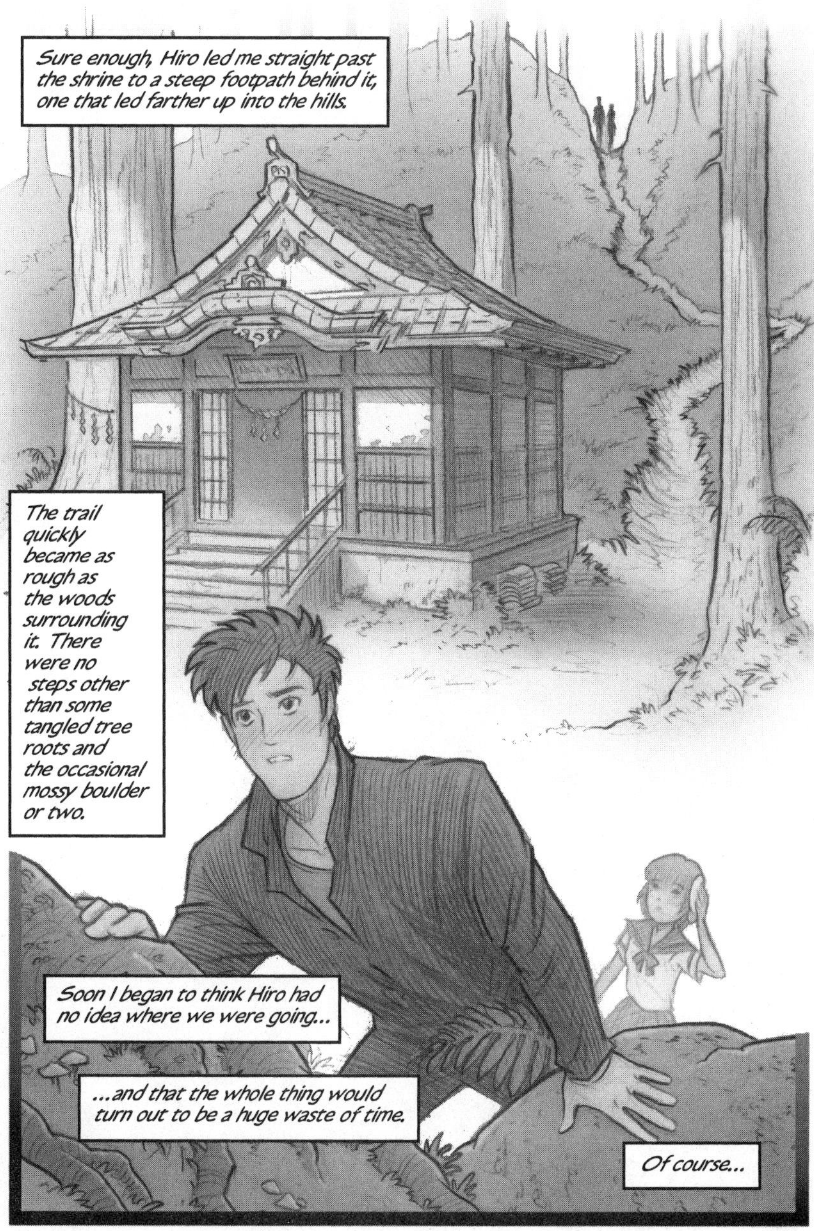

Sure enough, Hiro led me straight past the shrine to a steep footpath behind it, one that led farther up into the hills.
The trail quickly became as rough as the woods surrounding it. There were no steps other than some tangled tree roots and the occasional mossy boulder or two.
Soon I began to think Hiro had no idea where we were going...
...and that the whole thing would turn out to be a huge waste of time.
Of course...

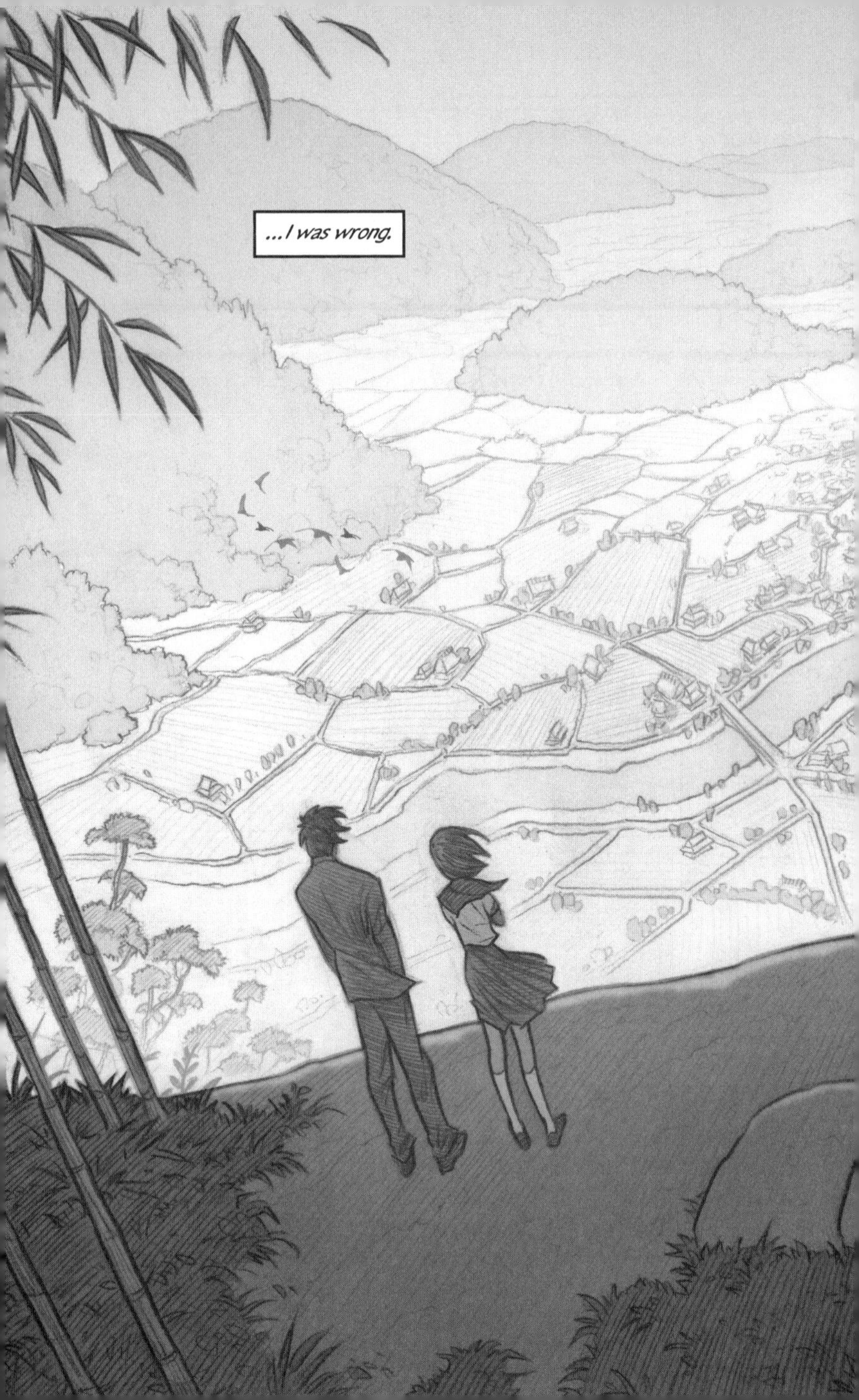
...I was wrong.

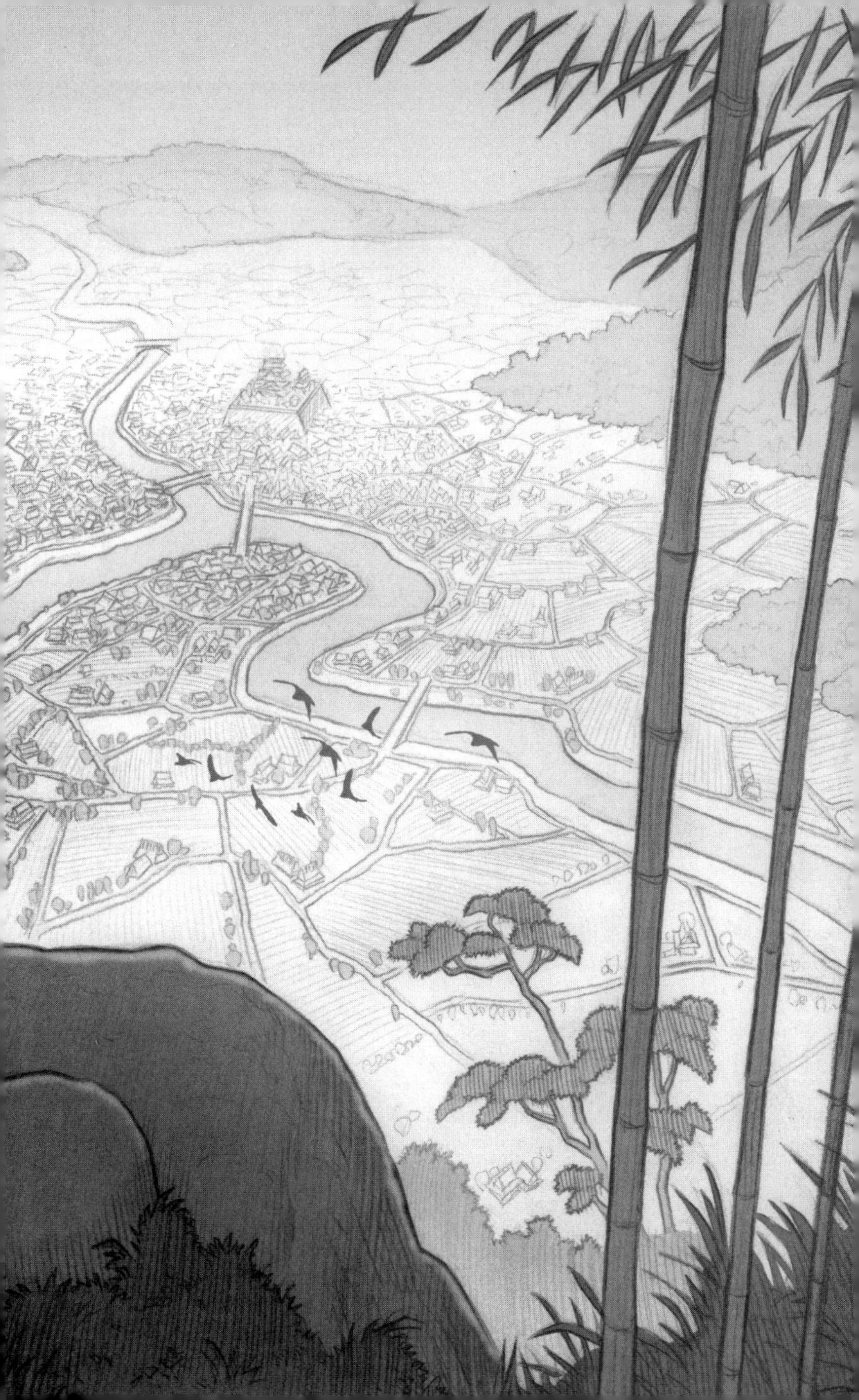

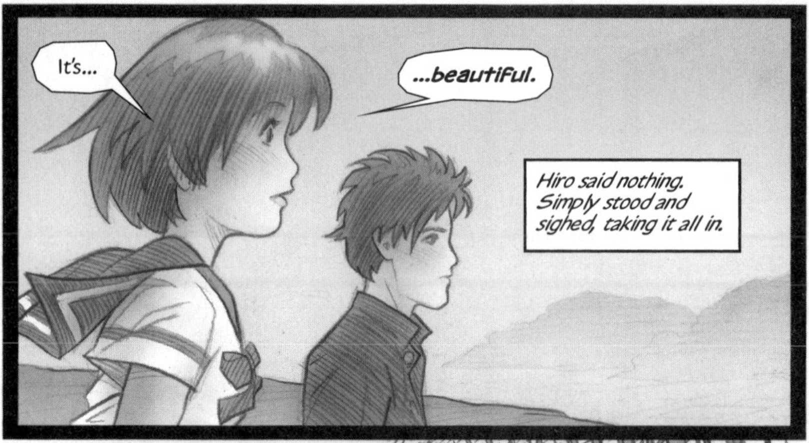
It's...
...beautiful.
Hiro said nothing. Simply stood and sighed, taking it all in.

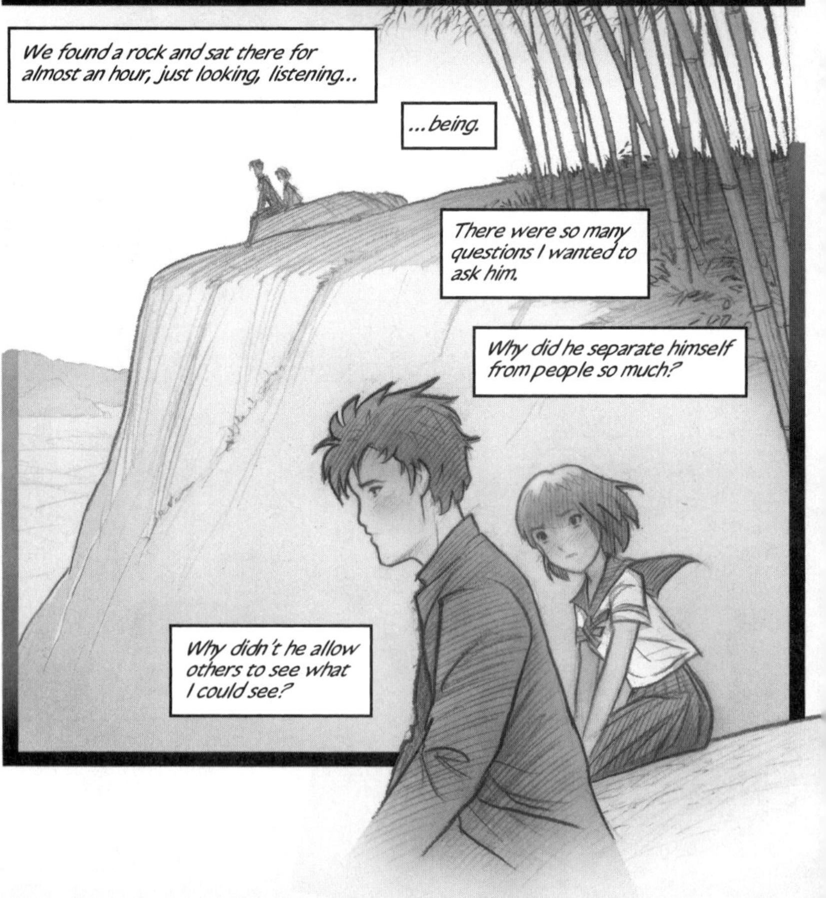
We found a rock and sat there for almost an hour, just looking, listening...
...being.
There were so many questions I wanted to ask him.
Why did he separate himself from people so much?
Why didn't he allow others to see what I could see?

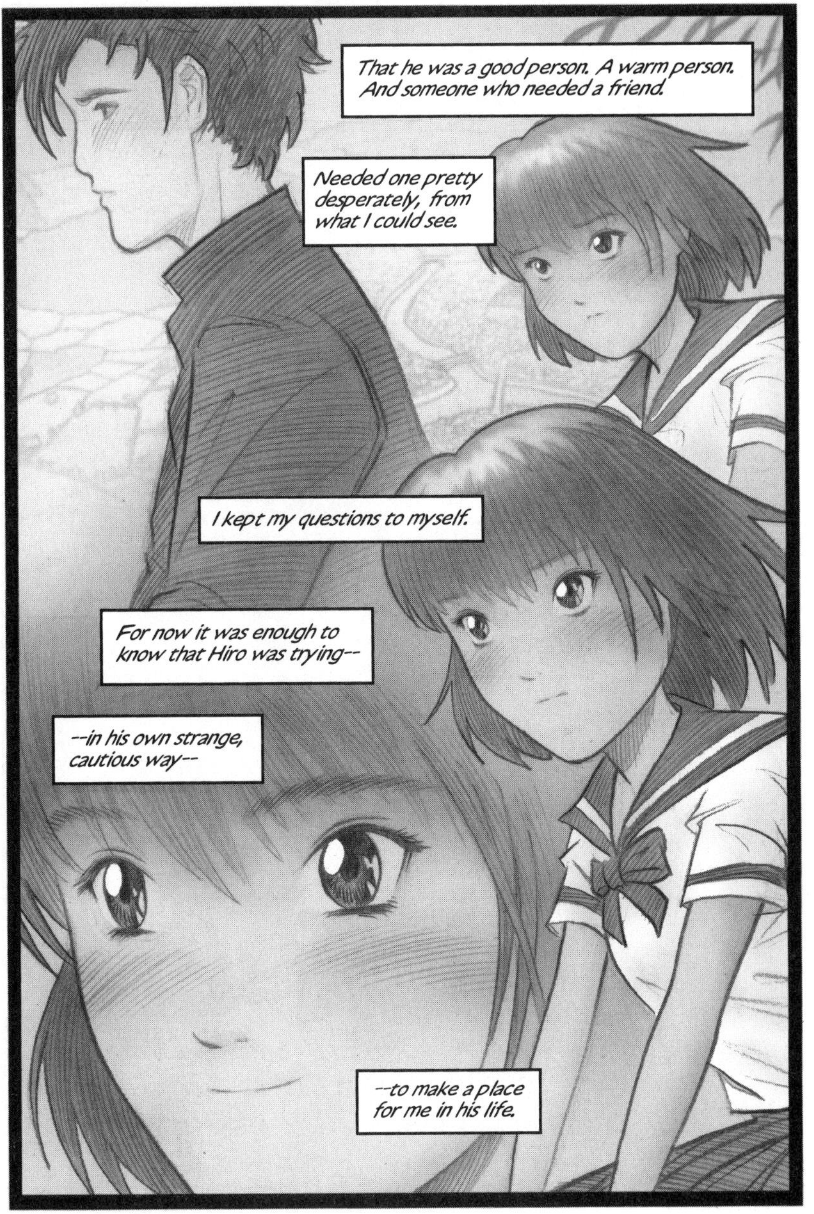
That he was a good person. A warm person. And someone who needed a friend.
Needed one pretty desperately, from what I could see.
I kept my questions to myself.
For now it was enough to know that Hiro was trying--
--in his own strange, cautious way--
--to make a place for me in his life.

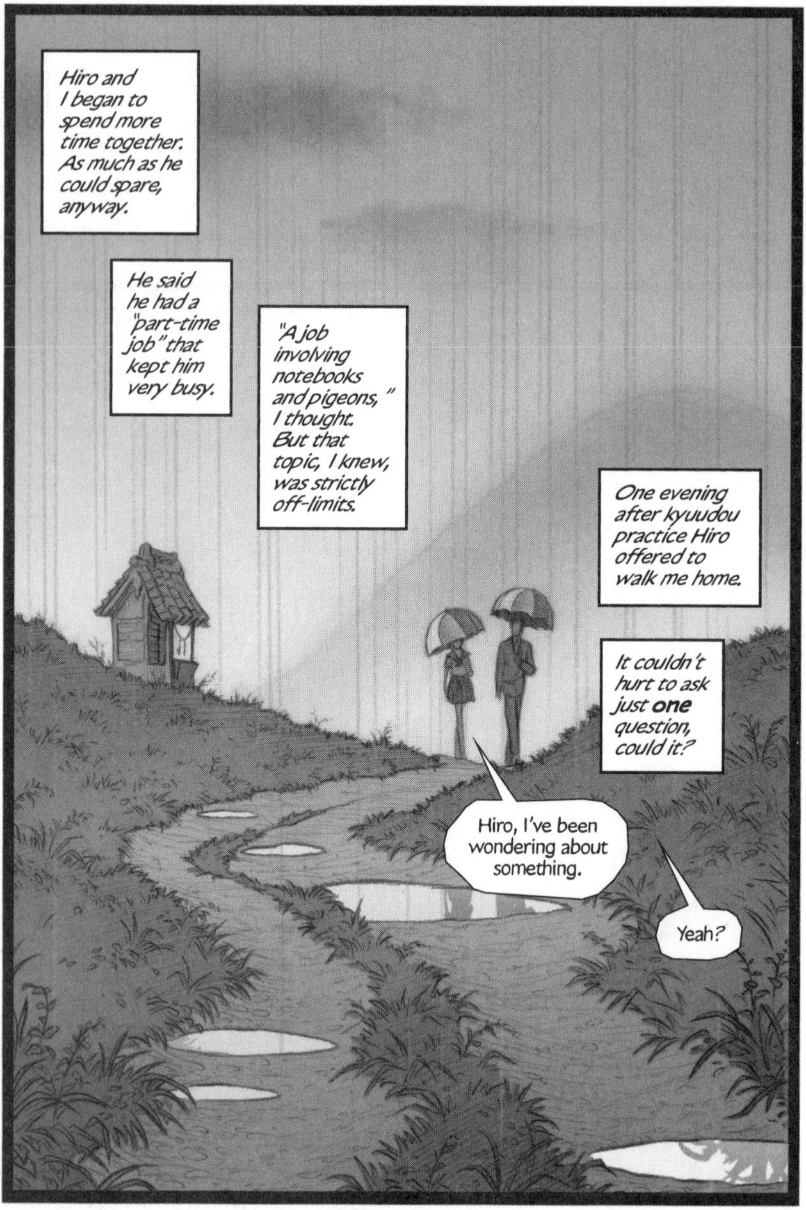
Hiro and I began to spend more time together. As much as he could spare, anyway.
He said he had a "part-time job" that kept him very busy.
"A job involving notebooks and pigeons," I thought. But that topic, I knew, was strictly off-limits.
One evening after kyuudou practice Hiro offered to walk me home.
It couldn't hurt to ask just **one** question, could it?
Hiro, I've been wondering about something.
Yeah?

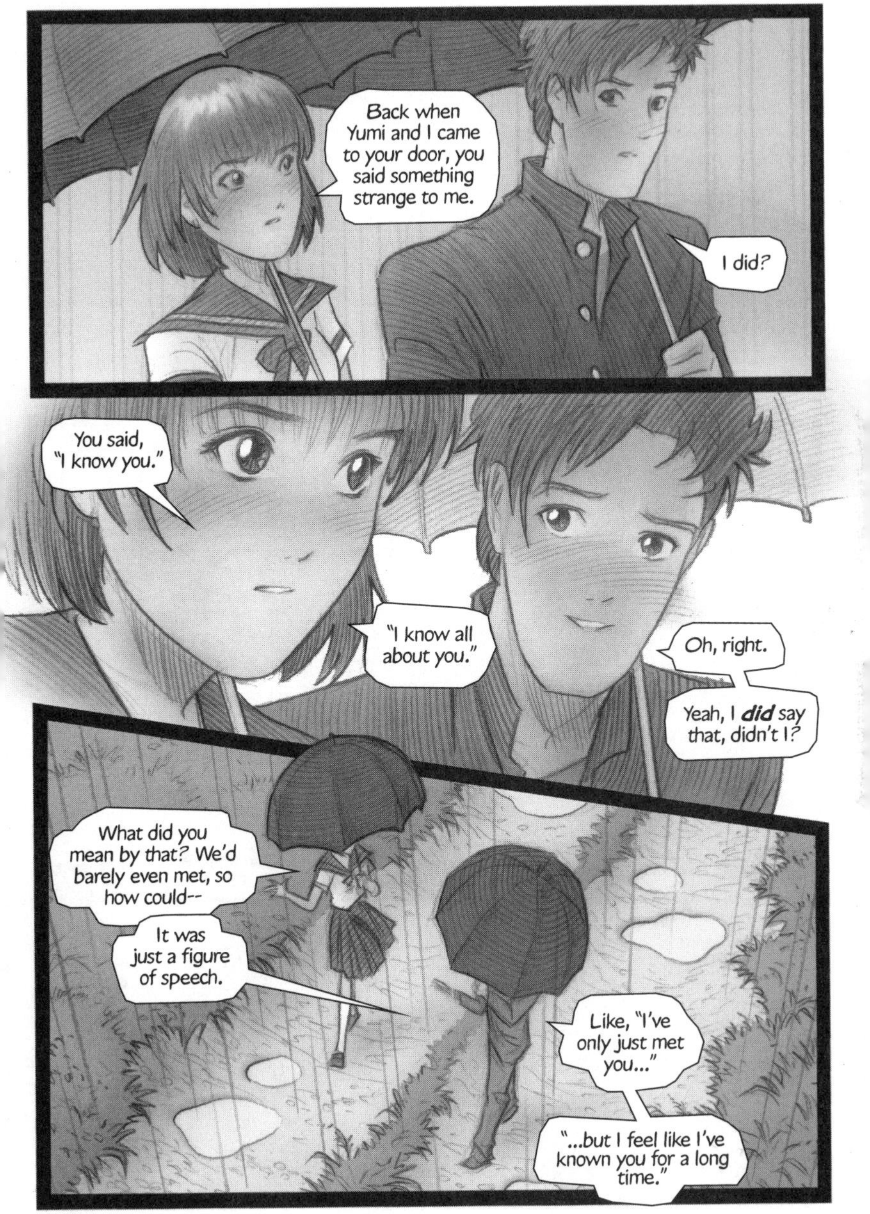
Back when Yumi and I came to your door, you said something strange to me.
I did?
You said, "I know you."
"I know all about you."
Oh, right.
Yeah, I ***did*** say that, didn't I?
What did you mean by that? We'd barely even met, so how could--
It was just a figure of speech.
Like, "I've only just met you..."
"...but I feel like I've known you for a long time."

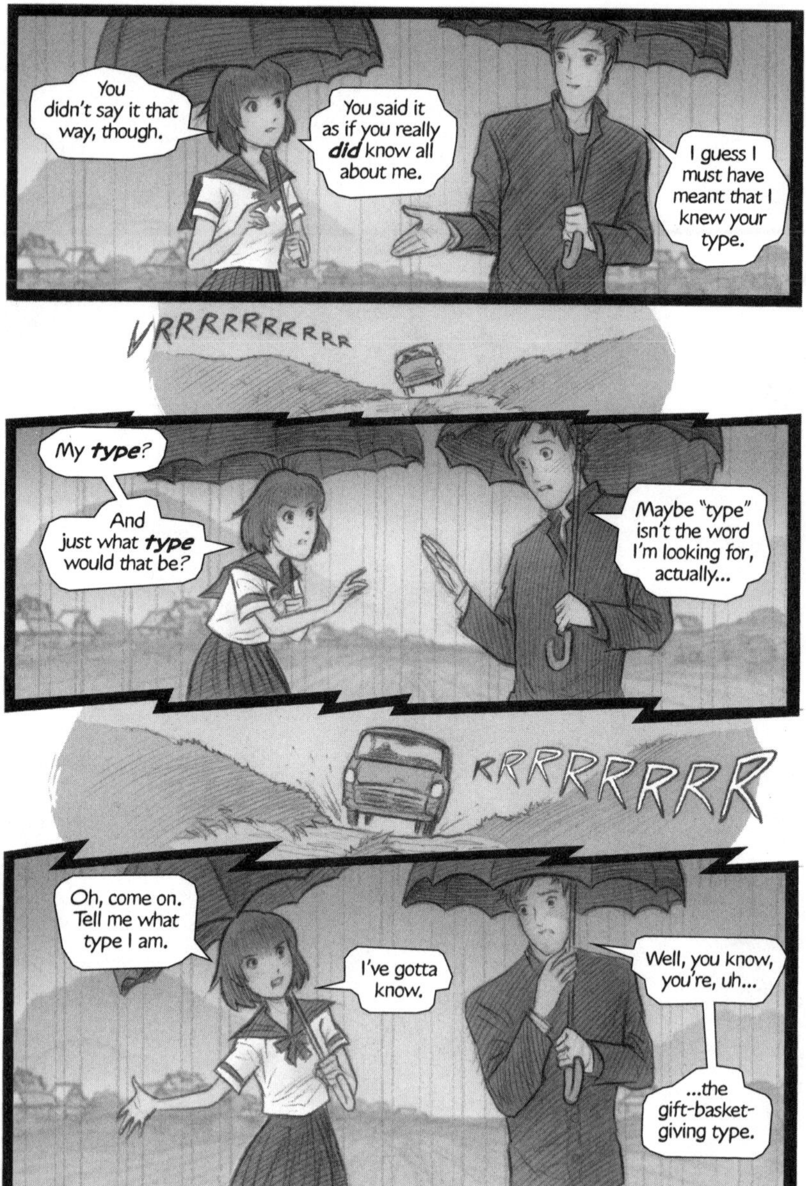
You didn't say it that way, though.
You said it as if you really *did* know all about me.
I guess I must have meant that I knew your type.
VRRRRRRRRRR
My *type*?
And just what *type* would that be?
Maybe "type" isn't the word I'm looking for, actually...
RRRRRRRRR
Oh, come on. Tell me what type I am.
I've gotta know.
Well, you know, you're, uh...
...the gift-basket-giving type.

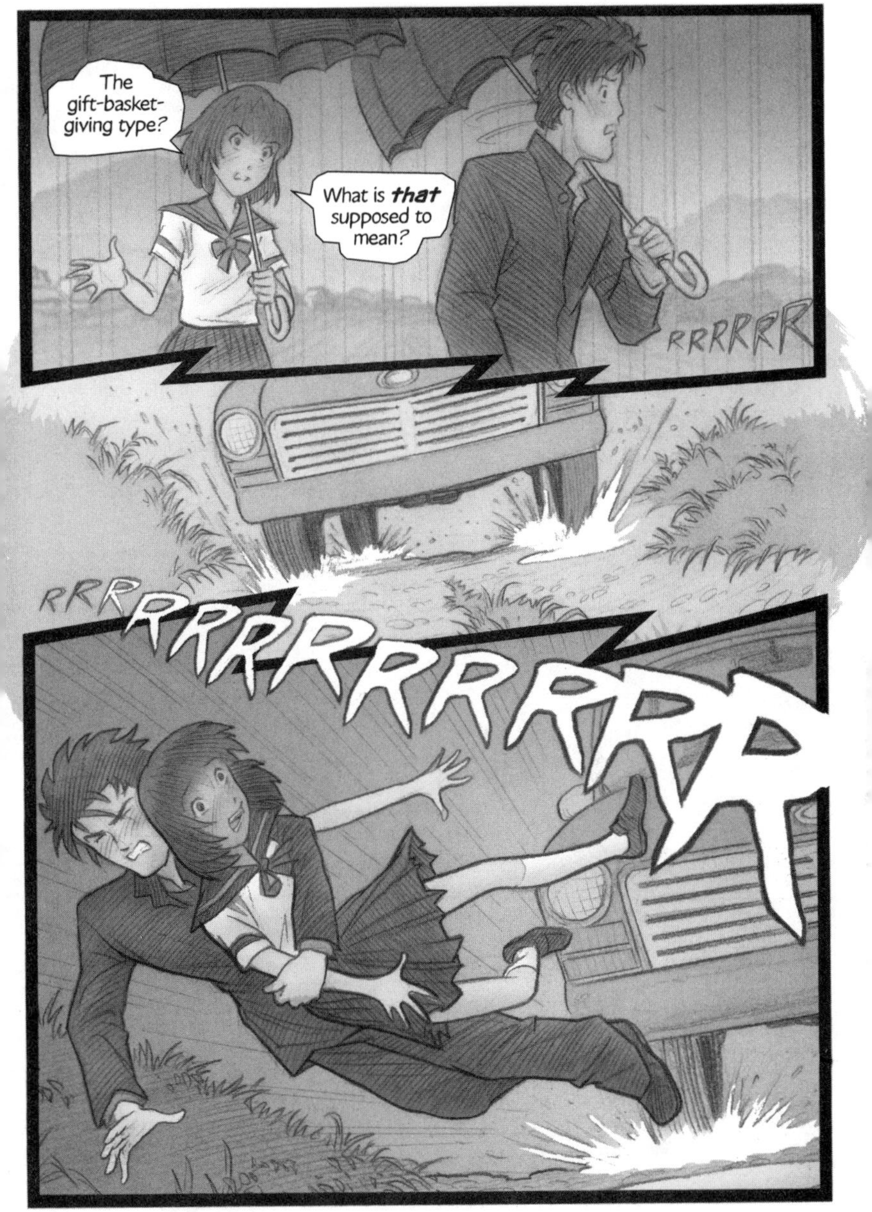
The gift-basket-giving type?
What is ***that*** supposed to mean?
RRRRRR
RRRRRRRRRRRRRR

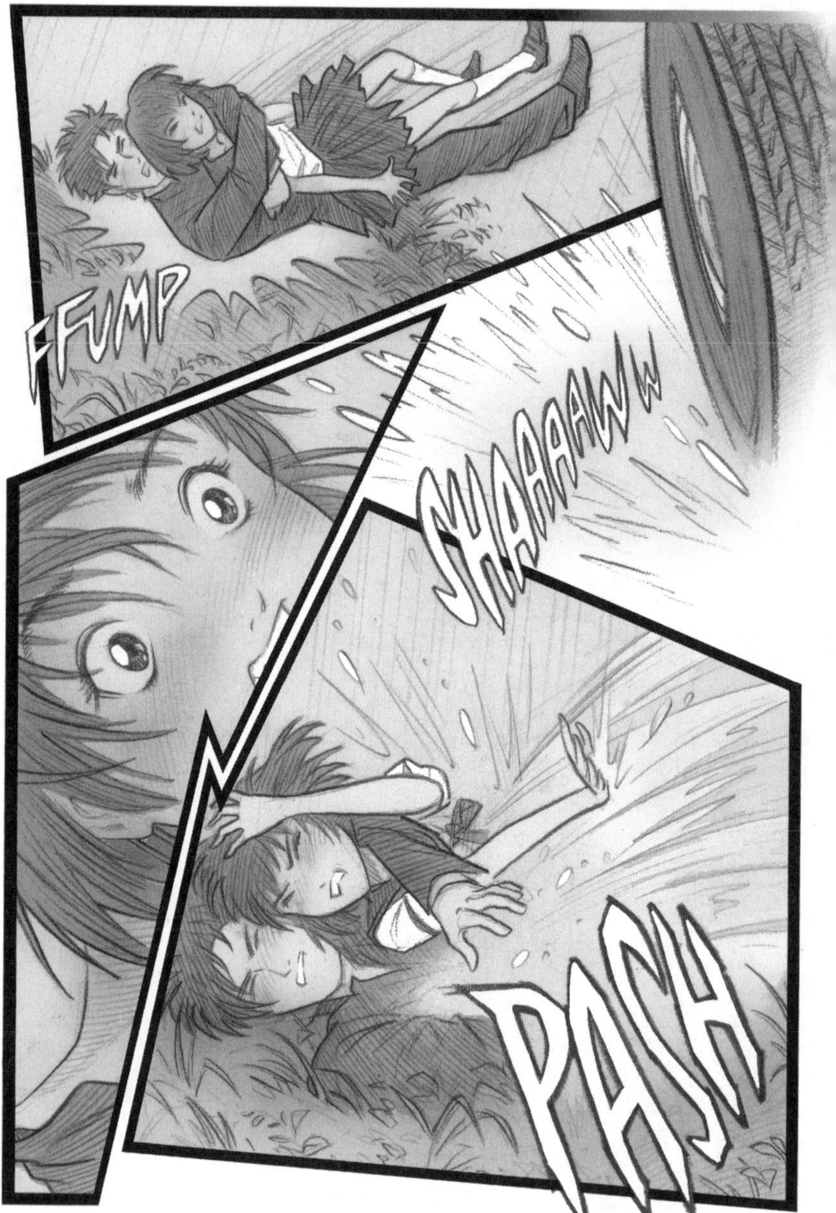
FFUMP
SHAAAAW w
PASH

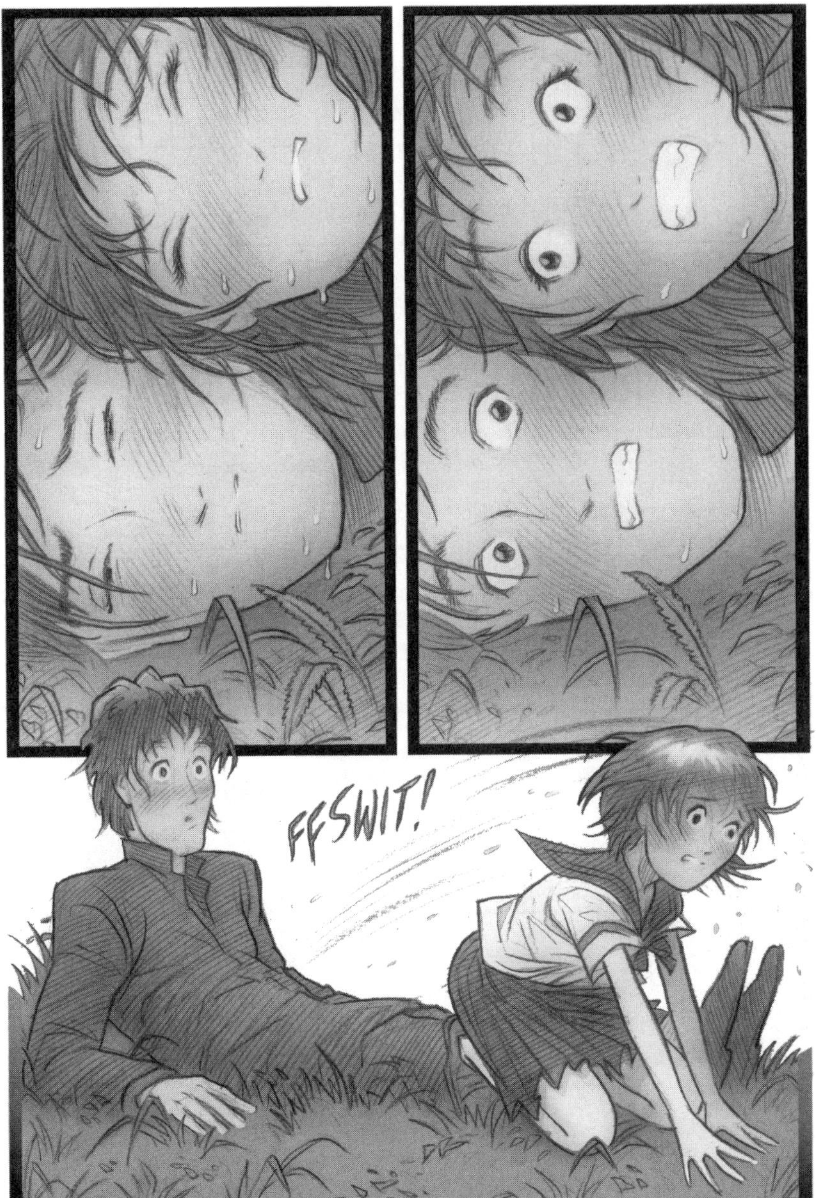
FFSWIT!

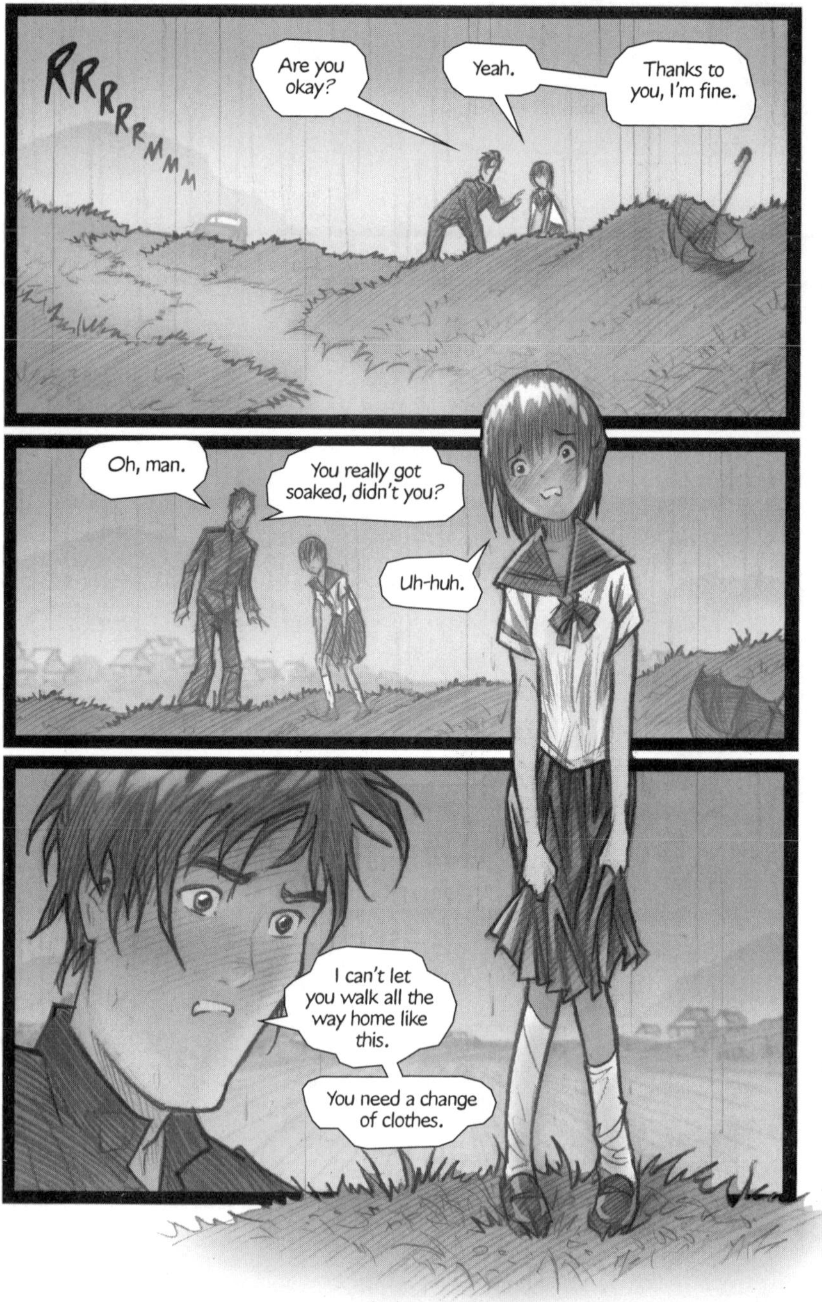
RRRRRMMM
Are you okay?
Yeah.
Thanks to you, I'm fine.
Oh, man.
You really got soaked, didn't you?
Uh-huh.
I can't let you walk all the way home like this.
You need a change of clothes.

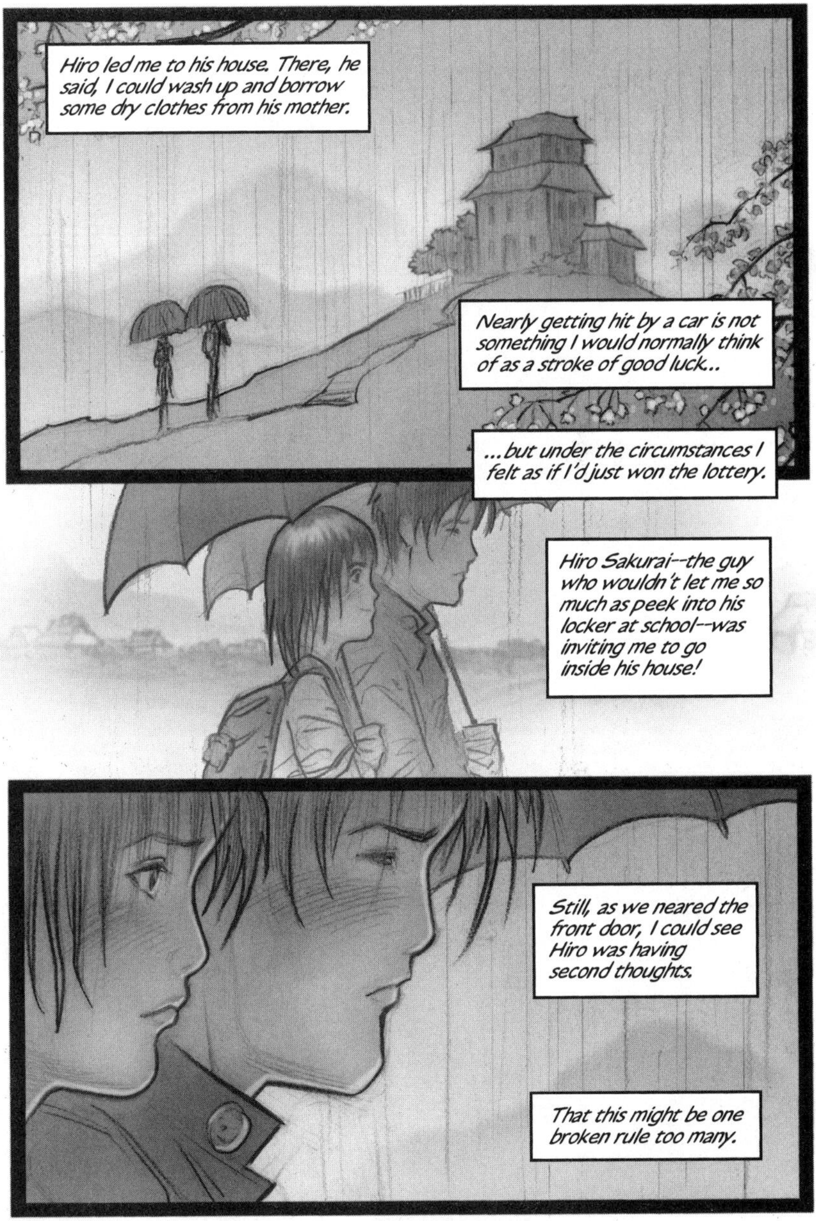
Hiro led me to his house. There, he said, I could wash up and borrow some dry clothes from his mother.
Nearly getting hit by a car is not something I would normally think of as a stroke of good luck...
...but under the circumstances I felt as if I'd just won the lottery.
Hiro Sakurai--the guy who wouldn't let me so much as peek into his locker at school--was inviting me to go inside his house!
Still, as we neared the front door, I could see Hiro was having second thoughts.
That this might be one broken rule too many.

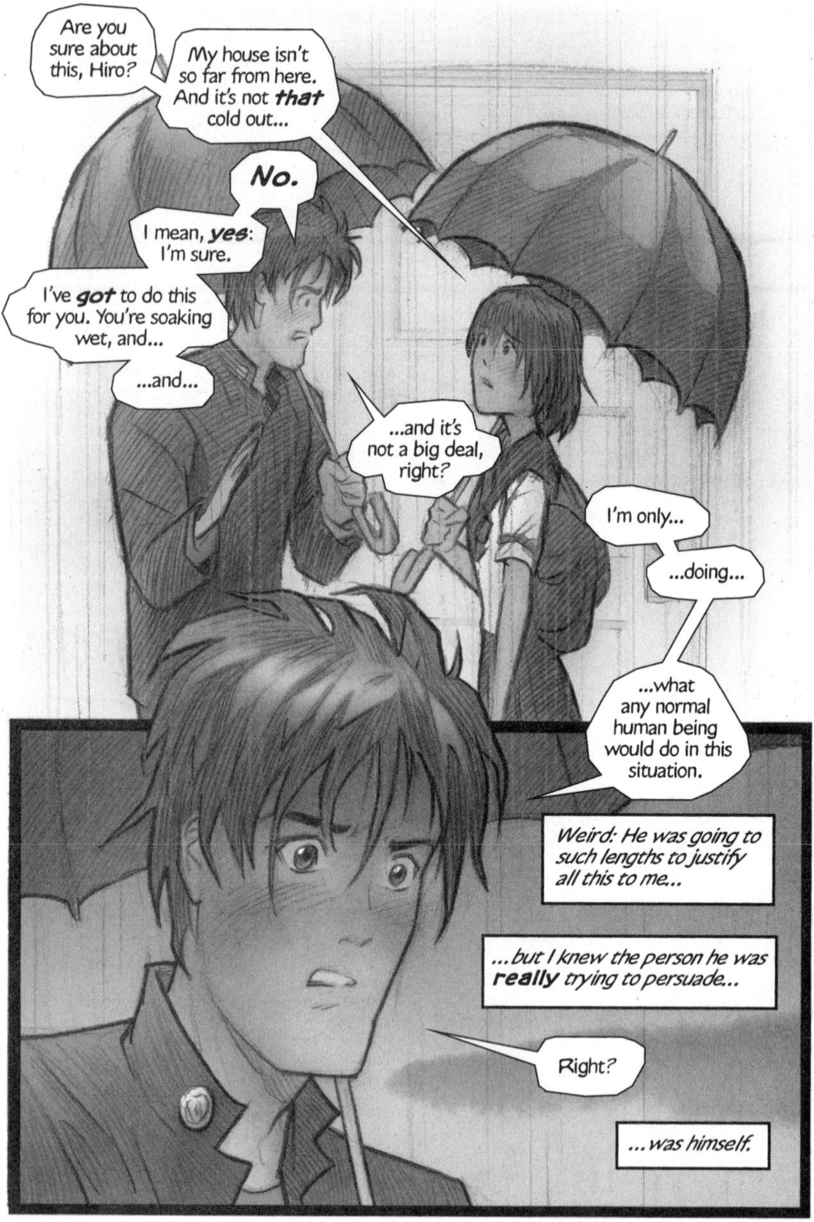
Are you sure about this, Hiro?
My house isn't so far from here. And it's not **that** cold out...
No.
I mean, **yes**: I'm sure.
I've **got** to do this for you. You're soaking wet, and...
...and...
...and it's not a big deal, right?
I'm only...
...doing...
...what any normal human being would do in this situation.
Weird: He was going to such lengths to justify all this to me...
*...but I knew the person he was **really** trying to persuade...*
Right?
...was himself.

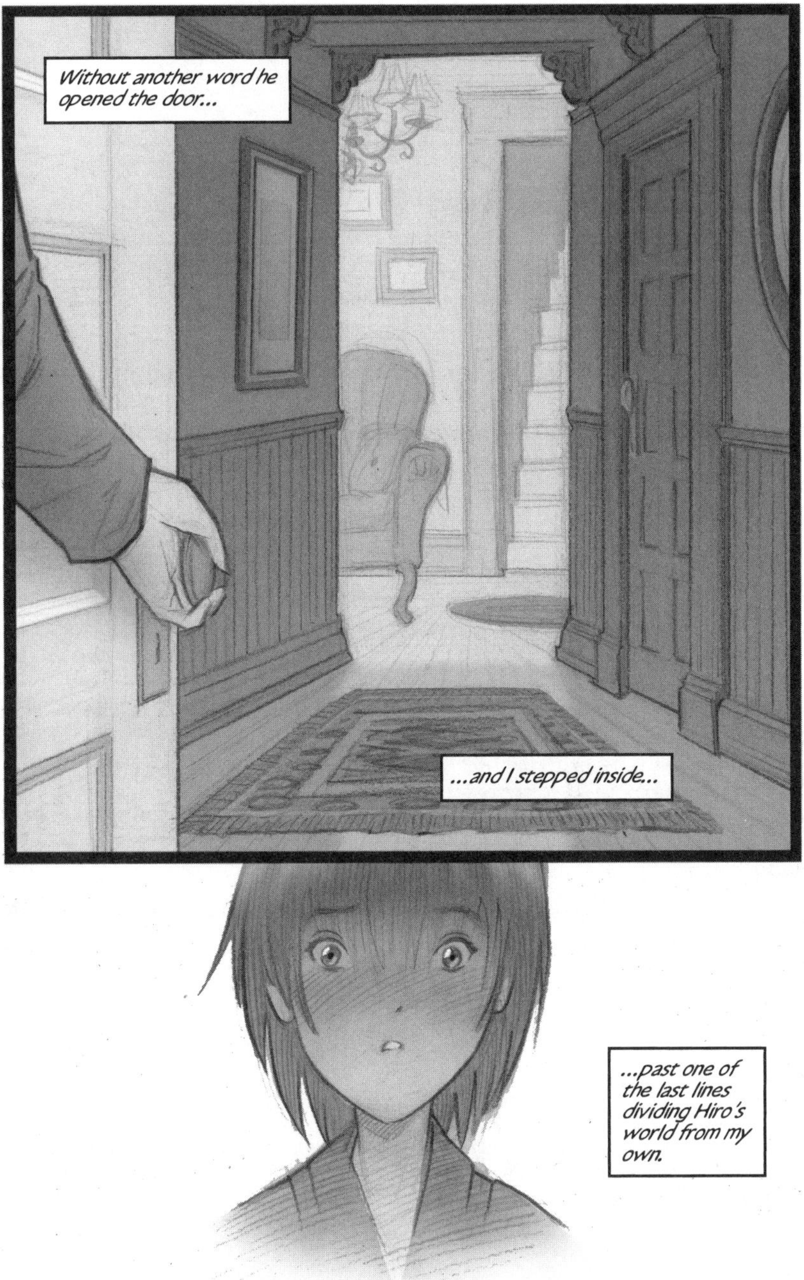
Without another word he opened the door...
...and I stepped inside...
...past one of the last lines dividing Hiro's world from my own.

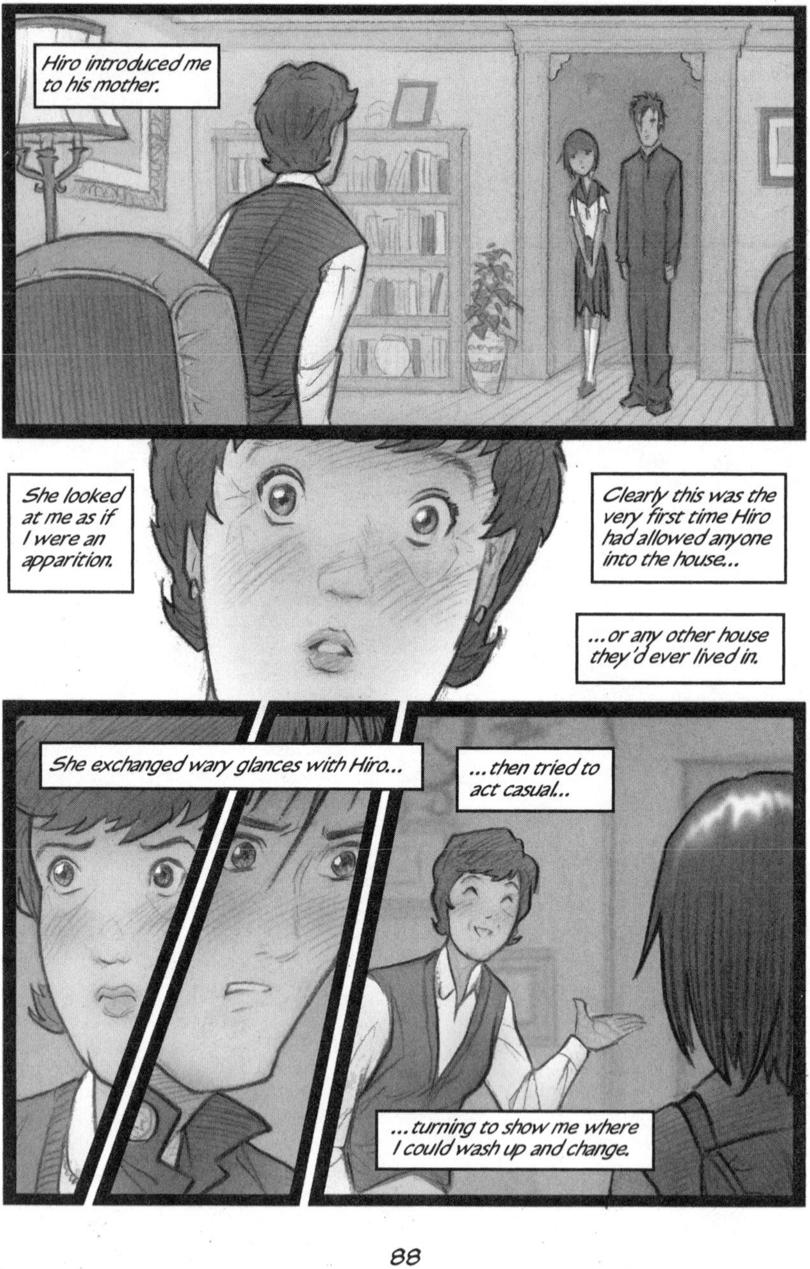
Hiro introduced me to his mother.
She looked at me as if I were an apparition.
Clearly this was the very first time Hiro had allowed anyone into the house...
...or any other house they'd ever lived in.
She exchanged wary glances with Hiro...
...then tried to act casual...
...turning to show me where I could wash up and change.

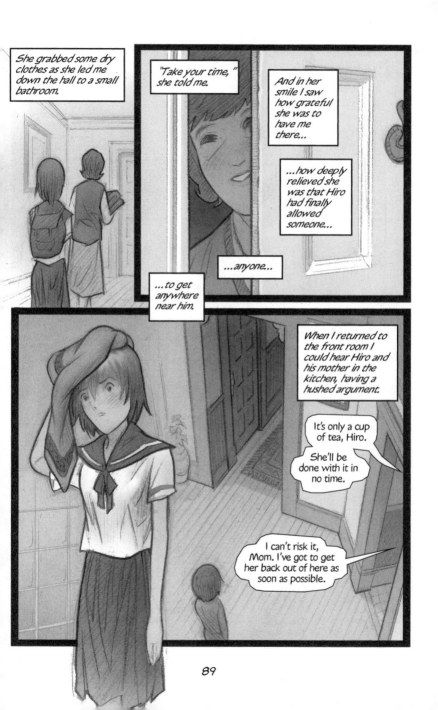

She grabbed some dry clothes as she led me down the hall to a small bathroom.

"Take your time," she told me.

And in her smile I saw how grateful she was to have me there...

...how deeply relieved she was that Hiro had finally allowed someone...

...anyone...

...to get anywhere near him.

When I returned to the front room I could hear Hiro and his mother in the kitchen, having a hushed argument.

It's only a cup of tea, Hiro.

She'll be done with it in no time.

I can't risk it, Mom. I've got to get her back out of here as soon as possible.

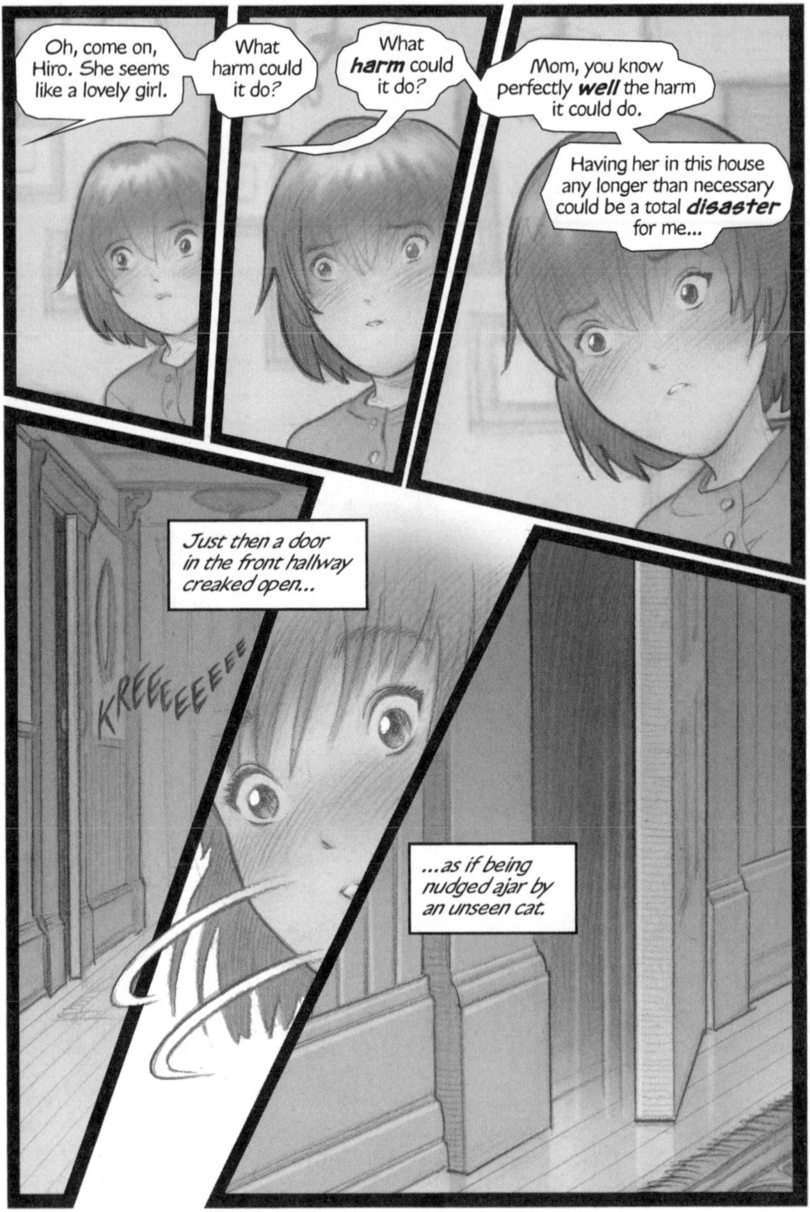
Oh, come on, Hiro. She seems like a lovely girl.
What harm could it do?
What **harm** could it do?
Mom, you know perfectly **well** the harm it could do.
Having her in this house any longer than necessary could be a total **disaster** for me...
Just then a door in the front hallway creaked open...
KREEEEEEEEE
...as if being nudged ajar by an unseen cat.

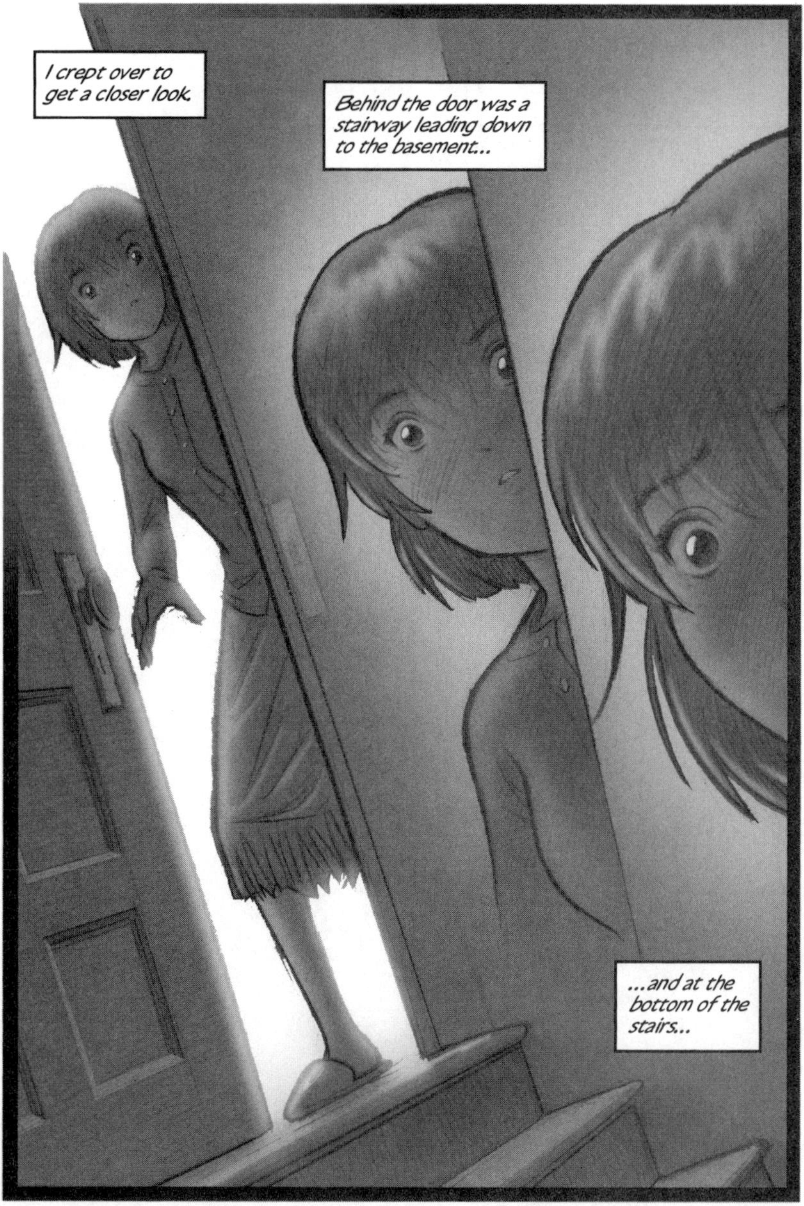
I crept over to get a closer look.
Behind the door was a stairway leading down to the basement...
...and at the bottom of the stairs...

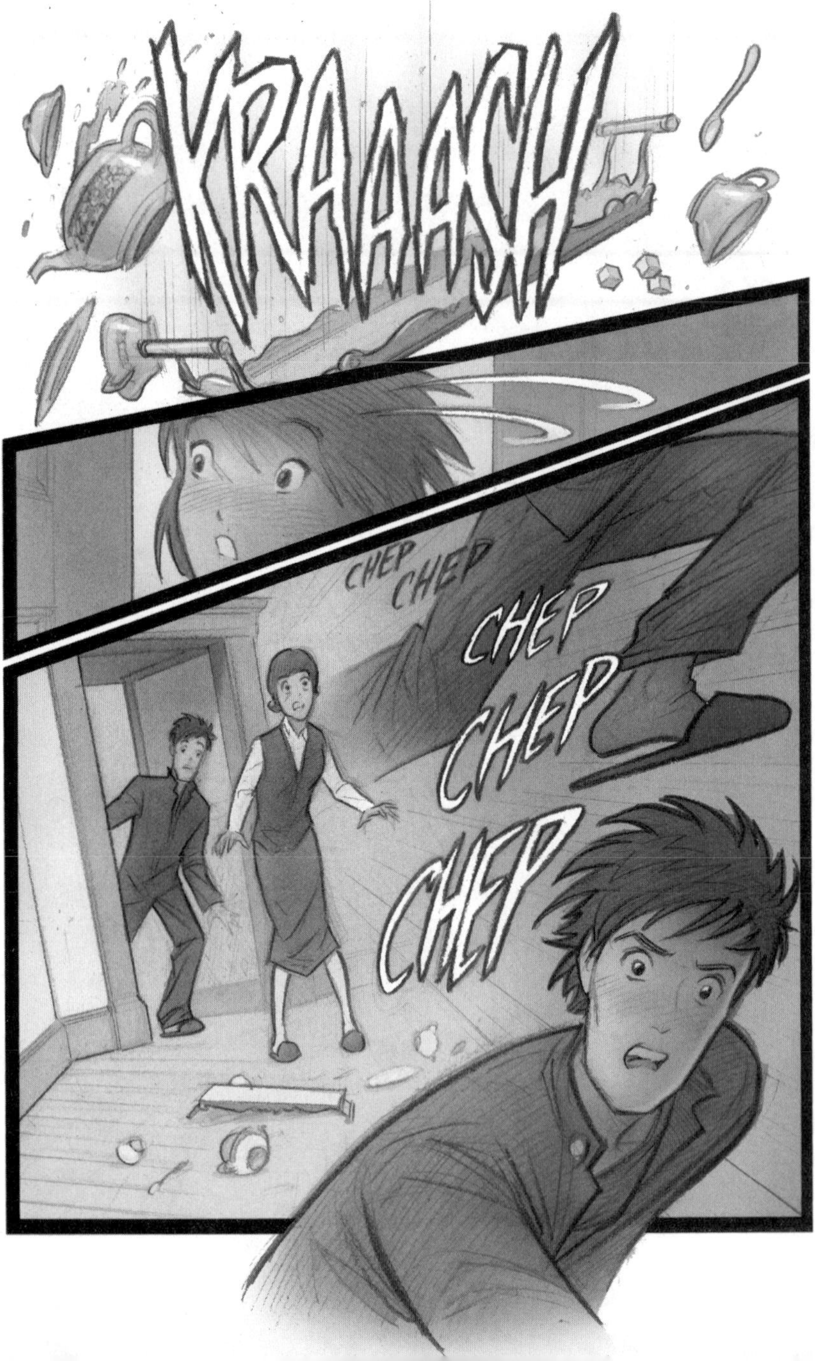
KRAAASH
CHEP
CHEP
CHEP
CHEP
CHEP

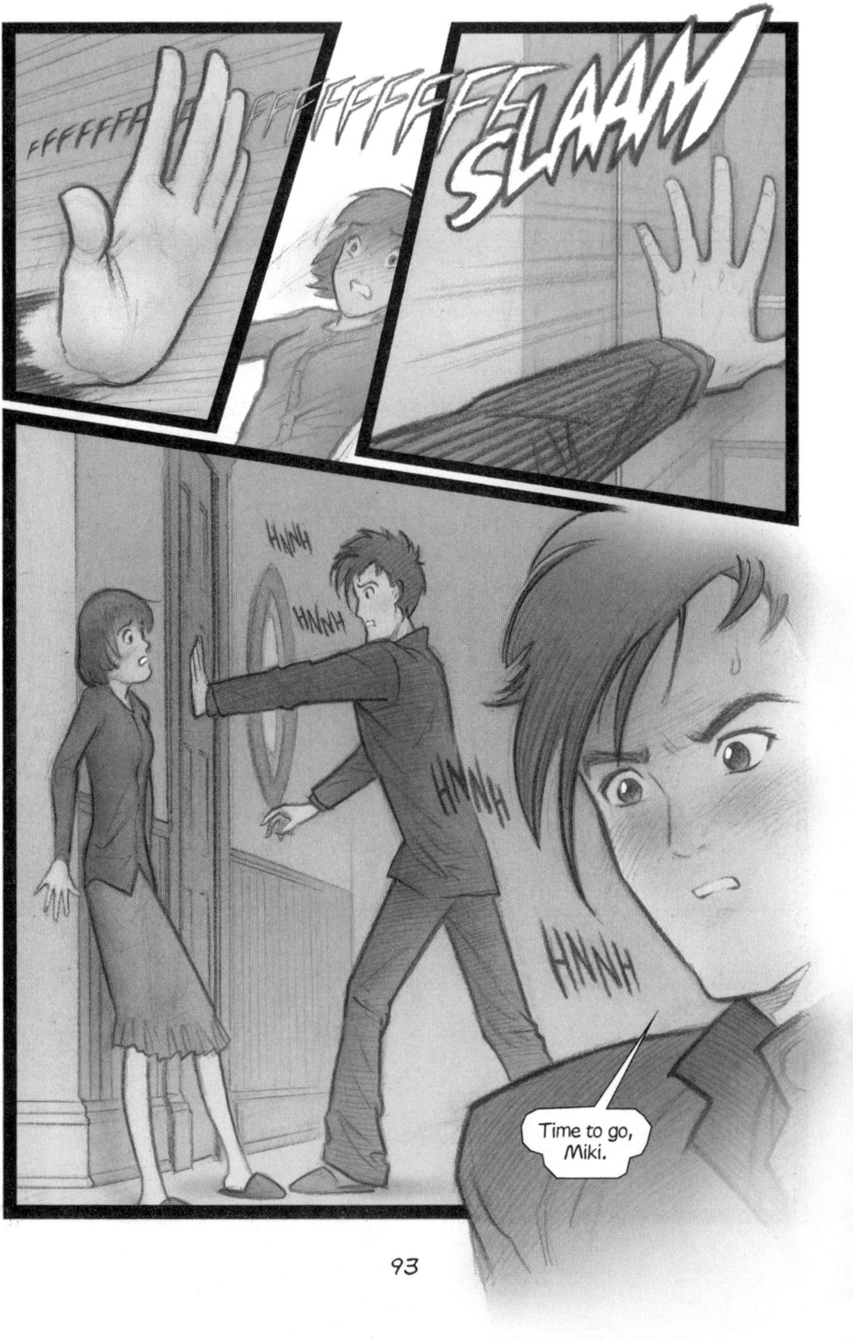
FFFFFFF
FFFFFFFFFF
SLAAM
HNNH
HNNH
HNNH
HNNH
Time to go, Miki.

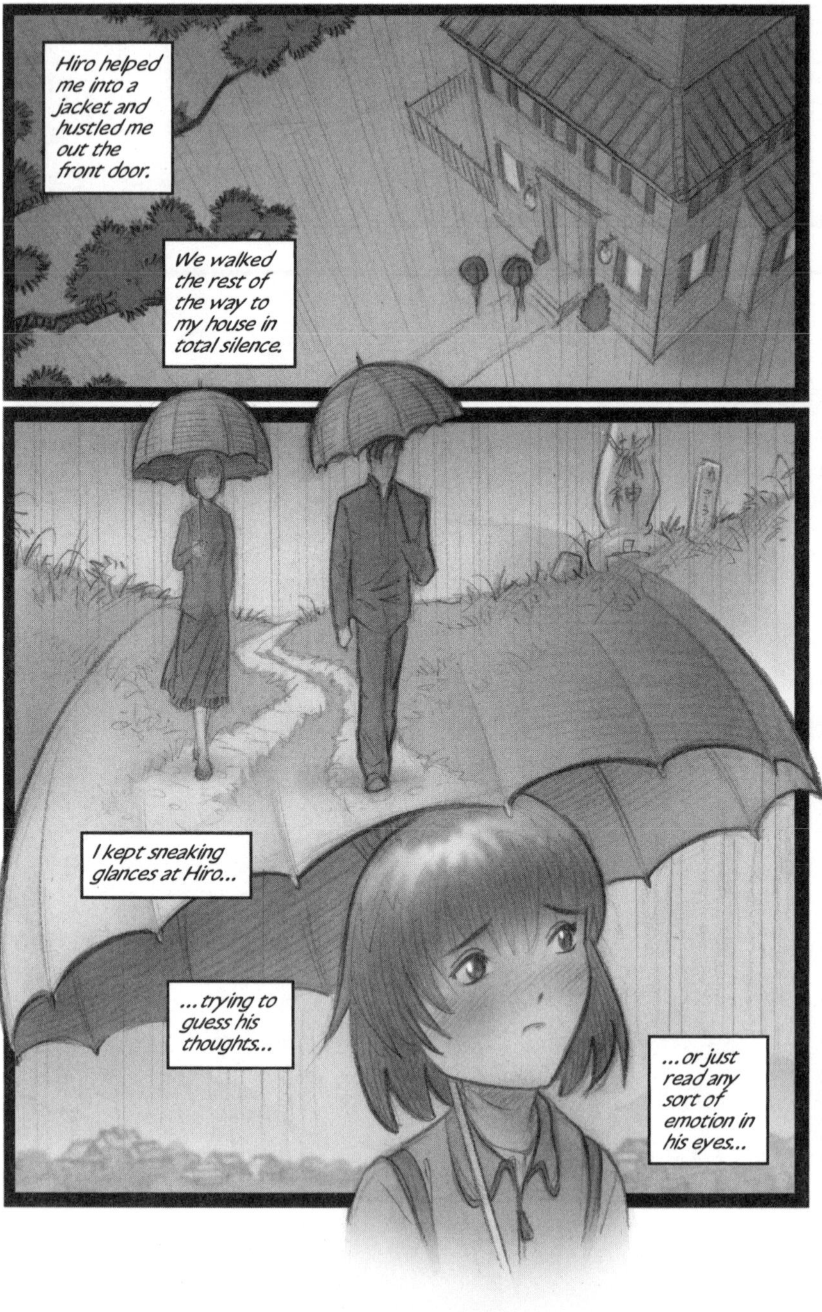
Hiro helped me into a jacket and hustled me out the front door.
We walked the rest of the way to my house in total silence.
I kept sneaking glances at Hiro...
...trying to guess his thoughts...
...or just read any sort of emotion in his eyes...

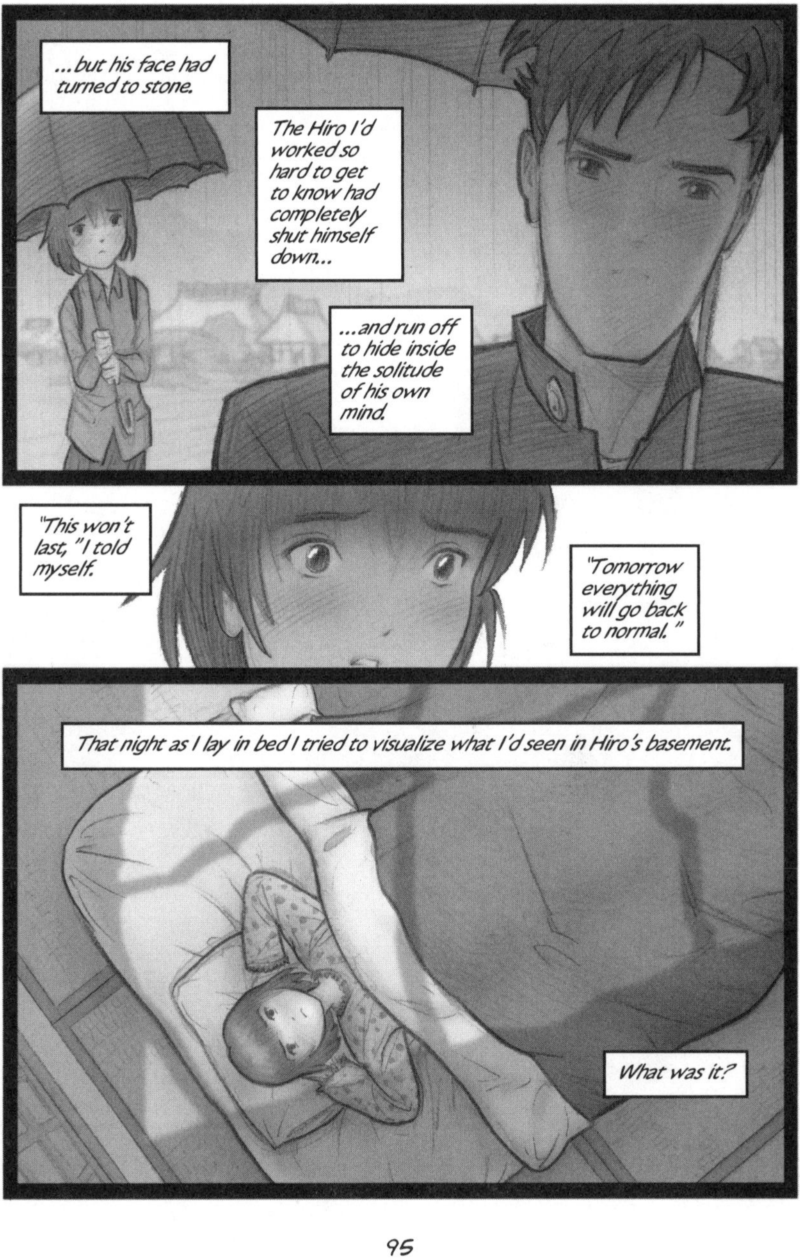
...but his face had turned to stone.
The Hiro I'd worked so hard to get to know had completely shut himself down...
...and run off to hide inside the solitude of his own mind.
"This won't last," I told myself.
"Tomorrow everything will go back to normal."
That night as I lay in bed I tried to visualize what I'd seen in Hiro's basement.
What was it?

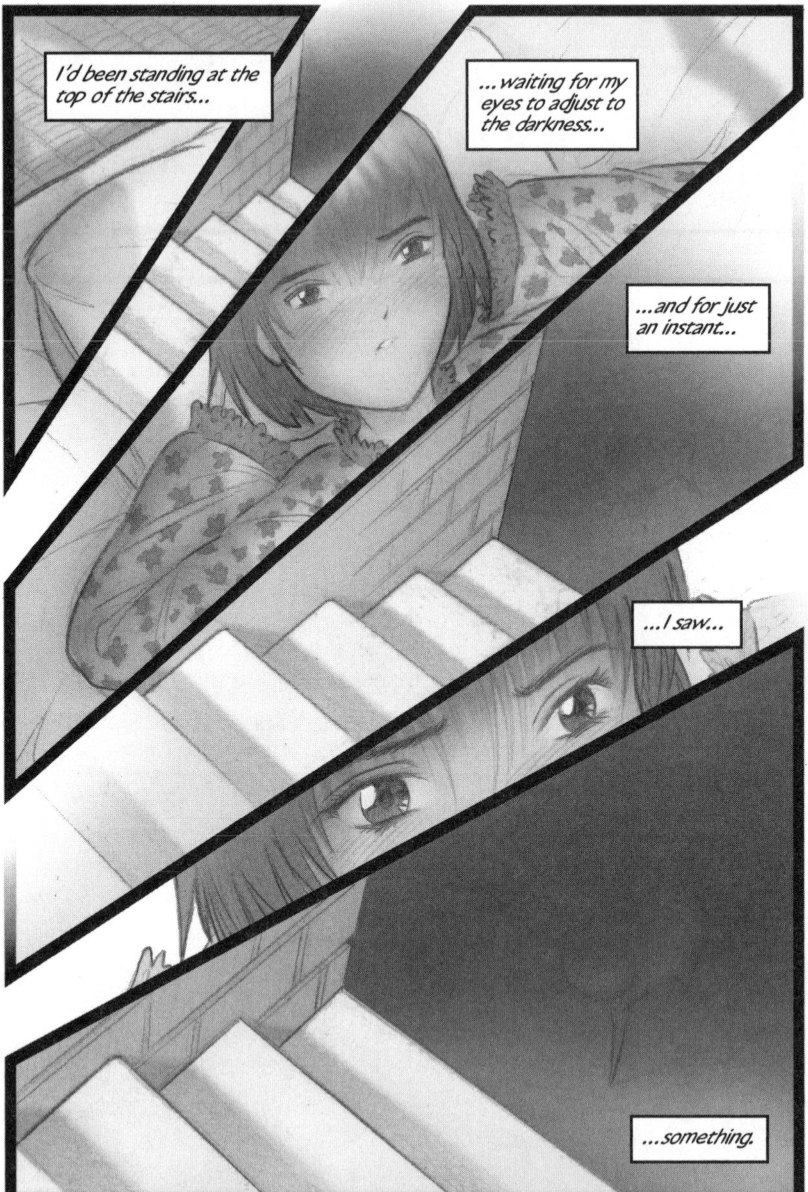
I'd been standing at the top of the stairs...
...waiting for my eyes to adjust to the darkness...
...and for just an instant...
...I saw...
...something.

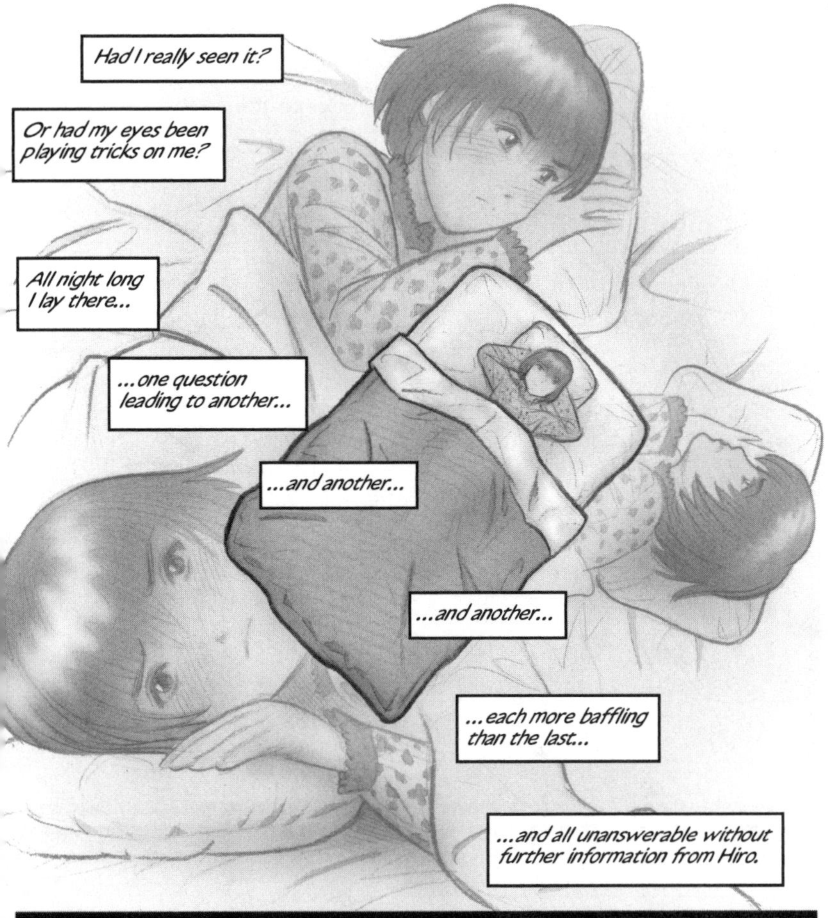
Had I really seen it?
Or had my eyes been playing tricks on me?
All night long I lay there...
...one question leading to another...
...and another...
...and another...
...each more baffling than the last...
...and all unanswerable without further information from Hiro.

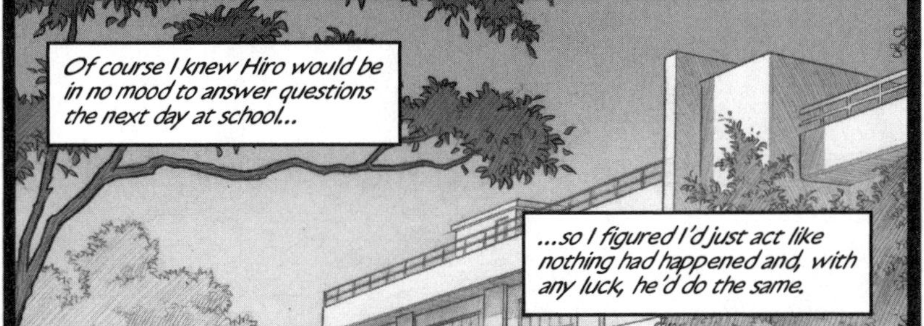
Of course I knew Hiro would be in no mood to answer questions the next day at school...
...so I figured I'd just act like nothing had happened and, with any luck, he'd do the same.

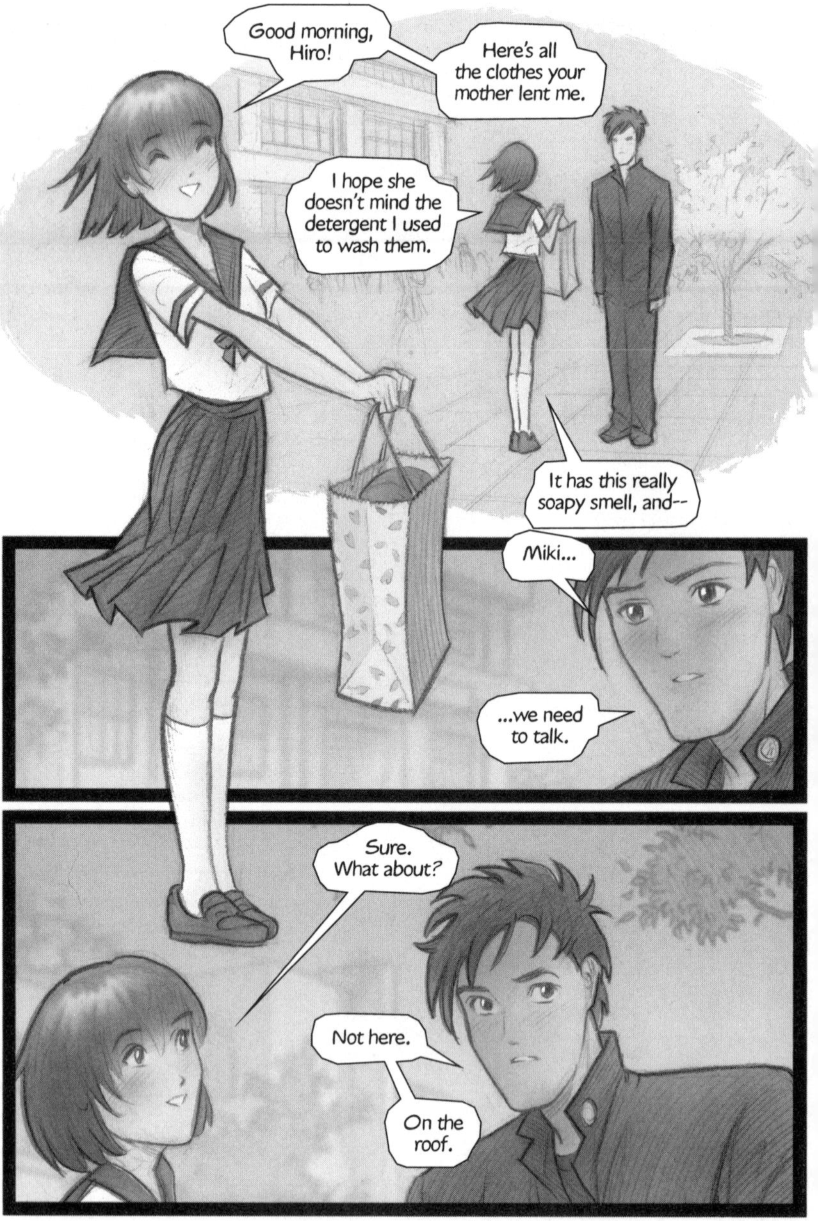
Good morning, Hiro!
Here's all the clothes your mother lent me.
I hope she doesn't mind the detergent I used to wash them.
It has this really soapy smell, and--
Miki...
...we need to talk.
Sure. What about?
Not here.
On the roof.

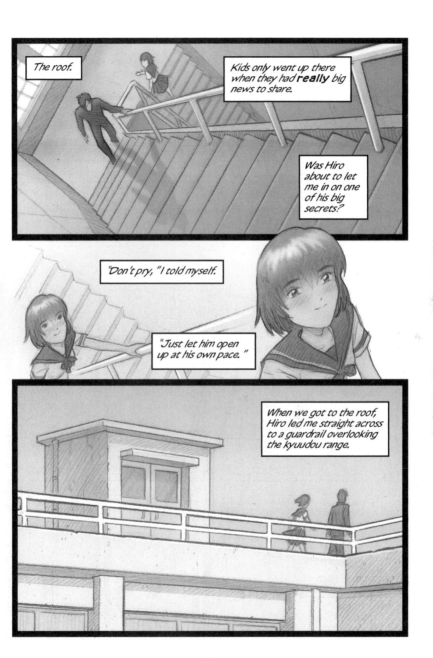

The roof.

Kids only went up there when they had **really** big news to share.

Was Hiro about to let me in on one of his big secrets?

"Don't pry," I told myself.

"Just let him open up at his own pace."

When we got to the roof, Hiro led me straight across to a guardrail overlooking the kyuudou range.

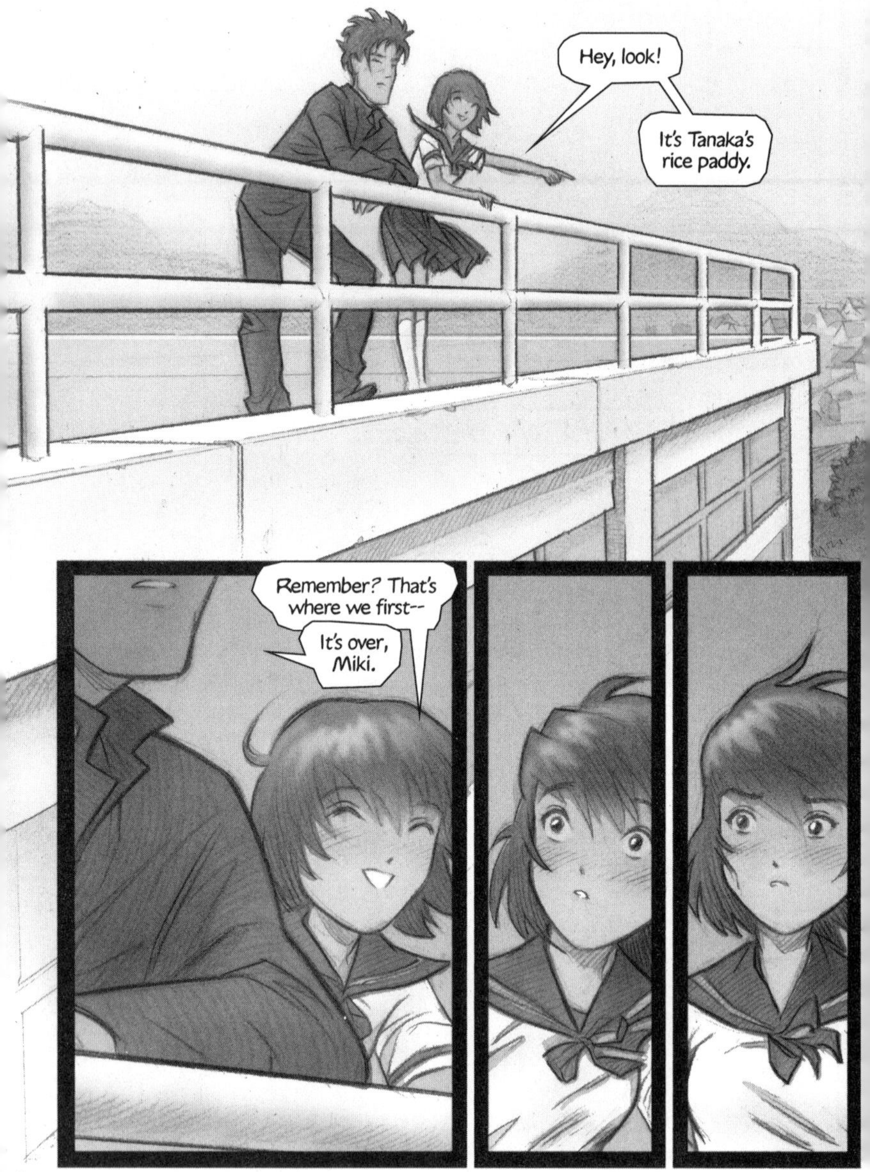
Hey, look!
It's Tanaka's rice paddy.
Remember? That's where we first--
It's over, Miki.

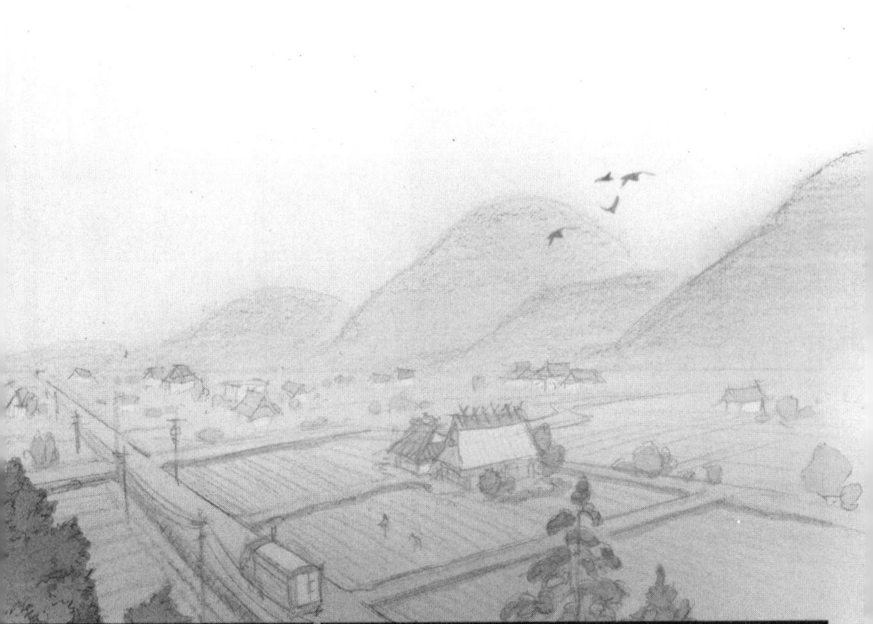

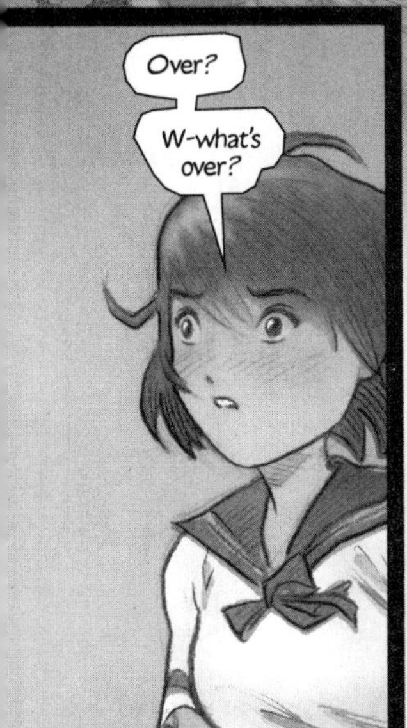
Over?
W-what's over?

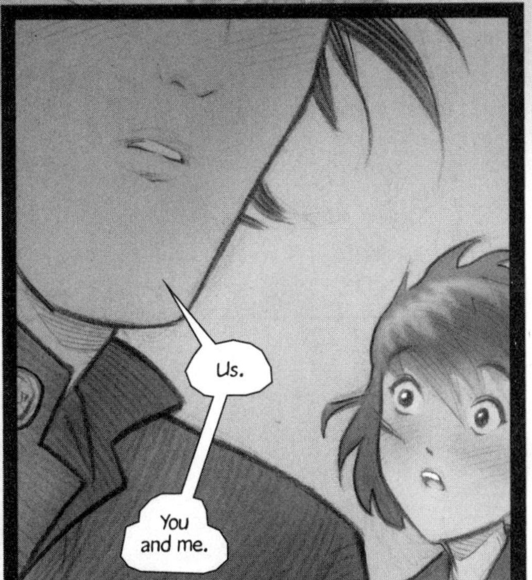
Us.
You and me.

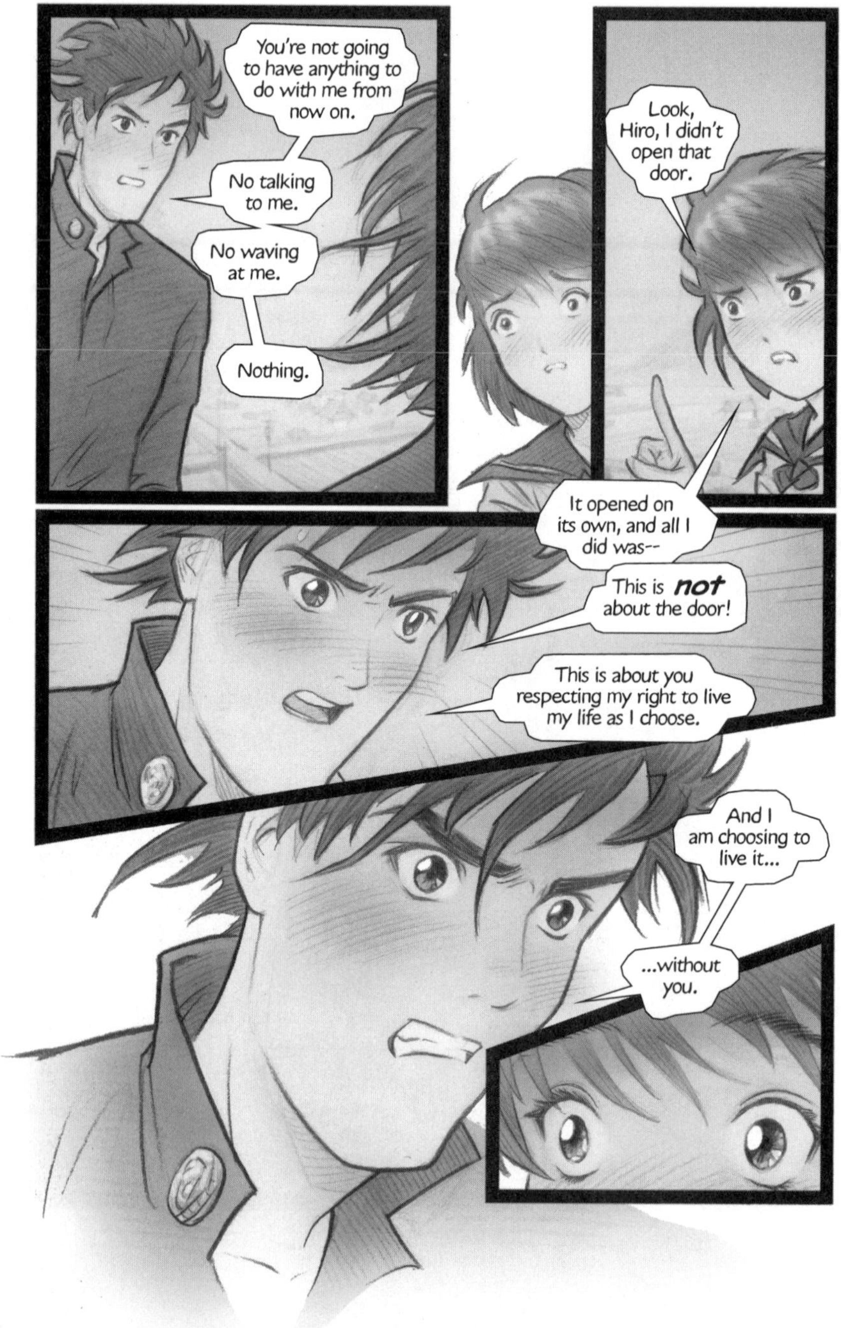
You're not going to have anything to do with me from now on.
No talking to me.
No waving at me.
Nothing.
Look, Hiro, I didn't open that door.
It opened on its own, and all I did was--
This is **not** about the door!
This is about you respecting my right to live my life as I choose.
And I am choosing to live it...
...without you.

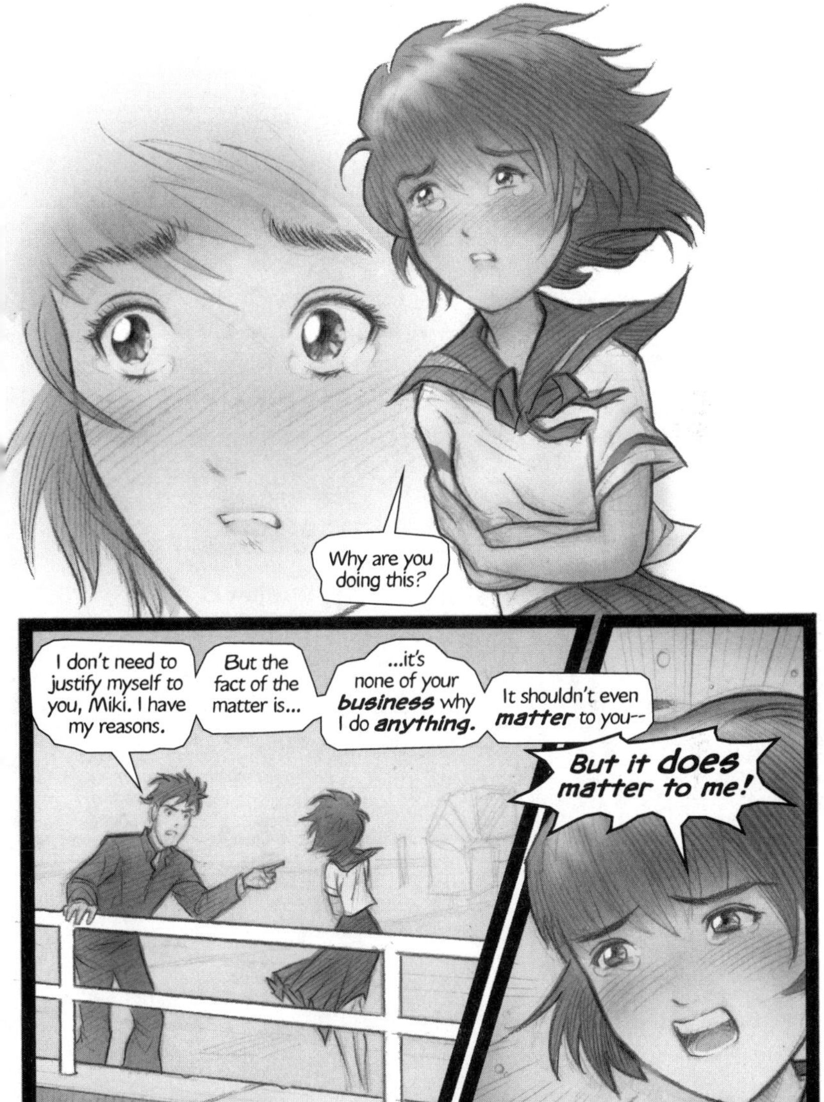
Why are you doing this?
I don't need to justify myself to you, Miki. I have my reasons.
But the fact of the matter is...
...it's none of your **business** why I do **anything.**
It shouldn't even **matter** to you--
But it does matter to me!

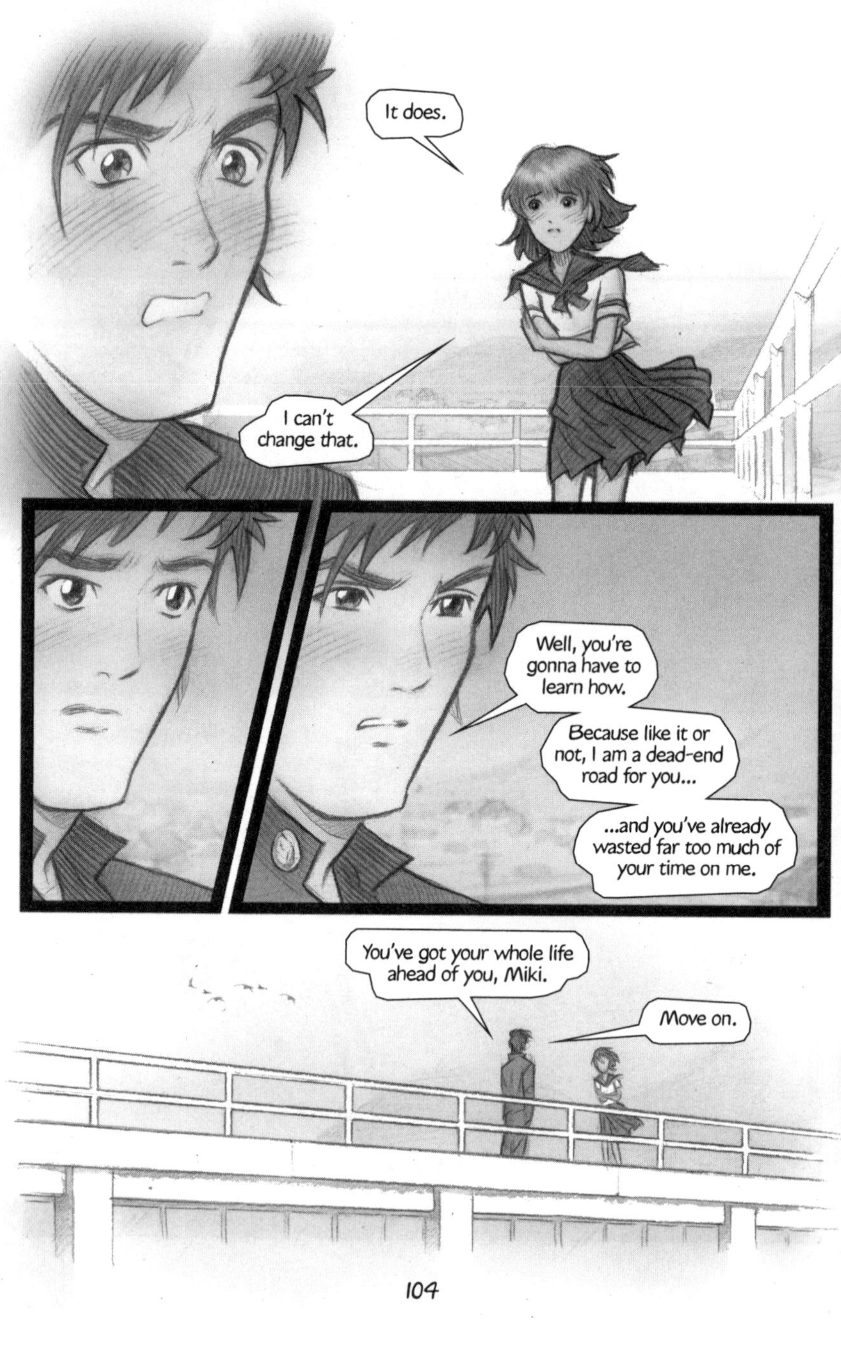
It does.
I can't change that.
Well, you're gonna have to learn how.
Because like it or not, I am a dead-end road for you...
...and you've already wasted far too much of your time on me.
You've got your whole life ahead of you, Miki.
Move on.

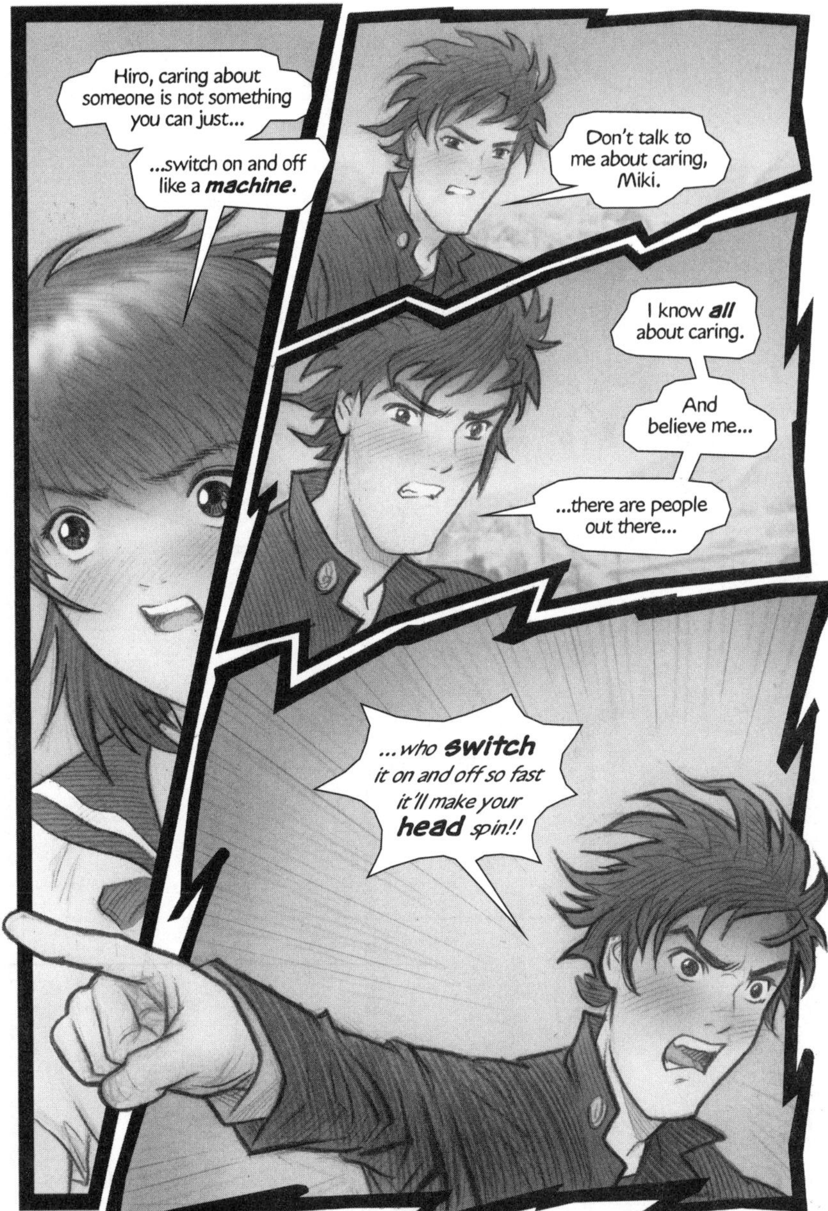
Hiro, caring about someone is not something you can just...
...switch on and off like a **machine**.
Don't talk to me about caring, Miki.
I know ***all*** about caring.
And believe me...
...there are people out there...
*...who **switch** it on and off so fast it'll make your **head** spin!!*

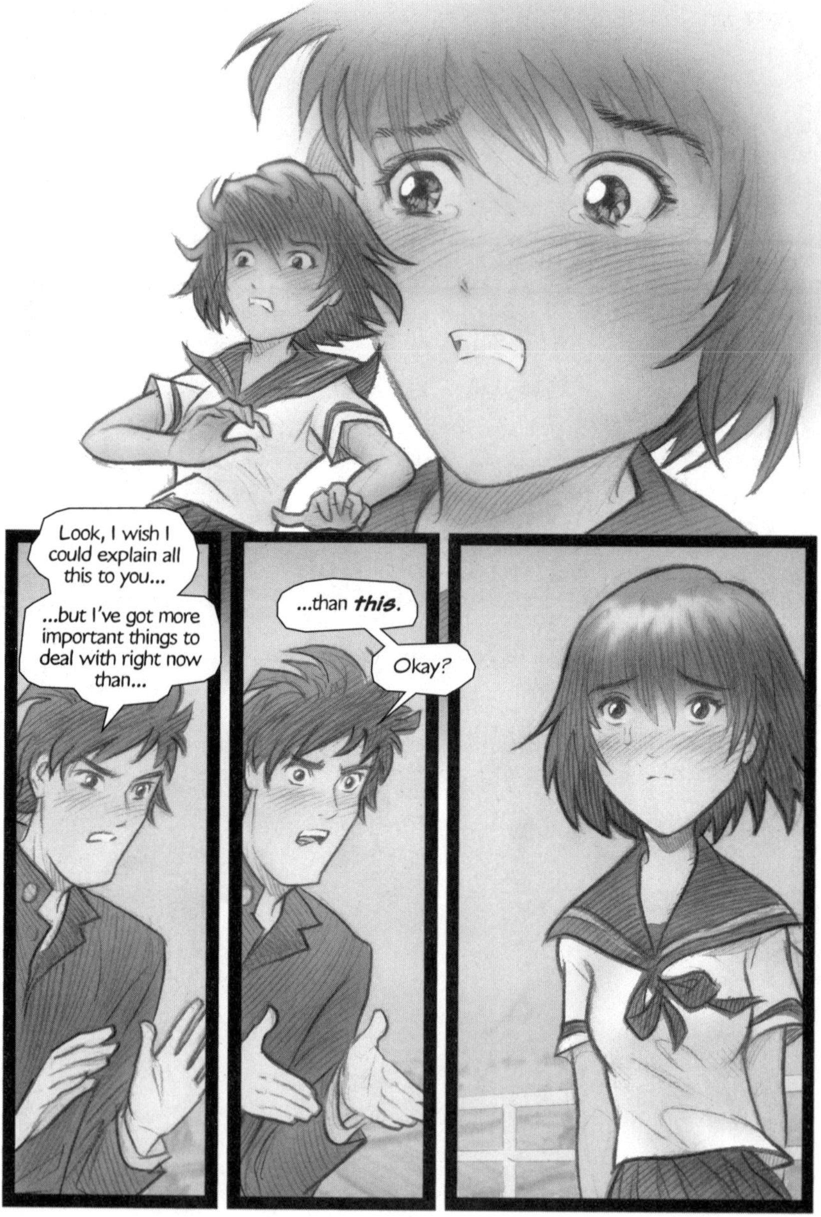
Look, I wish I could explain all this to you...
...but I've got more important things to deal with right now than...
...than *this*.
Okay?

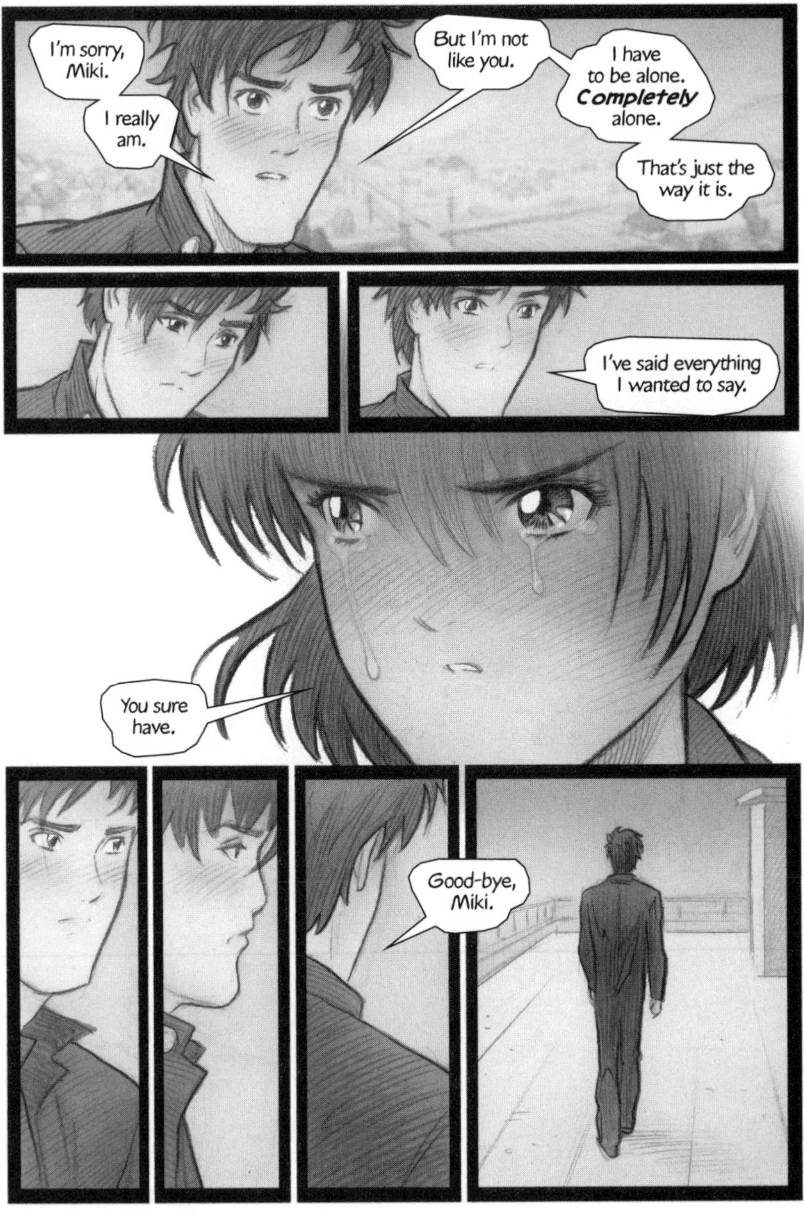
I'm sorry, Miki.
I really am.
But I'm not like you.
I have to be alone. Completely alone.
That's just the way it is.
I've said everything I wanted to say.
You sure have.
Good-bye, Miki.

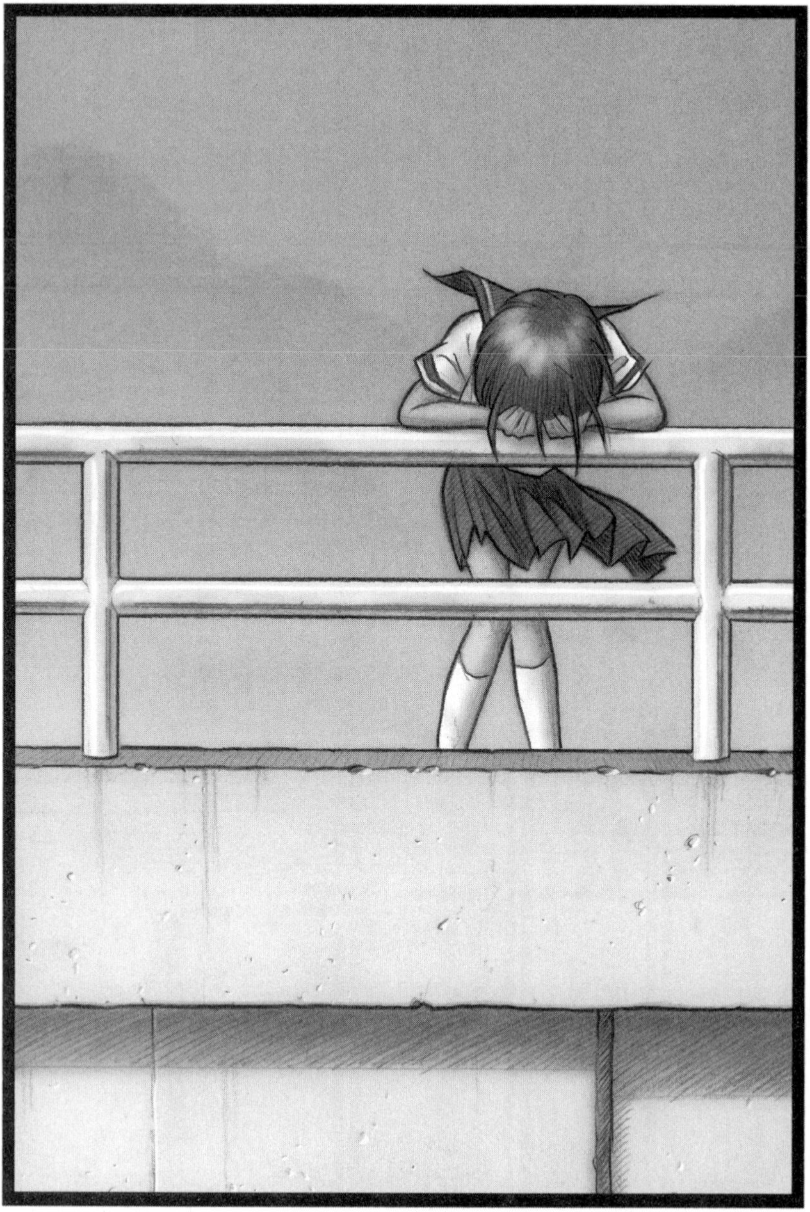

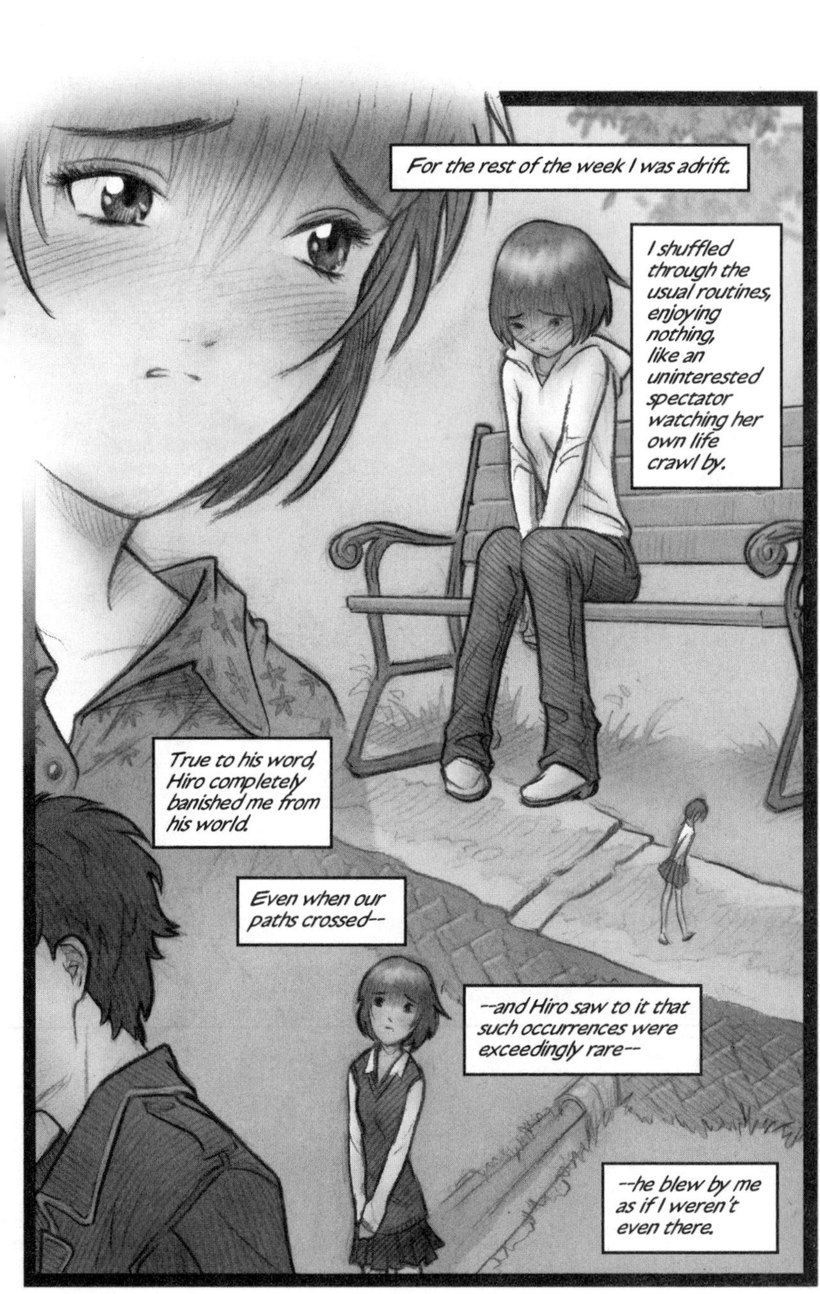
For the rest of the week I was adrift.
I shuffled through the usual routines, enjoying nothing, like an uninterested spectator watching her own life crawl by.
True to his word, Hiro completely banished me from his world.
Even when our paths crossed--
--and Hiro saw to it that such occurrences were exceedingly rare--
--he blew by me as if I weren't even there.

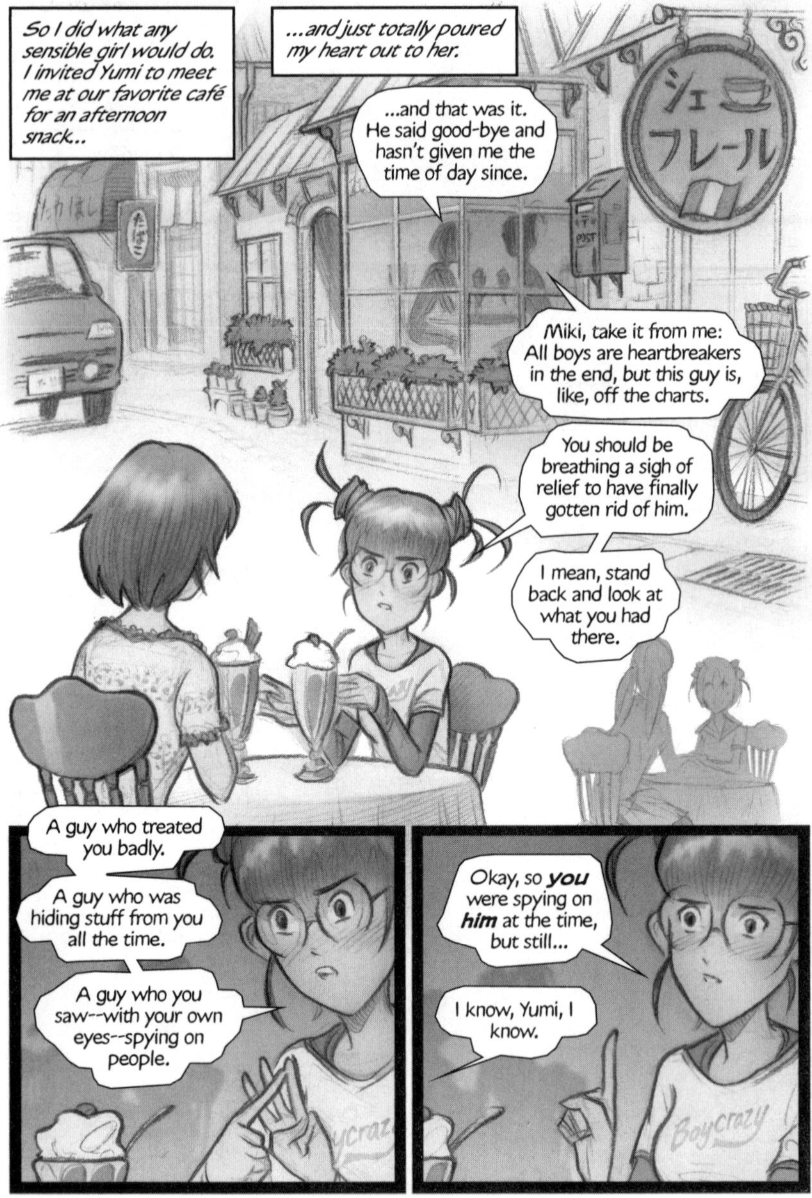

So I did what any sensible girl would do. I invited Yumi to meet me at our favorite café for an afternoon snack...
...and just totally poured my heart out to her.
...and that was it. He said good-bye and hasn't given me the time of day since.
シェ フレール
POST
Miki, take it from me: All boys are heartbreakers in the end, but this guy is, like, off the charts.
You should be breathing a sigh of relief to have finally gotten rid of him.
I mean, stand back and look at what you had there.
A guy who treated you badly.
A guy who was hiding stuff from you all the time.
A guy who you saw--with your own eyes--spying on people.
Okay, so **you** were spying on **him** at the time, but still...
I know, Yumi, I know.
Boycrazy

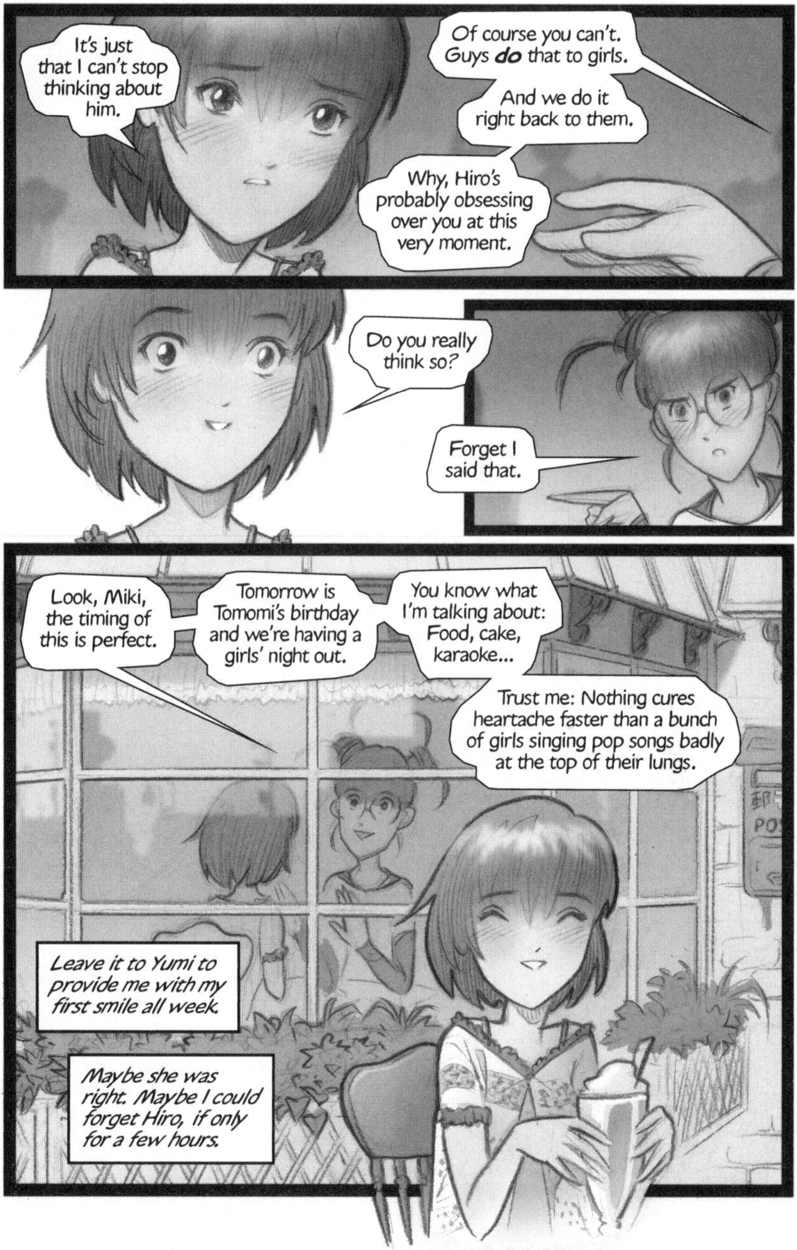
It's just that I can't stop thinking about him.
Of course you can't. Guys **do** that to girls.
And we do it right back to them.
Why, Hiro's probably obsessing over you at this very moment.
Do you really think so?
Forget I said that.
Look, Miki, the timing of this is perfect.
Tomorrow is Tomomi's birthday and we're having a girls' night out.
You know what I'm talking about: Food, cake, karaoke...
Trust me: Nothing cures heartache faster than a bunch of girls singing pop songs badly at the top of their lungs.
Leave it to Yumi to provide me with my first smile all week.
Maybe she was right. Maybe I could forget Hiro, if only for a few hours.

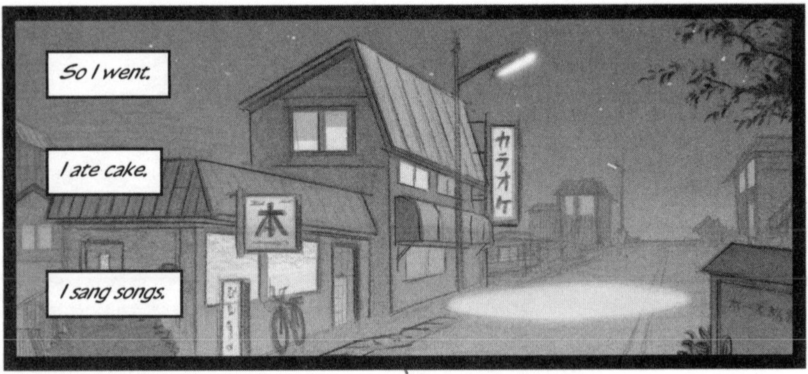
So I went.
I ate cake.
I sang songs.

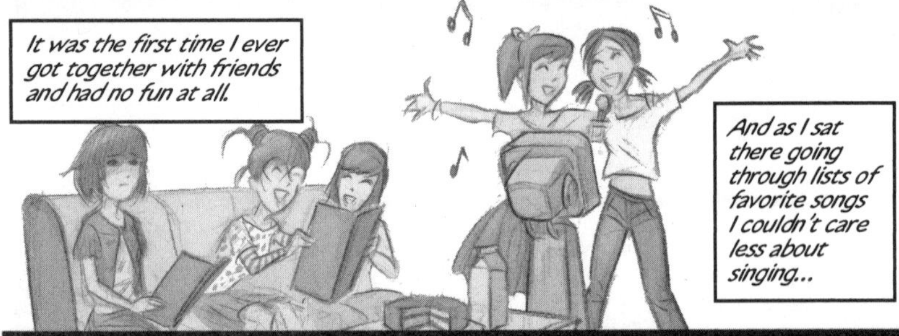
It was the first time I ever got together with friends and had no fun at all.
And as I sat there going through lists of favorite songs I couldn't care less about singing...

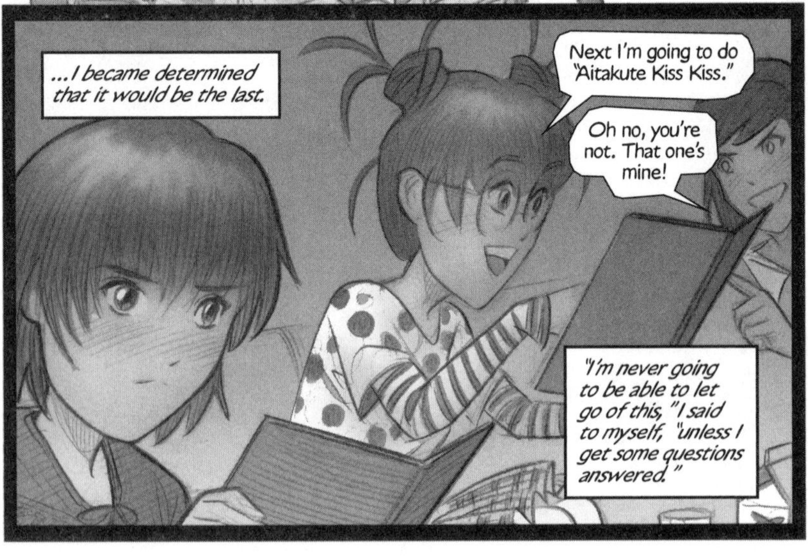
...I became determined that it would be the last.
Next I'm going to do "Aitakute Kiss Kiss."
Oh no, you're not. That one's mine!
"I'm never going to be able to let go of this," I said to myself, "unless I get some questions answered."

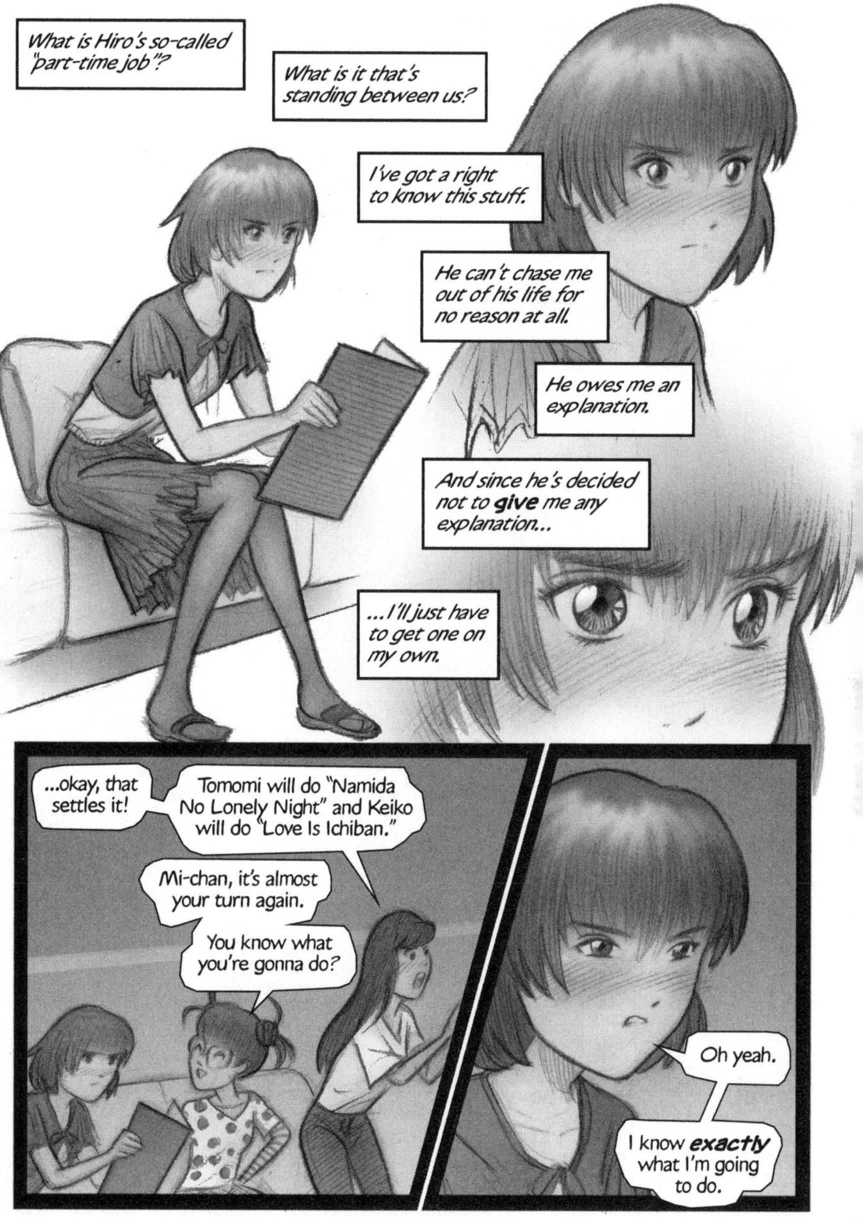
What is Hiro's so-called "part-time job"?
What is it that's standing between us?
I've got a right to know this stuff.
He can't chase me out of his life for no reason at all.
He owes me an explanation.
And since he's decided not to **give** me any explanation...
...I'll just have to get one on my own.
...okay, that settles it!
Tomomi will do "Namida No Lonely Night" and Keiko will do "Love Is Ichiban."
Mi-chan, it's almost your turn again.
You know what you're gonna do?
Oh yeah.
I know **exactly** what I'm going to do.

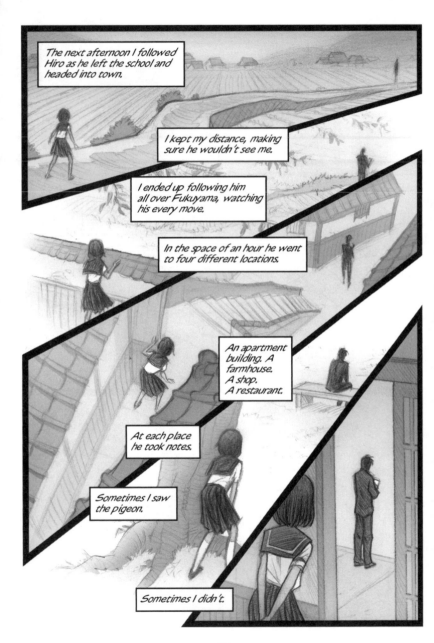

The next afternoon I followed Hiro as he left the school and headed into town.

I kept my distance, making sure he wouldn't see me.

I ended up following him all over Fukuyama, watching his every move.

In the space of an hour he went to four different locations.

An apartment building. A farmhouse. A shop. A restaurant.

At each place he took notes.

Sometimes I saw the pigeon.

Sometimes I didn't.

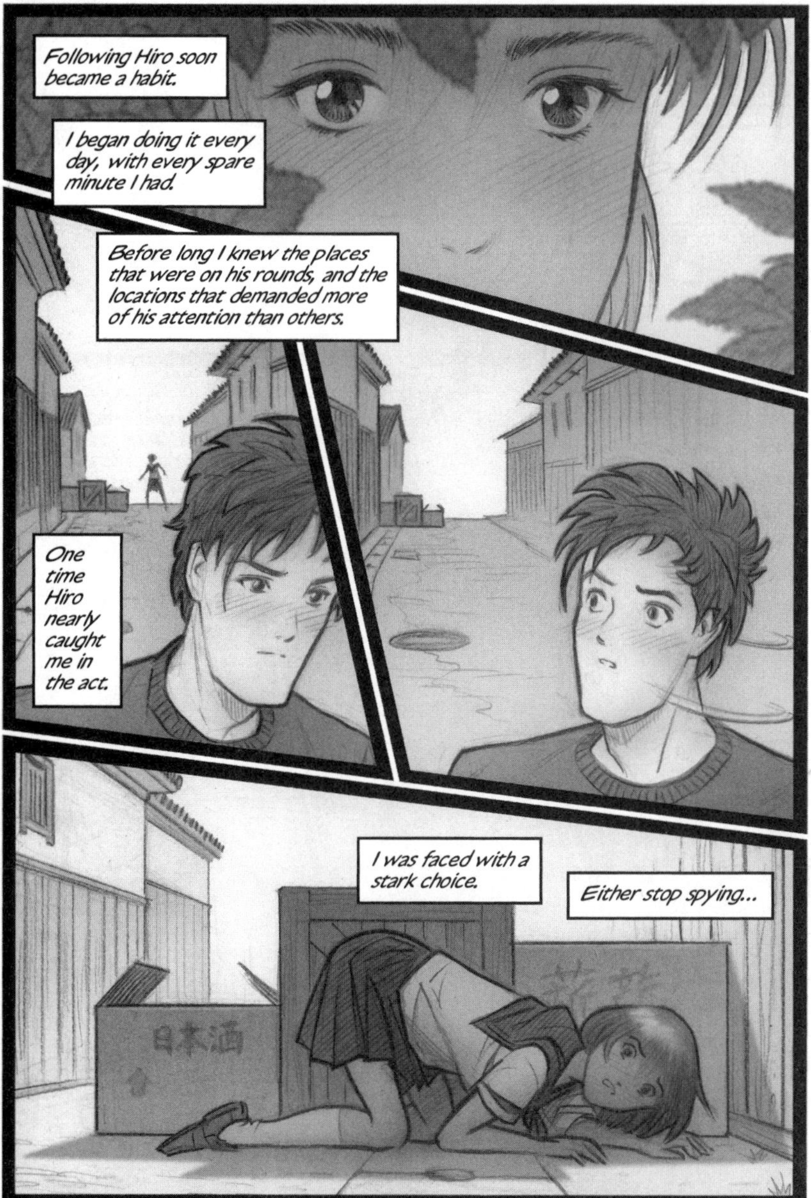
Following Hiro soon became a habit.
I began doing it every day, with every spare minute I had.
Before long I knew the places that were on his rounds, and the locations that demanded more of his attention than others.
One time Hiro nearly caught me in the act.
I was faced with a stark choice.
Either stop spying...
日本酒

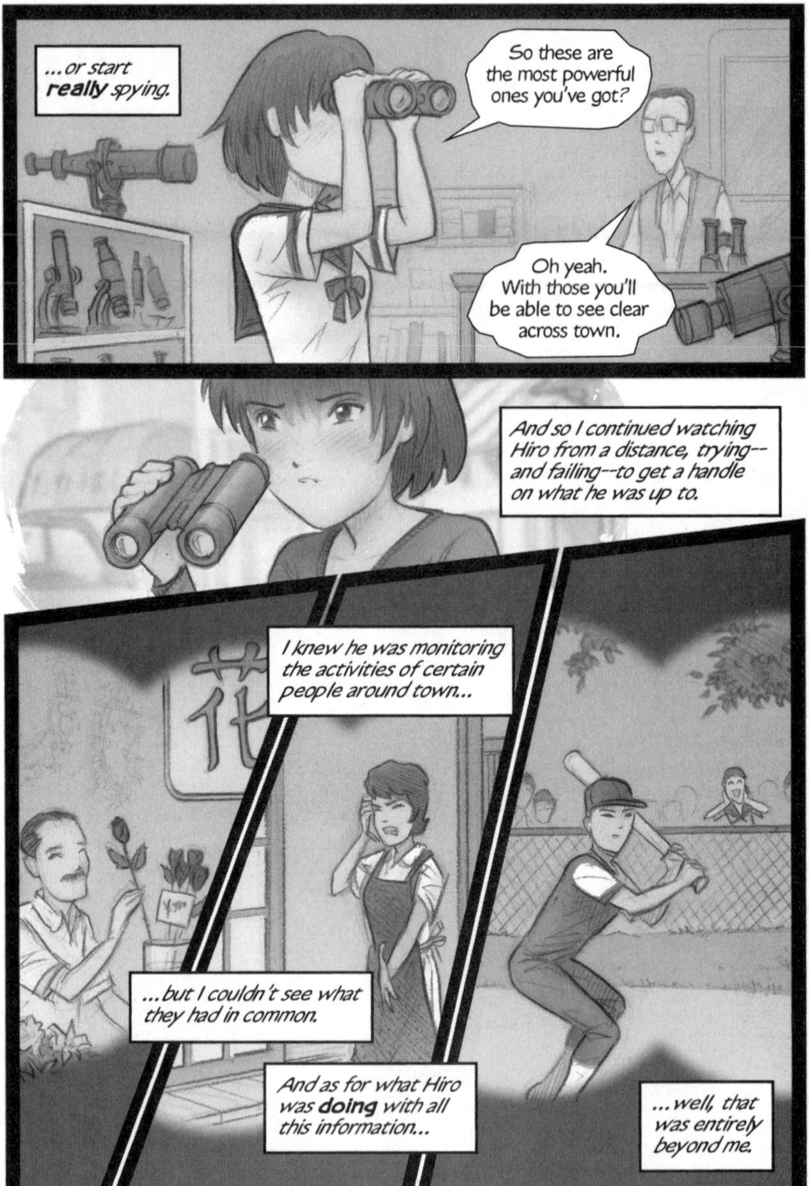
...or start **really** spying.
So these are the most powerful ones you've got?
Oh yeah. With those you'll be able to see clear across town.
And so I continued watching Hiro from a distance, trying--and failing--to get a handle on what he was up to.
I knew he was monitoring the activities of certain people around town...
花
...but I couldn't see what they had in common.
And as for what Hiro was **doing** with all this information...
...well, that was entirely beyond me.

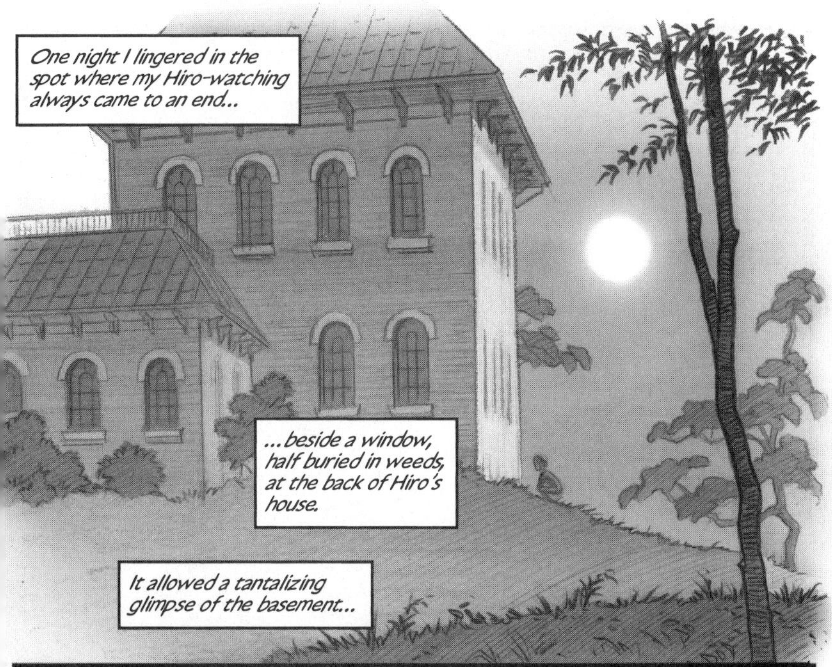
One night I lingered in the spot where my Hiro-watching always came to an end...
...beside a window, half buried in weeds, at the back of Hiro's house.
It allowed a tantalizing glimpse of the basement...

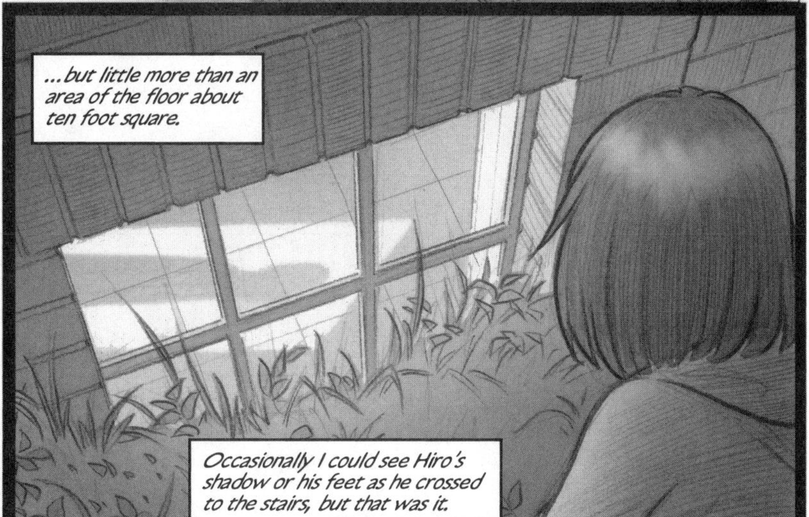
...but little more than an area of the floor about ten foot square.
Occasionally I could see Hiro's shadow or his feet as he crossed to the stairs, but that was it.

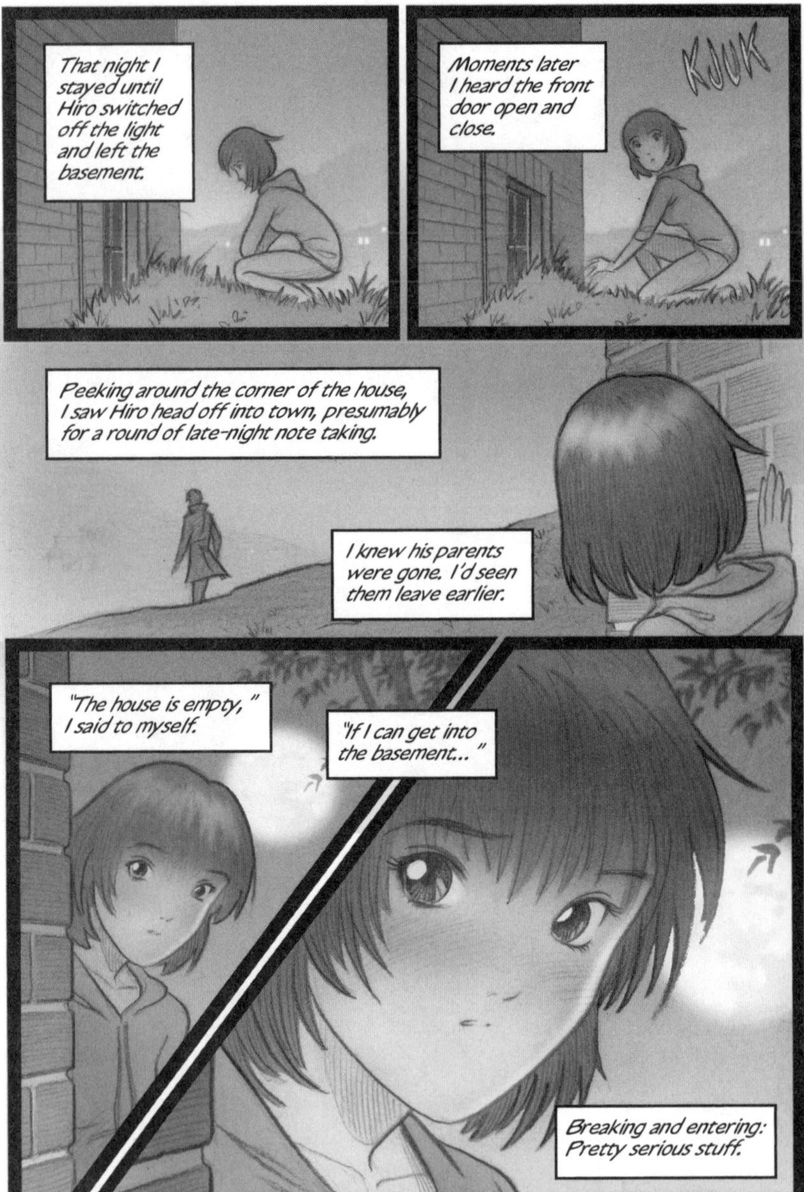
That night I stayed until Hiro switched off the light and left the basement.
Moments later I heard the front door open and close.
KJUK
Peeking around the corner of the house, I saw Hiro head off into town, presumably for a round of late-night note taking.
I knew his parents were gone. I'd seen them leave earlier.
"The house is empty," I said to myself.
"If I can get into the basement..."
Breaking and entering: Pretty serious stuff.

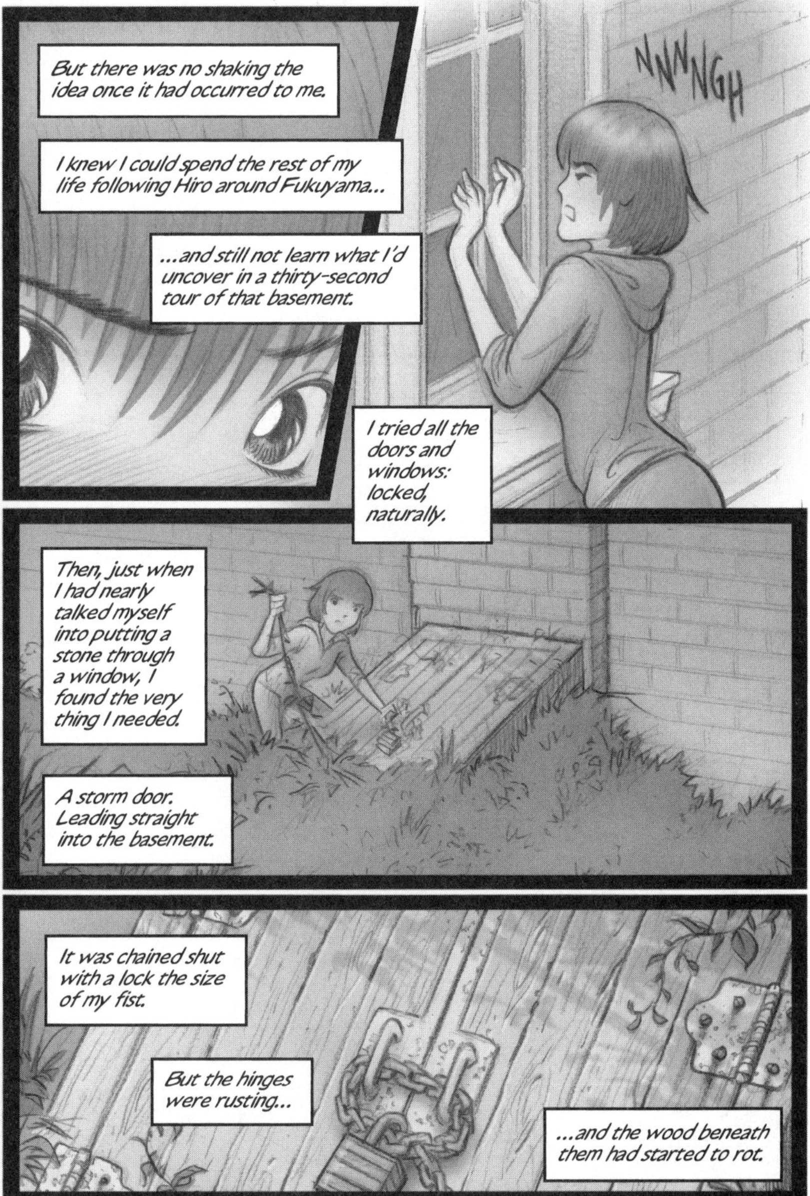
But there was no shaking the idea once it had occurred to me.
I knew I could spend the rest of my life following Hiro around Fukuyama...
...and still not learn what I'd uncover in a thirty-second tour of that basement.
NNNNGH
I tried all the doors and windows: locked, naturally.
Then, just when I had nearly talked myself into putting a stone through a window, I found the very thing I needed.
A storm door. Leading straight into the basement.
It was chained shut with a lock the size of my fist.
But the hinges were rusting...
...and the wood beneath them had started to rot.

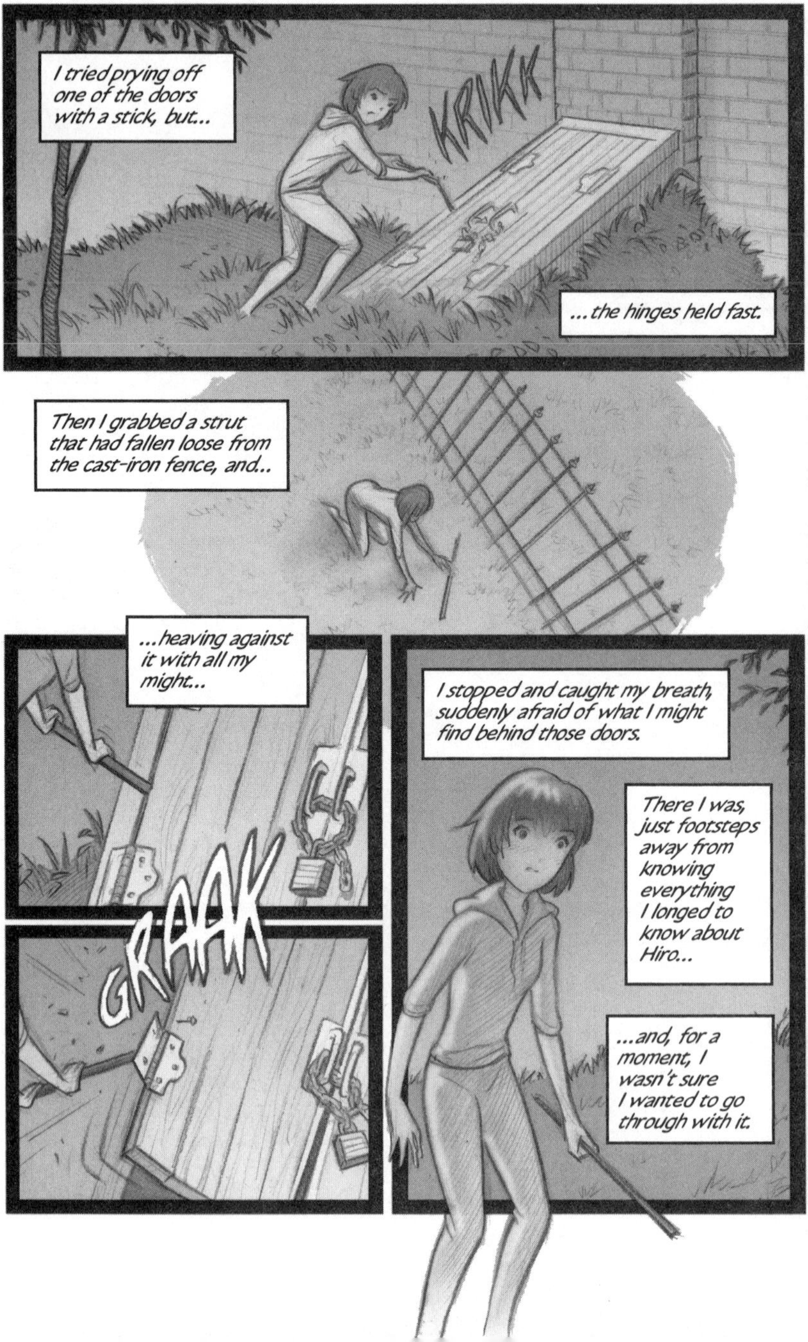
I tried prying off one of the doors with a stick, but...
KRIKK
...the hinges held fast.
Then I grabbed a strut that had fallen loose from the cast-iron fence, and...
...heaving against it with all my might...
GRAAK
I stopped and caught my breath, suddenly afraid of what I might find behind those doors.
There I was, just footsteps away from knowing everything I longed to know about Hiro...
...and, for a moment, I wasn't sure I wanted to go through with it.

But there was no turning back.

I realized now that my every move over the last days and weeks had brought me to this place...

...and that I could no more turn away at this point than cease to breathe, or command my heart to stop beating.

I moved the unhinged door aside and stepped down into the darkness.

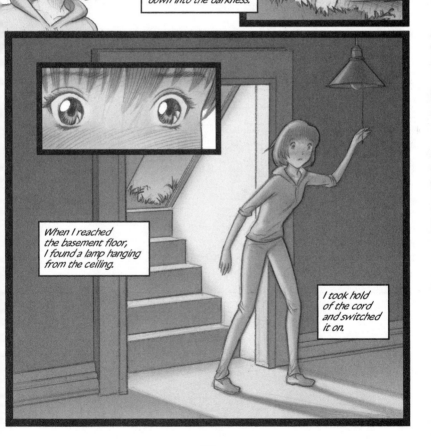

When I reached the basement floor, I found a lamp hanging from the ceiling.

I took hold of the cord and switched it on.

121

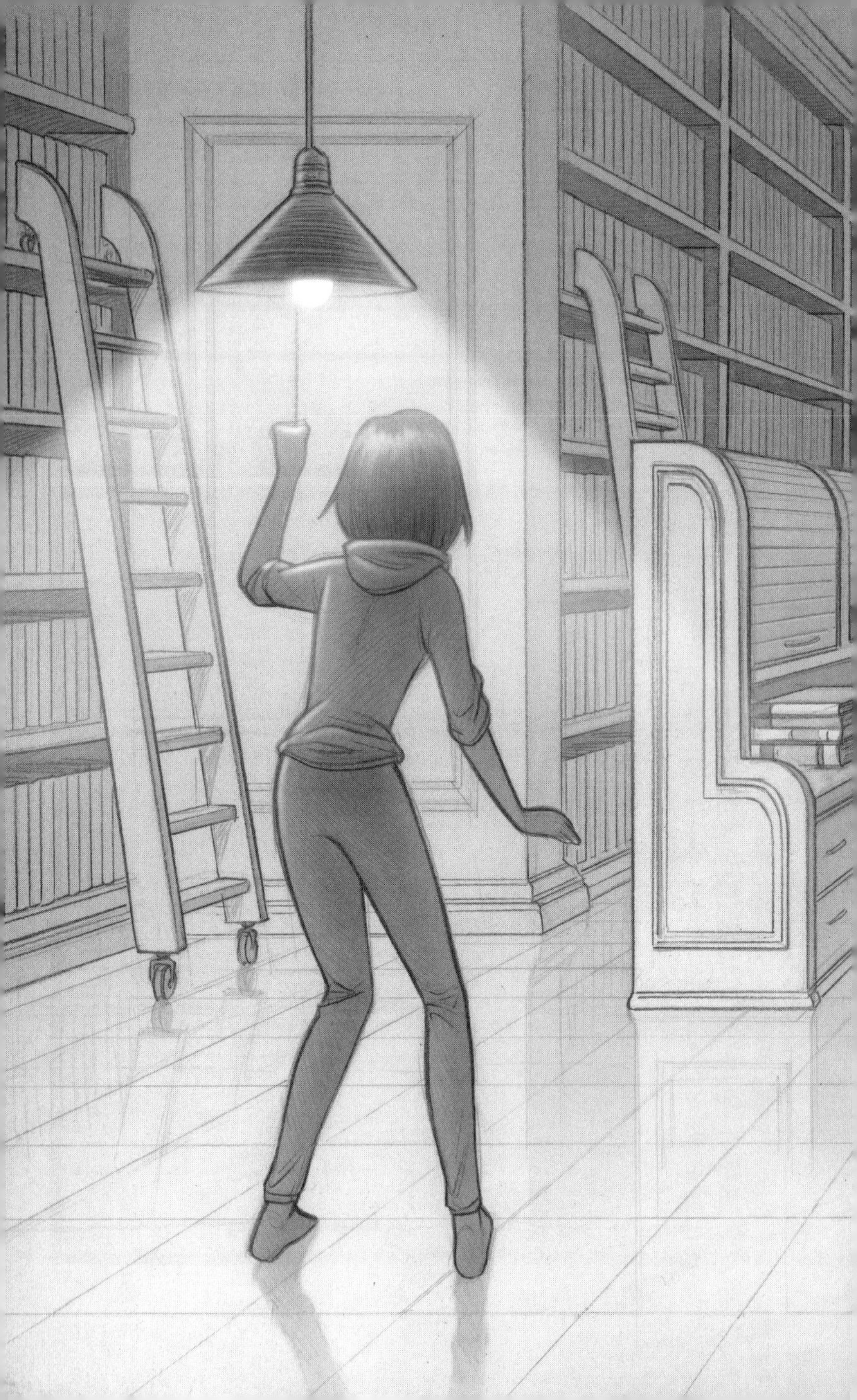

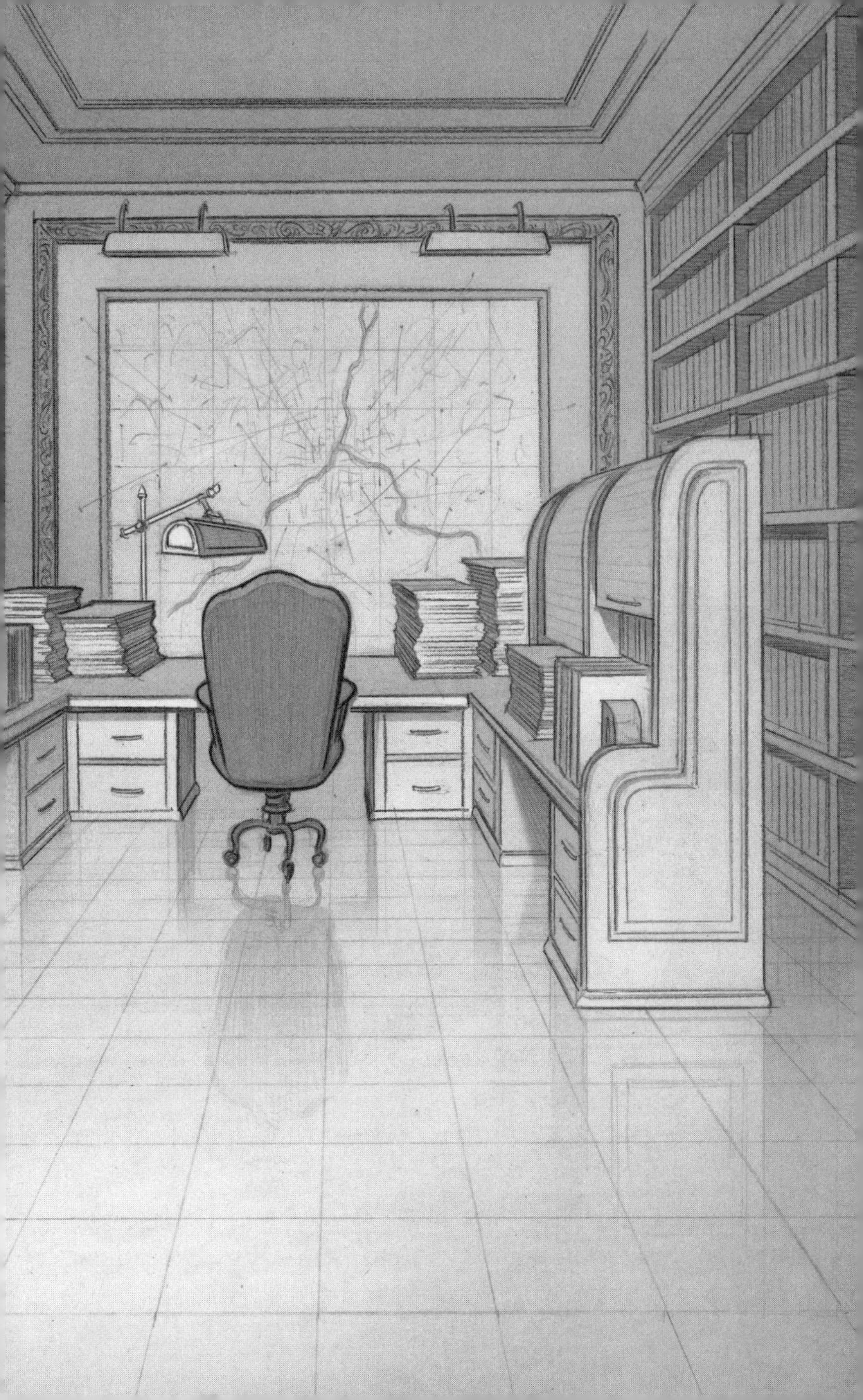

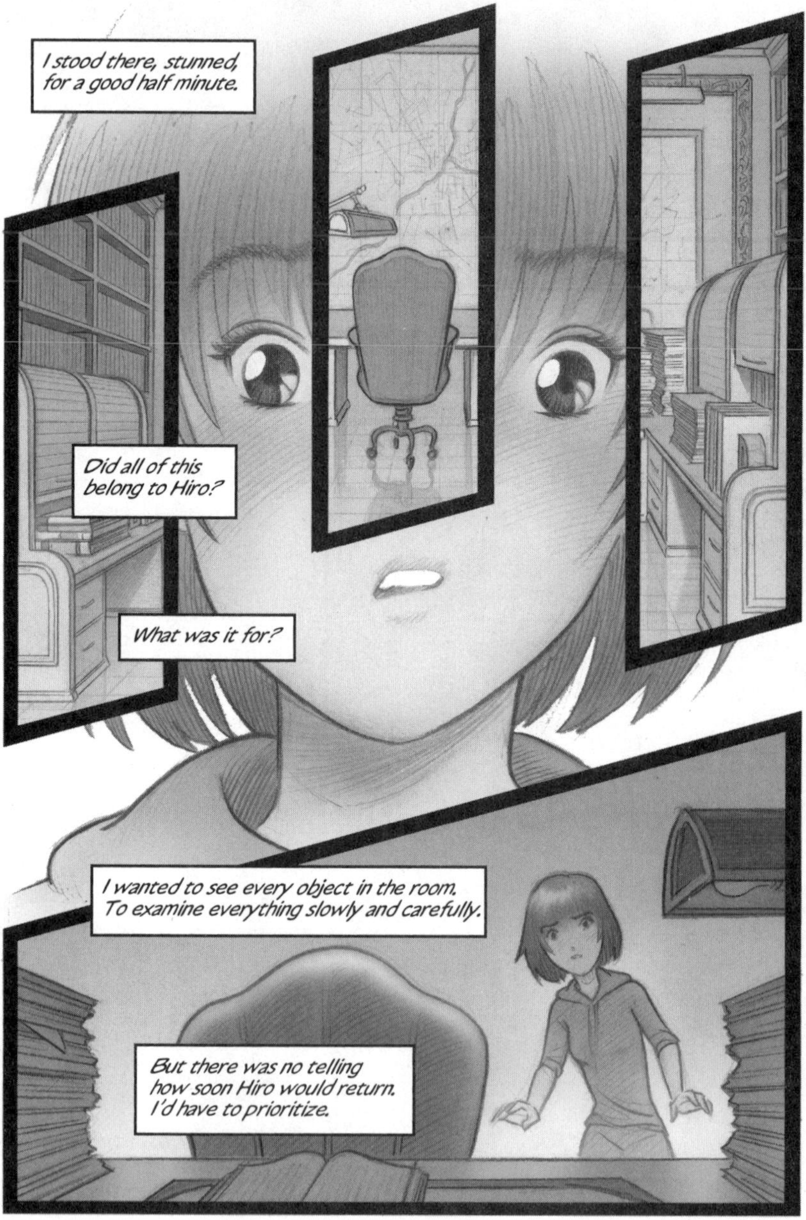
I stood there, stunned, for a good half minute.
Did all of this belong to Hiro?
What was it for?
I wanted to see every object in the room. To examine everything slowly and carefully.
But there was no telling how soon Hiro would return. I'd have to prioritize.

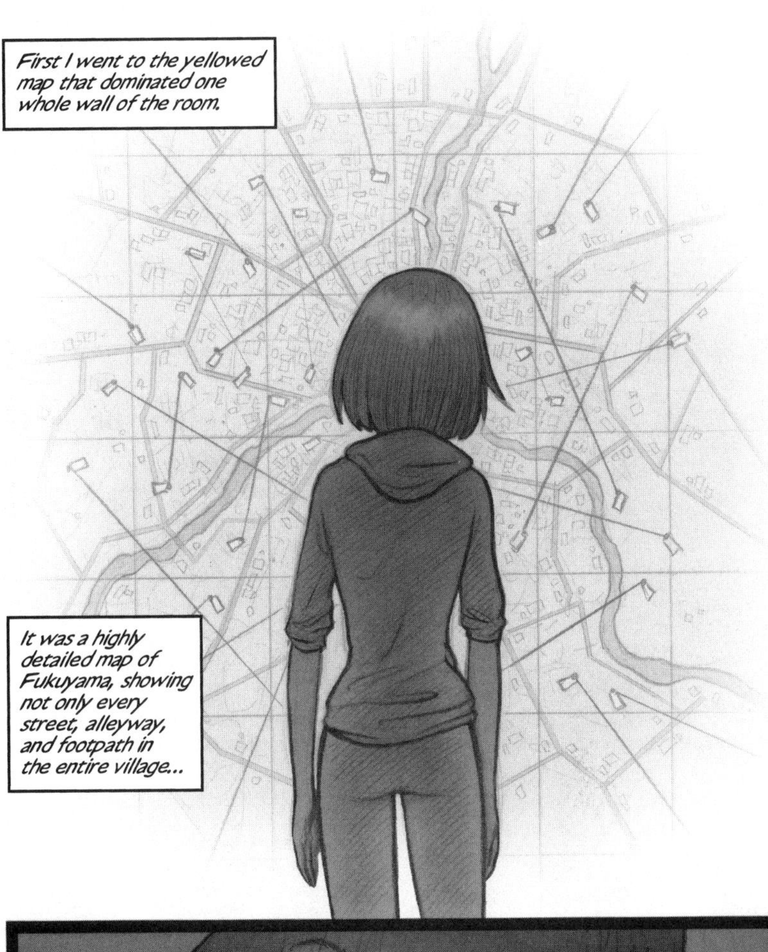
First I went to the yellowed map that dominated one whole wall of the room.
It was a highly detailed map of Fukuyama, showing not only every street, alleyway, and footpath in the entire village...

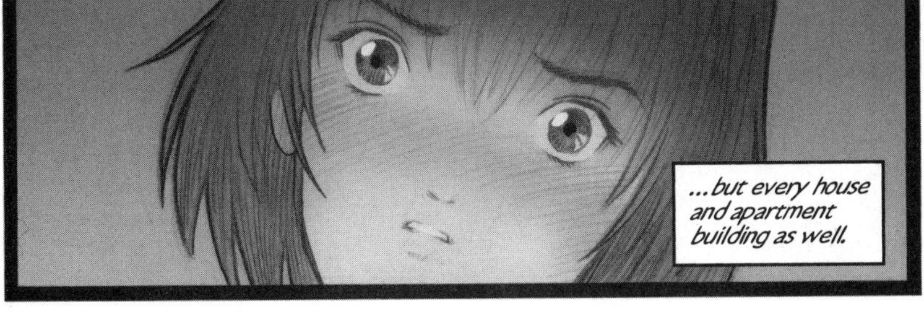
...but every house and apartment building as well.

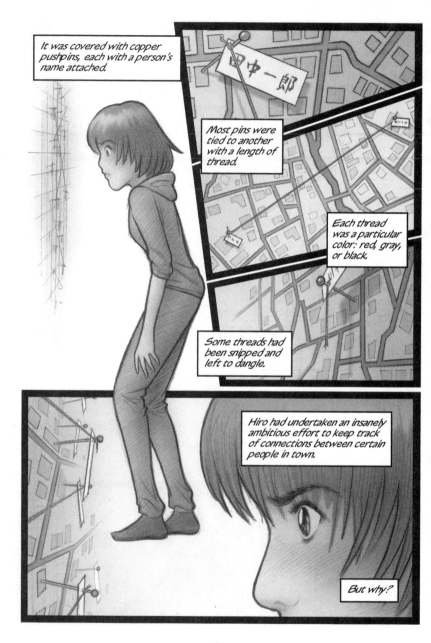

It was covered with copper pushpins, each with a person's name attached.

田中一郎

Most pins were tied to another with a length of thread.

Each thread was a particular color: red, gray, or black.

Some threads had been snipped and left to dangle.

Hiro had undertaken an insanely ambitious effort to keep track of connections between certain people in town.

But why?

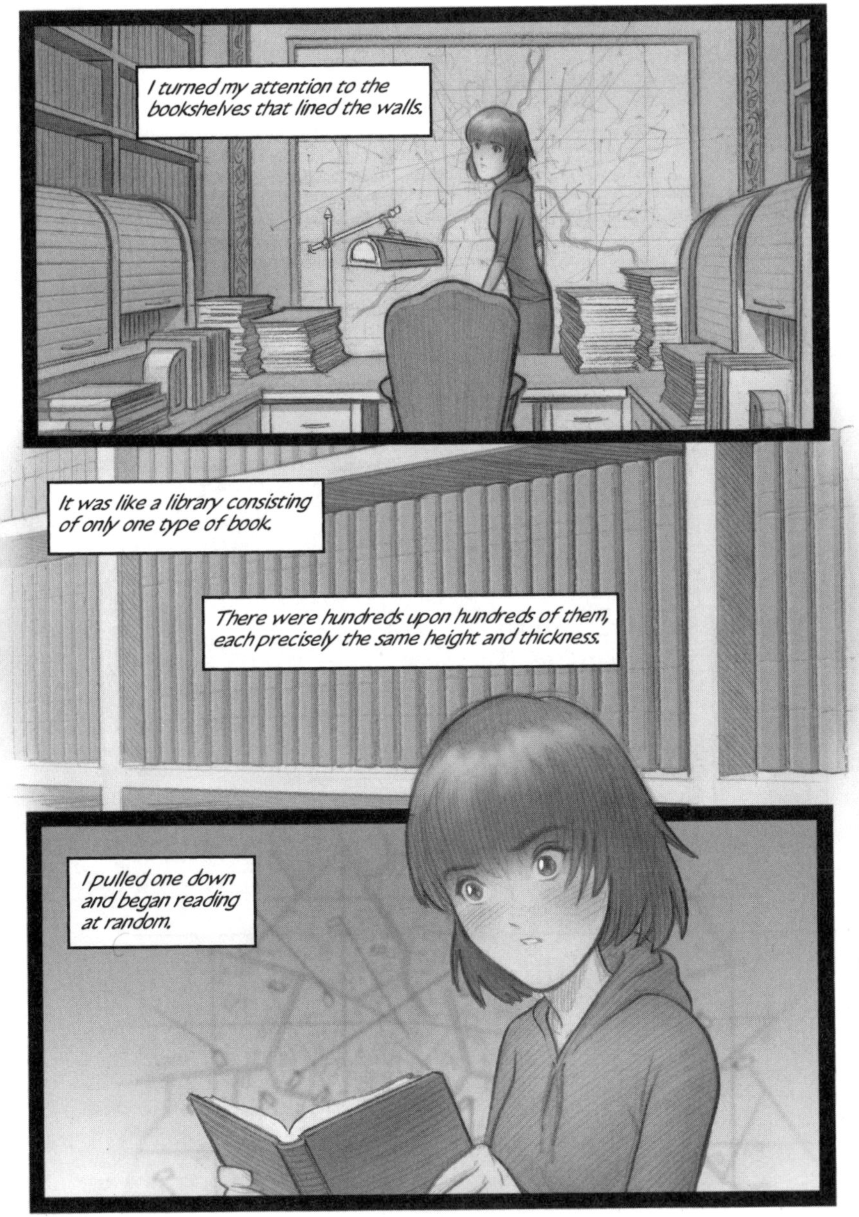
I turned my attention to the bookshelves that lined the walls.
It was like a library consisting of only one type of book.
There were hundreds upon hundreds of them, each precisely the same height and thickness.
I pulled one down and began reading at random.

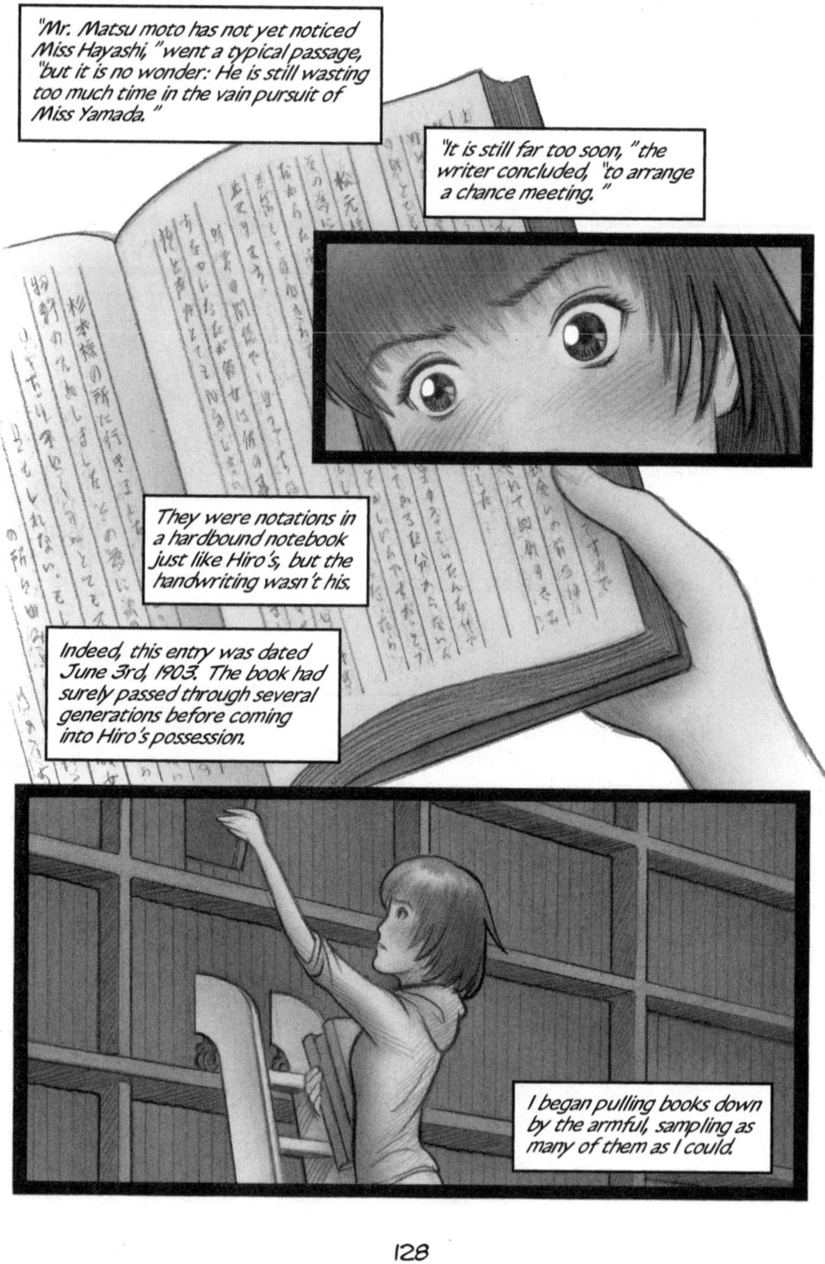
"Mr. Matsu moto has not yet noticed Miss Hayashi," went a typical passage, "but it is no wonder: He is still wasting too much time in the vain pursuit of Miss Yamada."
"It is still far too soon," the writer concluded, "to arrange a chance meeting."
They were notations in a hardbound notebook just like Hiro's, but the handwriting wasn't his.
Indeed, this entry was dated June 3rd, 1903. The book had surely passed through several generations before coming into Hiro's possession.
I began pulling books down by the armful, sampling as many of them as I could.

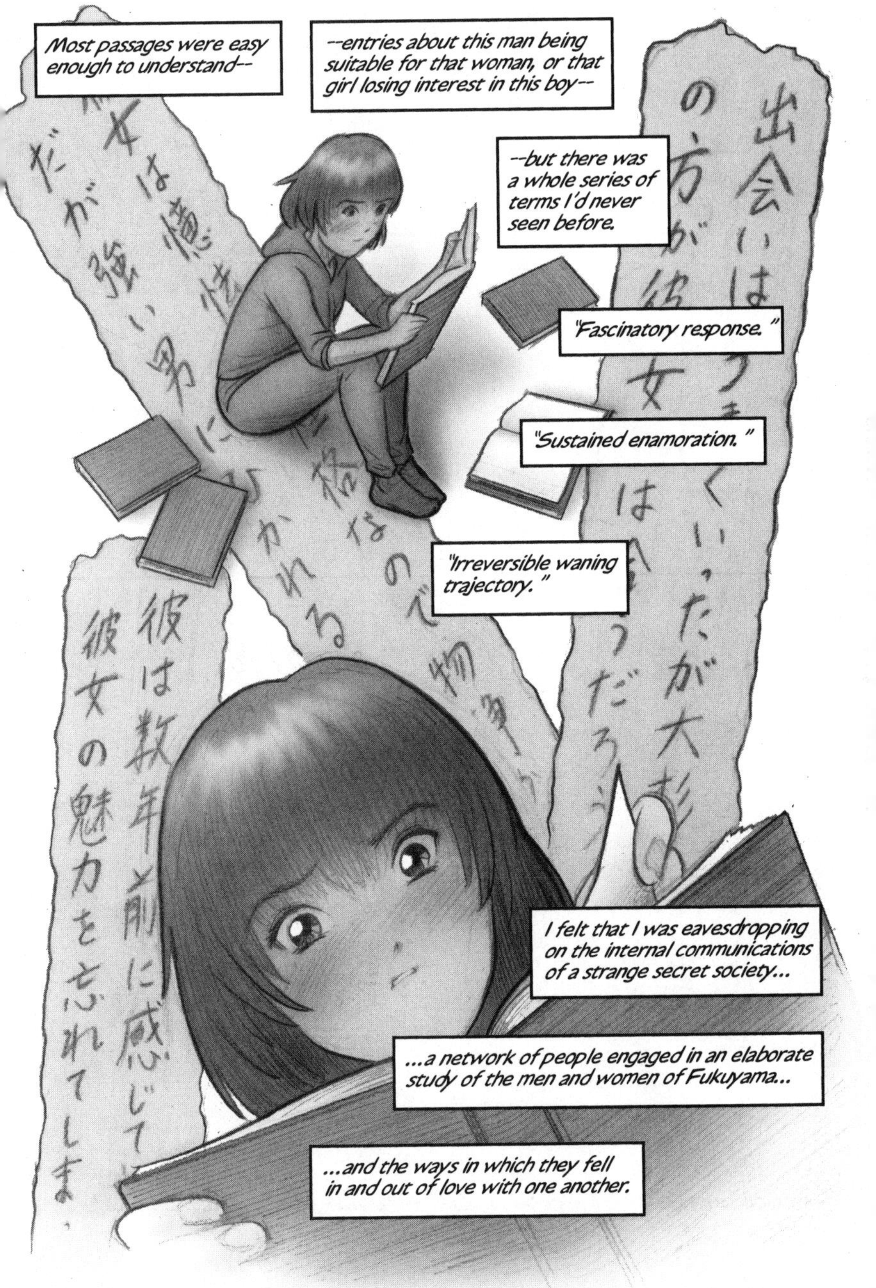
Most passages were easy enough to understand--
--entries about this man being suitable for that woman, or that girl losing interest in this boy--
--but there was a whole series of terms I'd never seen before.
"Fascinatory response."
"Sustained enamoration."
"Irreversible waning trajectory."
I felt that I was eavesdropping on the internal communications of a strange secret society...
...a network of people engaged in an elaborate study of the men and women of Fukuyama...
...and the ways in which they fell in and out of love with one another.

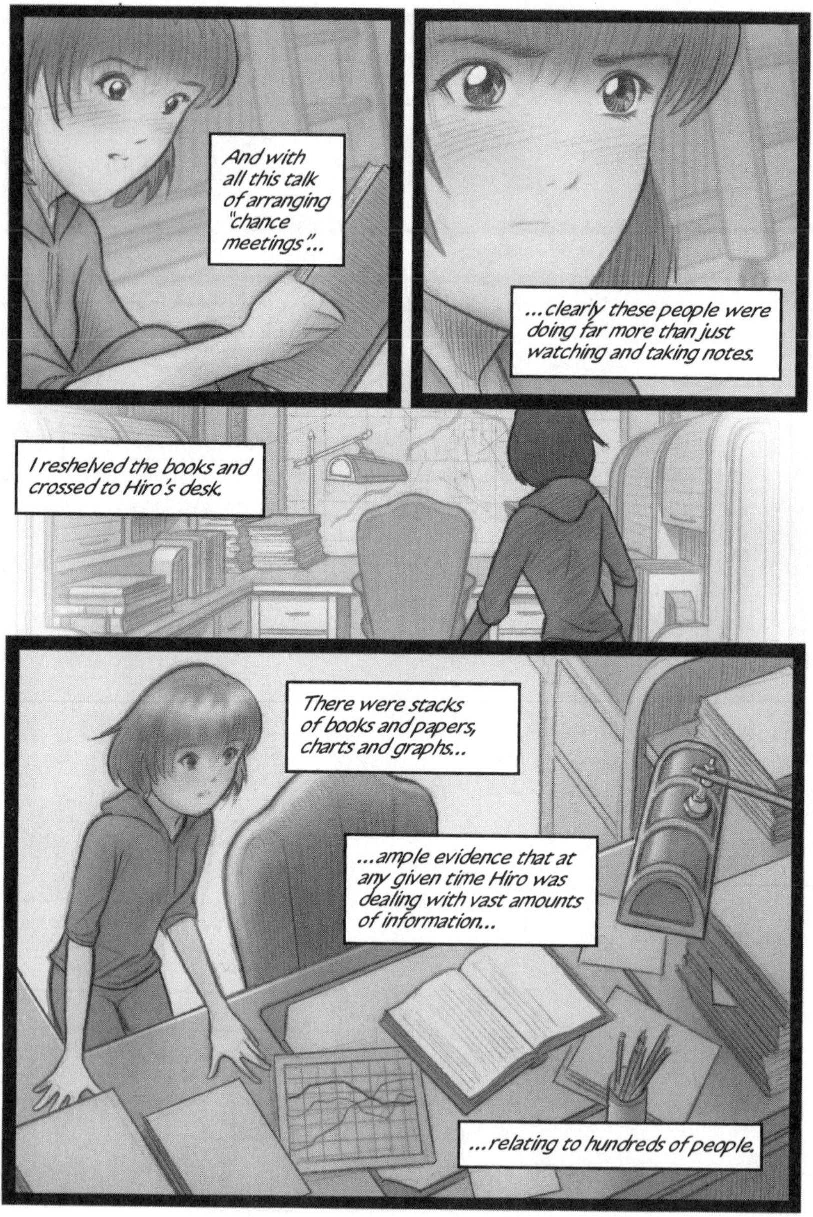
And with all this talk of arranging "chance meetings"...
...clearly these people were doing far more than just watching and taking notes.
I reshelved the books and crossed to Hiro's desk.
There were stacks of books and papers, charts and graphs...
...ample evidence that at any given time Hiro was dealing with vast amounts of information...
...relating to hundreds of people.

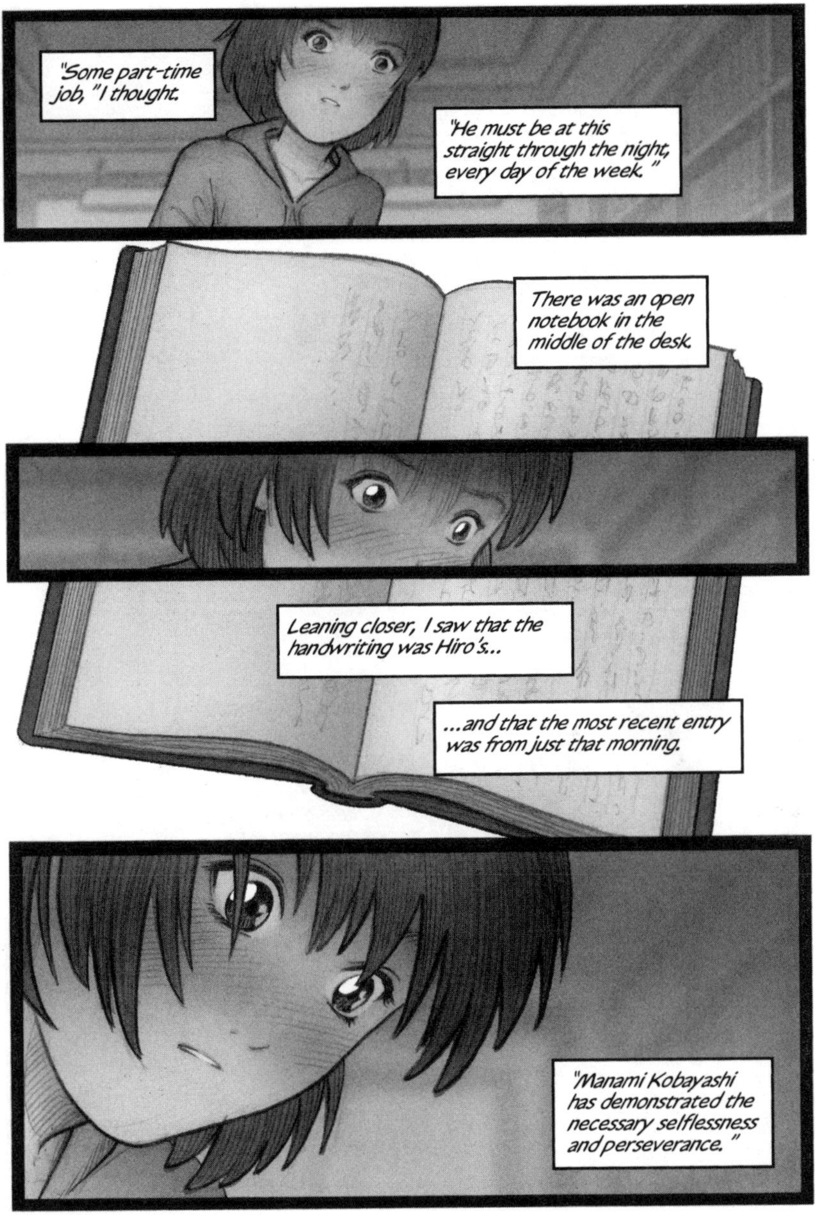
"Some part-time job," I thought.
"He must be at this straight through the night, every day of the week."
There was an open notebook in the middle of the desk.
Leaning closer, I saw that the handwriting was Hiro's...
...and that the most recent entry was from just that morning.
"Manami Kobayashi has demonstrated the necessary selflessness and perseverance."

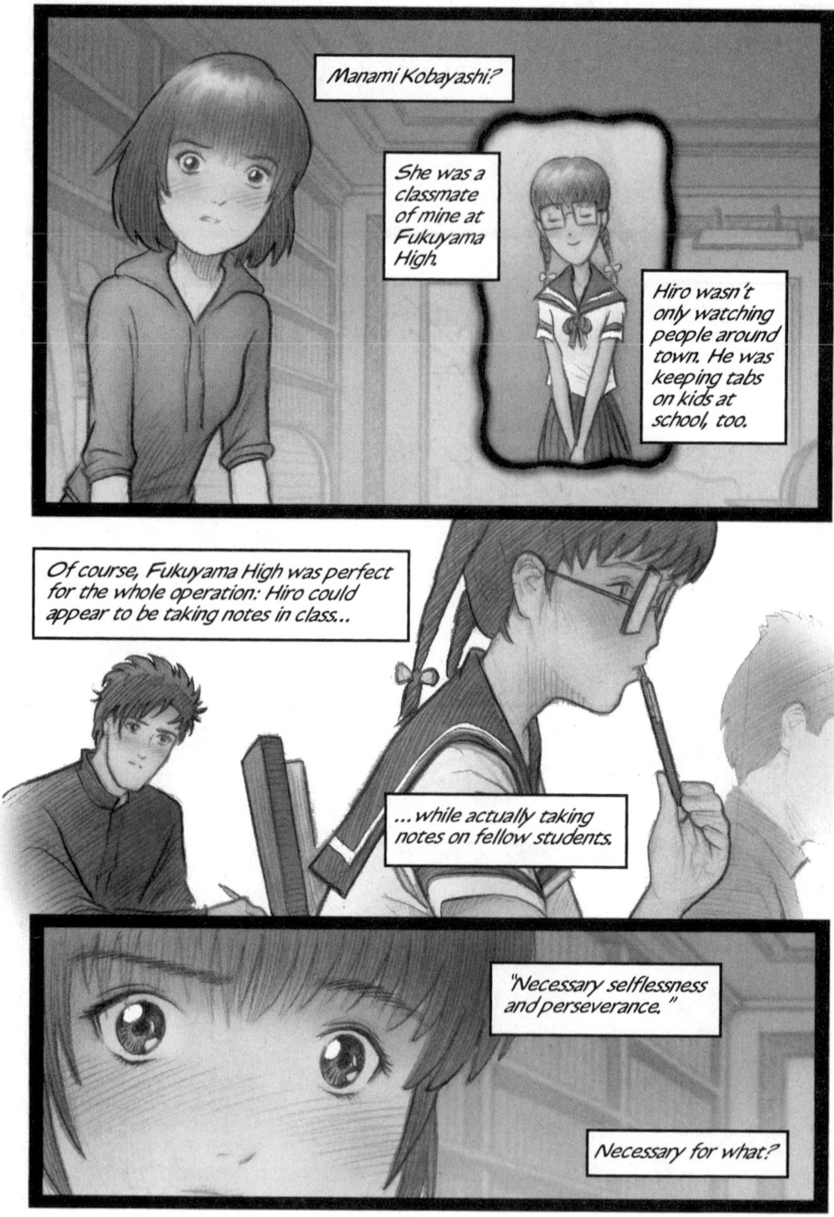
Manami Kobayashi?
She was a classmate of mine at Fukuyama High.
Hiro wasn't only watching people around town. He was keeping tabs on kids at school, too.
Of course, Fukuyama High was perfect for the whole operation: Hiro could appear to be taking notes in class...
...while actually taking notes on fellow students.
"Necessary selflessness and perseverance."
Necessary for what?

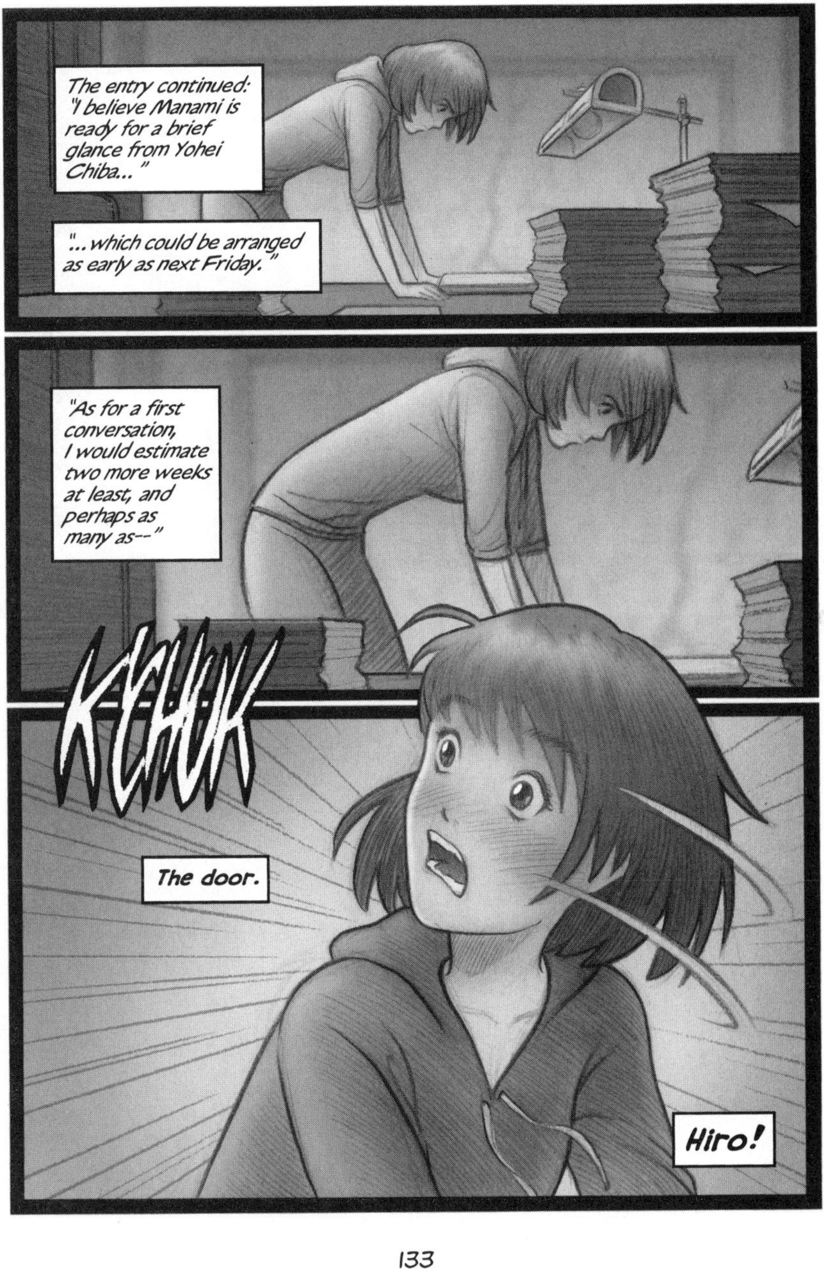
The entry continued: "I believe Manami is ready for a brief glance from Yohei Chiba..."
"...which could be arranged as early as next Friday."
"As for a first conversation, I would estimate two more weeks at least, and perhaps as many as--"
KYCHUK
The door.
Hiro!

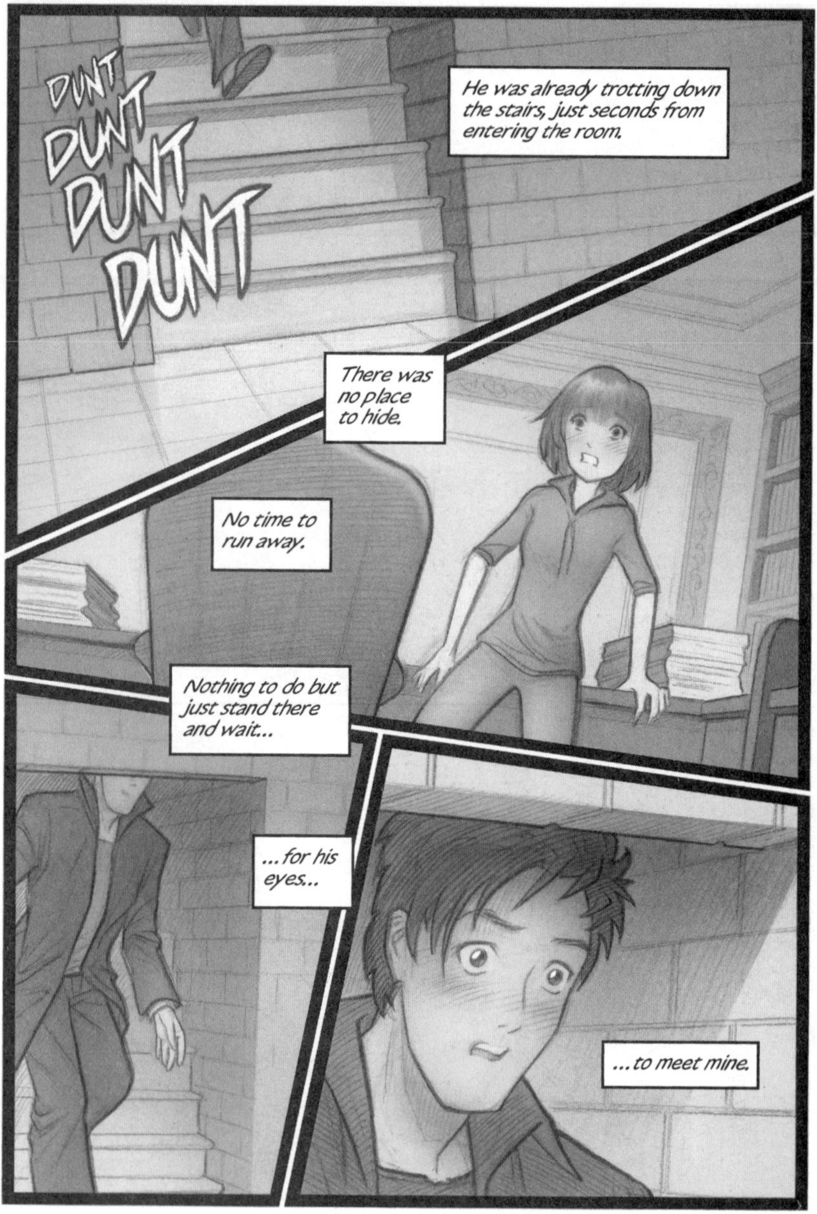
DUNT
DUNT
DUNT
DUNT
He was already trotting down the stairs, just seconds from entering the room.
There was no place to hide.
No time to run away.
Nothing to do but just stand there and wait...
...for his eyes...
...to meet mine.

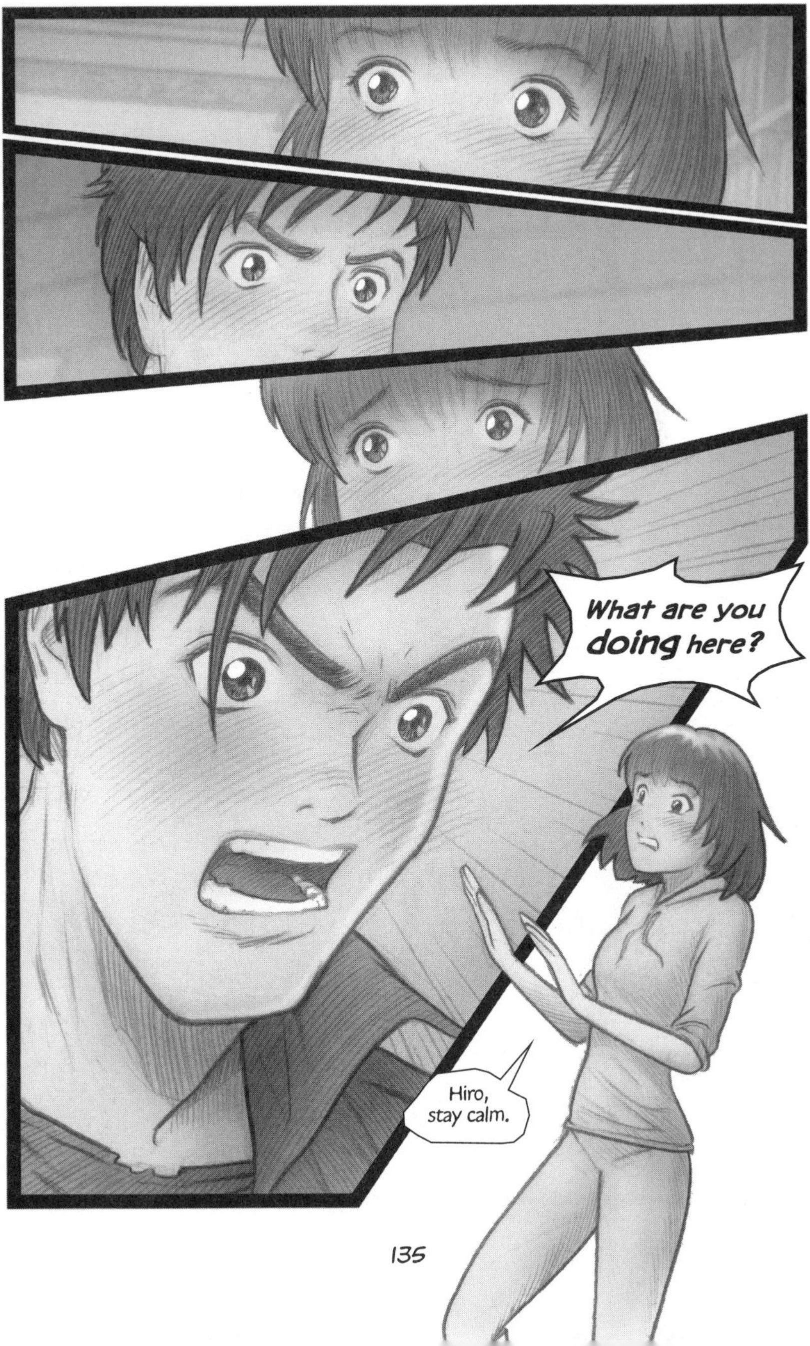
What are you doing here?
Hiro, stay calm.

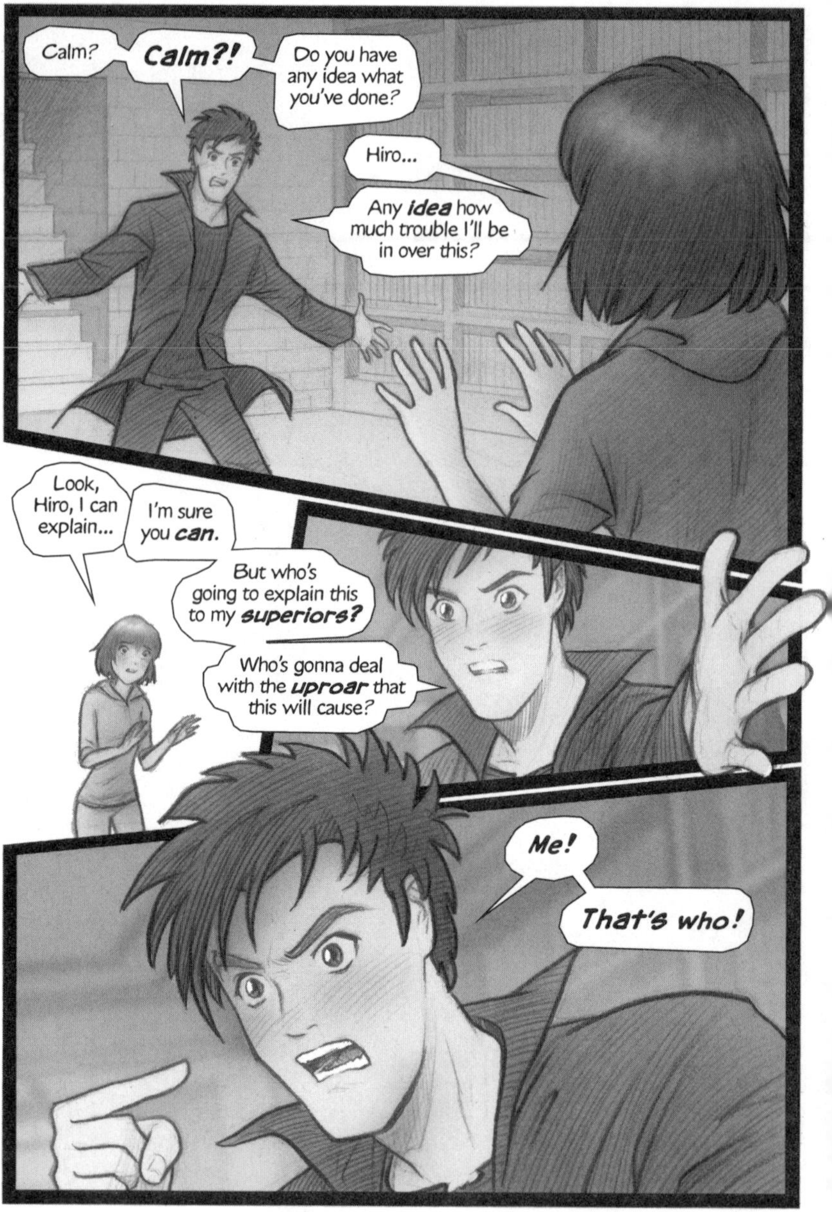
Calm?
Calm?!
Do you have any idea what you've done?
Hiro...
Any idea how much trouble I'll be in over this?
Look, Hiro, I can explain...
I'm sure you can.
But who's going to explain this to my superiors?
Who's gonna deal with the uproar that this will cause?
Me!
That's who!

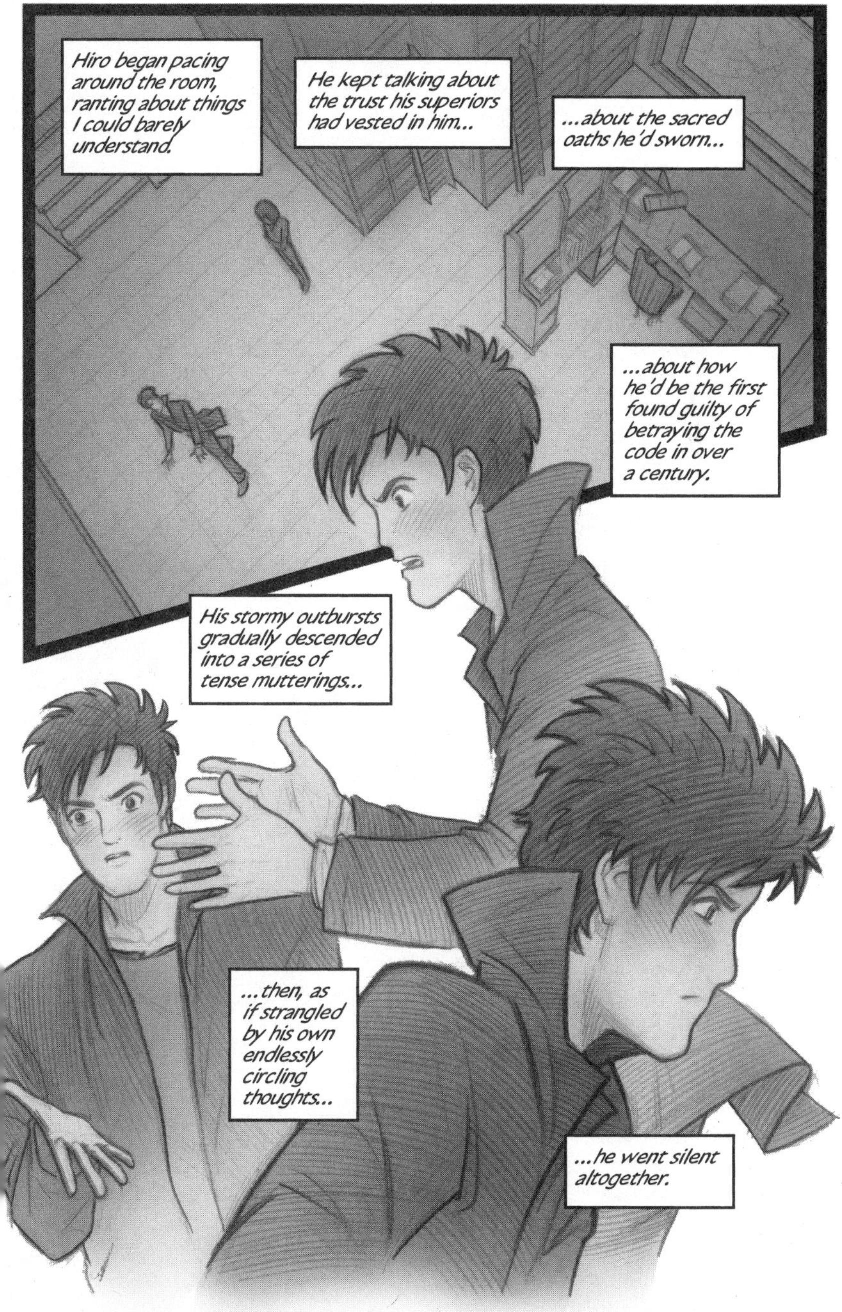
Hiro began pacing around the room, ranting about things I could barely understand.
He kept talking about the trust his superiors had vested in him...
...about the sacred oaths he'd sworn...
...about how he'd be the first found guilty of betraying the code in over a century.
His stormy outbursts gradually descended into a series of tense mutterings...
...then, as if strangled by his own endlessly circling thoughts...
...he went silent altogether.

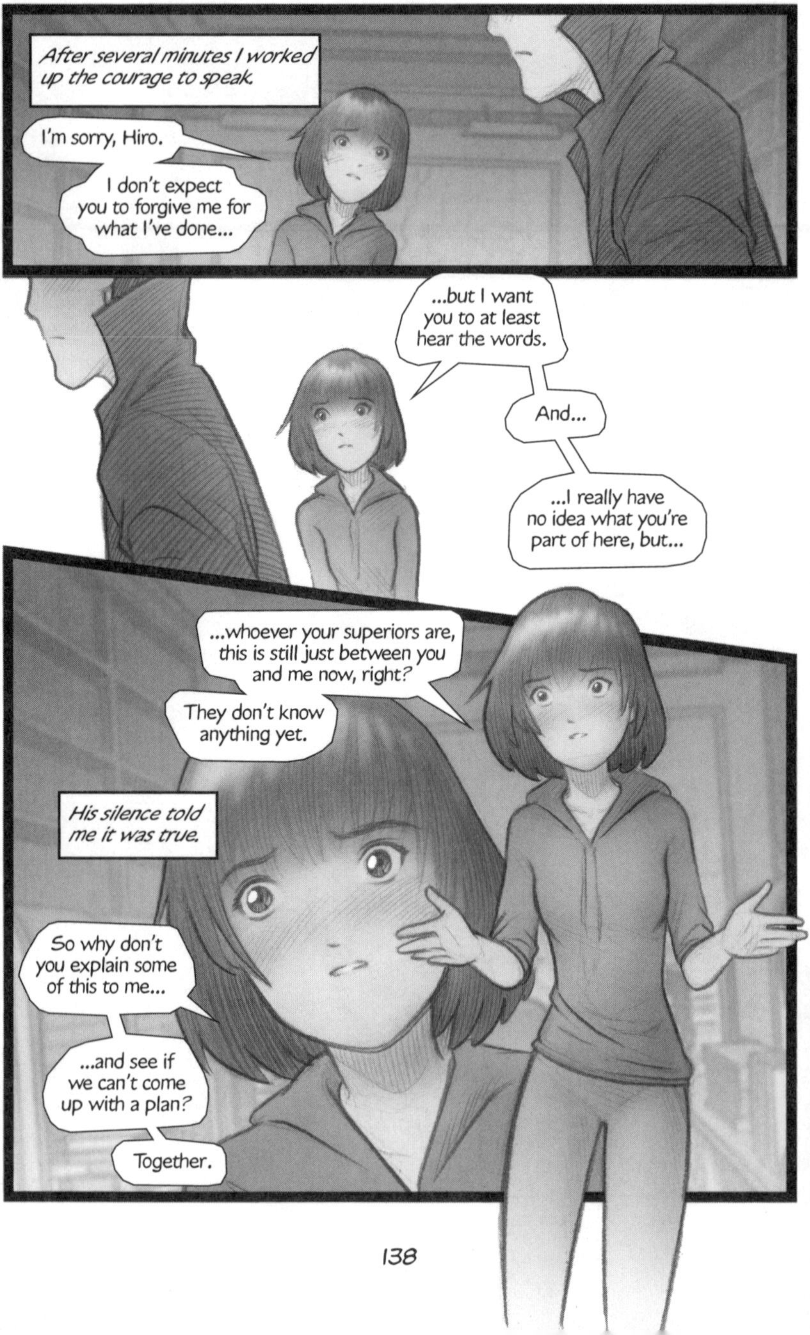
After several minutes I worked up the courage to speak.
I'm sorry, Hiro.
I don't expect you to forgive me for what I've done...
...but I want you to at least hear the words.
And...
...I really have no idea what you're part of here, but...
...whoever your superiors are, this is still just between you and me now, right?
They don't know anything yet.
His silence told me it was true.
So why don't you explain some of this to me...
...and see if we can't come up with a plan?
Together.

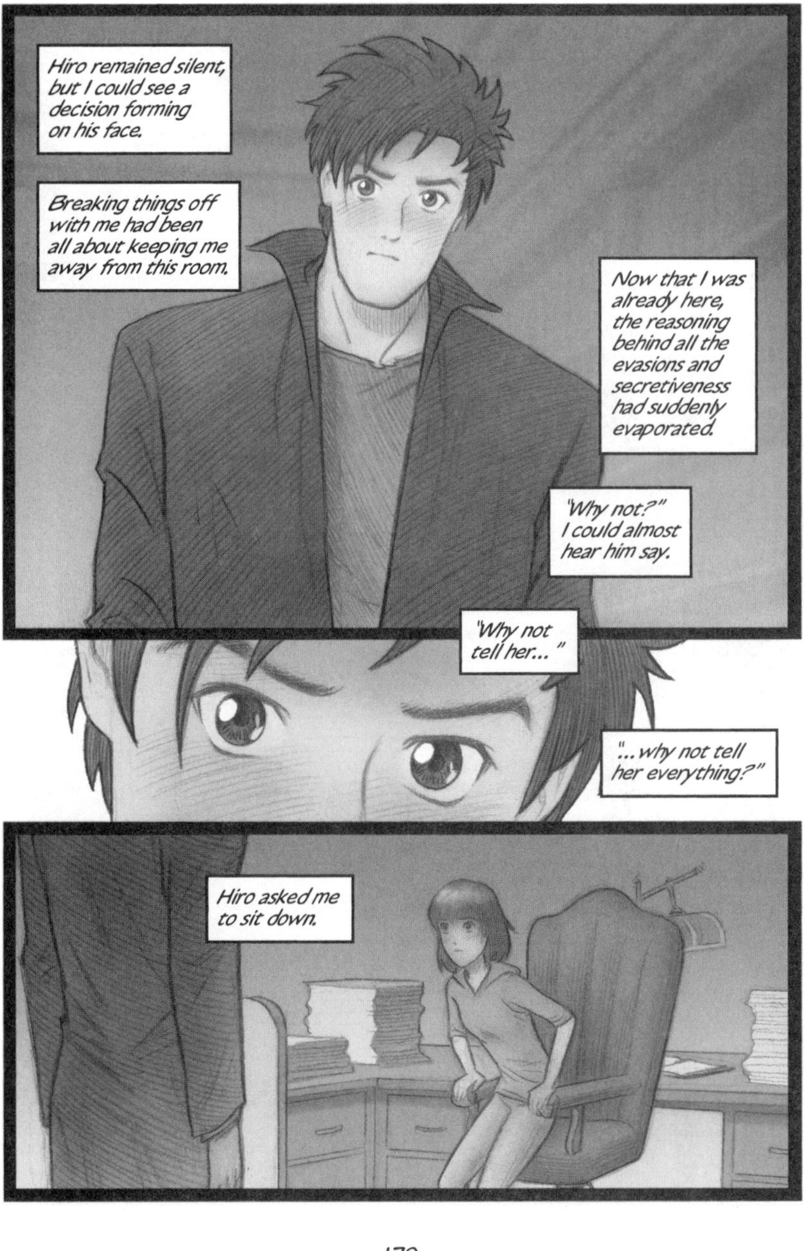
Hiro remained silent, but I could see a decision forming on his face.
Breaking things off with me had been all about keeping me away from this room.
Now that I was already here, the reasoning behind all the evasions and secretiveness had suddenly evaporated.
"Why not?" I could almost hear him say.
"Why not tell her... "
"...why not tell her everything?"
Hiro asked me to sit down.

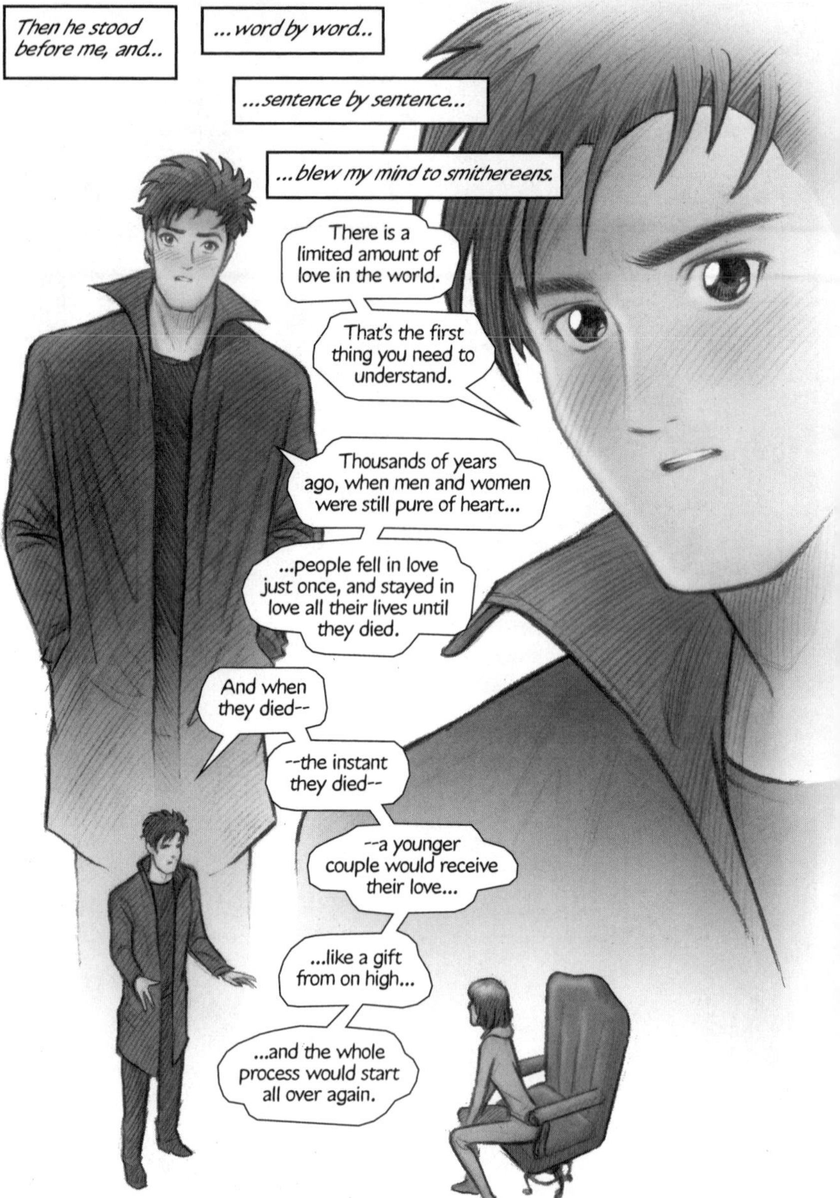
Then he stood before me, and..
...word by word..
...sentence by sentence...
...blew my mind to smithereens.
There is a limited amount of love in the world.
That's the first thing you need to understand.
Thousands of years ago, when men and women were still pure of heart...
...people fell in love just once, and stayed in love all their lives until they died.
And when they died--
--the instant they died--
--a younger couple would receive their love...
...like a gift from on high...
...and the whole process would start all over again.

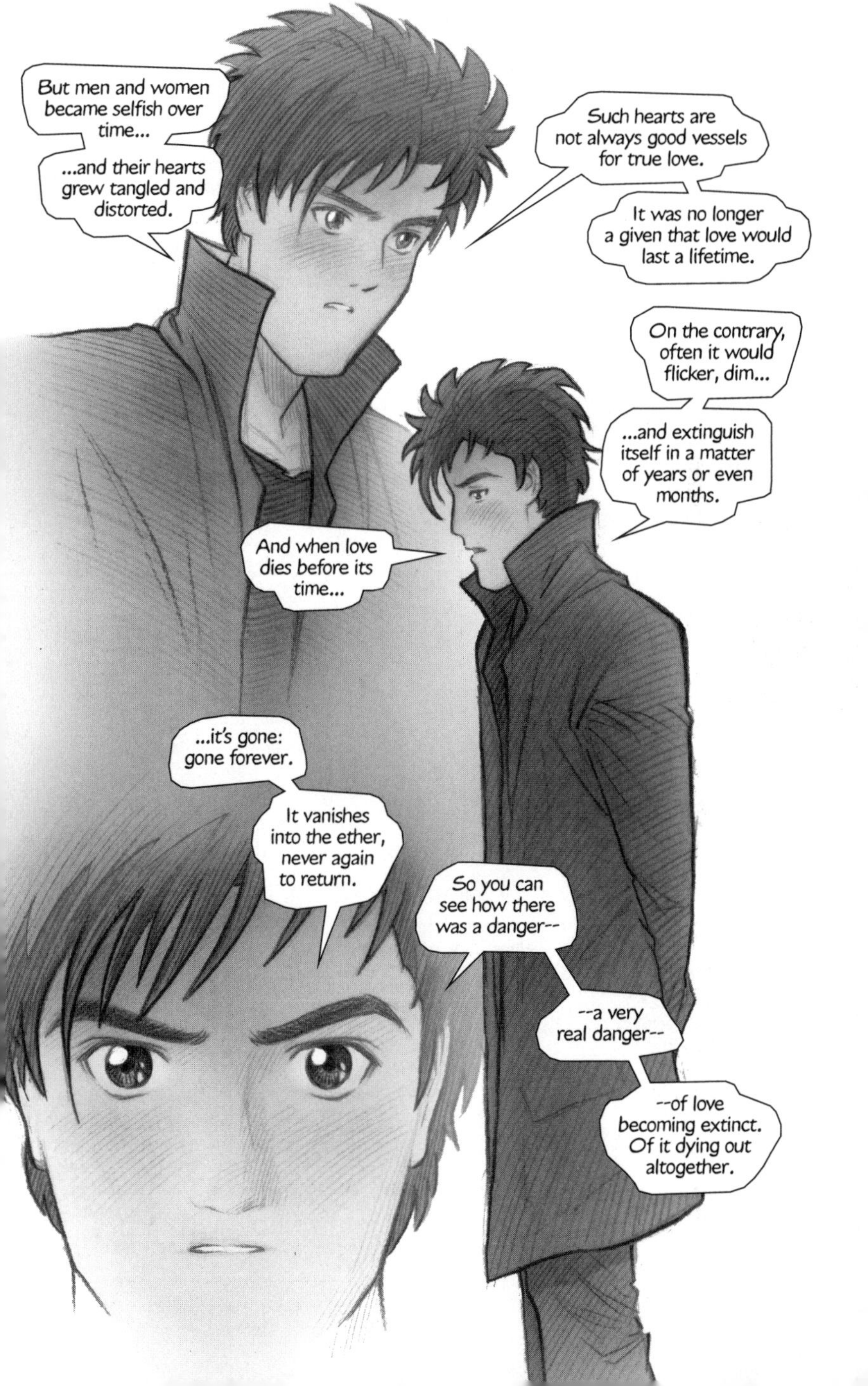
But men and women became selfish over time...
...and their hearts grew tangled and distorted.
Such hearts are not always good vessels for true love.
It was no longer a given that love would last a lifetime.
On the contrary, often it would flicker, dim...
...and extinguish itself in a matter of years or even months.
And when love dies before its time...
...it's gone: gone forever.
It vanishes into the ether, never again to return.
So you can see how there was a danger--
--a very real danger--
--of love becoming extinct. Of it dying out altogether.

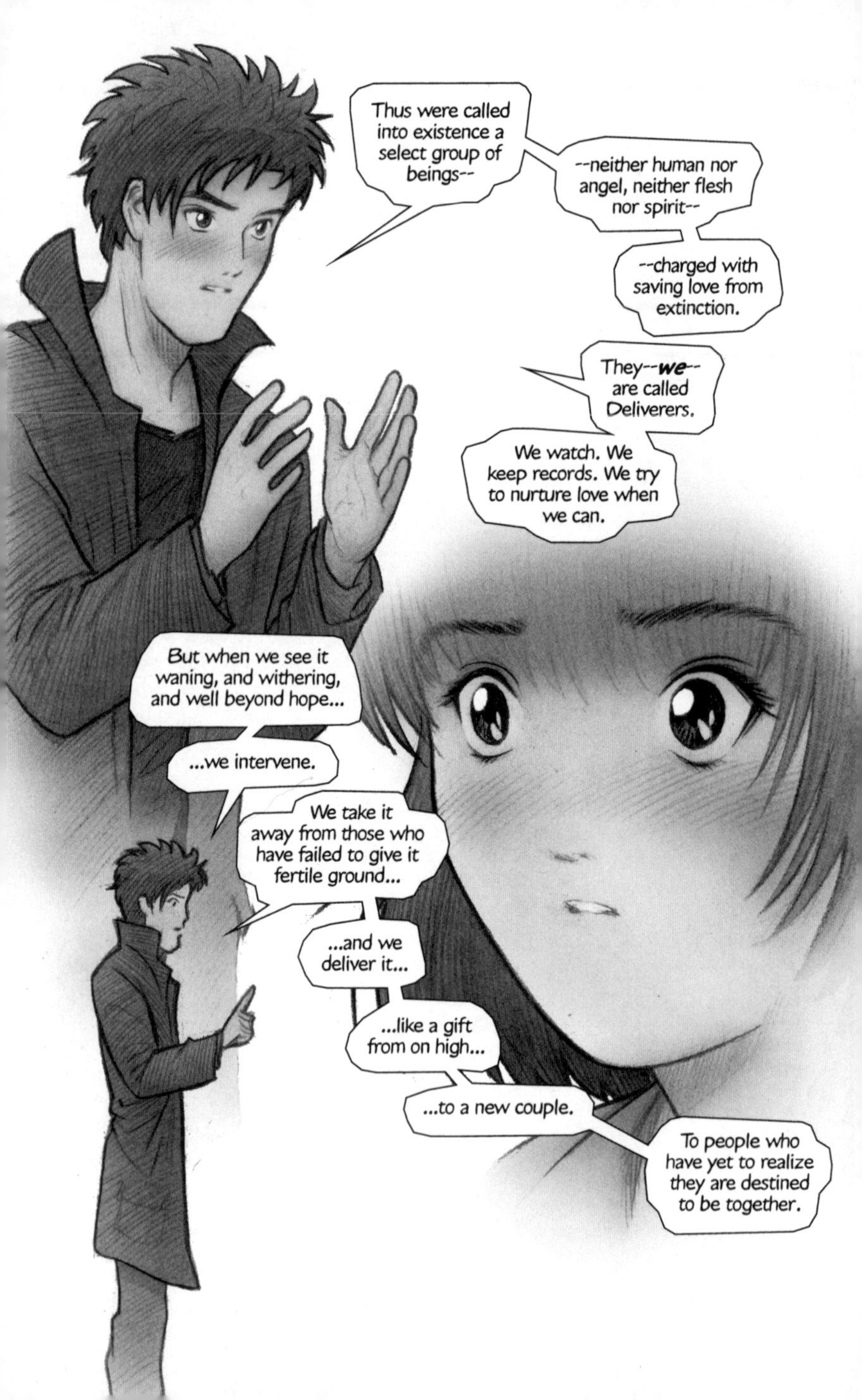
Thus were called into existence a select group of beings--
--neither human nor angel, neither flesh nor spirit--
--charged with saving love from extinction.
They--**we**--are called Deliverers.
We watch. We keep records. We try to nurture love when we can.
But when we see it waning, and withering, and well beyond hope...
...we intervene.
We take it away from those who have failed to give it fertile ground...
...and we deliver it...
...like a gift from on high...
...to a new couple.
To people who have yet to realize they are destined to be together.

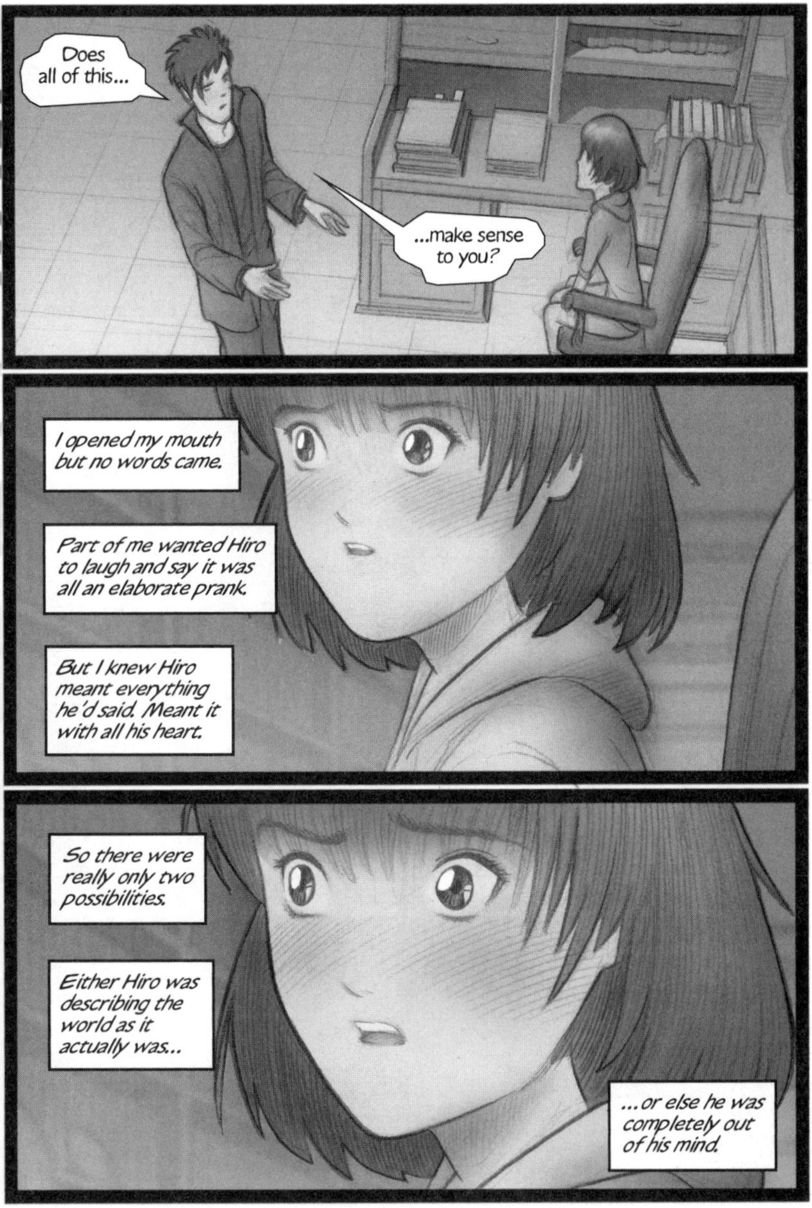
Does all of this...
...make sense to you?
I opened my mouth but no words came.
Part of me wanted Hiro to laugh and say it was all an elaborate prank.
But I knew Hiro meant everything he'd said. Meant it with all his heart.
So there were really only two possibilities.
Either Hiro was describing the world as it actually was...
...or else he was completely out of his mind.

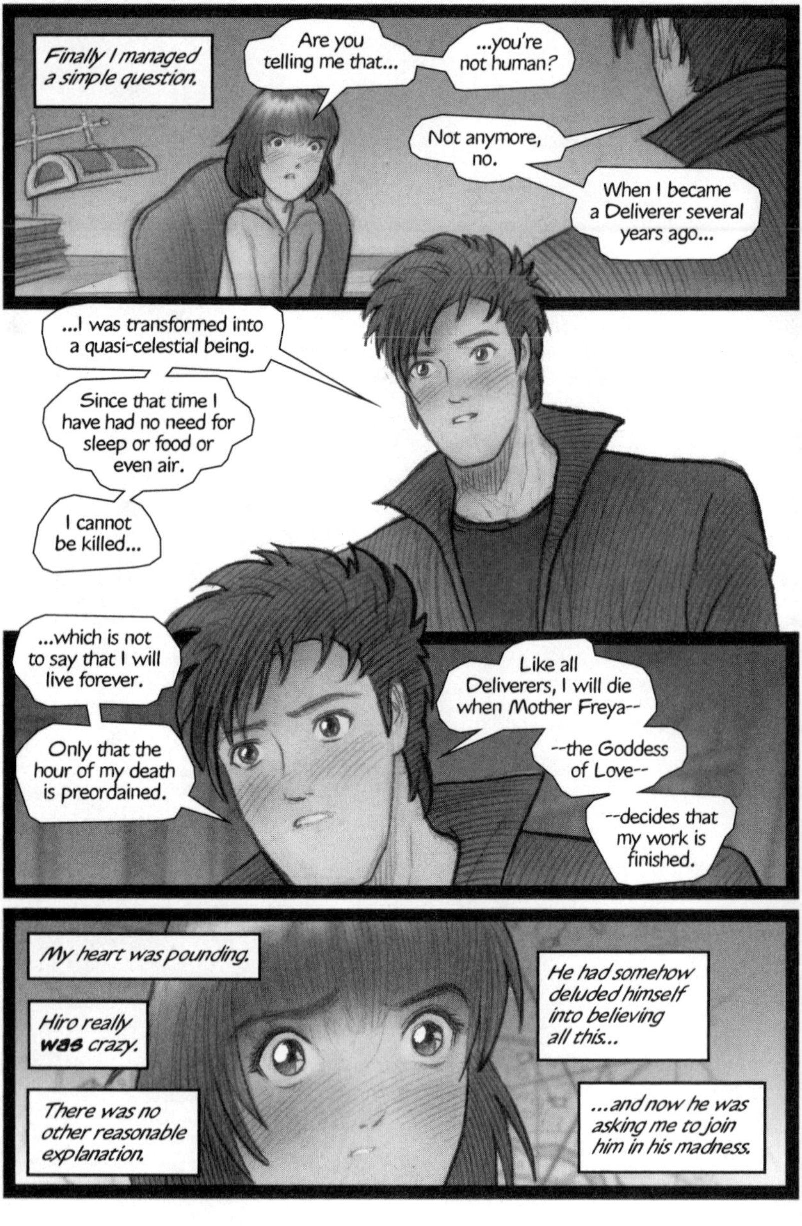
Finally I managed a simple question.
Are you telling me that...
...you're not human?
Not anymore, no.
When I became a Deliverer several years ago...
...I was transformed into a quasi-celestial being.
Since that time I have had no need for sleep or food or even air.
I cannot be killed...
...which is not to say that I will live forever.
Only that the hour of my death is preordained.
Like all Deliverers, I will die when Mother Freya--
--the Goddess of Love--
--decides that my work is finished.
My heart was pounding.
Hiro really **was** crazy.
There was no other reasonable explanation.
He had somehow deluded himself into believing all this...
...and now he was asking me to join him in his madness.

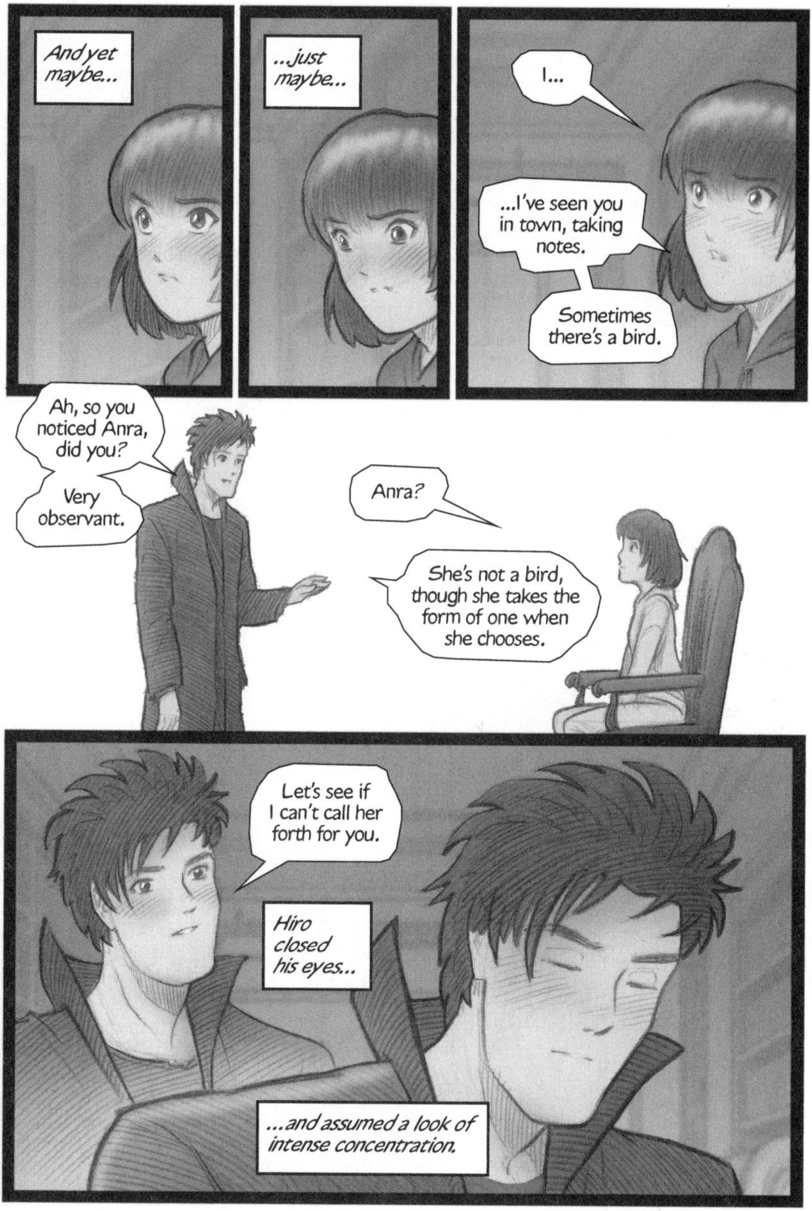
And yet maybe...
...just maybe...
I...
...I've seen you in town, taking notes.
Sometimes there's a bird.
Ah, so you noticed Anra, did you?
Very observant.
Anra?
She's not a bird, though she takes the form of one when she chooses.
Let's see if I can't call her forth for you.
Hiro closed his eyes...
...and assumed a look of intense concentration.

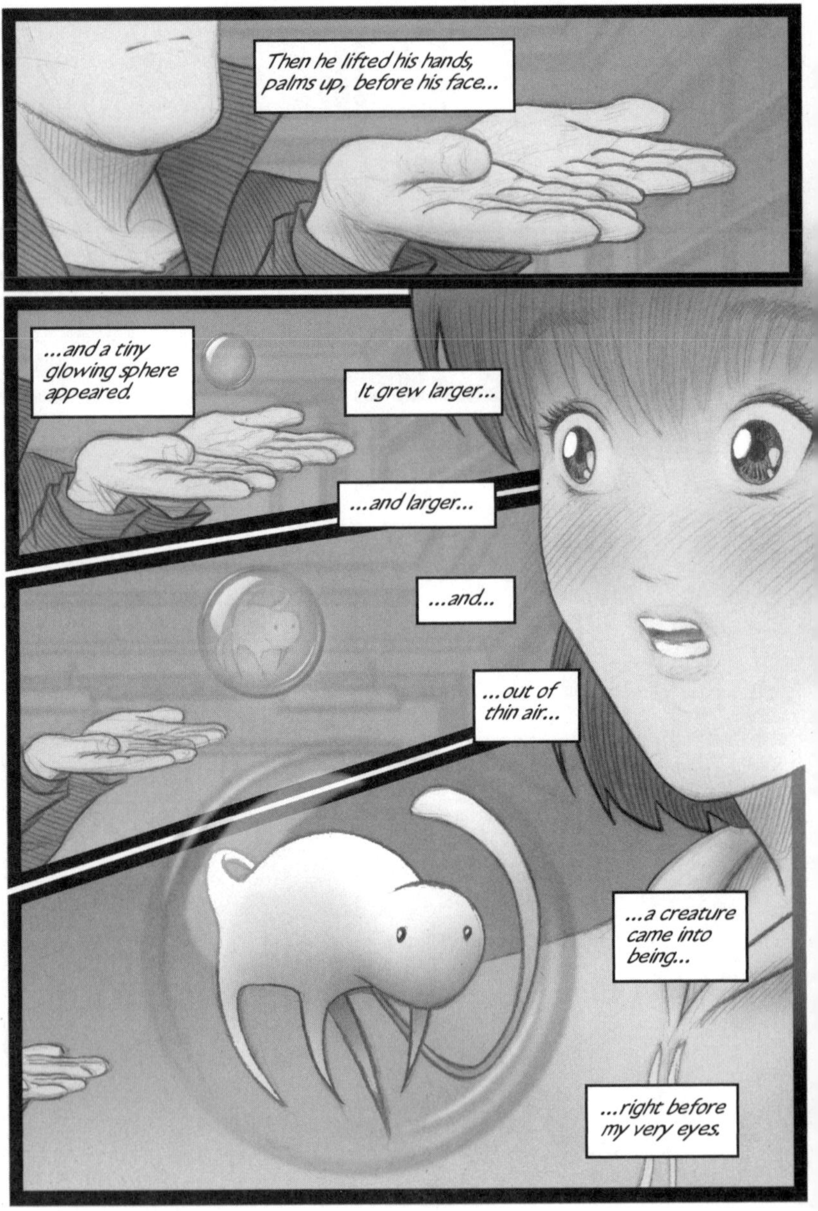
Then he lifted his hands, palms up, before his face...
...and a tiny glowing sphere appeared.
It grew larger...
...and larger...
...and...
...out of thin air...
...a creature came into being...
...right before my very eyes.

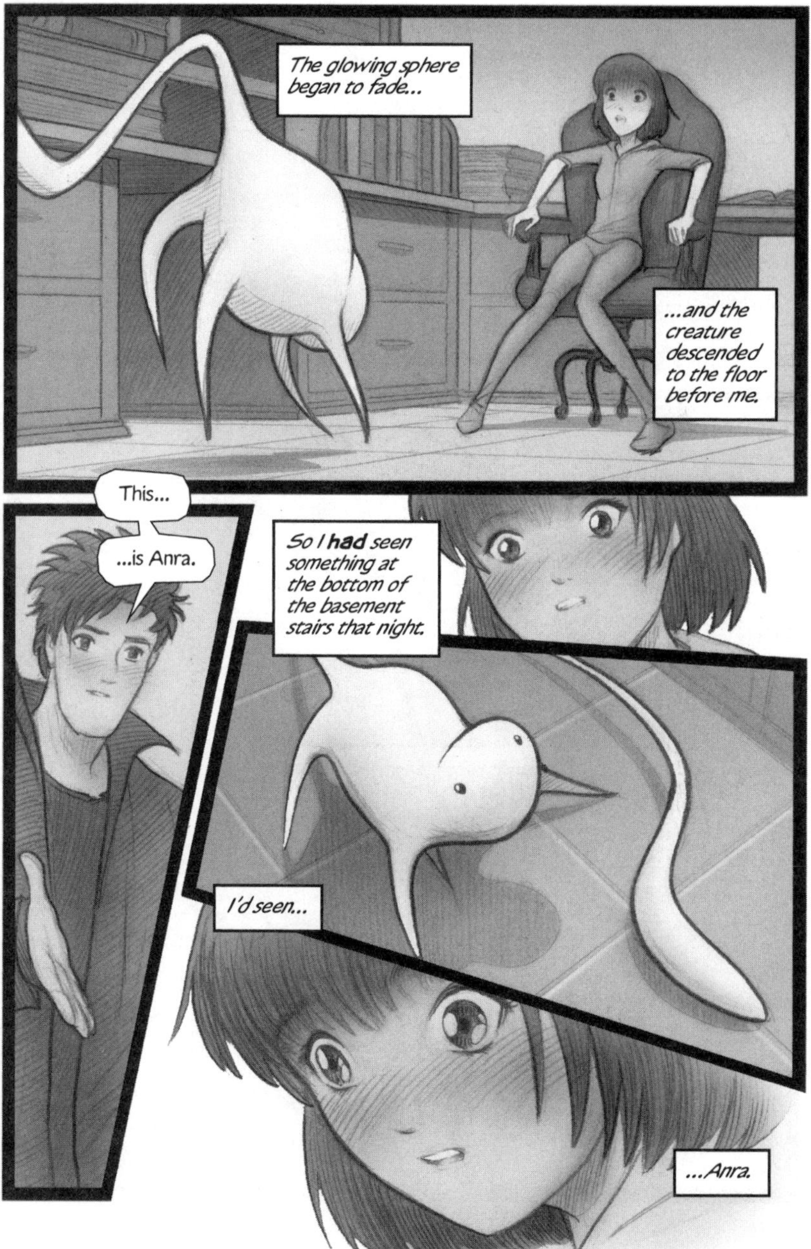
The glowing sphere began to fade...
...and the creature descended to the floor before me.
This...
...is Anra.
So I **had** seen something at the bottom of the basement stairs that night.
I'd seen...
...Anra.

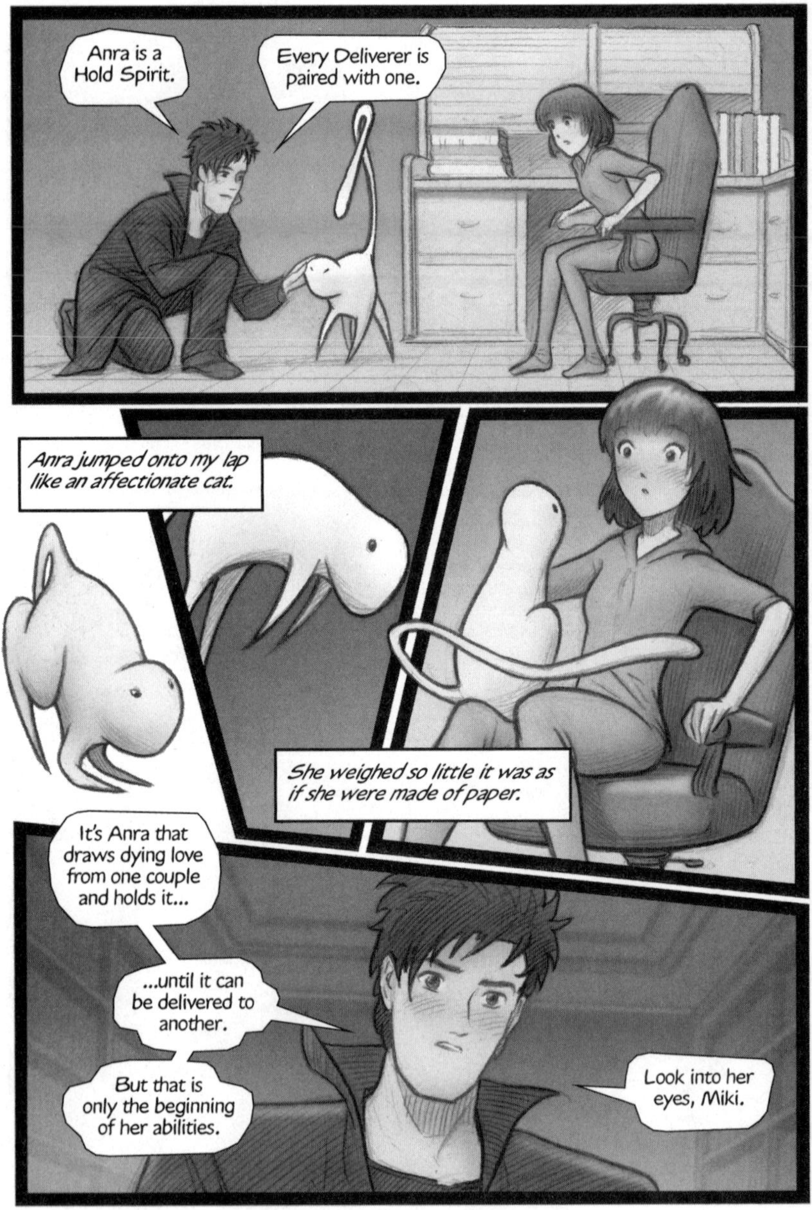
Anra is a Hold Spirit.
Every Deliverer is paired with one.
Anra jumped onto my lap like an affectionate cat.
She weighed so little it was as if she were made of paper.
It's Anra that draws dying love from one couple and holds it...
...until it can be delivered to another.
But that is only the beginning of her abilities.
Look into her eyes, Miki.

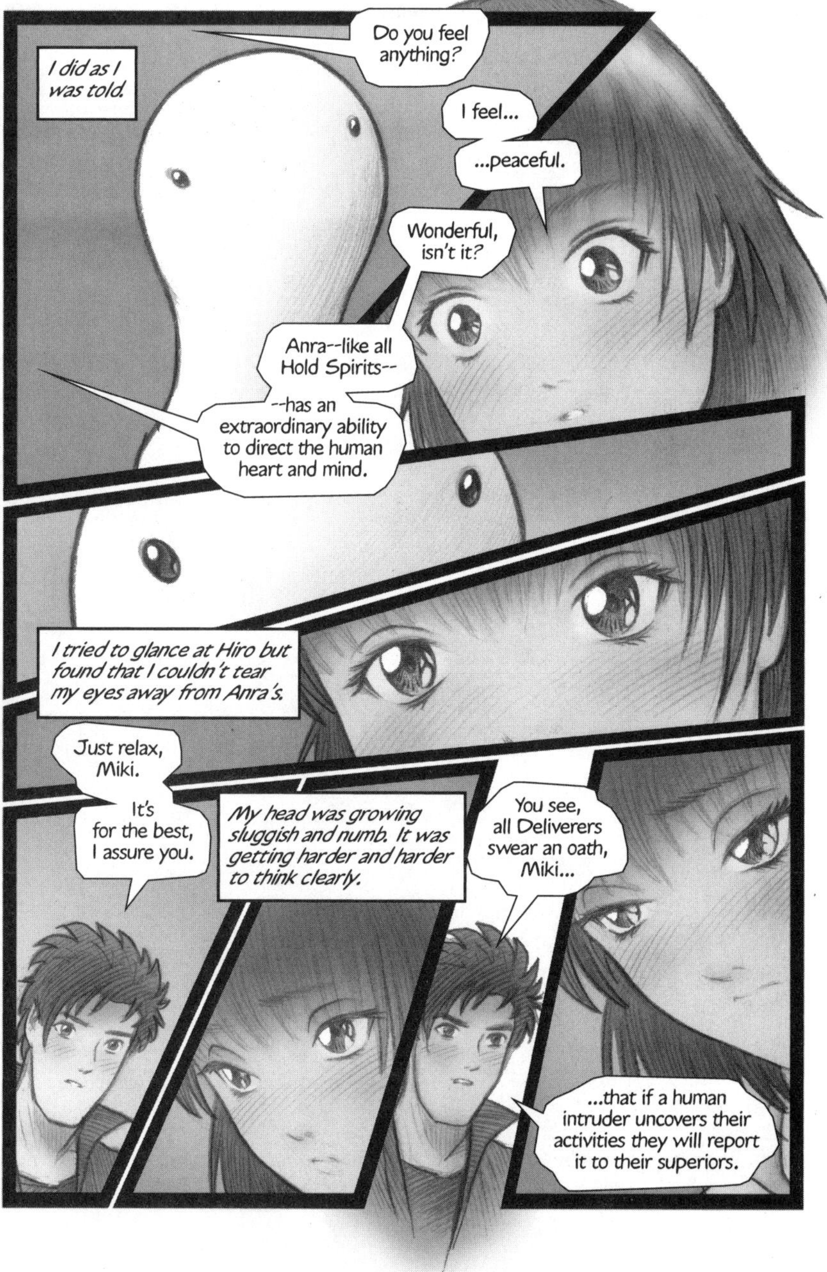
I did as I was told.
Do you feel anything?
I feel...
...peaceful.
Wonderful, isn't it?
Anra--like all Hold Spirits--
--has an extraordinary ability to direct the human heart and mind.
I tried to glance at Hiro but found that I couldn't tear my eyes away from Anra's.
Just relax, Miki.
It's for the best, I assure you.
My head was growing sluggish and numb. It was getting harder and harder to think clearly.
You see, all Deliverers swear an oath, Miki...
...that if a human intruder uncovers their activities they will report it to their superiors.

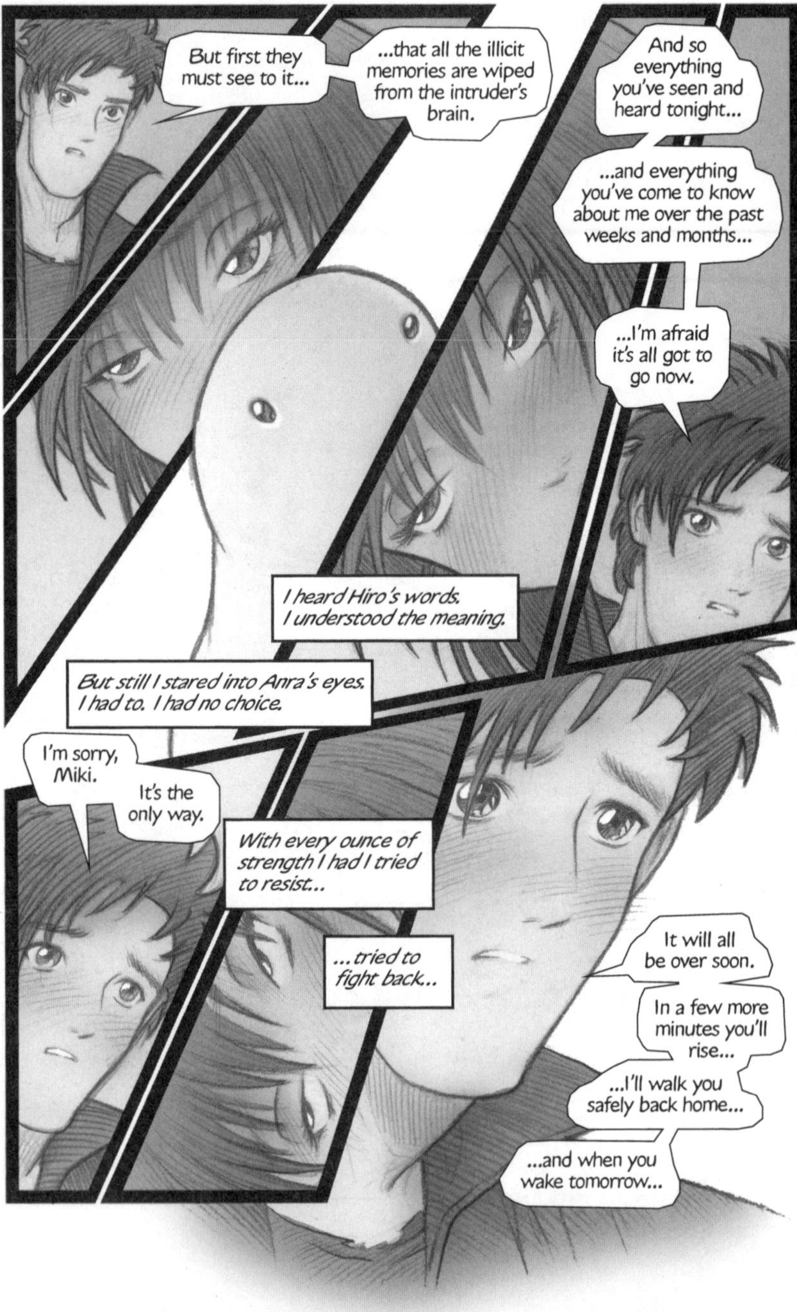

But first they must see to it...
...that all the illicit memories are wiped from the intruder's brain.
And so everything you've seen and heard tonight...
...and everything you've come to know about me over the past weeks and months...
...I'm afraid it's all got to go now.
I heard Hiro's words. I understood the meaning.
But still I stared into Anra's eyes. I had to. I had no choice.
I'm sorry, Miki.
It's the only way.
With every ounce of strength I had I tried to resist...
...tried to fight back...
It will all be over soon.
In a few more minutes you'll rise...
...I'll walk you safely back home...
...and when you wake tomorrow...

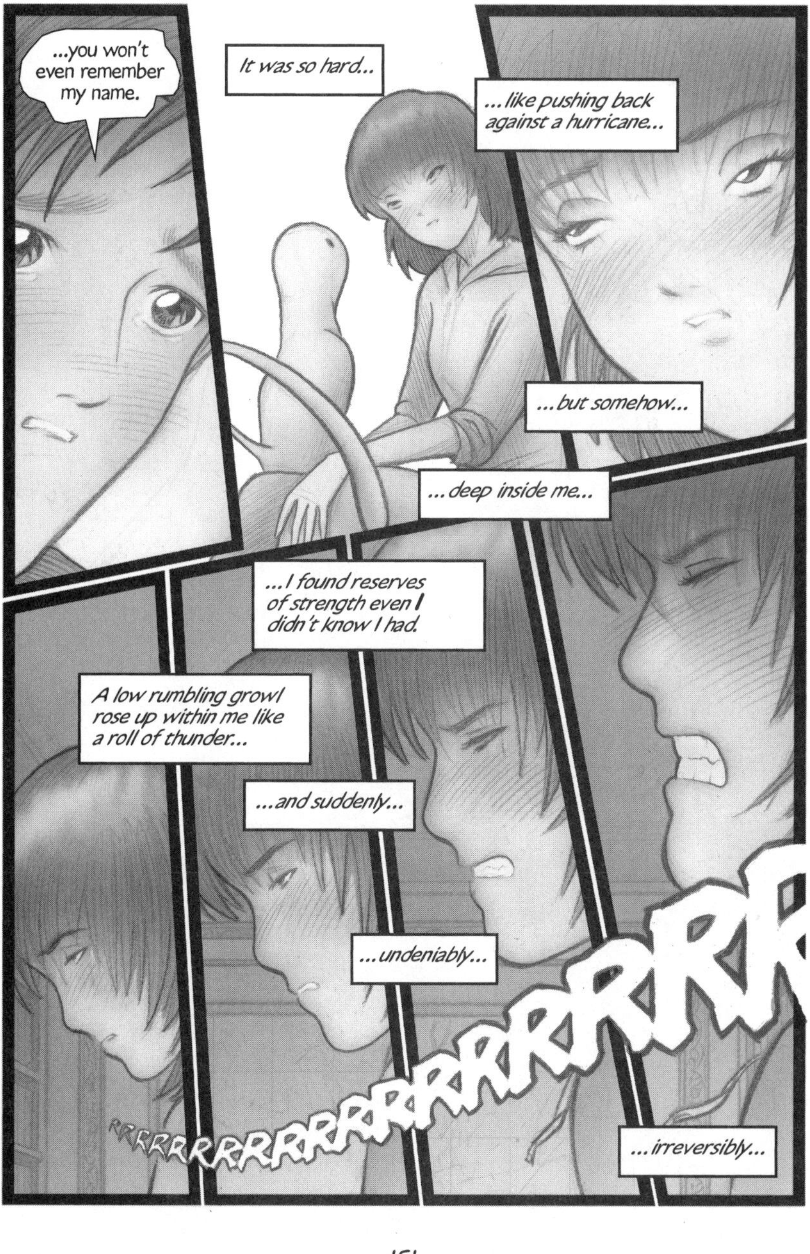
...you won't even remember my name.
It was so hard...
...like pushing back against a hurricane...
...but somehow...
...deep inside me...
...I found reserves of strength even I didn't know I had.
A low rumbling growl rose up within me like a roll of thunder...
...and suddenly...
...undeniably...
RRRRRRRRRRRRRRRRRRRRRRRR
...irreversibly...

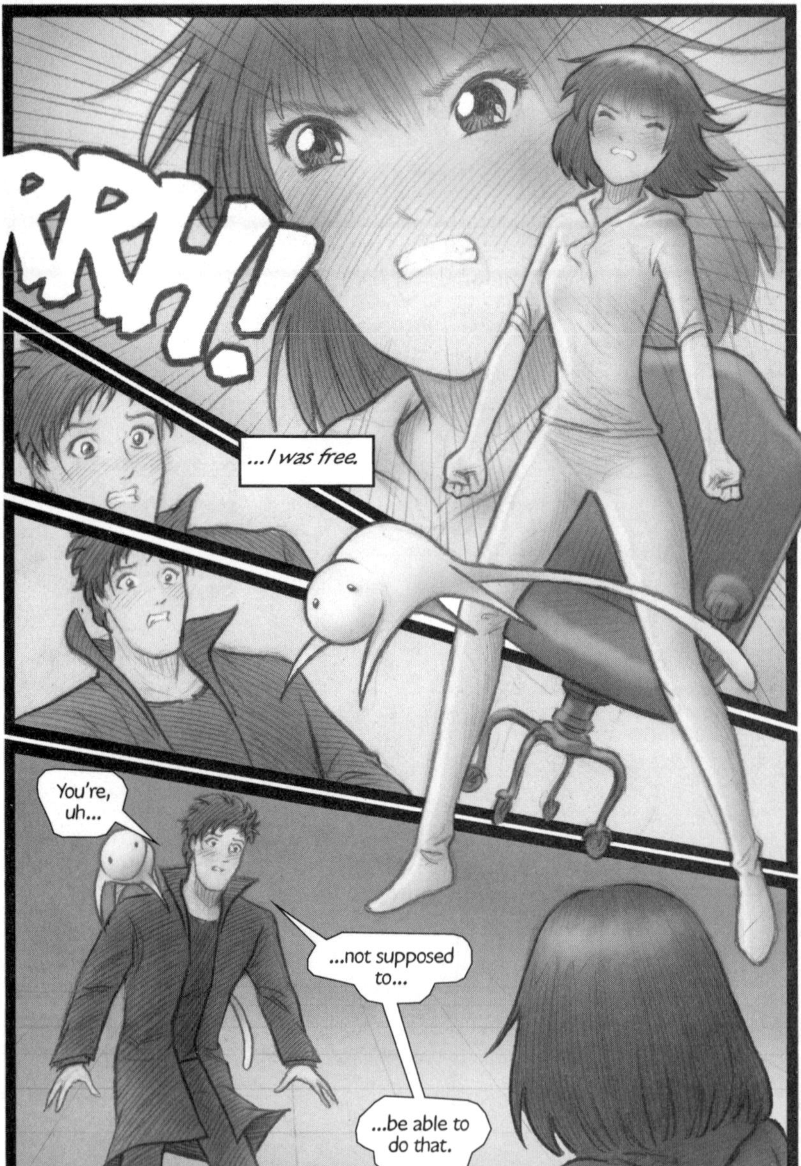

RRH!
...I was free.
You're, uh...
...not supposed to...
...be able to do that.

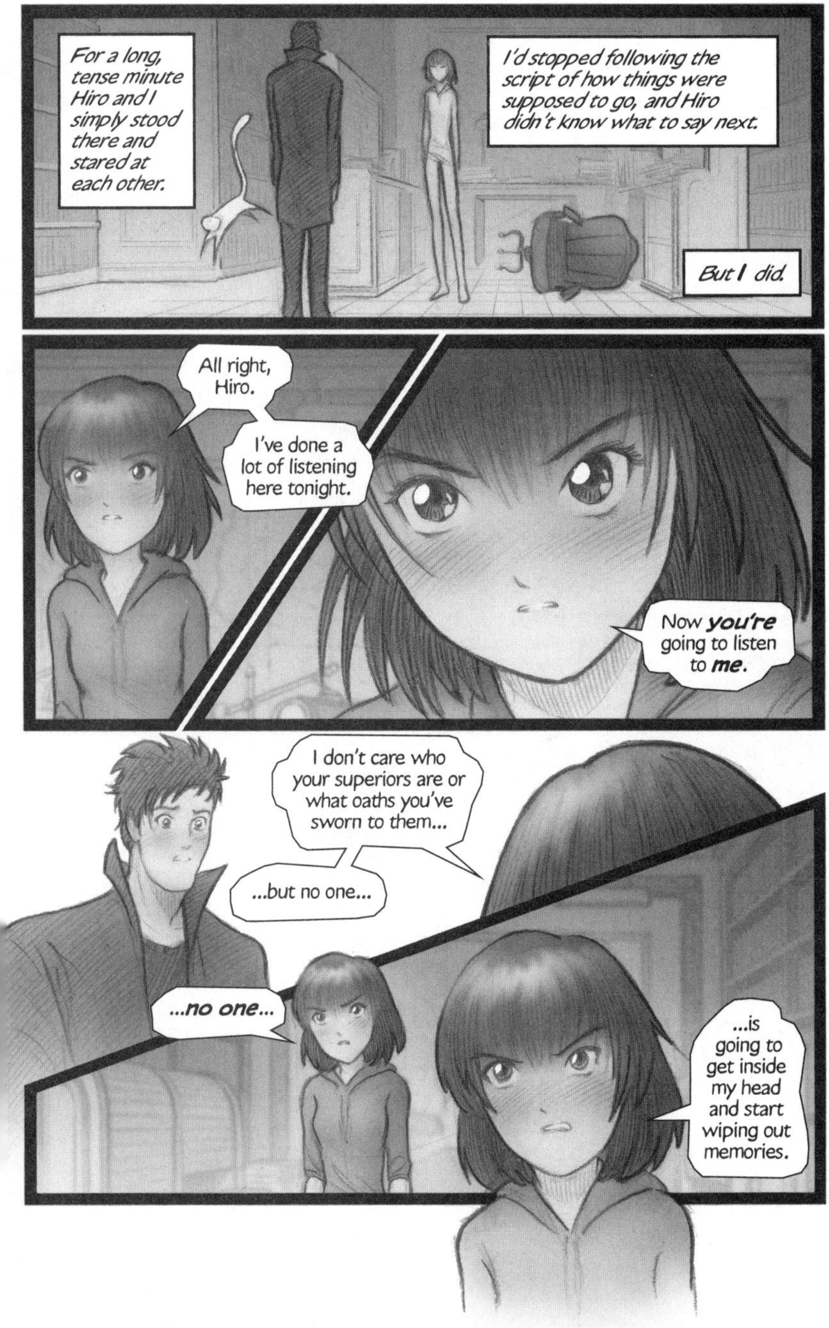

For a long, tense minute Hiro and I simply stood there and stared at each other.
I'd stopped following the script of how things were supposed to go, and Hiro didn't know what to say next.
*But **I** did.*
All right, Hiro.
I've done a lot of listening here tonight.
Now ***you're*** going to listen to ***me***.
I don't care who your superiors are or what oaths you've sworn to them...
...but no one...
*...**no one**...*
...is going to get inside my head and start wiping out memories.

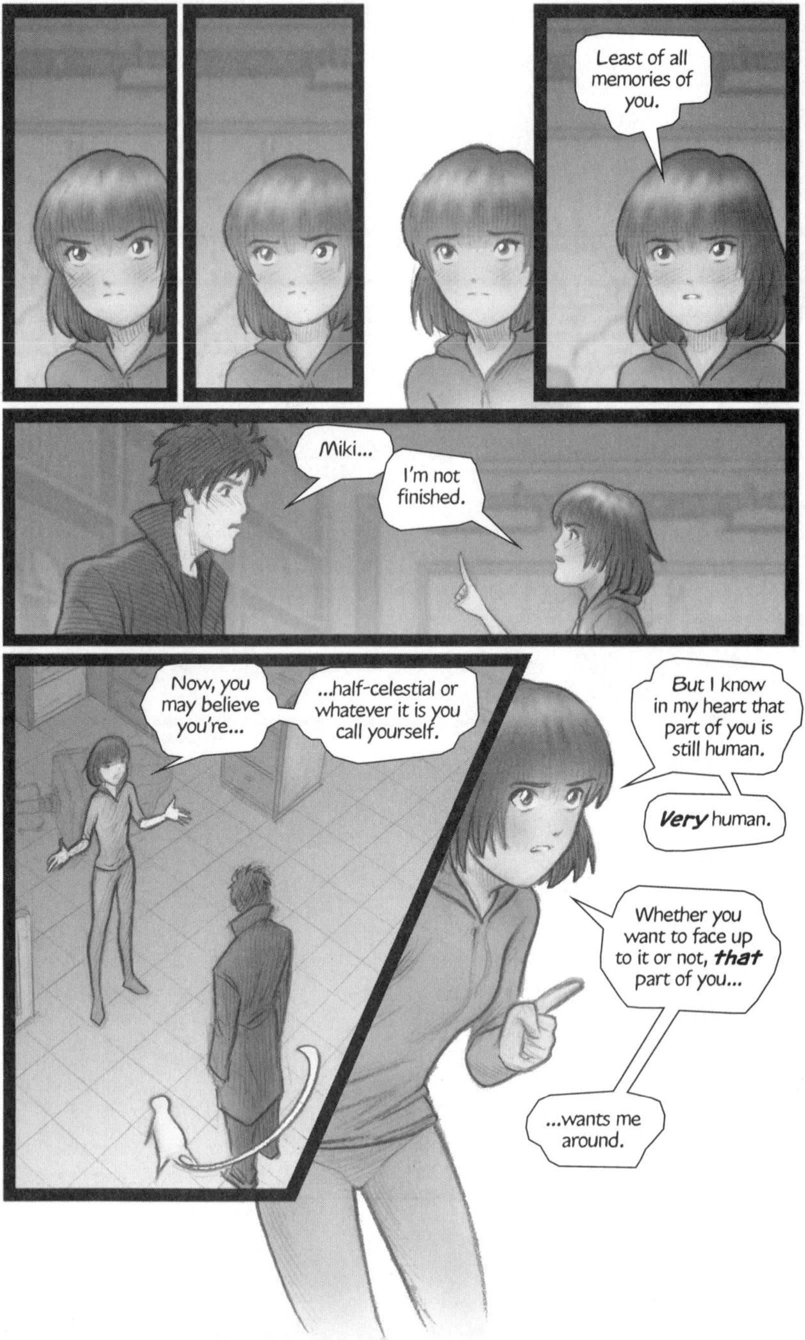
Least of all memories of you.
Miki...
I'm not finished.
Now, you may believe you're...
...half-celestial or whatever it is you call yourself.
But I know in my heart that part of you is still human.
Very human.
Whether you want to face up to it or not, *that* part of you...
...wants me around.

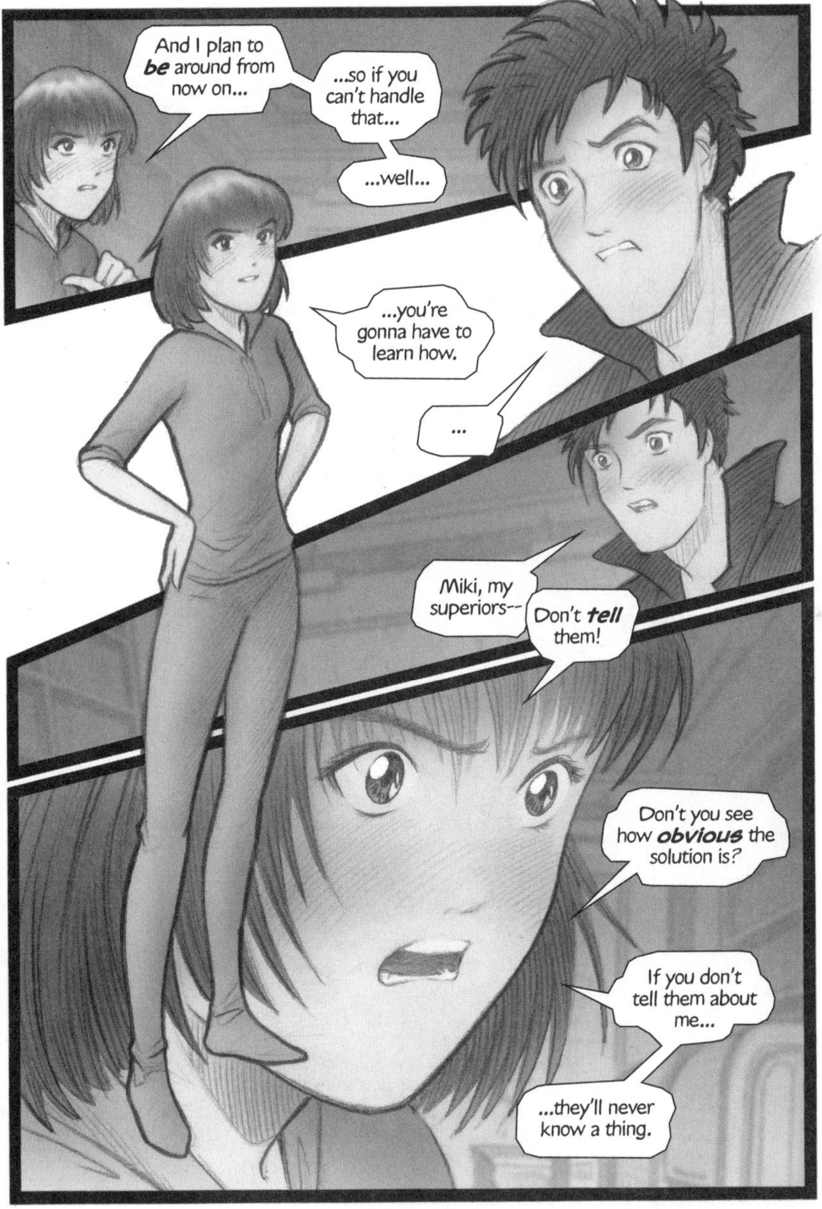
And I plan to *be* around from now on...
...so if you can't handle that...
...well...
...you're gonna have to learn how.
...
Miki, my superiors--
Don't *tell* them!
Don't you see how *obvious* the solution is?
If you don't tell them about me...
...they'll never know a thing.

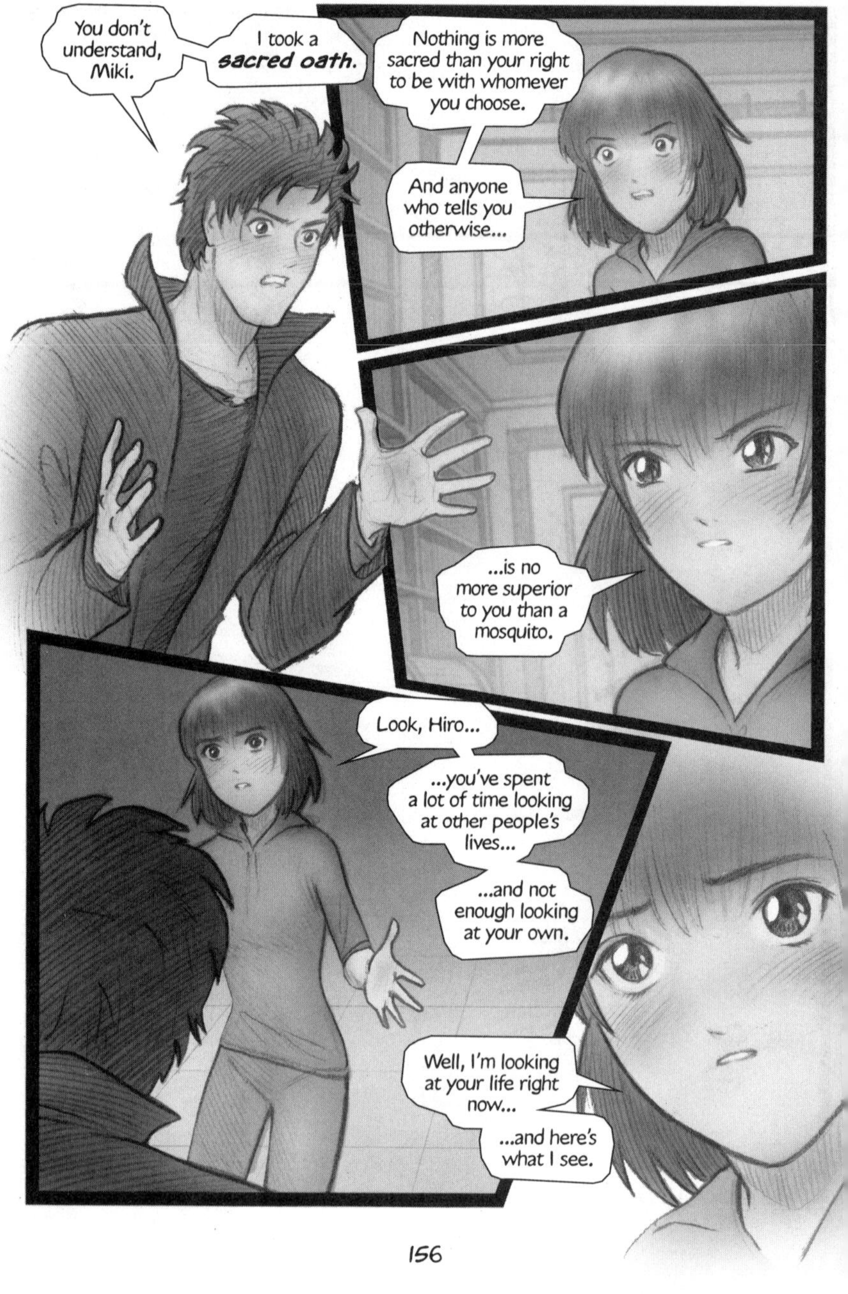
You don't understand, Miki.
I took a **sacred oath.**
Nothing is more sacred than your right to be with whomever you choose.
And anyone who tells you otherwise...
...is no more superior to you than a mosquito.
Look, Hiro...
...you've spent a lot of time looking at other people's lives...
...and not enough looking at your own.
Well, I'm looking at your life right now...
...and here's what I see.

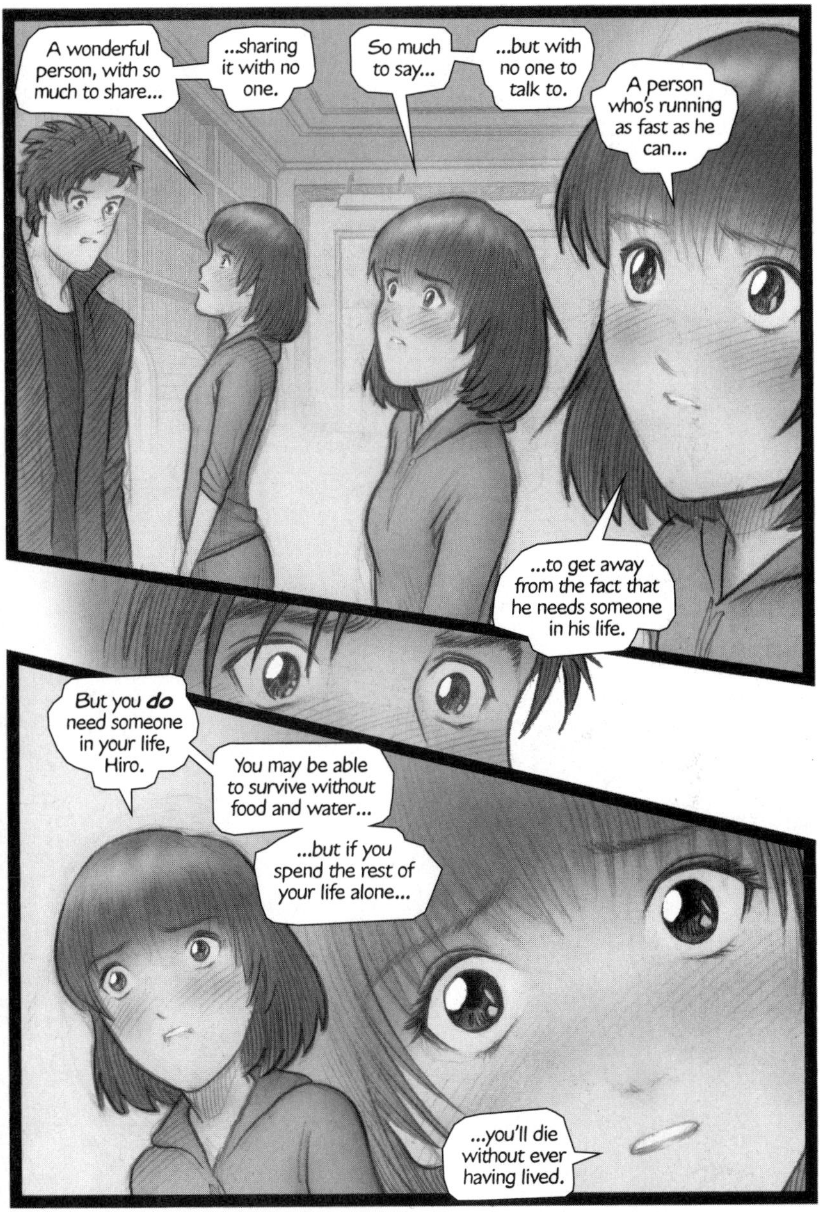
A wonderful person, with so much to share...
...sharing it with no one.
So much to say...
...but with no one to talk to.
A person who's running as fast as he can...
...to get away from the fact that he needs someone in his life.
But you **do** need someone in your life, Hiro.
You may be able to survive without food and water...
...but if you spend the rest of your life alone...
...you'll die without ever having lived.

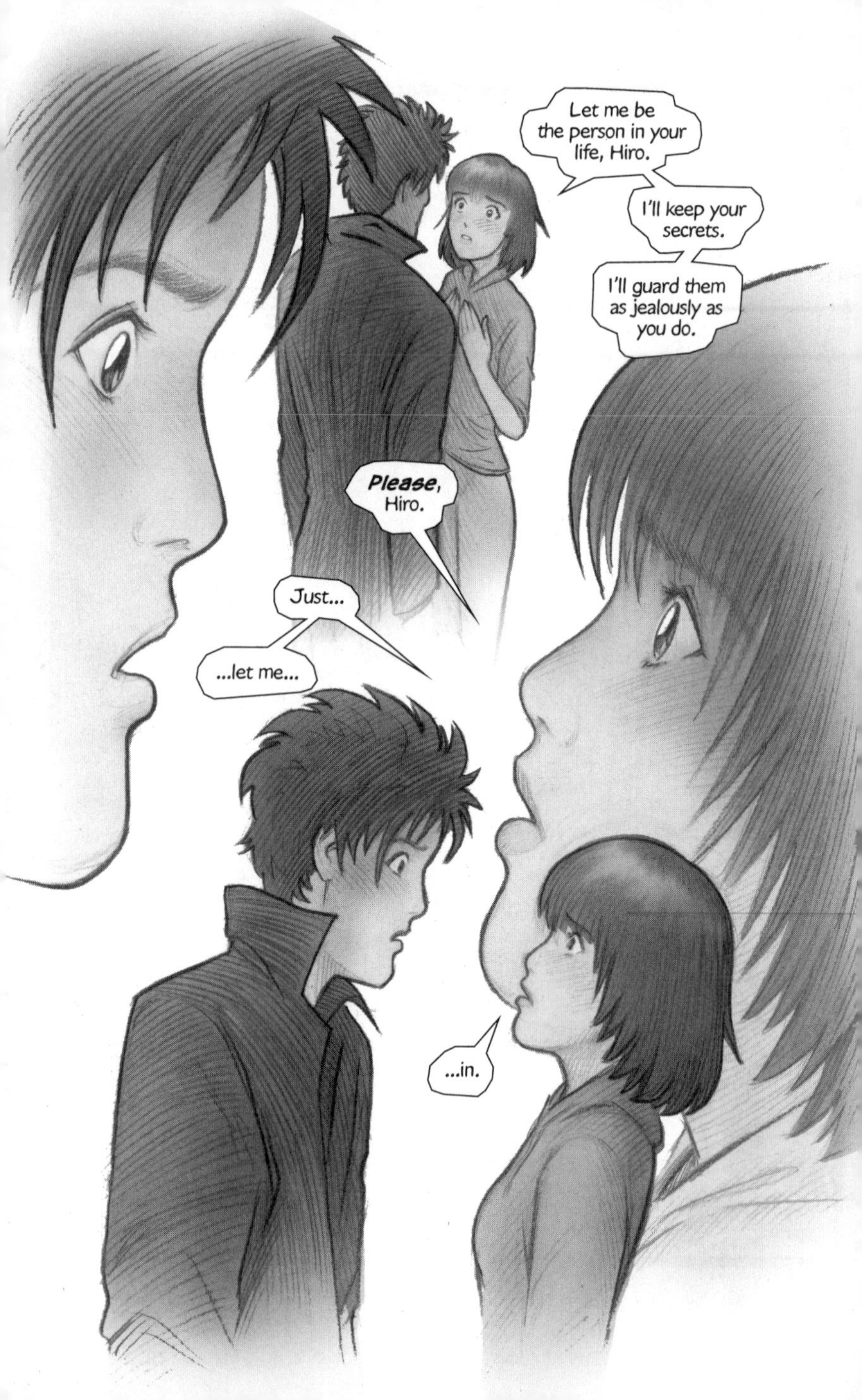
Let me be the person in your life, Hiro.
I'll keep your secrets.
I'll guard them as jealously as you do.
Please, Hiro.
Just...
...let me...
...in.

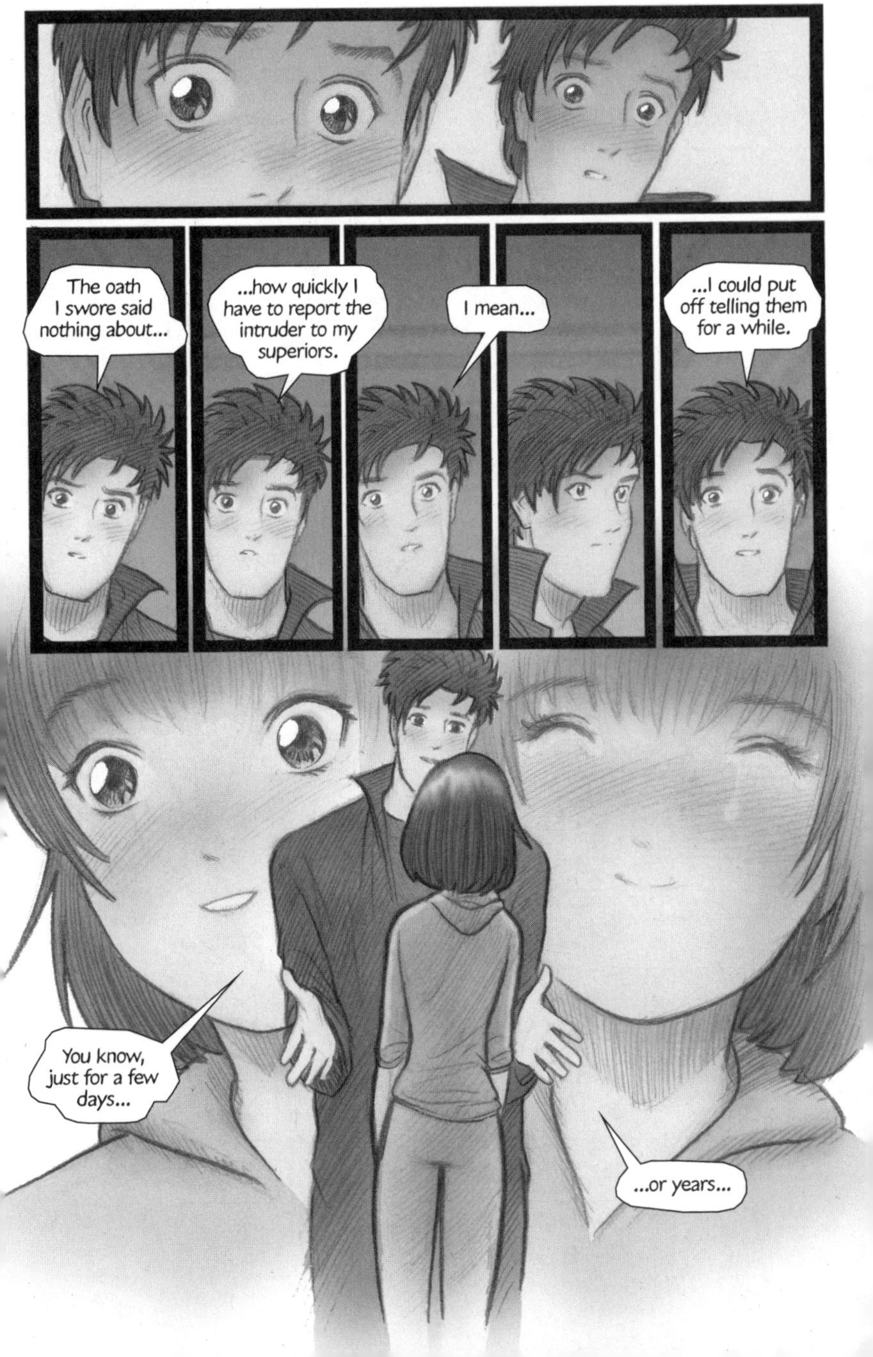
The oath I swore said nothing about...
...how quickly I have to report the intruder to my superiors.
I mean...
...I could put off telling them for a while.
You know, just for a few days...
...or years...

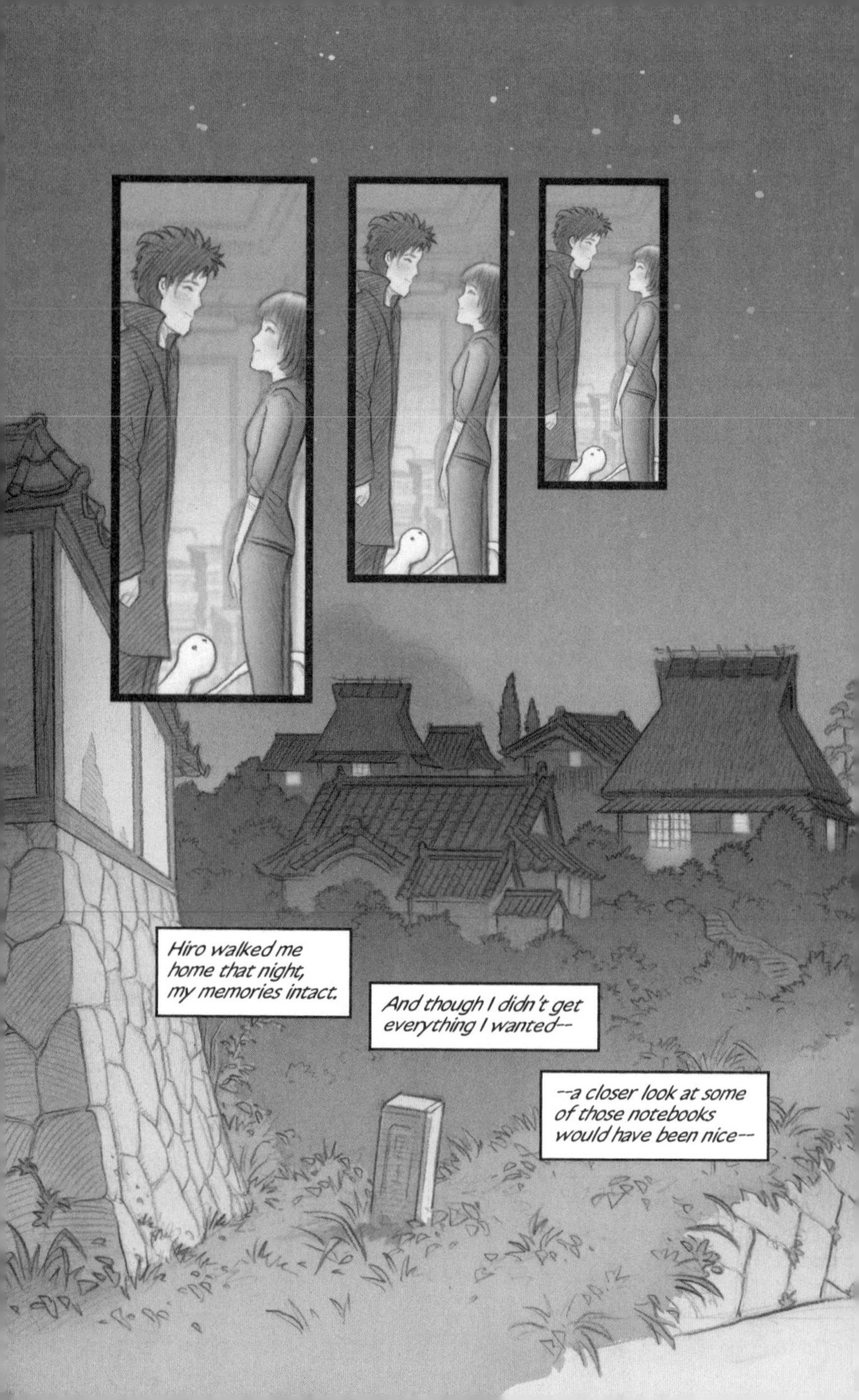
Hiro walked me home that night, my memories intact.
And though I didn't get everything I wanted--
--a closer look at some of those notebooks would have been nice--

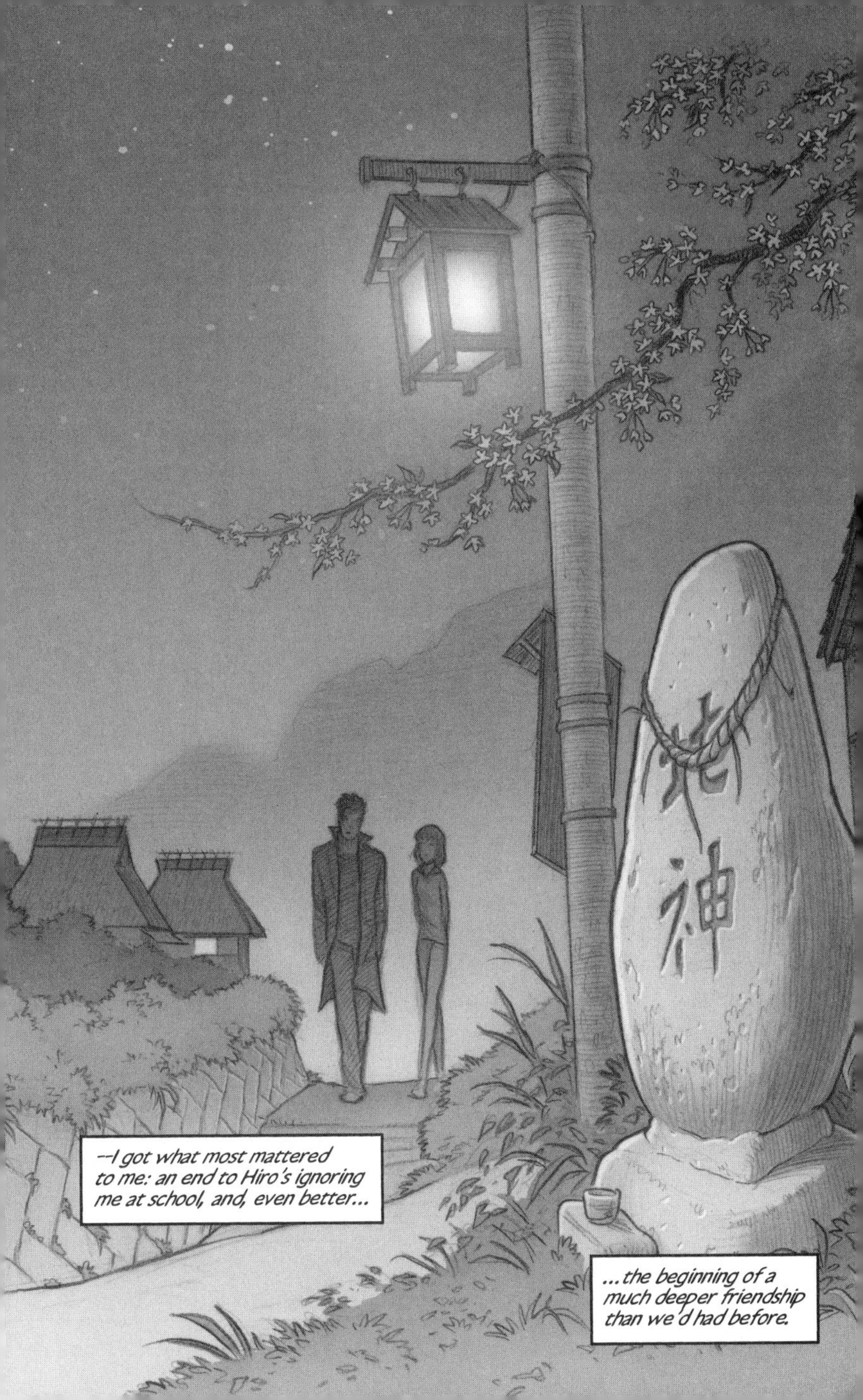
--I got what most mattered to me: an end to Hiro's ignoring me at school, and, even better...
...the beginning of a much deeper friendship than we'd had before.

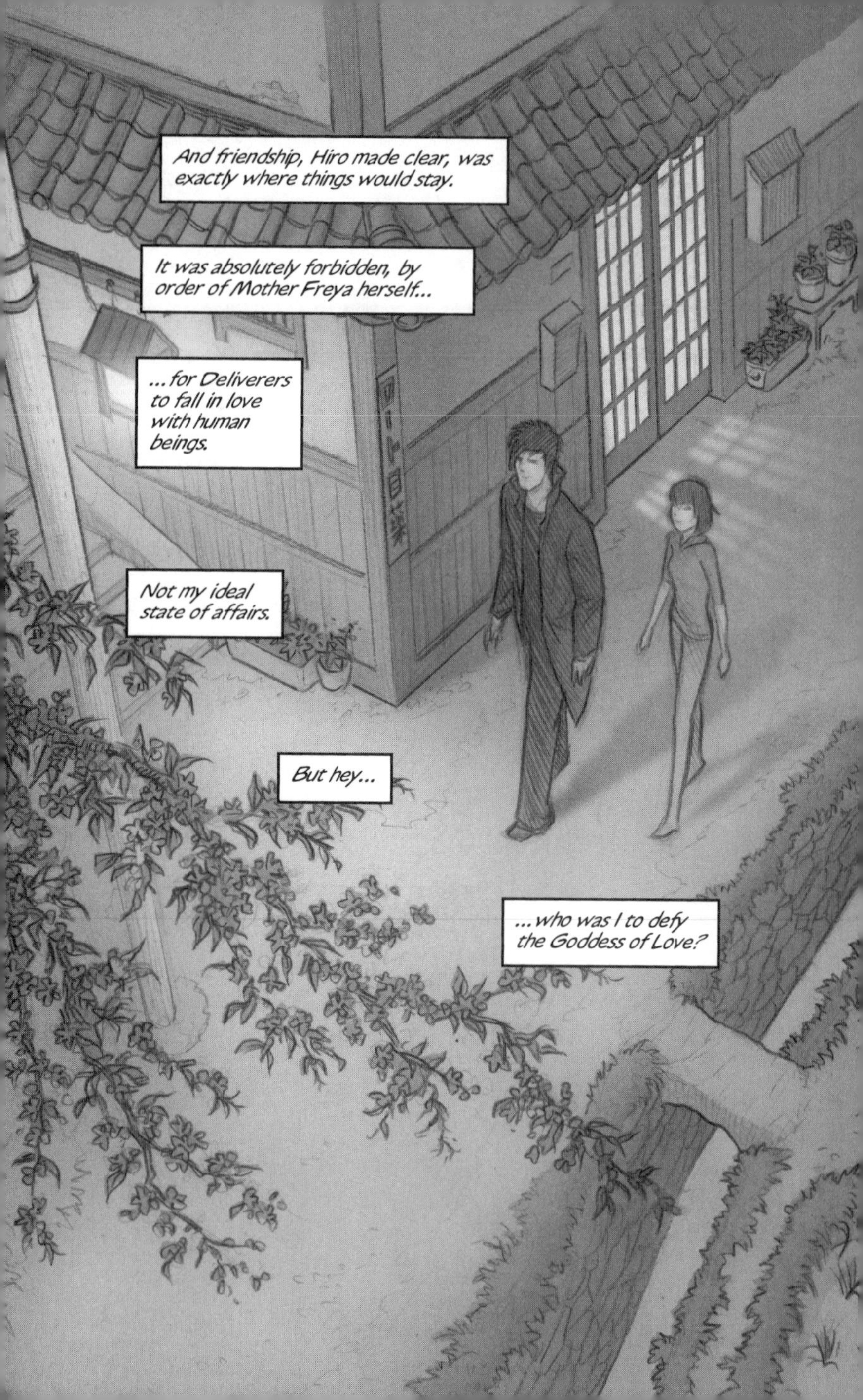
And friendship, Hiro made clear, was exactly where things would stay.
It was absolutely forbidden, by order of Mother Freya herself...
...for Deliverers to fall in love with human beings.
Not my ideal state of affairs.
But hey...
...who was I to defy the Goddess of Love?

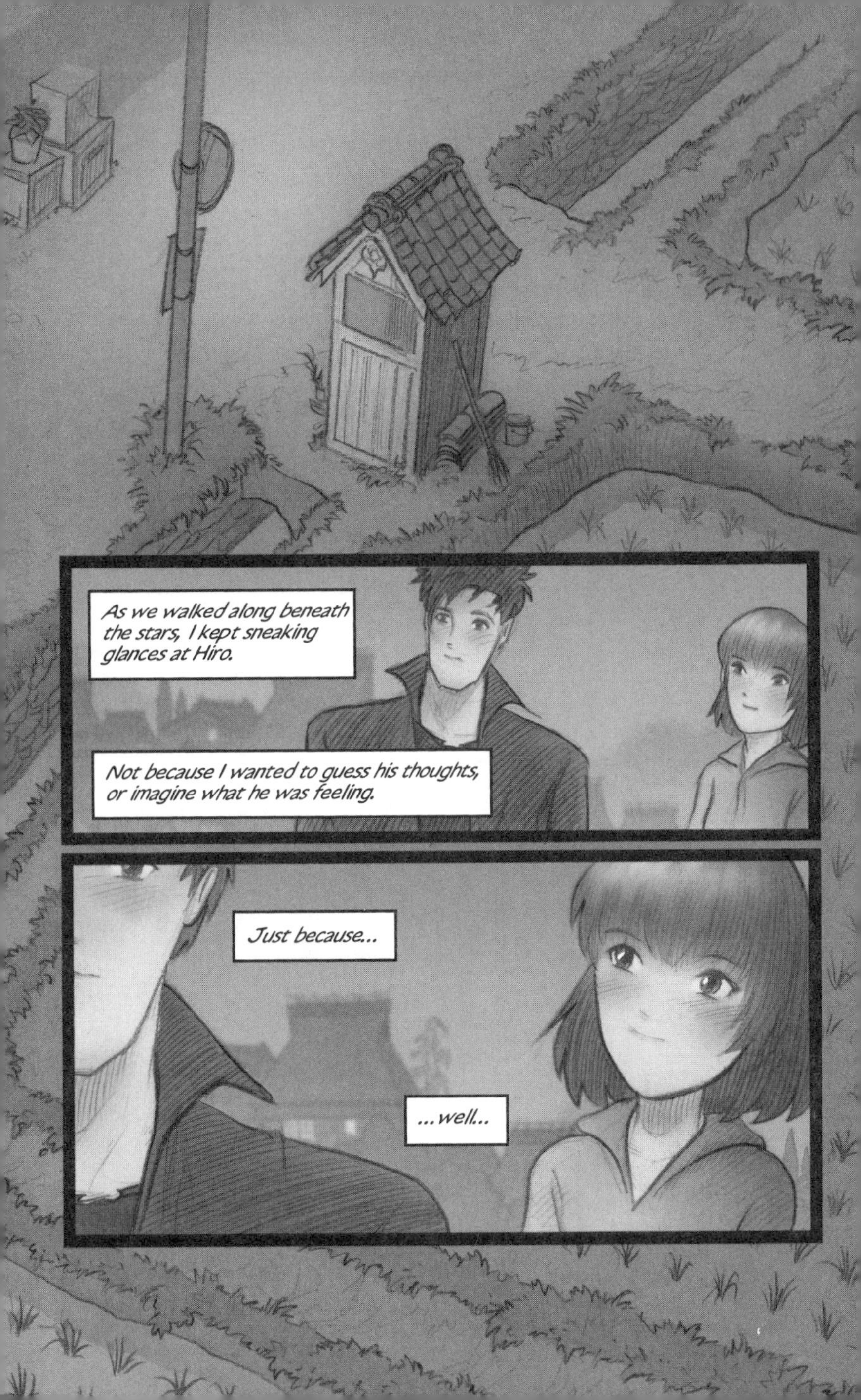
As we walked along beneath the stars, I kept sneaking glances at Hiro.
Not because I wanted to guess his thoughts, or imagine what he was feeling.
Just because...
...well...

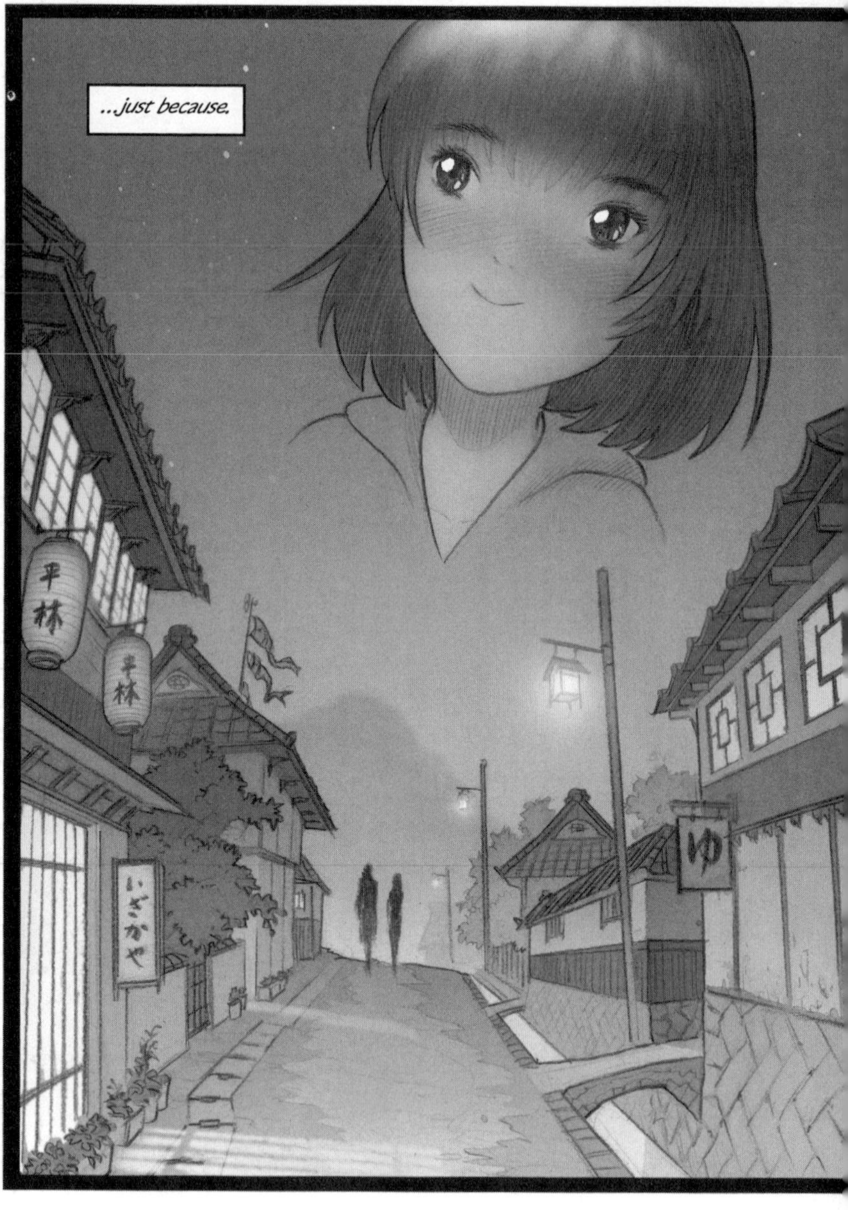
...just because.
平林
平林
いさかや
ゆ

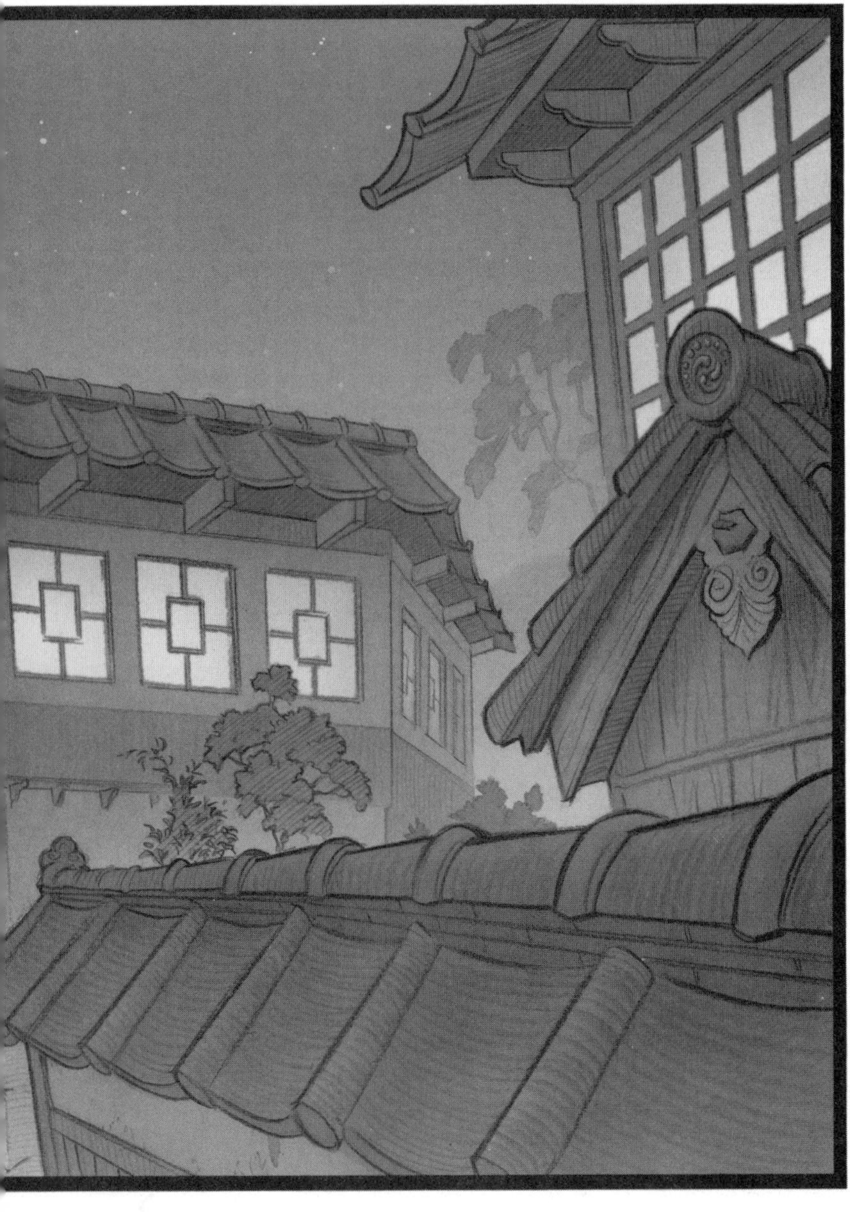

To the real Miki,
for whom I fall a little more
every day

HarperTeen is an imprint of HarperCollins Publishers.

Miki Falls: Spring
Copyright © 2007 by Mark Crilley
All rights reserved. Printed in the United States of America.
No part of this book may be used or reproduced in any manner whatsoever
without written permission except in the case of brief
quotations embodied in critical articles and reviews.
For information address HarperCollins Children's Books,
a division of HarperCollins Publishers,
10 East 53rd Street,
New York, NY 10022.
www.harperteen.com
Library of Congress Catalog Card Number is available
ISBN-10: 0-06-084616-X — ISBN-13: 978-0-06-084616-9

❖

14 LP/RRDH 10 9 8
First Edition

Has Miki fallen too hard?
Keep reading to find out more!

Turn the page for a preview of

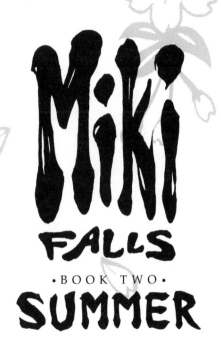

Miki

FALLS

·BOOK TWO·

SUMMER

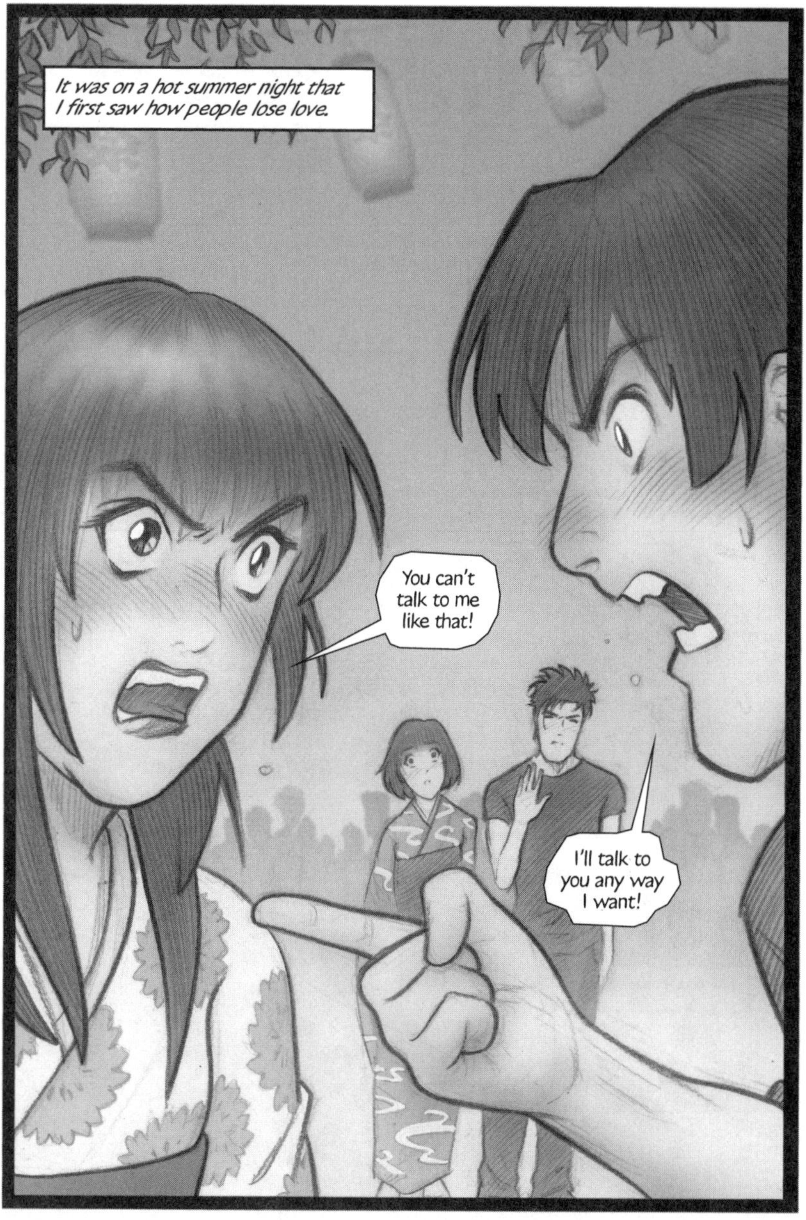
It was on a hot summer night that I first saw how people lose love.
You can't talk to me like that!
I'll talk to you any way I want!

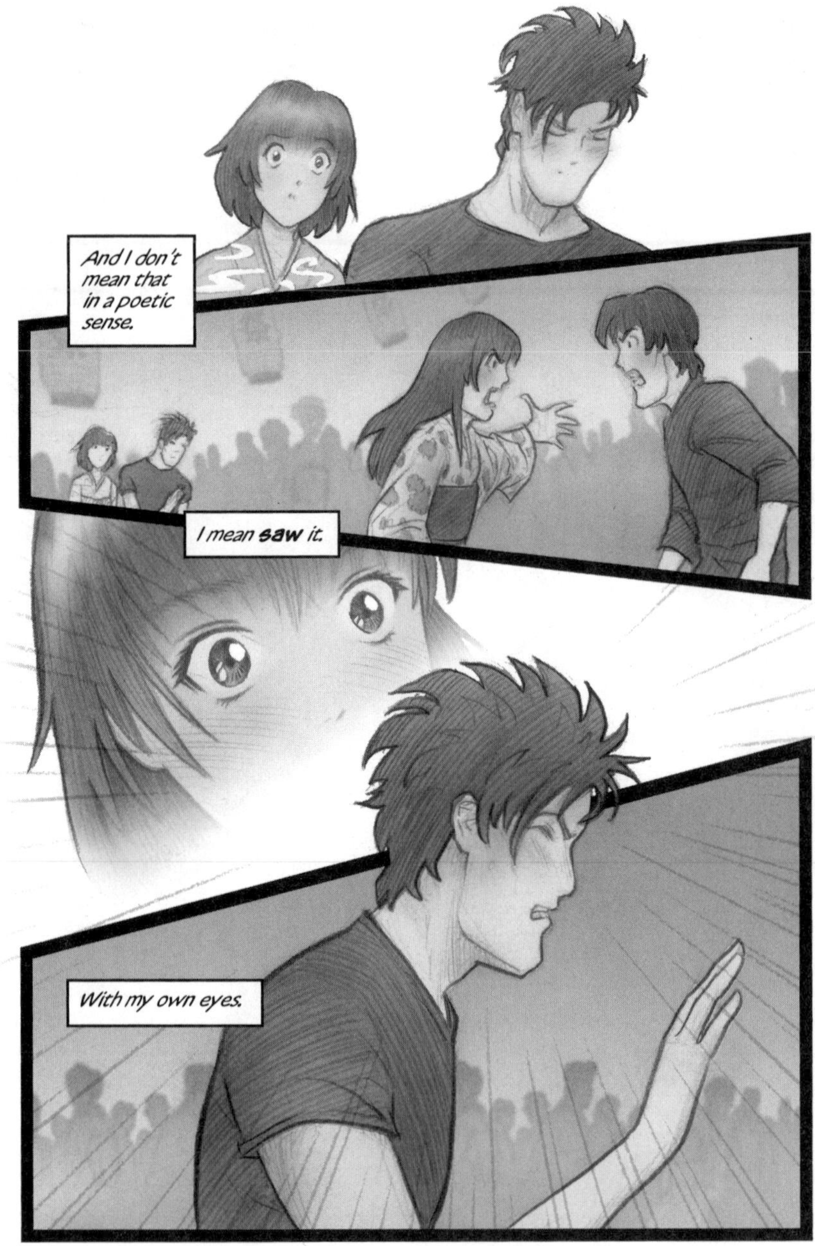
And I don't mean that in a poetic sense.
I mean **saw** it.
With my own eyes.

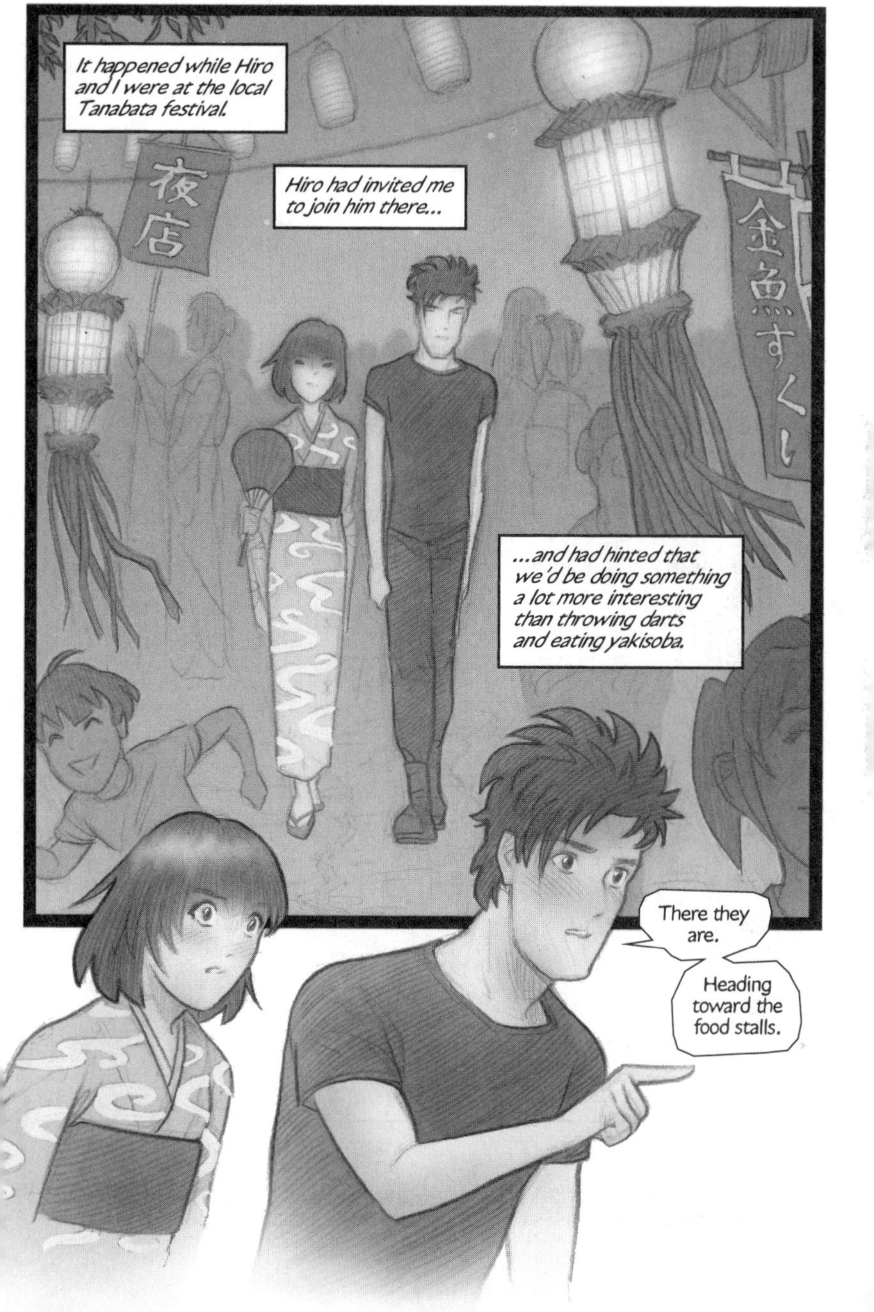
It happened while Hiro and I were at the local Tanabata festival.
夜店
Hiro had invited me to join him there...
金魚すくい
...and had hinted that we'd be doing something a lot more interesting than throwing darts and eating yakisoba.
There they are.
Heading toward the food stalls.

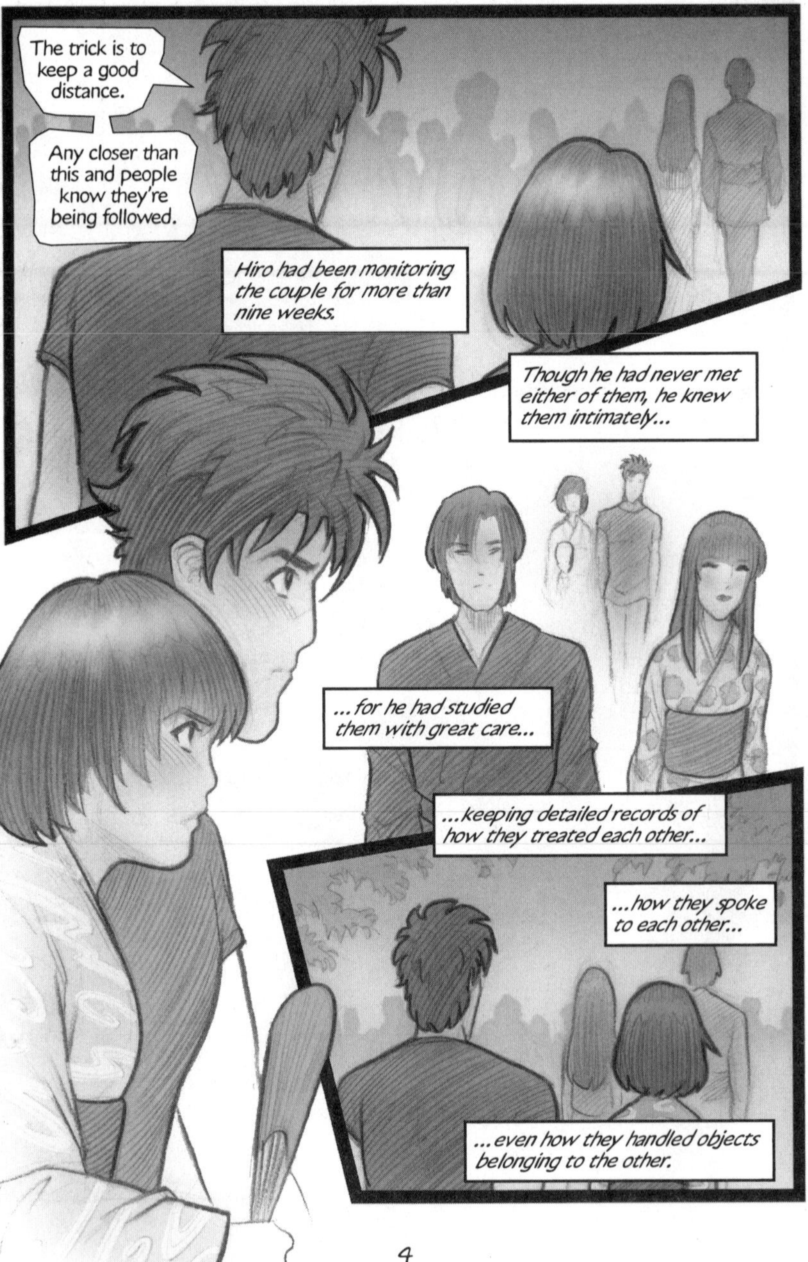
The trick is to keep a good distance.
Any closer than this and people know they're being followed.
Hiro had been monitoring the couple for more than nine weeks.
Though he had never met either of them, he knew them intimately...
...for he had studied them with great care...
...keeping detailed records of how they treated each other...
...how they spoke to each other...
...even how they handled objects belonging to the other.

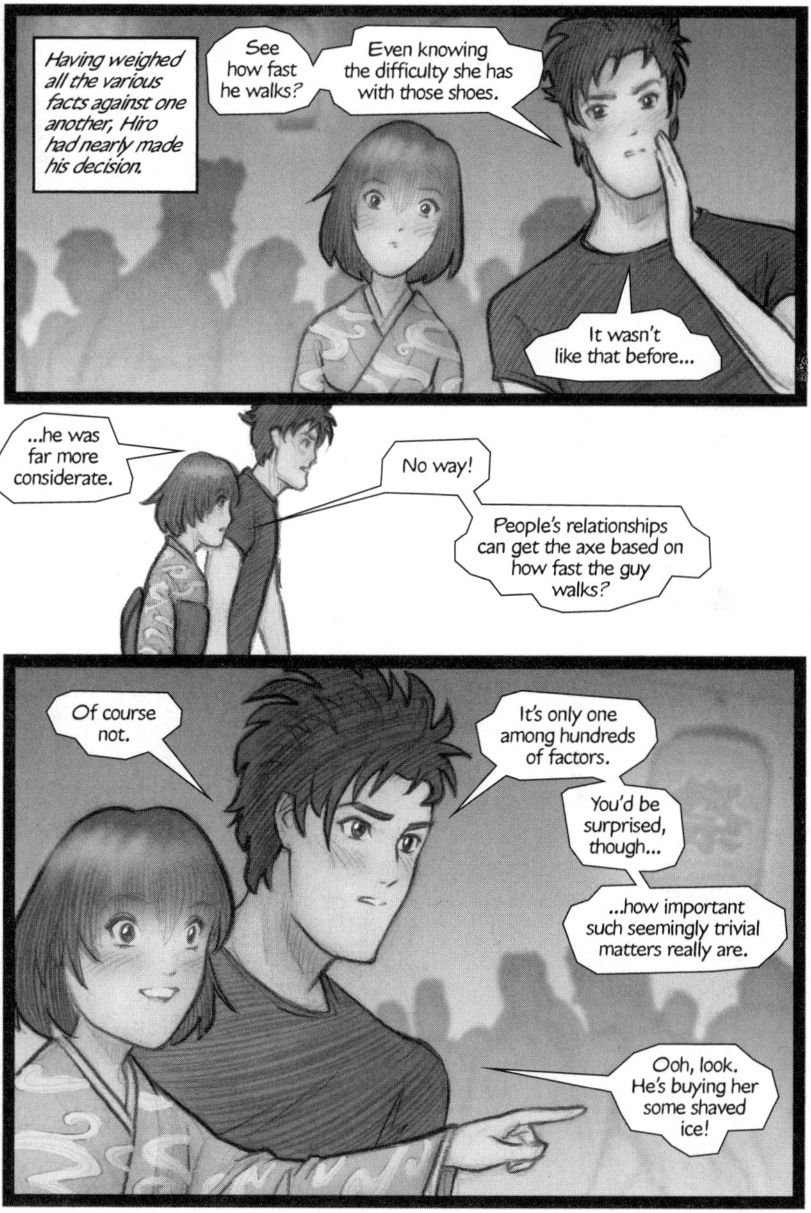
Having weighed all the various facts against one another, Hiro had nearly made his decision.
See how fast he walks?
Even knowing the difficulty she has with those shoes.
It wasn't like that before...
...he was far more considerate.
No way!
People's relationships can get the axe based on how fast the guy walks?
Of course not.
It's only one among hundreds of factors.
You'd be surprised, though...
...how important such seemingly trivial matters really are.
Ooh, look. He's buying her some shaved ice!

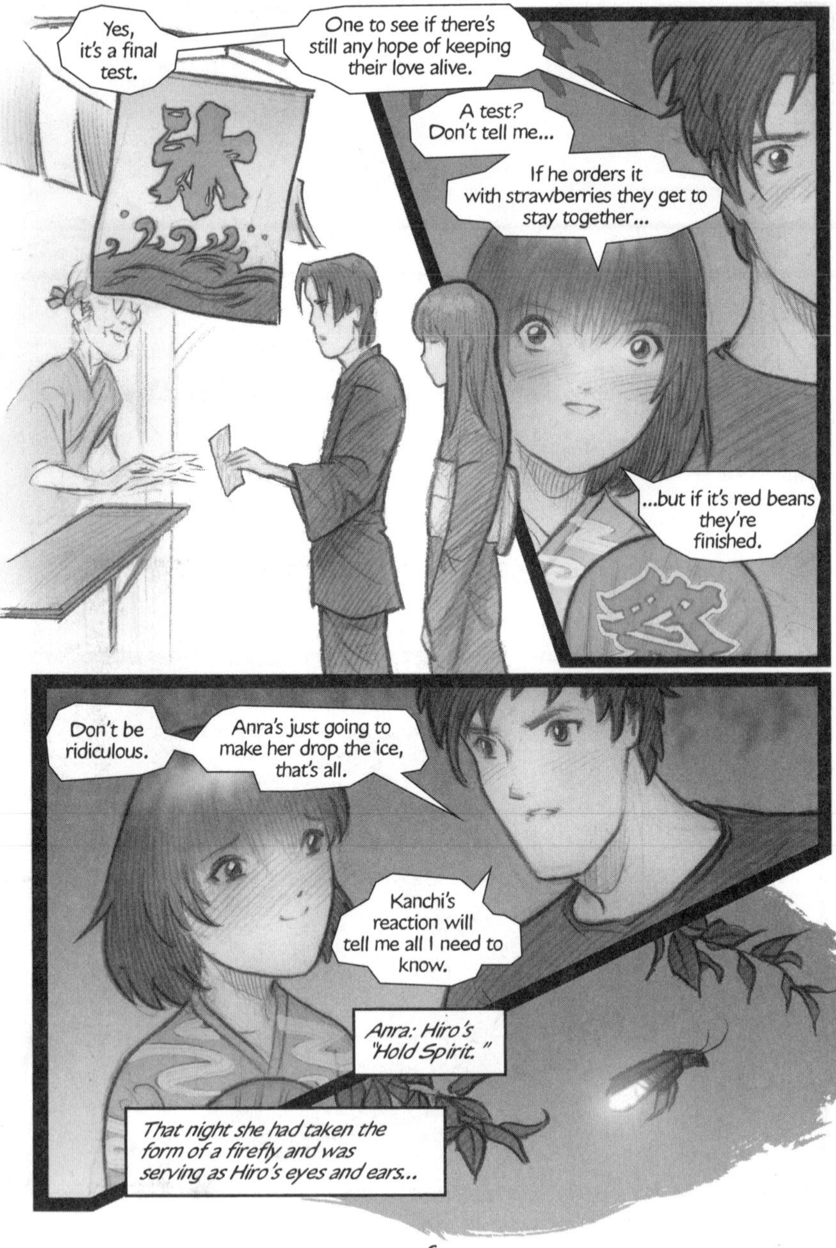
Yes, it's a final test.
One to see if there's still any hope of keeping their love alive.
A test? Don't tell me...
If he orders it with strawberries they get to stay together...
...but if it's red beans they're finished.
Don't be ridiculous.
Anra's just going to make her drop the ice, that's all.
Kanchi's reaction will tell me all I need to know.
Anra: Hiro's "Hold Spirit."
That night she had taken the form of a firefly and was serving as Hiro's eyes and ears...

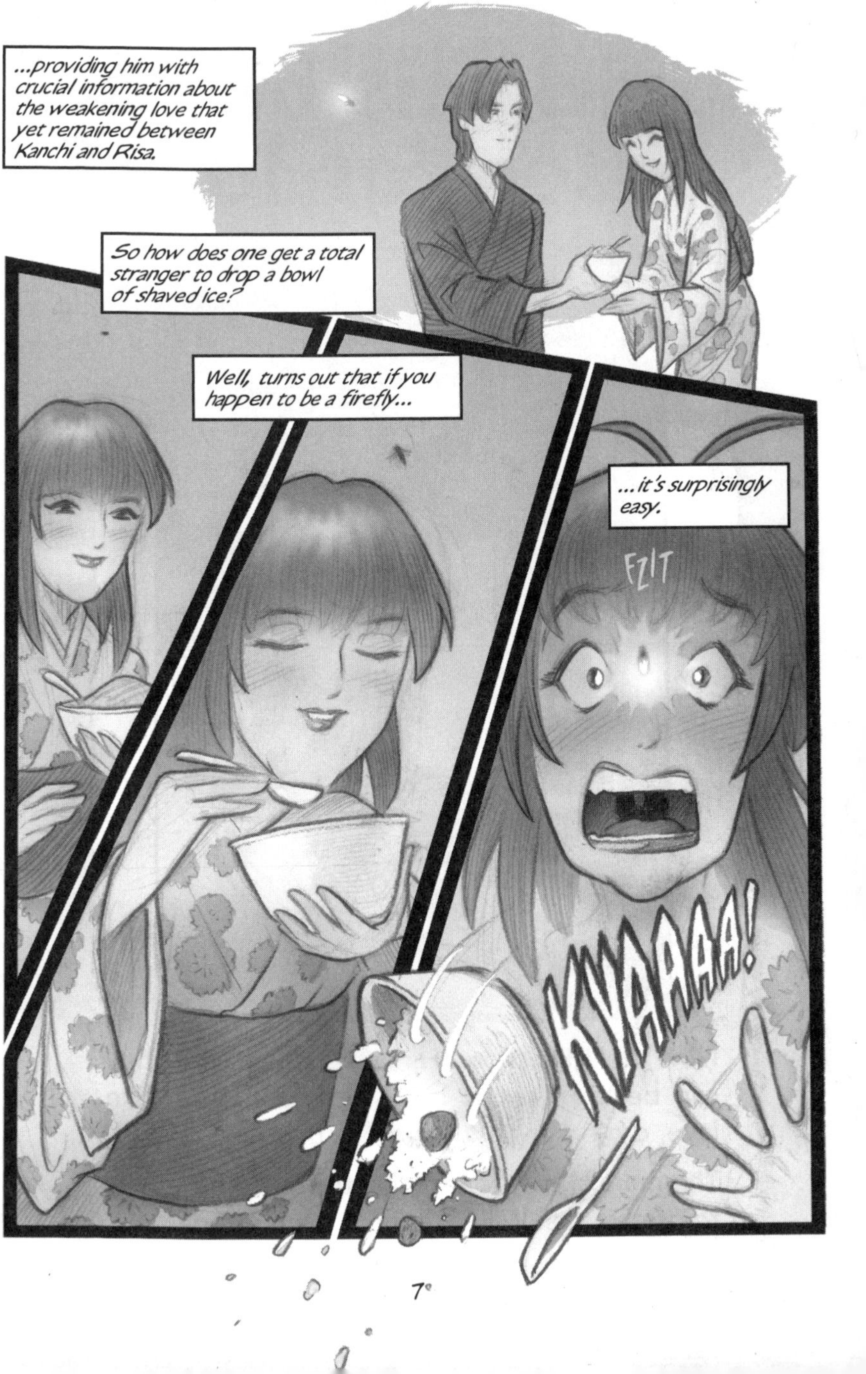
...providing him with crucial information about the weakening love that yet remained between Kanchi and Risa.
So how does one get a total stranger to drop a bowl of shaved ice?
Well, turns out that if you happen to be a firefly...
...it's surprisingly easy.
FZIT
KYAAAAA!

Could this be the season for love?

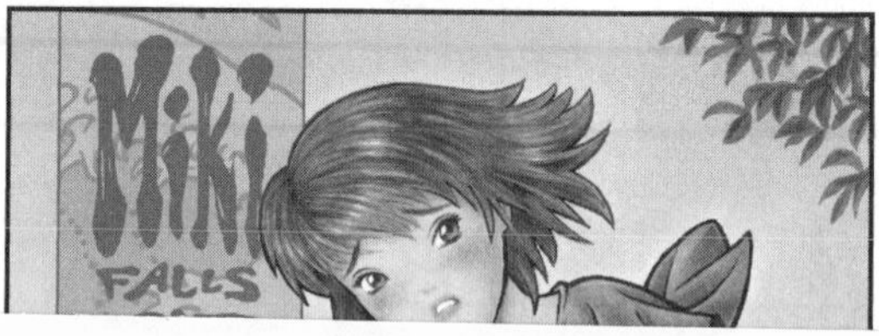
Miki
FALLS